Seaman

Between the innocence of infancy and the recklessness of adulthood comes that unique specimen of humanity called a seaman.

Seamen can be found in bars, in arguments, in bed and intoxicated. They are tall, short, fat, thin, dark, fair but never normal.

They dislike ships' food, Chief Engineers, writing letters, sailing on Saturdays and dry ships. They like receiving mail, pay off day, nude pin-ups, sympathy, complaining and beer.

A seaman's ambition is to change places with the shipowner for just one voyage, to own a brewery and to be loved by everyone in the world.

A seaman is a Sir Galahad in a Japanese brothel, a psychoanalyst with Reader's Digest on the table, Don Quixote with a discharge book, the saviour of mankind with his back teeth awash, Valentino with a fiver in his pocket, and democracy personified in a Red Chinese gaol cell.

A seaman is a provider in war and a parasite in peace. No one is subjected to so much abuse, wrongly accused, so often misunderstood by so many as a seaman. He has the patience of Job, the honesty of a fool and the heaven sent ability to laugh at himself.

When he returns home at the end of a long voyage no one but a seaman can create such an atmosphere of suspense and mysticism with an account of his travels -or perhaps more intriguingly, the tales he leaves untold.

i

Sunshine, Sugi & Salt

A Sea Story – of Sorts

By

Terry Smith

Introduction

First and foremost this is a novel so the tale is entirely fictitious. None of the incidents are real, all persons featured are imaginary as is the Australasian and Pacific Steam Navigation Company and the vessels it operated. Therefore, any reference to any actual person, living or otherwise, is purely coincidental. The reader may recognise some other famous shipping companies and the vessels in their ownership, although the ships themselves may not have been in the specified part of the world at the times alluded to. Whatever, like so much that was good they no longer exist, except in our memories and daydreams.

The various locations are for the most part real with the exception of Manoao, the small country town on the Canterbury Plains. Manoao – it is actually a native species of tree – could easily have been anywhere in New Zealand, but for convenience' sake I have situated it close to Timaru on the country's South Island. For similar purposes, Norris Street in St Kilda is also an invention.

As for The Contacts: they were in fact one of the most popular bands in New Zealand, and for at least some of the 'sixties' were resident at the Top Hat dance hall in Napier.

The narrative does contain some specimens of bad language and what some may regard as offensive terminology and if this causes umbrage then I apologize. However, after a period of deliberation I decided on its inclusion to more authentically reflect what was after all an almost exclusively male, often unenlightened, largely Anglo-Saxon workplace environment.

Some of the phraseology is unique to the seaman, so for the benefit of those with no seafaring background I recommend reading the glossary at the end of this work before you set sail. So with those few words of advice, here's wishing you, *Bon Voyage.*

Preface

There was a time in the recent past when a boy in his teens, with parental consent and following a period of training, could become a seaman and travel the world in a way that most of his contemporaries could only dream about. This tale relates the experiences of one such boy – we shall call him Steve – who left a comfortable home at a tender age, and after a spell of instruction at the training ship, *Vindicatrix,* set out to see the world as a catering rating aboard one of the cargo liners that formed Britain's lifeblood.

This book will, I hope, provide the reader with an insight to what life was like aboard those once-numerous freighters. You'll be able to follow Steve across storm-tossed oceans, to countries that bask in the sun, to places with weird and wonderful names, some of which are easily recognized while others you may never have heard of. You can join in his adventures, and meet some of the delightful – and in some instances, less delightful – characters he worked, lived and played with. You may learn, as Steve learnt, some things you'd rather not know, but knowledge is the essence of life and we'd all be the poorer for not knowing.

In the days being spoken of Britain possessed a vast fleet of merchant ships, with around sixty percent of the world's tonnage flying the Red Ensign. The decline in the fortunes of that once mighty armada has been so swift and dramatic that nowadays the flag is seldom seen on other than cross-channel ferries, the occasional cruise liner and the pleasure craft that ply our coastal and inland waterways. As the ships disappeared, so did the seamen who manned them, so that today it is virtually impossible for a British teenager to become a seafarer unless he has aspirations of becoming an officer and is extremely fortunate in gaining one of the handful of places at a nautical college. There are tentative signs that this dwindling number of both ships and seamen is at last being arrested, with the prospect of healthier times ahead, although it is difficult to envisage the situation returning to the halcyon days of the mid twentieth century - but only time will prove the judge of that.

I have tried my best to give an entertaining account of a way of life that sadly no longer exists. If I've failed then I'm sorry; but whatever, I feel certain that those of you who have also served as seafarers will recognize at least some of the situations Steve was confronted with, and be able to relate to him as he takes his first faltering steps as a seaman.

Acknowledgement

Many thanks to Rose Miles for her advice regarding grammar and punctuation, and to her husband, Bob, who never once complained at the ceaseless stream of questions as I endeavoured to transform a rather amateurish manuscript into something that others might enjoy. To Paul Mallett for his computer wizardry in helping prepare the manuscript for publication. To the apparently anonymous author of 'Seaman' - which I have taken the liberty of altering slightly - whose work appears everywhere but whose signature is invariably different and always illegible. But above all to my wife, Diana, for her patience, understanding and encouragement throughout the hours I spent at the keyboard; and to my parents for allowing me to go to sea in the first place and gain first-hand experience, subsequently making this work possible.

1

Steve Chapman, shift-working railwayman and a native of a small country town where the biggest attraction was the cinema. He was a steady enough bloke in a solid occupation; he hadn't really been anywhere apart from during his summer holidays or on day-trips to London - so what could possibly have fired this ambition?

Wanderlust! That's what it was, there was no other word to describe it.

It stemmed largely from those childhood holidays, when the ocean liners had passed his family's summer retreat on Hayling Island, especially those that had been nosing their way through Spithead, outward bound from Southampton. He'd imagine himself sailing away to some faraway tropical paradise; nowhere specific so long as the sea was blue, the sun shone warmly and palm fronds waved in the breeze. He'd sit and fantasize, promising himself that somehow, sometime in the future, he'd see the world for himself and if his dreams came true, aboard one of those wonderful liners.

His present situation obviously had its roots in those seaside holidays but had oddly evolved in the unlikely surroundings of a railway signal box. What had happened was this. A railway enthusiast for as long as he could remember, his age had prevented him becoming a seafarer upon leaving school so he became a railwayman instead. After a spell of training at the area signalling academy he'd started work as a telegraph lad in his home-town signal box where he was to remain for the next eighteen months.

It was during a shift at the signal box, while flicking through the situations vacant columns of his daily newspaper, that he spotted an advertisement placed by the Cunard Steamship Company. Cunard were seeking bakers and confectioners for their liners, and were inviting applicants to send their credentials to the company's offices in Liverpool. Steve knew absolutely nothing about food preparation; indeed, he'd never made so much as a slice of toast in his life, and in the signal box they even boiled their eggs in the kettle whilst making the tea. He wasn't deterred, his premise being that if he did nothing when the opportunity presented itself he probably never would; so in spite of his inability to bake so much as a jacket potato he'd written to Cunard regardless.

The shipping company had duly replied and as expected couldn't consider anyone with Steve's lack of experience. However, they'd suggested that if he was really keen on becoming a seafarer he should apply to the British Shipping Federation at their offices at Prescott Street in London. Eager to keep the ball rolling he'd done exactly that with the outcome that he'd been accepted as a catering trainee at the National Sea Training Schools' Gloucestershire establishment. The fact that he wore spectacles had precluded him becoming a deck trainee but that didn't matter. He'd never been one for getting his hands dirty and catering sounded ideal.

He'd tendered his resignation to the local stationmaster and left his job as a telegraph lad shortly before Christmas; and following six weeks of intensive training in various aspects of catering and seamanship in the most arduous of surroundings, had been instructed to attend the Shipping Federation's office at the western end of London's King George V Dock. Now here he was, a naive seventeen year-old, about to embark on one of life's greatest adventures.

'Just arrived from the Vindi have you, Lad?' asked the officer behind the counter at the Federation, as he studied the details in Steve's pristine and empty discharge book (Vindi was short for *Vindicatrix*, the dismasted sailing ship that had formed the nucleus of the sea training school at Sharpness in Gloucestershire). 'Well, with a bit of luck you'll find it a lot less primitive where you're going. Here,' he added, handing back the discharge book along with a neatly folded slip of paper, 'give this to the Catering Superintendent of the Australasian and Pacific Steam Navigation Company. You'll find their office opposite number four shed, immediately before the P&O building.'

Taking his discharge book and the slip of paper Steve thanked the officer, hoping he hadn't been joking. His six weeks training at the *Vindicatrix* had brought a rude awakening. It had been a cold and hungry interlude in a life that had previously been warm and well nourished. The winter sun had never penetrated into the canal berth where the poorly-heated Vindi was moored with the result that he and his fellow trainees had been frozen. Their circumstances hadn't been improved by a diet that was both meagre and poor. The inadequate fare on offer had been appallingly prepared and this, allied with the fact that the Vindi was infested with cockroaches that routinely invaded the rations, had made mealtimes something of an ordeal. But, as is often repeated, when you're hungry you'll eat anything and so it had transpired. But that was now history - or so he fervently hoped - and the reassuring words of the Federation officer had significantly boosted his morale.

Striding along the dock road he caught glimpses of ships at their moorings. It was February 1962; London could boast of being the biggest and busiest seaport in the world and this was reflected in the number of vessels lining the quaysides. Many of the funnel colours were easily recognised and the ships bore some fascinating names. There was: *Dominion Monarch*, *Port Lyttleton*, *Kenya Castle*, *Adelaide Star*, *Hinakura*, *City of Port Elizabeth* and goodness knows how many more, but with the exception of the *Dominion Monarch* and *Kenya Castle* none of them resembled the liners he'd known and remembered; and he knew very well that the Australasian and Pacific Steam Navigation Company's vessels were equally anonymous. As the company's name suggested, they traded between the United Kingdom and Australia, calling at ports in New Zealand and other countries encircling the Pacific Ocean along with the intermingling islands. In common with the majority of cargo ships they had black-painted hulls and white upper works, while the legend 'A&P' in bright yellow lettering was emblazoned on their emerald-green funnels. To complete the picture, the company had named each of their vessels after a town, city or other notable location in the antipodes.

As Steve hurried on, his battered suitcase in one hand and slip of paper in the other, the siren of an outward-bound Glen liner echoed around the neighbouring communities as her attendant PLA tugs

3

guided her towards the dock system's river entrance. Whilst a forest of cranes plumbed the hatches of the assembled freighters, either loading or discharging merchandise, the sound of clanking buffers reverberated around the sheds as a diminutive tank locomotive shunted a train of vans alongside a Houlder Line steamer that had recently arrived from The Argentine. Dockers and stevedores swarmed about the business of shifting imports and exports as lorries loaded down to their springs rumbled noisily over the concrete. The entire acreage of the Royal Docks was a hive of industry, an intoxicating cocktail of sight, sound and activity.

It was a trillion miles away from the outside world. Out there a humdrum assuredness had governed Steve's very existence. His life had been ruled by the clock, the calendar and his place of work. He'd known within reason just what he'd be doing at any given instant; well, as sure as he could have been in a daily cycle that was always capable of throwing up the occasional surprise. But in here, within the walls and fences that encompassed the complex micro-universe of the capital's dockland, everything was new; he'd detected the difference as soon as he walked through the gates. In here nothing could be taken for granted. Even tomorrow - perhaps even the next few hours - was an imponderable. For all he knew he might be on his way to Australia by nightfall, and the same uncertainty held true for any seaman between ships; although in Steve's case the ship would be his first which made it all the more tantalizing. His weeks at the Vindi had given him the merest taste of the hereafter but had failed to prepare him for the present. It was an exciting new medium of which he was now part and he loped through the docks rejoicing.

Passing the Union-Castle and Port Line offices he could see the P&O building in the distance and just before that, with their house flag flying from the rooftop, the offices of the Australasian and Pacific Steam Navigation Company. He stopped to shake a grit from his shoe and felt suddenly nervous, the sight of the flag having dented his confidence. But there was no going back; he was almost there so he carried on walking and was soon standing flush with the entrance. Well, this is it, he thought, drawing himself up to his full height and straightening his tie in the reflection from a window - this is where it really begins. He pushed open the door to find a pretty

4

brunette looking up from her desk, the clatter of her typewriter ceasing the moment she spoke.

'Hello - what can I do for you?' she asked, pleasantly, with a beaming smile on her face.

'I have to report to the Catering Superintendent,' answered Steve, in a fluster, dropping his suitcase and smoothing his hair with one hand while handing her his slip of paper with the other.

The brunette, who wasn't much older than Steve, handed back the slip, and said, 'Okay, you'll find his office on the first floor. Just tap on the door and walk in.'

'Thanks,' said Steve, as he picked up his suitcase and mounted the stairs. 'Um........what's he like? Is he easy to get on with?'

'You'll have no trouble with him. He's a good enough boss so long as you do your job properly - well, I think so at any rate.'

Feeling suitably comforted Steve climbed the stairs, knocked on the door bearing the Catering Superintendent's name, and stepped boldly over the threshold. The Superintendent, a smartly-dressed man with greying hair combed back with a centre parting, glanced up from the papers on his desk and regarded Steve's Vindi uniform tunic.

'A first tripper, eh! Well, never mind, we all have to start somewhere. What's your name, Lad?'

'Chapman, Sir - Steve Chapman,' replied Steve, who remembering the slip of paper, passed it to the beckoning fingers.

'All right, Chapman, I need a catering boy for the *Alice Springs*. She's just down the road at number six shed. Report to the Second Steward - he'll be expecting you. You'll be working in the ship's pantry with another catering boy, and you're on pay as from today.'

Steve thanked the Superintendent and prepared to leave, but suddenly turned, and asked, 'Where's the *Alice Springs* going, Sir?'

'Nowhere at the moment,' came the reply, as the Superintendent returned to his papers. 'She broke down on her way home from Auckland and is currently undergoing repair. Her engineers are working on the problem and if all goes according to schedule they'll soon have it sorted. You'll know as soon as everyone else.'

Closing the door behind him Steve descended the stairs and walked out into the fresh morning air, exchanging smiles with the brunette as he passed. Despite the weak February sunshine he felt cold and was surprised to find that his underclothes were sticking to his skin. He'd been sweating profusely in the presence of the Superintendent but the fact had gone completely unnoticed.

Steve had seen the *Alice Springs* on his way from the Federation office; but there was another of the company's vessels tied up astern and he'd wondered to which, if either, he'd be assigned. It was a mystery that had been recently solved. Drawing a deep breath he crossed the road and picked his way over a maze of railway tracks. He rounded the corner of number six shed and there, towering above him, rose the bulk of an ocean-going freighter.

The quayside in front of him had the look of an obstacle course. Dodging a forklift truck, he skirted a group of dockers who were busily removing a net of frozen lamb from a crane hook. Further along the wharf were stacked cases of apples and pears, while adjacent to the shed stood boxes of butter and cheese. Virtually everything emerging from the *Alice Springs'* holds was the produce of the orchards and fertile farmlands of New Zealand.

Reaching the foot of the accommodation ladder Steve became suddenly tense. Most of the cargo had been discharged, so with the ship sitting high in the water the ladder seemed exceedingly steep. The ascent looked formidable; but he was slightly reassured by the underlying netting, a precaution should anyone slip. He began the climb, nervously at first, one tread at a time, dragging his suitcase behind him. He stopped for a breather at the half-way mark and scanned the decks forming the superstructure. Nearly there, he ruminated, contemplating a pair of faces peering at him over a bulwark. Only another few steps.

'Here he comes, another first tripper,' he heard one of the characters mumble through a haze of exhaled tobacco smoke. The remark was irritating. The last thing he needed was to be reminded that he was a novice even if it was patently obvious. He resolved there and then to rid himself of his Vindi uniform tunic just as soon as it was humanly possible, unwelcome aid that it was to easy identification.

As it happened, one of the men was the gangway watchman and he proved to be extremely helpful. He offered to take Steve to the

Second Steward while the individual who'd made the unwarranted comment drifted aimlessly off, flicking his extinguished cigarette-butt overboard. 'Don't take any notice of him,' said the watchman, as he led the way through a warren of alleyways. 'Get a couple of trips under their belts and they think they're Sinbad the Sailor. He's a relative newcomer himself.' Steve felt instantly brighter. The seaman's words made him feel less of an intruder and more like a member of crew.

In due course they arrived at a pair of doors that opened into an expansive dining area. 'Right,' said the watchman, ushering Steve through the doorway. 'This is the dining saloon and that fellow over there, the one with the zigzag stripe on the sleeves of his uniform jacket, chatting to the guy in the chef's outfit - well, he's the Second Steward. Okay?'

'Yeah, sure,' replied Steve, gratefully, gazing in awe at the dining room's impressive décor, 'and thanks very much for your help.'

As his chaperone disappeared into the network of alleyways, Steve approached the men whom the watchman had indicated, wondering at his likely reception. Seeing Steve making his way towards him the Second Steward turned from his companion with the words, 'See you in The Roundhouse later,' and fixing his gaze on Steve, he observed. 'Now then youngster, you must be the catering boy who's just been sent over from the office. Let's get you fixed up and settled.'

Steve wilted visibly as the Second Steward scrutinized his uniform tunic. By this stage of the proceedings he was wishing he'd ditched it the previous weekend. He could easily have worn his Harris Tweed sports jacket but he'd wanted to show off, to be seen strutting around in his tunic. Now he considered it a liability. Thankfully, there was a waterproof wind-cheater in his suitcase so he'd still have protection from the elements once the tunic had been finally disposed of.

'First of all,' said the Second Steward, beckoning for Steve to follow, 'I'll show you to your cabin, issue you with some bedlinen, then you can change into working gear and report back to me at the pantry.'

'Right - thank you, Sir,' replied Steve, as he followed the Second

Steward out of the saloon and down a companionway. They negotiated a short athwartships corridor before swinging right into a lengthy alleyway with cabins located to starboard. The opposite side of the alleyway was occupied by a number of built-in lockers that bore labels reading: clean linen, dry stores, soiled linen, cleaning materials; along with sundry other storerooms for items associated with the efficient running of the *Alice Springs'* catering department.

'This is the working alleyway,' said the Second Steward, waving a casual hand at the entire length of passageway. 'All the catering staff live here, all except the Chief Steward - he's got a cabin topside. This is your accommodation,' he announced, throwing open a door to reveal a two-berth room that at first glance seemed little larger than a broom cupboard. 'Sling your suitcase in there then follow me - I'll sort you out some towels, sheets and pillowcases.' Steve did as he was told and a couple of minutes later was on his way back beneath a burden of crisp white linen along with hand and bath towels and a tablet of Palmolive soap. It was all a far cry from the Vindi where his linen issue had comprised a rough cotton sleeping bag that was meant for a midget - one of the principal reasons he hadn't been able to keep warm at nights - and a solitary pillowcase. A couple of threadbare blankets had already occupied his bunk and he'd supplied his own towels and soap. 'Don't forget, as soon as you've made up your bunk and changed into working gear we'll find you a job,' reminded the Second Steward, and then as a parting shot, he added. Oh! and another thing. You call me Sec, not Sir - all right?' And with that, Steve was left to take stock of his new surroundings.

With time to reflect, he could see that the cabin was roomier than first impressions had created. A pair of bunks were located against the forward bulkhead while opposite were a table and chair. There was a locker for each of the room's occupants, one behind the cabin door, the other against the after bulkhead. Running along the starboard bulkhead between the bunks and the table was a small settee and above that a porthole with its dead-light in the raised position. Beneath the bunks there was ample drawer space, and for heating and ventilation purposes a pair of ball vents, often referred to as 'Punka Louvres', protruded from a deck-head conduit. The vents could be swivelled in any direction, including to a position that smothered the airflow.

Steve noticed that the lower bunk had already been claimed so he laid his linen on the upper of the two before unlatching his suitcase. He quickly slipped out of his shore-going clothes and into a striped pee-jacket and blue dungarees. He found an empty drawer for his shirts, socks and underwear then hung the rest of his clothing in the locker against the after bulkhead. The empty suitcase was then stowed upright in the locker along with his other possessions. He made up his bunk, W-fold fashion as he'd been taught at the Vindi, then went to look out of the porthole.

The water in the King George V Dock appeared cold and dark and the surface was littered with debris. Pieces of timber drifted hither and thither while all sorts of unpleasantness could be seen lurking beneath the ripples. 'You'll need your stomach pumped out if you fall in there - that's assuming you don't drown in the meantime.' Steve started at the voice behind him. The cabin door had silently opened and a lad of about his own age and dressed in identical garb had begun rummaging through a drawer in search of some mystery item. 'Hi, I'm Peter - Peter Grimble,' said the boy, breaking off his quest and joining Steve at the porthole. 'I'm your room-mate and you'll be working with me in the pantry - as well as carrying out all the side jobs that the Second Steward finds for you. He sent me to see where you'd got to.'

'It's okay - I'm just coming,' replied Steve. 'I was just looking at the state of the dock. It's absolutely filthy. Isn't it ever cleaned out?'

'Waste of time,' said Peter, now rifling another drawer until he found what he was looking for. Stuffing a clean handkerchief into his pocket, he continued, 'If they cleared it out today it'd be full of shite again tomorrow. Sometimes a driftwood patrol comes around to remove the larger pieces of timber, the ones that could damage a ship's propeller or the lock gate mechanism, otherwise it's left as it is. Come along - we'd better get going.'

Casting a glance at P&O's *Patonga* which was tied up at the opposite quayside, Steve turned and followed Peter into the working alleyway. He belatedly introduced himself, and commented, 'The *Alice Springs* seems a nice ship. What's she like compared with some of the others - the *Patonga*, for instance, over the way?'

9

'No comparison,' replied Peter, over his shoulder as they scaled a companionway. 'Most of the boats that trade out east carry Asian crews and theirs is a totally different lifestyle. The British crewed ships are usually all right although a few of the older ones, especially those belonging to the tramping outfits, can be rough. They reckon the grub on some of those - Hogarth's, and the like - is worse than at the Vindi and that's saying something. Unless you get a really old stager the liner companies are generally okay, and the food's pretty decent as well. This company's one of the better ones and this is as good a ship as any. This'll be my third trip on the *Alice Springs* - that's providing they fix the engines.'

'You were a Vindi Boy as well, then?' queried Steve, rhetorically, as they reached the topside accommodation area. 'What did you make of it?'

'Bloody awful. Still, I don't suppose it'll have done us any harm in the long run. It'll have toughened us up that's for sure, and at least we've got something to brag about - not like them as went to the Gravesend sea school. They always get the piss taken out of them cos it's reckoned that they had it easy. Now, here we are - this here's the pantry.'

They were back at the dining saloon, but ignoring the main entrance they entered an adjoining area that was mostly stainless steel and lit by fluorescent strips. The glare was dazzling, and Steve was momentarily blinded. 'Just in time for smoke-ho,' said the Second Steward, removing a trio of mugs from their hooks and filling them with coffee from a percolator. 'Enjoy your break, then I want the pair of you to sugi the deck-head in the passengers' smoke room. There's still an hour before lunch so you should get the bulk of it finished.'

'And what do we do at lunchtime?' asked Steve, shovelling a couple of spoonfuls of sugar into his coffee, now that his eyes had adjusted.

'You'll be working your socks off,' replied the Second Steward, winking craftily at Peter. 'By a quarter past one you'll be wondering what you've let yourself in for.'

'Ignore him,' said Peter, adding extra milk to his coffee. 'It isn't that bad, but you'll certainly have your work cut out. Even so, it'd be

10

busier still if we had a full load of passengers.'

There ensued some general conversation about life on board before Steve drained his coffee and followed Peter's example in filling a bucket from the hot and cold water taps. 'Here, stir that in,' said Peter, scooping a couple of handfuls of soft soap from a five-gallon drum into the two brimming buckets. 'Bloody good stuff for making sugi that is - easier than shaving slices off a bar of Sunlight.' As they made to leave the pantry Peter handed Steve several strips of mutton cloth, saying, 'Use one bit for washing and the rest of it for wiping down afterwards. You won't leave any smear marks that way.'

The passenger accommodation was located above and abaft the dining area, and as the boys climbed the companionway Steve remarked that the Second Steward seemed a decent enough fellow.

'Yeah - he's all right is Sec,' answered Peter, hauling himself up by the handrail. 'Pity they're not all like him. Some of them are right bastards. Give 'em a bit of gold braid and they turn into little bleedin' fascists. Mind you, if you're work-shy or start buggering about he'll be down on you like a ton of bricks, but keep your nose clean and he'll be as good a friend as you could wish for. Away from the ship he's one of the boys. In fact, we're all going to the Bedroom Steward's birthday shindig tonight. We're kicking off in The Roundhouse at about seven o'clock - should be a bloody good do. I suppose you'll be coming, won't you?'

Steve was astonished at the assumption. 'How can I go to his birthday party?' he protested, staring at Peter as if the suggestion had been made by a lunatic. 'I don't even know the man - and not only that. I've only got seven-bob to last me till pay-day. I can't afford to go drinking.'

'Don't you worry about that,' answered Peter, nodding towards the smoke room at the after end of the alleyway. 'The other blokes'll see you all right. The likes of you and me'll only have to stick a few bob in the kitty and they'll take care of the rest.' And with a knowing smile on his face, he added, 'Being on a low rate of pay does have some advantages, you know.'

Steve wasn't entirely happy with the idea of sponging his way through a pub-crawl but had to admit, the prospect of a night ashore with his shipmates sounded infinitely appealing. 'Okay,' he agreed, as they reached the door to the smoke room. 'I'll come - so long as no-one else minds.'

'No, they won't mind - and anyway, it'll give you a chance to meet the rest of the catering crowd.'

The deck-head could be reached without steps, so commencing above the doorway they began washing the tobacco-stained paint-work, exposing the underlying shade of magnolia so that it assumed the appearance of a completely new paint-job. The work wasn't particularly exacting, and apart from the water that trickled down to his armpits Steve was feeling largely content. He seemed to have fallen on his feet, and first impressions suggested that the *Alice Springs* was as happy a ship as he was ever likely to come across. Still, it was early days and as he dried a section of deck-head he wondered what it would be like with a fully-paid-up complement of passengers. 'I didn't realize the *Alice Springs* carried passengers,' he voiced, wringing out his mutton cloth in a bucket of already-discoloured water. 'I thought she was just a straightforward cargo liner.'

'Yeah,' replied Peter, energetically rubbing away at a stubborn patch of stain in a corner. 'She carries twelve - in single and two-berth staterooms. It's a nice enough way to see the world, and a bloody sight cheaper than on the big ships. Having said that, there's not much in the way of entertainment on here. There's the bar in the corner there, and there's a small library and a radiogram in the lounge, but otherwise they have to make their own amusement - playing cards or scrabble, and so on.' He paused and wrung out his cloth, wiping a pool of spilt water from the deck before resuming. 'Tell you what though. It's a lot easier working on one of these. There's none of the bullshit you get on the passenger liners, and you get longer in port.'

That final statement was like the signature tune from 'Desert Island Discs'. From Steve's point of view a long time in port in some faraway country - provided it wasn't war-riven or blighted with famine - sounded magical, and the wait to discover the *Alice Springs'* eventual sailing date was becoming increasingly frustrating. Nevertheless, he carried on working, his colourful daydreams becoming ever more vivid.

'You know, we're not gonna finish this,' bemoaned Peter, with a trace of annoyance. 'It's nearly twelve o'clock now and it's only three-quarters done. Bloody nuisance that is. I wanted to nip into Plaistow this afternoon to do some shopping. Now it'll have to wait till tomorrow.'

'Do we normally get the afternoons off then?' asked Steve, wondering how Peter was going to find time to go shopping.

'Course we don't,' replied Peter, scornfully, regarding Steve as some kind of nincompoop. 'What d'ya think this is - Daddy's fuckin' yacht? It's just that provided we've finished the morning's side jobs we usually get a break after lunch. Most of the blokes turn in or catch up with their dhobying, especially when we're at sea, but in port it's handy for things like shopping or getting your hair cut. Anyway, we'd better leave this for the time being and get back to the pantry. We can finish it off later.'

Leaving their buckets in the smoke room they returned to the pantry where Steve was about to discover the true meaning of the phrase, "working your socks off". 'Now then,' said Peter, sliding open the doors of a large cabinet located directly beneath the servery. 'This here's the hot-press - hand me some of those soup plates and I'll show you how it works.' Removing the plates from the rack on the after bulkhead, Steve handed them to Peter who began stacking them into a carousel within the walls of the cabinet. 'This contraption's got four compartments,' continued Peter from his crouched position, spinning the revolving appliance in a hands-on demonstration. 'There's one each for soup, entrée and dinner plates and another for sweet dishes. You just turn it in any direction until you come to whichever you're looking for.' Straightening up, he gestured to several large holes in the surface. 'That's where you put the veg and sauce dixies,' and pointing at the sliding doors, he added, 'and your meats and puddings go inside. It's simple really, and it keeps everything hot till it's needed. Still, you and me only have to worry about loading it up and emptying it out afterwards. We don't get involved in the serving - the Second Steward and Archie see to that,'

'Archie? That's the Bedroom Steward you were talking about - isn't it?' enquired Steve.

'Yeah!' replied Peter, tying a pantry cloth around his midriff. 'He's sixty years old today but from the way he tears around you wouldn't think it. Tell you what though. I wouldn't turn my back on him if I was you, not till you get to know him at any rate. He's as queer as a six-bob note, and it's my guess that with you being a new boy he'll try tickling your fancy - if you get me. He tried it with me in the beginning. I just told him to fuck off and he's left me alone ever since. Apart from that Archie's all right, and he'll always buy you a beer if you're skint.' Handing Steve a pantry cloth from the pile on the work surface, he continued. 'Knot that around your waist while you're strapping up and your dungarees won't get wet.' Just then a buzzer sounded and Peter walked over to an as yet closed hatchway. Pressing the upper of a pair of buttons, he said. 'This here's a dumb waiter, and that buzzer was the galley telling us the food's ready. It'll be on its way up in a jiffy.'

'I thought a dumb waiter was a kind of sideboard,' said Steve, surprised by Peter's revelation. 'Well, that's what they taught us at the Vindi. Said it was the saloon steward's best friend so long as it was kept clean and tidy.'

'It can be either,' answered Peter, leaning lazily against the bulkhead while awaiting the arrival of what was in fact a food elevator. 'This one's electric, but on some of the older ships they're rope operated. Those you're talking about are wooden and don't go anywhere.'

Peter had hardly stopped speaking when a light flashed on next to the upper button and the door of the hatch slid open to reveal half-a dozen piping-hot dixies. 'These are the vegetables and sauces I was telling you about,' said Peter, indicating to Steve that he should help remove the containers from the lift and stow them in the appropriate holes. 'As soon as it's empty we'll send it back down to the galley and then they'll send up the rest.'

Protecting his hands with a pantry cloth, Steve lowered a dixieful of boiled potatoes into the waiting cavity and was reaching for the lid when the Second Steward entered the pantry accompanied by a beanpole of a fellow with a balding head and what appeared to be a pencil-lined moustache. Steve instinctively dropped the lid and as it clattered to the deck he spun around to confront Archie whose face crumpled into a grin.

'I see young Peter's been blabbing his mouth off again,' said the Bedroom Steward, as he minced over to the sink and began scrubbing his hands beneath the hot water tap. 'It's all right sweetie, you don't have to worry about me. You're not my type and even if you were I wouldn't take advantage without your say-so. I'll say this for you though - you're a nice looking boy.........but that Peter, spreading malicious rumours. He'd better watch his bum from now on.'

Steve reddened, exchanging glances with Peter, who sniggered, and said. 'You've got to catch me first, Archie. I know you're quick but you've got to remember you're sixty now. Wouldn't want you having a heart attack on your birthday and missing tonight's piss-up.'

'Cheeky young bitch,' said Archie, as he finished drying his hands and set about placing serving spoons in each of the dixies. 'Any more of that my girl and you'll be going ashore on your own tonight and no mistake.' Steve felt confused and looked to Sec for enlightenment; but the Second Steward just shrugged and opened the doors of the servery.

Steve couldn't believe it. Peter, a homosexual? Archie almost certainly - but Peter? Surely not - not after the way he'd been talking about Archie. He certainly hoped not, not with them sharing a cabin. He'd have to tackle Peter just as soon as the two of them were alone together, but for the time being he needed to focus on the job.

On the dot of twelve-thirty one of the stewards stood at the entrance to the saloon beating a gong with a muffled drumstick, summoning the hierarchy to lunch. Within seconds, officers and engineers began to occupy their seats and shortly thereafter the initial orders began to arrive at the servery. If the stewards had their hands full then so did the lads in the pantry. As fast as the courses were served the soiled tableware was returned to the sink where Steve was overwhelmed by the influx. Suds and perspiration flew in all directions as he fought to keep up with the rush. As fast as an item of crockery or silverware was placed on the drainer it was grabbed by Peter who dried it and returned it to its repository; plates and dishes to their racks and cutlery into wickerwork baskets. The pace was frenzied, but to have paused would have resulted in backlog. It was simply a matter of persisting; for at least three-quarters of an hour, after which there were signs of a gradual slowdown. Through the open doors of the servery Steve could see that little-by-little the saloon was emptying. The flow of dirty dishes and silverware reduced to a dribble and after what seemed a prolonged eternity, ceased altogether. Drying his hands on a pantry cloth, he exclaimed, 'Phew! Is it always like this?'

'Yeah - pretty much,' replied Peter, untying the pantry cloth from around his waist and laying it on the work surface. 'It'll be even busier with passengers on board, but you'll soon get used to it.'

Steve could only wonder what it was like with a full load of passengers, but for the time being he was simply grateful for the respite. 'What do we do now?' he asked.

'Get our own grub,' replied Peter, swiping a couple of plates from the carousel and placing them on top of the hot-press. 'Here, grab yourself a knife and fork and get stuck in before those hungry-gutted stewards get in here and clear everything up.' Archie and the Second Steward were already loading their plates and as soon as the press was clear Peter and Steve followed suit.

'Where do we eat?' asked Steve. 'Do we have our own mess-room?'

'Sure, but no one uses it,' answered Peter, pouring gravy over a handsome helping of steak-and-kidney pudding. 'We usually eat in the saloon. If we were to use the mess-room off the working alleyway the food would be cold when we got there.' Steve, whose plate was overflowing with roast pork and vegetables, followed Peter out of the pantry and into the saloon, making for a large circular table that was already occupied by Archie and the Second Steward. They were shortly joined by the three assistant stewards who until recently had been waiting on the higher echelons of the pecking order.

For a while the seven of them ate in silence and Steve, between mouthfuls, contemplated the view through the windows. From up here, overlooking the fore-deck, he could see almost the entire length of the King George V Dock, and the ships that he'd passed in the morning. He was about to ask if there was any more news about a prospective sailing date, when Archie interrupted, 'Well then, young Steve. What's it feel like to be eating at the Captain's table?'

Steve gulped and glanced quickly at the gathering, wondering if this was just a slice of hokum for the benefit of the newly-joined greenhorn; but they were all munching away, seemingly engrossed in their meal.

'Captain's table? You're joking,' said Steve. 'Honest?'

'It most certainly is,' replied Archie, daintily forking a Brussels sprout into his mouth. 'Only the best is good enough for the catering staff of the *Alice Springs*. When we're at sea the 'Old Man' and half the passengers eat at this table. The rest of the bloods eat with the Chief Engineer - over there,' continued Archie, waving his fork in the direction of a similarly sized table on the other side of the saloon. You should consider yourself a very privileged young man.'

'Blood's?' whispered Steve to Peter, as Archie carried on eating. 'What's he talking about?'

'Passengers,' replied Peter, sitting with his knife and fork erect, his elbows on the table. 'Bloods is what they're known as to the likes of us - and their cabins, or staterooms if you want to be posh, are called sheds. Old Archie here has eight sheds to service each morning - four doubles and four singles. No wonder he's showing his age.'

'I've warned you once already today, Peter,' cautioned the Bedroom Steward, with mock irritation. 'Any more of that and you know what's coming to you.'

'Promises, promises,' chortled Peter, as he resumed eating, leaving Steve in even more of a quandary as to the sexual status of his cheeky cabin mate. 'I'll believe it when it happens.'

One by one they finished their lunches and settled to enjoy their cigarettes, lapsing into general conversation, most of it chit-chat and no mention was made of any sailing date. Eventually, they rose and dispersed, the stewards to wherever leaving the boys to clear away and to finish cleaning down in the pantry. Archie was the last to leave and as he exited the saloon, he called, 'See you later, Steve,' and with a kiss blown in Peter's direction, he added. 'And you too, Peter.'

As Steve gathered up an armful of soiled crockery he flashed a look at Peter who was collecting up the cruets and serviette rings. Now was as good a time as any, he thought, wondering how best he should pose the question. Suddenly, it all gushed out. 'Peter, you're not........you're not........?' he stammered, unable to complete the

17

sentence which Peter finished for him.

'Queer?' said Peter, as he slid the silverware on to a dumb waiter. 'No, course I'm bloody well not. It was all part of a game between Archie and me for your benefit and everyone else played along. That's something else you're going to have to get used to, leg pulling and the like. You'll get the piss taken out of you something rotten at times, especially being a first tripper - but it happens to us all and there isn't any harm meant.'

Steve felt mightily relieved. He could put up with the odd bit of leg pulling - just as long as he didn't have to sleep with his back to the bulkhead. In fact, he felt so good about things that he volunteered, 'Tell you what, if you want to go into Plaistow this afternoon I'll finish sugiing that deck-head. I'm not going anywhere.'

'You sure?' replied Peter, wiping a smudge of apple sauce from the tablecloth. 'I shan't be gone long - it's just that I need some new socks. The ones I'm wearing are nearly worn out.'

'Sure,' answered Steve. 'So long as Sec doesn't mind.'

'He won't mind as long as the job gets done,' said Peter. 'Thanks a lot. We'll get the pantry squared away and then I'll get going. I'll be back before afternoon tea.'

The deck in the pantry was washed at the end of each sitting, so as Peter dashed aft to empty the rosie Steve made a start on the scrub-out. When Peter returned, he offered, 'You can empty the rosie this evening while I do the scrub-out - it's only fair that we take it in turns.' And with a breezy, 'Cheerio - see you later,' he left Steve to carry on single-handed.

Steve reflected that he had little to grumble about as he left the pantry and ambled back to the passengers' smoke room. All right, he'd fallen victim to some good-natured banter but that was only to be expected, and if he bided his time he was certain to get even in the long-run. In the meantime he simply had to remain vigilant, and avoid becoming a stooge for the pranksters.

Left with his thoughts Steve worked steadily and it wasn't long before the deck-head was free of tobacco stains. Standing back to admire his handiwork he dried his hands on his dungarees and took a Rothmans from the pack in his pocket. He'd just lit up when the Second Steward unexpectedly appeared, and queried, 'All finished,

18

Lad?' Steve almost jumped out of his skin, suddenly concerned that the leading hand would want to know Peter's whereabouts. 'It's okay,' reassured Sec, 'he asked my permission before leaving.' Expressing his satisfaction with the newly-washed deck-head, he continued, 'You may as well knock off for an hour or so. Everyone else has got their head down so there's no reason why you shouldn't.' Then, almost as an afterthought, he enquired. 'By the way, what do you think of shipboard life now that you've tasted it?'

'All right,' answered Steve, glad that he was able to engage in conversation with someone with a stripe on his sleeve without feeling intimidated. 'Everyone seems friendly enough - that's what I was worried about more than anything. I'm not afraid of hard work.'

'That's just as well, because you'll be grafting for more than seventy hours a week when we're at sea, so make the most of it while you're able.'

'That's something else I wanted to ask,' said Steve, following Sec into the alleyway. 'Has there been any further talk of a sailing date? The Superintendent seemed pretty coy about it when I mentioned it earlier.'

'I'll let you into a secret,' replied the Second Steward, tapping the side of his nose. 'I've just been chatting with the Chief Engineer and he reckons they'll have everything up and running within the next forty-eight hours. If that's the case we should get a sailing date shortly afterwards. At one stage it looked like a shipyard job, but the Chief knows his engines and managed to convince them otherwise.'

It was encouraging news, and as Steve collected his bucket and returned to the pantry there was an additional spring in his step. He was eager to be away, and was hoping that the Chief Engineer's word was as good as his supposed expertise.

2

Instead of going to his cabin as the Second Steward had suggested, Steve climbed up to the starboard side of the boat deck for a wider-ranging view of the most famous group of docks in the world. The scene that greeted him was breathtaking. Everywhere he looked there was industry of some sort: tugs fussing about with lighters, an old Thames sailing barge that was barely moving but making her way to somewhere or other, while directly opposite a floating crane was hoisting an enormous generator from a pontoon on to the deck of the *Patonga*. Further afield he could see upper works and funnels amid the cranes and derricks in the Royal Albert Dock, and further west in the Royal Victoria Dock. At the western end of King George V Dock, furthest from the lock gates and adjacent to the dry dock, a freighter was being eased from her moorings, a tug with a line attached leading. At this stage she was some way away, so he wandered around to the opposite side of the funnel casing and scrutinized the once-busy quayside. In sharp contrast with the morning, when it had been seething with labourers and commerce, it was completely deserted. That's odd, he thought, wondering at the lack of activity, so seeing a fellow in a white boiler-suit, working on the propeller of one of the lifeboats, he approached, and asked, politely, 'Excuse me, but do you know where the dockers and stevedores have disappeared to?'

'Finished for the day.' answered the boiler-suit, as he slapped a handful of grease on to the lifeboat's propeller shaft. 'There's nothing left to discharge, and we won't begin loading until they're satisfied the engines are functioning properly.'

Steve nodded, satisfied with the explanation - but then asked, 'Are you one of the engineers?'

'Yes - I'm the Junior Fourth,' answered the overalled workman, wiping his hands on a wad of cotton-waste. 'Why do you ask?'

'Oooh........no particular reason,' fibbed Steve, staring vacantly at the *Alice Springs'* funnel. 'I was just wondering how the work on the engines was progressing - that's all.'

'Well, unless things have changed while I've been fiddling about up here the Chief reckons sometime tomorrow - but don't repeat it in case anything else goes pear-shaped.'

That was good enough for Steve - two different people singing from more or less the same hymn sheet. Thanking the engineer and promising to keep his mouth shut he climbed down to the after well-deck and up to the poop, from where rubbish was dumped into a lighter that was lashed to the outboard quarter. Tonight it would be his turn to empty the rosie so it was important he knew where to come.

Idling away the minutes, high on the poop, directly aft of the petty officers' accommodation in the after deck house, Steve leant on the taffrail and surveyed the vessel immediately astern. She was the second of the company's ships he'd seen in the morning and the name on her bows was clearly legible. The *Lilac Hill* appeared considerably older than the *Alice Springs* which was relatively modern, and although her colour-scheme was identical he imagined the A&P symbol looking squashed and insipid on the sides of her spindle-thin funnel.

And then, without warning, the stillness was shattered by a siren. Steve swung around and there, sliding serenely past was a British India line freighter, outward bound for Chittagong, Chalna and Calcutta. She was the *Chakdara,* and the ship he'd seen earlier from the boat deck. Her name evoked visions of all kinds of places on the Indian sub-continent, whereas the dusky, expressionless faces of her crewmen suggested it was nothing extraordinary and just another word that was vaguely related to their homeland. He waved to the men on her fo'c'sle and several waved back; and one of them smiled, exposing two of the whitest rows of teeth that the pantry boy had ever laid eyes on. As the *Chakdara* slipped by, her attendant tugs guiding her safely between the two rows of shipping, Steve had a glance at his watch. It was past four o'clock, and Peter should be back from his shopping.

Back at the pantry he found tea plates and teacups piled up in the sink, but Peter was notably absent. He was wondering where all the soiled crockery had come from when the puzzle was duly resolved. The Second Mate shoved his way through the door and laid a tray on the drainer, saying, 'Here you are, Lad, the steward forgot to collect it from my cabin.' As the officer departed Steve suddenly realized that this was the sequel to afternoon tea which he'd completely forgotten, and that strapping it up would be part of his afternoon schedule.

It was getting on for a quarter to five by the time he'd finished; so with high tea due to be served at five o'clock he began removing plates from their racks and loading them into the hot-press. All of a sudden the door flew open and in burst Peter. 'Sorry, Mate,' gasped the other boy in a breathless gabble. 'I didn't mean to be this long. It's just that I bumped into an old pal from the Vindi. He left the week before me and we've been swinging the lamp together. He's sailing for Canada tonight on the *Beaverlake*. I don't envy him at this time of year.'

High tea was nowhere near as frenetic as lunch. Half the officers were ashore so didn't need feeding, and Archie had left a huge plate of sandwiches in the duty mess fridge for those engineers who were working. By six o'clock Steve and Peter were busily engaged in the strap-up which didn't take long and didn't consume many calories. 'Right,' said Peter, noisily slamming the doors of the hot-press,' I'll scrub down while you go and empty the rosie - and don't forget to wash it out afterwards. There's a hosepipe next to the chute.'

Leaving the scrub-out to Peter, Steve lifted the rosie and made his way aft; but instead of taking the outboard route he hurried down to the working alleyway and headed straight for his locker and his Vindi uniform tunic. With the offending garment draped over his forearm he proceeded to the poop and the chute that was attached to the taffrail. At sea, the chute would be suspended from the lee-side rail so that any rubbish would be taken clear of the ship, away from the *Alice Springs'* hull; but in port it was affixed to whichever side the lighter was moored to, which in this specific instance was starboard.

Darkness had fallen, and a gentle breeze ruffled his hair as Steve scanned the ships at their moorings. Although the outlines of the vessels were barely visible every deck and superstructure was floodlit, while several of the more modern examples had their names illuminated in neon, immediately abaft of the wheelhouse. His surroundings were spellbinding and Steve could have stayed there indefinitely; but then it dawned that he'd better get moving if he wanted to go ashore with the rest of the crowd to celebrate Archie's birthday.

The rosie was speedily upended; and as the rubbish plopped into the lighter, and before he could think better of it, his uniform tunic followed suit. As the last material vestige of his days at the Vindi landed among the leftovers Steve took hold of the hosepipe, happily satisfied that although he was still a first tripper, and would be until the voyage was completed, he'd no longer stand out like a gargoyle.

By a quarter to seven virtually the entire catering department was piling down the *Alice Springs'* gangway and on to the quayside. Steve, dressed in his wind-cheater jacket, felt completely relaxed, and participated in the conversation feeling for all the world like a seasoned old salt rather than a newly-joined débutante. He looked at Peter who winked, and said, 'No worries, Mate. You look just like the rest of us now.'

The assortment of cooks and stewards, a dozen in total, hurried along the dock road, past the P&O office towards number sixteen gate KG5 where the whole assemblage wheeled right on to Woolwich Manor Way. After continuing on for another sixty seconds they approached a solidly-built edifice of slightly rounded configuration which was clearly where the party was heading for. There was a large scarlet barrel suspended above the doorway, and shiny gold lettering proclaimed that this was indeed the legendary Roundhouse, a shrine of immense significance to seamen whose ships were berthed towards the eastern end of the Royal group.

'Right,' called Archie, who along with the Second Steward and Ted the Chief Cook, was several yards ahead of the rest of them. 'The first drinks are on me, and then we'll be having a kitty. I'll collect the money once we're inside. Okay?' No one answered and Archie's second, 'Okay?' was completely drowned out as the Bedroom Steward was bundled through the doorway into an explosion of sound and humanity. Archie was swept along to the bar where other drinkers made room for the newly-celebrated sexagenarian who drew a pound from his wallet, and bellowed, 'Twelve pints of Red Barrel, please, Landlord.'

There was nowhere to sit - all seats were taken, but to Steve this was a just minor inconvenience. He was more than happy just to wallow in the confinement of the first dockside tavern he'd ever set foot in. It was so completely at odds with his regular watering holes. They were of the more 'local' variety where the weekly highlights were the darts and domino matches. The Roundhouse, by comparison, was an altogether different proposition.

Through the smoke-laden atmosphere the hand-painted murals adorning the upper walls appeared almost lifelike, such was the accuracy of detail. The artwork depicted scenes from the Royal Docks but was discoloured with age and tobacco smoke. Many of the vessels portrayed were long since gone; but whether it was the Blue Star 'A' class liner, all of which had been wartime casualties, or the *Dominion Monarch*, some of whose crew were probably drinking in this very establishment, they were a credit to the artist's dexterity.

'Wha'd'ya think?' bawled Peter, waving an arm at the room in general. 'Opens your eyes, doesn't it? Most of these blokes are off ships in the docks, and every pub within miles will be just as busy. Peter took a draught from his glass, wiped his mouth on the back of his hand; and turning to grab the shoulder of a boy behind him, declared, 'This is Jimmy Craddock, the ship's galley boy. He comes from Glasgow and he's a right piss artist, just like the rest of the galley rats.'

The other boy turned, smiled and acknowledged the newcomer. 'Hi - how are y'doin? I'd ignore this little tosser if I were you. He's the piss artist if anyone is.' Steve responded easily to Jimmy's friendliness and nodded in turn to Ted the Chief Cook, Norman the Second Cook, Davy the Baker and John the Butcher as Peter rattled off their names. 'Right, that's about it,' said Peter. 'I think you know everyone now so let's get stuck in and enjoy ourselves.'

'What about the Chief Steward?' asked Steve. 'Doesn't he socialize with the rest of us?'

'What, him? The Boss - miserable bastard,' complained Peter. 'There wouldn't be any beer on the ship if he had his way. He's

24

fuckin' teetotal - and a Scouse to boot if you've ever heard of such a thing.' Steve hadn't heard of such a thing; in fact, even the word Scouse was alien so he asked Peter to elucidate.

'Cor! stone the fuckin' crows,' retorted Peter, in shell-shocked amazement. 'Don't you know anything? Scouses come from Liverpool and they're usually a bigger bunch of piss artists than the Jocks - and that's saying something.' At that very moment a table close to the jukebox became vacant as several drinkers, fed up with the racket, emptied up their glasses and left. Peter had been on the lookout for just such an opening, and no sooner had the previous occupants evacuated then he pushed through the crowd and took possession of the table for themselves. 'Here, get yourselves sat down,' he called to Steve and Jimmy who were in hot pursuit, shortly to be joined by Archie who was in the process of collecting the kitty, 'it looks like we've got to fork out.'

'Now then you boys,' sang the Bedroom Steward, limp-wristedly, swinging a bagful of coins. 'I hope you're going to have a good time without making pigs of yourselves, otherwise it'll be duff for you three rather than birthday cake - and you know what that means.'

'Oh! We should be so lucky,' cried Peter, mimicking Archie's effeminate mannerisms as he rose to his feet, shoved a hand into his hip pocket, and demanded, 'How much d'ya want?'

'Three shillings each off you lads,' replied Archie, flicking a feigned slap in the direction of Peter who ducked out of the way - and nearly brained himself on the perspex cover of the jukebox. 'Serves you right for being so cheeky,' shrilled Archie, in a fit of laughter, before enquiring in a more conciliatory tone. 'Are you all right?'

'Yeah,' replied Peter, ruefully, massaging his scalp while aiming a kick at the jukebox. 'But no thanks to you, you old bugger.'

'Hey, steady on,' reproved the birthday boy, with an accusing wag of an index finger 'Have a go at me by all means, but don't get us thrown out of here for damaging brewery property. You've only yourself to blame.'

Peter grimaced and sat down, still favouring a tender spot where his head had collided with the jukebox. 'How long do you reckon on staying here, Archie? There's hardly room to swing a cat.'

'We're going to have one more in here and then go round to The Royal Oak,' said Archie, collecting nine shillings worth of loose change from the table. 'There might be more room in there. Be about fifteen minutes - I'll let you know when we're leaving.'

As Archie moved away, Peter said, 'There, told you, didn't I? Three bob for a night on the piss isn't bad. Cost us a darn sight more if we were out on our own and no mistake.'

Jimmy, who'd been virtually silent up until then, nodded in agreement. 'No doubt about it. We'd be lucky to get a couple of pints each for that money.'

Apart from acknowledging Jimmy and the rest of the galley staff Steve had hardly spoken himself since entering The Roundhouse. But following Archie's announcement, he asked, 'If you reckon all the other pubs'll be crowded, what's the point of moving elsewhere?'

'Because if we get round to the Royal Oak early enough we should all get a seat,' said Jimmy, 'and not only that, it's not usually as rowdy as this.' For the following few minutes they engaged in the kind of conversation that youngsters were noted for. They talked about cars and motorbikes, girls and Rock 'n' Roll music, sometimes straining to be heard above Brenda Lee, Fats Domino and Del Shannon who were pouring forth from the jukebox.

Suddenly, Peter said, 'Here we go,' as he spotted the Second Steward beckoning them from the doorway. Without further delay they sprung to their feet, swallowed what was left in their glasses and pushed through the squash into the dimly-lit street where an annoying drizzle was falling on to an already damp pavement.

'Good job it isn't very far,' said Jimmy, as they followed the rest of the group through a maze of narrow side streets. 'If it sets in any harder I'm going to get soaked. I only came ashore in this woolly.'

Steve was thankful for his waterproof wind-cheater as they neared the Royal Oak, an odd-looking construction that looked as if the roof and upper stories had been completely stripped off and supplanted by a temporary covering.

'It looks a bit of a dump,' observed Steve, studying the flat-roofed abnormality. 'What happened to the rest of it?'

'It got blown off in a wartime air raid,' informed Peter, knowledgeably. 'They reckon the bomb obliterated a row of houses a couple of streets away, but the blast blew the roof and upper floors off the 'Oak'. After the rubble was cleared they decided that instead of going for a complete rebuild they'd just cover what was left and make do.'

Outward appearances can be deceptive, as Steve discovered as they entered a spacious main bar that was comfortably furnished and tastefully decorated. As an added refinement the floor was carpeted, as if the licensees were aiming for a more polished clientèle than the average waterfront pot-house. However, their efforts had been spoilt because if the bar was a model of discernment the same wasn't true of the toilets. They were spotlessly clean, but had been the subject of a makeshift repair job; for as Peter explained, 'When they bodged up the roof they fixed the drainpipes so that they emptied into the urinals, but if it rains really hard then you know what happens - they overflow on to the floor.'

'That's right,' agreed Jimmy, 'and just to keep a check on the water-level there's a Plimsoll Line painted on the wall.'

Steve took a sip from his pint. He imagined the Plimsoll Line tale to be a shaggy-dog story - although the artwork actually existed - but he made a mental note to be heedful when using the loo.

There was little doubt that the group from the *Alice Springs* had arrived at the Royal Oak in the nick of time because within minutes of their arrival the room was full, and not all of the latecomers were seamen. Several of those now making an entrance were female, dripping with jewellery and dressed in the most expensive of costumes. They gathered at one end of the bar, perching on stools and ordering their drinks whilst lighting up filter-tipped cigarettes. Steve could only gawp in amazement as one of the girls, a striking brunette with long flowing hair and ruby-red lips, seeing the young man's eyes popping out of their sockets, smiled seductively, the invitation as plain as a pikestaff. Steve grinned sheepishly and blushed, averting his gaze, pretending he hadn't been staring.

'Don't get too carried away, Son,' murmured a voice beside him. 'It's what's in your wallet she's interested in, not what's hidden in your underpants.'

The voice was that of the Second Steward, and Steve guessed he was in for a sermon. He glanced again at the girl who was now eyeing-up a fellow with 'Union-Castle Line' emblazoned across the front of his jumper. 'You mean she's a prostitute, don't you?'

'Exactly,' answered the Second Steward, 'and so are the rest of them. All right, they'll give you the time of your life but it'll cost you - a lot more than you can afford, and they'll likely present you with more than you bargained for, if you get my meaning?'

Steve understood, remembering an extremely graphic lecture that his squad had been given shortly before their departure from the Vindi. A local GP had visited the school with the express purpose of warning the boys against the dangers of tropical and sexually transmitted diseases. The discourse had been vividly illustrated and some of the photographs had been sufficient to suppress any immediate thoughts of sexual activity - and were far more effective than the bromide that was reputedly added to the cocoa. He smiled as he remembered the medic's preamble - when he'd introduced himself as a pox doctor. The GP had reiterated the point by stressing that he was a pox doctor - not a 'poxy' doctor.

While Steve's train of thought had meandered back to the Vindi, the Second Steward had been relating how the Albert Dock Seaman's Hospital was frequently the first port of call for homeward-bound philanderers. Their purpose was to avail themselves of a dose of penicillin, hoping it would rid them of a different kind of dose before making their way home to their partners. Steve was jolted back to the present as the Second Steward concluded, 'And if penicillin doesn't do the trick then God help them. The alternatives don't bear thinking about.'

The remarks had certainly struck home and from that moment on, apart from the occasional peep, Steve ignored the assembled pulchritude. In due course, the brunette who'd quickened his pulse at the outset, slipped on her coat and strolled out on the arm of a fifty-year-old. Sec rolled his eyes in despair. 'Stupid bastard,' he sighed, shaking his head in bewilderment. 'They never learn. He'll be lucky if he's got the price of a pint in his pocket by morning.'

Steve was also surprised by the number of homosexual seamen who were present, openly flaunting their sexuality, holding their cigarettes female fashion and calling each other 'Duckie', or 'Deary', or if one of their number was out of favour, referring to them as,

"That silly cow".

'You have to remember that being a practising homosexual is a criminal offence in the UK,' explained Sec, continuing his lesson in morality. 'That's why they come away to sea - so they can carry on in their own sweet way without fear of either persecution or prosecution.' And gesticulating at the room in general, he added, 'You'll find most if not all of them are stewards, and that the majority of these are off the *Kenya Castle*.'

Thereafter, Archie's birthday was celebrated in typical seaman-like fashion, and by closing time most had exceeded their limits. As Jimmy had accurately predicted, Peter had drunk himself silly and ended up flat on his face in the toilets. He emerged soaked to the skin, having been helped to his feet by other drinkers who'd handled him cautiously, fully conscious of the dubious water quality.

The rain had stopped by the time the lads from the *Alice Springs* headed across the road and through gate seventeen, a handily-placed pedestrian entrance that opened into the docks, more or less right on their doorstep. Archie was still in the lead, seemingly as sober as ever when he of all people might have been excused for surpassing his parameters. Steve subsequently learnt that Archie had a copious capacity; and whereas it was customary for ordinary folk to begin each new day with a cuppa, it was Archie's practice to greet every new dawn with a 'livener'.

As for Peter: apart from some occasional drivel he was dead to the world as soon as his head hit the pillow. 'That'll do,' sighed Jimmy, mopping his brow on the sleeve of his pullover after he and Steve had stripped the delinquent of his saturated clothing and bundled him over his bunkboard. 'He'll feel like shit in the morning, but that's his lookout.' Anyway, I'm away to bed, and if I were you I'd do likewise.'

'Yeah! I probably will,' answered Steve, who by this time was close to bursting and in desperate need of the toilet, 'but first of all I'm going for a pee, and then I might go for a smoke.'

'That's up to you,' replied Jimmy, 'just as long as you remember it's a six o'clock turn to, and if you're thirty-seconds late the Second Steward'll be a totally different guy to the one you were drinking with earlier.'

29

Despite the lateness there was the hint of curry in the air that Steve suspected was wafting across from the *Patonga*. He was leaning on the outboard rail of the boat deck, in virtually the same position that he'd occupied that very afternoon. It all seemed so long ago now and so much had happened in the meantime. He drew heavily on his cigarette so that the tip flared redly, contrasting with the brilliance of the brightly lit ships at their moorings. So, this was the end of his first working day as a seaman, and although he hadn't actually been anywhere it had been thoroughly rewarding. He took another long drag from his Rothmans before pinching it out and tossing the dog-end overboard. He hunched his shoulders against the chill before making his way down to his cabin, quietly confident that the seafaring tradition was the ideal way to earn a living.

3

'Come on you blokes, shake a leg,' called a voice from beyond the darkness that symbolized Steve's current level of consciousness, 'If you're late turning to it won't be my fault. It'll be you that gets the bollocking - not me.' Steve was being aggressively shaken, and the speaker's words eventually penetrated; but even when he finally rolled over and stared straight into an unshaven face it was several seconds before he grasped that the voice was that of the night-watchman, who was making the rounds of the working alleyway, rousing the *Alice Springs'* catering staff.

'Thank goodness for that,' said the watchman, as Steve showed the first signs of life. 'I was beginning to think that you two were as dead as the Dinosaurs.'

'What's the time?' groaned Steve, wearily, propping himself up on an elbow while rubbing sleep from his eyes with his knuckles.

'Five-thirty,' grunted the watchman, who appeared not to be in the best of moods as he prodded the snoring Peter with a bony finger that might just have well have been a roll of tissue-paper. Finally, realizing he was flogging a dead horse, he grumbled, 'Bollocks to him - I've got to wake the others up yet.' And with that, he stalked grumpily out, slamming the door shut behind him.

As Steve swung his legs out of bed he heard Peter snort, but it was a false alarm and it soon became clear that his cabin mate was still in hibernation. He shook him vigorously, while struggling simultaneously into his underclothes. 'Come on you lazy bugger,' he yelled. 'I'm not going to be late for work just because you can't get up in the morning.'

'Piss off,' moaned Peter, unexpectedly. 'You're worse than that bloody watchman?'

31

Steve recoiled, peering at the figure lying flat on its back without a flicker to suggest it was living. 'Have you been awake all the time?' he quizzed, remembering Peter's fondness for nonsense.

'Course I have,' answered Peter, irritably, opening his eyes and shielding them from the glare of the light bulb. 'Couldn't be otherwise, could I? Not with that fuckin' night-watchman bawling his fuckin' head off - fuckin' foghorn.'

Steve winced at the foul-mouthed tirade, but still managed a smile as he clambered into his dungarees, and said, 'Well, as far as I'm concerned you can stay there - you can't say you haven't been warned.'

Steve's show of urgency had the desired effect and as he set off for the wash-room carrying his towel, soap and flannel, Peter showed the first signs of movement.

As Steve entered the pantry he was greeted with a mouth-watering aroma, and by Archie who was pouring himself some tea having downed his gin and tonic beforehand. Over at the salamander a steward called Donald was piling freshly-made toast on to a dinner plate while at the sink, another - whose name Steve had momentarily forgotten - was stirring up a bucketful of sugi.

'Morning! young Steve,' said Archie, breezily, as he removed a dishful of butter from the refrigerator. 'I trust you're feeling hale and hearty. I'm not sure about Peter, though. Made sure he had his three-bobs-worth, didn't he?' He smiled wickedly as he spread a huge smear of butter on his toast. 'With a bit of luck he'll have a cracking hangover this morning.'

With Steve showing all the initiative of a spare bouquet at a wedding, Archie motioned to the toast on the work top. 'Help yourself to a slice of toast and some tea,' he invited, dipping a spoon into a jar of marmalade, you won't get your breakfast for ages. Here,' he added, taking a fancy blue mug from its hook and placing it next to the teapot, 'this one's a spare so you might as well have it.'

Just then Peter tumbled into the pantry looking the colour of a half-rotten cabbage. His uncombed hair flopped over his forehead and his appearance was that of a scarecrow. He poured himself some tea but waved away the toast that was offered. Archie regarded him scornfully, and declared, 'Serves you right for being greedy.'

Steve ate his toast in silence, hoping Peter made a speedy recovery because if he didn't, with the breakfast strap-up on the horizon, he could see himself doing the job solo. As for what he should do in the meantime; the answer came floating through the ether.

'Steve!' called the Second Steward, from the saloon foyer. 'I want you to take a bucket of water and scrub out the engineers' alleyway.' Almost immediately a head appeared at the servery, and Sec continued. 'And use plenty of elbow grease - the whole shebang's like a shit-house. When you've finished the alleyway you can make a start on their duty mess - and if it isn't done and dusted by breakfast you can leave it till afterwards.'

The engineers' alleyway was exactly as Sec had described it; the filth on the deck was deeply ingrained and the pattern was virtually obscured. The problem had arisen owing to the engineers traipsing back and forth between their accommodation area and the engine room which had been labelled, 'Grease-pot Canyon', by the firemen.

Following the assertion that the place was a shit-house Steve hadn't been expecting a cakewalk - but nor had he expected hard labour. It was obvious from the start that soap and hot water alone would be useless and that something more stringent was needed. He was on the verge of seeking out Sec and asking his advice when he experienced a flash of genius. Leaving his scrubbing brush and bar of Sunlight he dashed back to the pantry and returned with a large tin of Ajax. This'll soon shift it, he thought, sprinkling the deck with a liberal dusting of scouring powder. The Ajax worked just as the instructions had suggested; but unluckily for Steve, it also scoured the decorative pattern from the oilcloth. His face registered absolute horror.

'Having a spot of bother?' enquired Donald, who'd arrived at the opportune time with a tray of tea for the Third Engineer. 'Try using a brush with a handle,' he proposed, 'like the one they use in the galley. And chuck in a spoonful of caustic - not too much mind you, otherwise you'll bugger up the lino.'

Steve was on the point of replying that the lino was already buggered but thought better of it. Instead, he thanked Donald for his counsel and did precisely as the steward had advocated. The caustic soda worked wonders. The job was completed in a trice and the engineers' alleyway, which was to become his regular early-morning scrub-out, was from that point onwards a model of exemplary housekeeping. And as for the scarred patch of lino: Steve developed a bout of amnesia and the engineers themselves got the blame; something to do with acid on the soles of their boots.

During the course of the morning the *Alice Springs'* crew, and Steve in particular, heard the news they'd been impatiently longing for. The Chief Engineer emerged from the engine room and declared the engines repaired and in perfect seagoing fettle. It appeared that the breakdown had been caused by contaminated boiler water. This was obviously a problem peculiar to steamships, and while steamers were generally regarded as more reliable than motor vessels, contaminated boilers were prone to costly and long-lasting damage. So thus it was that the refrigerated cargo liner *Alice Springs* was pronounced seaworthy, and that her eight-and-a-half thousand gross register tons were as fit to face the elements as they had been on the day she was launched.

The Chief Engineer had hardly completed his announcement when the Chief Steward entered the pantry and advised that shore leave had been temporarily suspended. 'We're shifting into the berth currently occupied by the *Lilac Hill*,' he informed. 'She's been sold to the Greeks and we'll be loading the cargo that she was due to take to Australia.'

Steve was instantly aroused. With unbridled spontaneity, and while others were still absorbing the information, he demanded, 'When are we supposed to be sailing?'

The senior catering officer paused briefly, before resuming, 'At the moment we're scheduled to call at Aden for bunkers, then: Adelaide, Melbourne, Sidney, Brisbane..................' Steve's equilibrium was in such a state of imbalance that the Chief Steward's following comments about continuing on to New Zealand before returning home via the Panama Canal went almost unnoticed; and it was only when his superior cast him a disdainful glance, and concluded, 'We'll be sailing on Saturday,' that the substance was fully digested.

A sea of smiles told their own story as the Chief stomped out of the pantry. 'Don't worry,' comforted Archie, patting Steve on the shoulder, 'we've all been in your position at some time or other. It's just that you got swept along with the excitement. I can't say I blame you. It's not every first-tripper that gets a round-the-world voyage for his christening. When I first went to sea it was on colliers, carrying coals from the Tyne to the Thames. How's that for a contrast?'

'My first trip was a run on the *Wollongong*,' chirped a now fully-revived Peter, keen to add his own two-pennyworth. 'We were only on articles for forty-eight hours while we delivered her to a shipyard at Sunderland. Mind you,' he stressed, proudly, proclaiming his subsequent achievements. 'I've already been to Australia and New Zealand on this ship, but they weren't round-the-world trips like this one.'

'Some fellows have been at sea for donkey's years and never been out of the Channel,' commented Archie, as the sound of the luncheon gong resounded around the alleyways. 'Then there's others who happily sail away to the other side of the world and only come home when they have to - like those on the MANZ run, for instance.'

'That's right,' said Peter. 'Those blokes on the MANZ run have certainly hit the jackpot and no mistake. Just imagine - months at a time on the New Zealand coast, and them Kiwi girls......... I'd be dead by the time I was twenty.'

'Hmph!' grunted Archie, with undisguised disapproval. 'Dirty little get. All you think about is boozing yourself silly and getting your end away. You can laugh all you like, my lad, but many a word has been spoken in jest and the speaker hasn't lived to regret it.'

Steve smiled and gave thought to the MANZ run. In his ignorance he'd misconstrued MANZ for 'man's', thinking that while it all sounded idyllic only a masochist could enjoy a two-year stint to wherever, despite Peter's lurid portrayal. It was only later that he learnt that the MANZ run was extremely popular among those who served on it, and that MANZ was an acronym for a Port Line service operating between Montreal, Australia and New Zealand, and that the crews involved were indeed engaged for twenty-four months at a time.

It was later that same afternoon that the *Alice Springs* shifted, taking up the berth recently vacated by the *Lilac Hill* which was being towed to the workshops close to the Connaught Road swing-bridge. There, she would undergo a change of name and have her funnel repainted in the colours of those who'd acquired her. In many respects it was a sad transition for a ship that had faithfully served the Australasian and Pacific Steam Navigation Company for several decades, for although she was to continue in revenue-earning service there were those who thought she would have met an altogether more dignified end at the breakers'.

'Fuckin' Greeks won't look after her like we have,' complained Peter, contemptuously, as they watched the *Lilac Hill* being edged away from the quayside. 'They'll run her on a shoestring until they've made all they can out of her then they'll run her aground on a reef somewhere and claim the insurance.'

Peter's cynicism was perhaps understandable given the Greeks' poor reputation as shipowners; but was it, Steve wondered, really justified? The Mediterranean country was notoriously lacking in the realms of ship husbandry; but as for the owners deliberately wrecking their vessels for the sole purpose of claiming the insurance - well, that was a different matter, and one he found hard to believe. But with time comes awareness, and he subsequently learnt that insurance swindles involving merchant vessels were far from uncommon, and that the Greeks weren't the only practitioners.

No sooner was the *Alice Springs* back alongside then dockers and stevedores set about stuffing her holds with all manner of merchandise for the antipodes. There were Vauxhall motor cars, unassembled and in crates, destined for showrooms all over Australia; electrical switch-gear for a new power station on the outskirts of Melbourne; half a dozen Land Rovers for the New South Wales Police Service; heavy-engineering equipment for a smelting plant deep in the Queensland hinterland - and just about any other manufactured item you could think of. In fact, the *Alice Springs'* was a literal exhibition hall for the workshops and production lines of Britain, a glowing testament to the excellence of the country's entrepreneurs, designers and tradesmen. While Australia was the eventual destination for most of the cargo a sizeable chunk of it would be deposited on the wharves of New Zealand, twelve thousand miles and half a world from its land of creation. When the ship

36

returned home, these very same holds would be bulging with foodstuffs and animal by-products, all of it bound for shopkeepers' counters the length and breadth of the kingdom.

When his duties permitted Steve took a special interest in the loading operations, fascinated as he was by the methods employed to stow even the most unwieldy parcels in the seemingly most inaccessible corners. Even negotiating the hatchways appeared a work of art; the Land Rovers, for instance, that on the face of it entered the holds with only the minimum of clearance. The work would continue from the early hours until evening, when the hatches were covered to prevent the ingress of overnight rainfall.

But it was a case of chasing his tail for the most part, with the mornings especially being particularly lively. In addition to scrubbing the engineers' alleyway and cleaning their duty mess, he'd also been charged with cleaning their heads, wash-room and showers; not the most sanitary of chores but one that was traditionally bestowed on the juniors. He also had a couple of cabins to service, including that of the Junior Fourth, the engineer he'd conversed with on the boat deck. He then had to help prepare morning coffee and complete the strap-up before - hopefully - enjoying a few minutes respite. However, if the Second Steward identified another task - cleaning and refilling the coffee percolator, for instance - then the prospect of a break was forgotten. The afternoons were generally more leisurely but even so, by the time he knocked off he was just about asleep on his feet. Nevertheless, he was far from disillusioned; in fact, he positively relished the workload as it added to his sense of belonging - which was just as well considering that come sailing day, and with a full complement of passengers to cater for, it would be well into the evening before the lights in the pantry were extinguished.

Steve had joined the *Alice Springs* on a Monday with seven shillings and tuppence in his pocket, three shillings of which had been collected by Archie in The Roundhouse. The remaining four and tuppence had to last until Friday when the ship would be signing on articles. That would be their ultimate pay-day until the voyage's completion, although they'd be eligible for an advance at the outset while subs could be drawn when allowed. He'd need a haircut before setting sail and that would account for one and threepence of his remaining money, leaving two and eleven-pence for the meantime. Therefore, any further drinking sprees were out of the question - at least until Friday when the crew would enjoy a final run ashore before sailing.

With Peter and Jimmy equally strapped for cash the Flying Angel, Missions to Seamen, was a haven that didn't cost a fortune. The mission that served the Royal Docks was situated in Victoria Dock Road, immediately opposite Custom House railway station. For any seaman at a loose end or deficient of funds it was a Godsend, selling food and drink at reasonable prices, as well as providing recreational facilities and affordable, short-term accommodation.

And so it was that they found themselves traipsing the mile and a quarter from number 4 shed KG5 to the mission, and while the Flying Angel was a world away from The Roundhouse it was at least a passable alternative. They played darts and snooker, and when tired of games they either read the newspapers or discussed whatever was fashionable - the voyage in the offing for one thing.

'How long does it take to get to Australia?' asked Steve, both Peter and Jimmy having made the trip previously. 'It looks a jolly long way on a map.'

'It's about a month's sailing to Adelaide,' answered Peter, picking his darts out of the dartboard, 'so long as the engines keep running.'

'Why? Are they likely to break down again?' asked Steve, mildly concerned that their arrival in Australia might be further delayed owing to the whims of the *Alice Springs'* boilers.

'Shouldn't think so,' replied Jimmy, with the air of someone who knew what he was talking about. 'The Chief Engineer wouldn't have given us the all clear if he thought there was any kind of uncertainty - not with passengers to consider.'

'You can never be a hundred per-cent sure, though,' voiced Peter, pessimistically. 'Might lose a propeller in the middle of the Indian Ocean and be stranded for weeks while it's sorted.'

'I'll be more than happy if it happened off the New Zealand coast,' enthused Jimmy, clearly relishing the prospect. 'It'd be worth a breakdown if only for the extra weeks in dry dock.'

'What's so special about New Zealand?' asked Steve, posing what many seasoned seafarers would regard as a lunatic question. 'It's either, "New Zealand this", or, "New Zealand that". No-one ever mentions Australia.'

His pals exchanged glances and grinned. 'Because it's so bloody fantastic,' replied Peter, rubbing his hands together in anticipation. 'The scenery's stupendous, the girls are gorgeous and........well, you'll find out when you get there.'

'Just so long as you wear Wrangler jeans and Old Spice aftershave lotion,' added Jimmy, with a gleam in his eye. 'The Kiwi girls can't resist anyone wearing Old Spice and Wranglers. Just remember that and you're laughing.'

That's interesting, thought Steve, whose knowledge of New Zealand was minuscule despite his fascination with travel. It was largely the fault of his schooling, where the main preoccupation had been science and maths while geography had been largely neglected. Apart from Europe, the Americas and Asia, the rest of the world seemed to have been overlooked - or fleetingly touched on at best. Australia and New Zealand, together with Africa and the polar regions, had fallen into this latter grouping, with Australia receiving greater attention than its neighbour in the livestock tradition. All Steve could remember being taught about New Zealand was that sheep outnumbered people by about eighteen-to-one and that the native inhabitants were Maoris. Perhaps he should have made better use of his local library; but even so, he'd spent hours poring over atlases and back-numbers of National Geographic. He even had a small pocket atlas among his belongings; but for some obscure reason, New Zealand had remained as an academic enigma - probably owing to its very remoteness.

The stores arrived on the Wednesday, and were deposited on to the quayside from a van bearing the slogan, 'Cheeseman & Son, Ships' Stores and Provisions', inscribed on its rear doors and side panels. A whole variety of foodstuffs was then craned onto the after well-deck, to be joined shortly thereafter by sufficient butchery products to send London Zoo's lions into raptures. Every member of the catering department, with the exception of the Chief and Second Stewards, then had to transfer the supplies to the storerooms. Storing ship was a back-breaker, especially for the boys who were tasked with shifting fifty, one-hundredweight sacks of potatoes up to the potato locker which was situated high on the poop, immediately for'ard of the deck house. Steve and Peter did the donkey-work while Jimmy had the relative sinecure of stacking the spuds in the locker. The work was exhausting, but arguably preferable to humping innumerable carcasses of frozen meat to the domestic fridges which were located adjacent to the galley. Over lunch, Keith, the steward whose name Steve had earlier forgotten, complained that his shoulder was still numb from the cold, as if it had been injected with a local anaesthetic.

Later that same afternoon Steve had his hair cut at the barber's in Woolwich Manor Way, before spending an hour in the pleasant surroundings of the Royal Victoria Gardens, close to the Woolwich Free Ferry. From the gardens he had a grandstand view of the river, and of the Clan liner *Clan Macrae*, outward bound from the West India Docks for Port Sudan, Beira and Madagascar. He felt quietly content, knowing that if all went according to plan - and barring any further mishaps - his own ship would shortly follow suit.

On Thursday morning the Second Steward toured the ship distributing mailing lists to the various departments. In the pantry, Archie glanced at his before folding it and slipping it into his pocket. Peter screwed his up and tossed it into the rosie while Steve asked, politely, 'What's all this about, Sec?'

'It's the names and addresses of the company's agents,' replied the Second Steward. 'Pop it in an envelope and post it home to your family so they can to write to you while you're away.'

The mailing list read like a Baedeker tour guide, but whereas the well-to-do among British society would willingly invest a small fortune in such a voyage, Steve would be paid for the privilege. He was well acquainted with many of the place names while others he'd never even heard of; but as he linked them together with an imaginary line he could see they encompassed the globe. Port Said, Aden, Adelaide, Melbourne, Sydney, Brisbane, Nelson, Timaru, Napier, Balboa, Christobal, Curacao - even Dunkirk in north-eastern France, the *Alice Springs'* final port of call.

His family would be just as excited as he was, knowing his precise whereabouts at any given moment of asking. But that was of only secondary importance, regular communication being paramount. They needed to know he was alive and well while he needed similar reassurance. Not that they'd have informed him had the case been otherwise - not with him being absent and likely to fret over anything more serious than flu. He remembered how his father had suffered a thrombosis while he was undergoing his six-weeks training at the Vindi. None of this had been mentioned in any of his parents' correspondence, and it was only after arriving home with his father fully recovered that he'd learnt of the illness. Taking a leaf out of Archie's book he carefully folded the mailing list and slid it into his pee-jacket pocket. Turning to Peter, he asked, 'Why did you chuck yours away? Don't you write home to your family?'

'Nah - no point,' answered Peter, his upper lip twisted in a curl. 'They wouldn't write back if I did. You see, we've never really got on. I've always looked after myself, you know, getting my own grub and the like - even when I came home from school. They didn't bother. Dad was always out on the piss while Mum was messing about with her boyfriends. That's why I came away to sea........among other things. Even when I'm on leave I stay with one of my mates - and I sometimes wonder if the only reason they put up with me is because I've usually got money in my pockets.'

Steve was appalled; but he knew from his recent spell at the Vindi that happy, family units like his weren't the only environment in which children were raised. While most of the lads had come from loving and respectable backgrounds there were those who, for whatever reason, had spent their childhoods in care or with relatives, tolerated but often not loved in the way that he and his brother were loved, or that other parents' children were cherished. But even living in an institution or with an elderly aunt sounded superior to fending for oneself. He suddenly found himself regarding Peter more highly. He may be rough around the edges, but he seemed to have made a reasonable enough job of self-parenting.

Steve slipped ashore after lunch and posted his mailing list, knowing his parents would relay the information to his grandmother who was also an enthusiastic letter writer. In addition to being a keen correspondent his grandmother also collected postage stamps, so Steve's letters home would add to her already extensive

41

accumulation.

On his return from the post office he climbed up to the boat deck and was immediately struck by the change. The *Patonga* had sailed and in her place lay a splendid white liner, similar to those he remembered. The *Amazon was* one of a new class of ship for the Royal Mail Line's South American service, and she looked suitably impressive in the watery afternoon sunshine. But oddly enough it was the vessel moored immediately astern of the *Amazon* that intrigued him. She was obviously a freighter - that much was clear from her extensive cargo-handling equipment - but she had the graceful lines of a small passenger liner, a feature exemplified by her two streamlined funnels, almost unique among cargo ships. Like the *Amazon* she was a morning arrival and her name was *Alsatia,* her funnels carrying the colours of Cunard.

'Nice looking thing - aint she?' opined a voice with a strong Cornish burr that Steve instantly recognized as the Bosun's. He turned and contemplated the elderly seaman whose weather-beaten features were wreathed in a pall of tobacco smoke. He was lighting his pipe while studying the *Alsatia's* profile. Steve had exchanged pleasantries with the Bosun on several occasions - usually when passing the after deck house on his way to the rubbish chute - and found him extremely likeable. In the months to come the petty officer would also become a valuable source of tutelage for the young first tripper who still had a great deal to learn.

'Exactly what I was thinking,' replied Steve, as he accepted a light from the Bosun's cigarette lighter. 'This is the first time I've seen a two-funnelled cargo ship.'

'I'll let you into a secret,' said the Bosun, extinguishing his lighter and concealing it in the depths his overalls. 'The front one's a dummy, and if you take a good look you'll see that it's moulded into the bridge structure. It houses the radio and chart rooms, radar equipment and the Captains quarters - and there's even a lookout post on top.' And seeing the expression of disbelief, he insisted, 'Honestly - no kidding.'

Steve stared at the freighter opposite, looking for some tell-tale sign that the *Alsatia's* forward funnel might function as the Bosun had suggested; but there was nothing obvious, and for the remainder of the afternoon he regarded the story with scepticism, until Archie confirmed that the Bosun's revelations were true.

On the Friday afternoon, with lunch squared away and the saloon vacant, three of the smaller tables were stripped of their tablecloths and rearranged in a row athwartships. A couple of officers from the Shipping Federation then established themselves at one end of the line while a representative of the National Union of Seaman occupied the other. In the centre, a shore-based company cashier sat behind a mountain of currency, and at two o'clock precisely the business of signing articles commenced.

Steve joined the queue with the others, signing the articles sheet alongside his personal details which a Federation officer had transcribed from his discharge book. The book, he was informed, would be retained until the voyage's completion. He noted that his monthly pay would be fourteen pounds, twelve-shillings-and-sixpence, but this would be enhanced by overtime payments and the accrual of leave-pay entitlements. He was making an allotment of five pounds a month to his bank, so even allowing for the occasional spree he was saving some money for the future. From the company cashier he collected two pounds nine and ten-pence in outstanding wages and a three-pound advance against his earnings. Therefore, with well over a fiver sitting snugly in his pocket he was more comfortably-off than he'd ever been. On Peter's recommendation he neatly avoided the union rep who was ostensibly there to resolve disputes, but was more actively engaged in collecting accumulated arrears. By a quarter past three the process had been entirely completed, and the saloon had reverted to normal.

That evening the ship was virtually deserted as almost the entire crew decamped to the waterside drinking dens. By closing time there was hardly a man among them - the possible exceptions being Steve and Archie - who wasn't liquored up to the eyeballs. Given his extraordinary capacity Archie's clear-headedness was perhaps to be expected, but Steve's relative sobriety had more to do with tomorrow than the present. It was because tomorrow was the day he'd been so eagerly awaiting, and he had no intention of allowing an evening's excesses to ruin it before it had started.

4

Saturday morning dawned frosty and fine with a thick coating of rime on the roofs of the surrounding buildings. A ridge of high pressure was keeping the Atlantic weather systems at bay, so in spite of the cold the *Alice Springs'* crew could hardly have wished for anything more clement.

It was on mornings like this that Steve offered thanks to the inventor of the maritime retention tank. He could think of nothing more irksome than having to walk ashore in the middle of the night to use the toilet, a journey that would have been unavoidable had she been a vessel of a more venerable vintage. On veterans such as the *Lilac Hill,* that had been built before retention tanks were commonplace, the toilets were kept locked until the ship was deemed clear of the coast; hence, unless a bucket was kept handy for just such a purpose a trek to the conveniences was inevitable - unless a porthole could be practically exploited. Owing to the *Alice Springs'* retention tanks her toilets had thankfully remained open; and the accumulated effluent would be pumped into the sea as soon as the ship cleared the estuary.

Steve flushed the toilet and burped. He'd completed his scrub-out and cleaned the engineers' duty mess but had then suffered a bout of the 'runs'. Wisely, and in an attempt to avoid any sort of hangover, his previous night's drinking had been moderate, so apart from the queasiness he felt reasonably fit although he still had a trace of a headache. However, he'd taken a couple of codeine with his early-morning cuppa and as usual they were working their magic.

Codeine was an ultra-effective analgesic, and formed the probable basis of almost every seagoing first-aid kit. In Steve's case it had largely stemmed from the Vindi where Sister Grey, the nurse in charge of the sickbay, had been such a codeine enthusiast that she'd gained the sobriquet, 'Codeine Annie', because, it was rumoured, she prescribed codeine whatever the ailment, be it the hint of a cold or the onset of double-pneumonia. Whatever, it had hastened the end of Steve's headache and he was now looking forward to his breakfast.

'At least you weren't paralytic,' said Archie, removing a clutch of warm teapots from the hot-press. 'You seem to have a sensible head on your shoulders, and don't get plastered like the rest of them. As for Peter, well - you saw the state of him earlier on.'

'You don't have to worry about me, Archie,' said Steve, with the confidence of someone who'd rapidly found his feet in a world where work and pleasure shared equal billing although not necessarily in that order, 'I can look after myself. I enjoy a drink like everyone else but I'm no piss artist. An occasional few pints and I'm happy.'

'I certainly hope so,' replied Archie, who'd heard similar stories a thousand and one times and taken them with hefty pinch of salt. 'Because if it gets out of hand you'll be down on your uppers and it's an awful long way to climb back.'

'I'll bear it in mind,' said Steve, who'd no intention of becoming a barfly, although he appreciated Archie's concern.

'Heard any news about a sailing time?' he enquired, not only for a change of subject but to satisfy his own curiosity.

'The notice board at the top of the gangway says one o'clock with shore leave expiring at twelve,' answered Archie, as he opened a large tin of grapefruit and emptied the contents into a serving bowl. 'Not that I'll be going anywhere - not with a dozen bloods to get settled after breakfast.'

'Are they aboard already?' queried Steve, as he removed a tray of fried eggs from the elevator and slid it into the bowels of the hot-press.

'Not yet,' replied the Bedroom Steward, wiping his hands on a pantry cloth. 'They've been advised to report from nine-thirty onwards, but if previous experience is anything to go by they'll probably be here on the dot.'

Steve and Archie were eventually joined by Peter who was late finishing his scrub-out, and by the Second Steward who breezed into the pantry, and declared, 'Well, this is it lads. Make the most of it because from lunchtime onwards there'll be twelve extra mouths to feed. Oh! And another thing. Lunch is half an hour early today on account of the one o'clock sailing time.'

At one point, earlier in the week, Steve had wondered how they were going to deal with the additional workload but the worries had been largely dispelled. Under Peter's guidance the job had become virtual child's play. His mate knew all the little wrinkles; tiddly things mostly like filling the smaller teapots from their own large enamel pot instead of allowing the smaller ones to brew individually. It only saved a minute but the minutes added up and it was time that could be better spent. He also realized that the *Alice Springs'* catering department had managed quite satisfactorily prior to his arrival, a state of affairs that would hopefully be perpetuated afterwards.

Archie had been correct in his prediction. The passengers were all aboard by ten; not that Steve noticed their arrival, busy as he was stowing a last-minute delivery of cleaning materials into the appropriate locker. The first he knew of their guests' embarkation was later in the morning when he was enjoying a smoke on the after well-deck. His attention was drawn to the promenade area adjoining the staterooms. They were few in number, a couple of handfuls at the most, milling around - and among them was a beautiful girl.

'You've spotted her, then,' gushed Peter, as he hurried on deck from the working alleyway.

'Spotted who?' replied Steve, knowing exactly who his friend was alluding to but pretending otherwise.

'Whad'ya mean, who? You know who,' answered Peter, incredulously, his brow furrowed in disbelief. 'Her of course - her up there........the doctor's daughter. The bird with the great big tits.'

Steve stared up in surprise. 'Oh! Her!' he exclaimed, acknowledging the girl's existence. 'Yeah, I noticed her earlier but hadn't actually studied the details.'

'What? You must be blind,' spluttered Peter, eyes like saucers as he ogled the well-endowed teenager who'd wandered to the after end of the boat deck and was regarding them from beneath lowered eyelids. It was clear that she wasn't prone to shyness. She turned to reveal a bosomy profile, her close-fitting sweater hugging the well-rounded contours. Her head drooped teasingly and a sidelong glance, suggested, Yes, I'm looking - but I'll keep you guessing as to which of you I fancy.

Steve turned away - but Peter stood transfixed, and it was only when he espied the Chief Officer prowling the boat deck that the spell was broken. When they looked again the girl had disappeared, summoned by her parents who, aware of her flirtatious tendency, were determined that a pair of young ruffians, and crew members at that, shouldn't become the focus of their daughter's affections.

'Oi! You two,' barked a voice from the entrance to the working alleyway. 'Have you forgotten what the Second Steward told you about lunch being early? And you haven't strapped up the coffee things yet, either.' The voice belonged to Danny Meeks, the Captains Tiger, the steward responsible for servicing the Captain's suite of rooms, for waiting at his table at mealtimes and for attending to all but his most personal requirements. 'You'll be in trouble if you don't get a shift on.'

A slight man in his mid-forties with dark greasy hair and a perpetual smirk, Danny Meeks never enjoyed the confidence of his workmates. He socialized well enough and stood his corner with the rest of them, but in spite of all that he was always suspected of being slimy. His cause was hampered by a toadying closeness to the Chief Steward but if the truth was known, his greatest handicap was his appearance.

'Who the fuck does he think he is?' rasped Peter, offering a two-fingered salute to the departing figure, before shouting, 'OK, Danny - we'll be there directly.' As the boys ambled back to the pantry, he continued, 'The trouble with that little tosser is that just 'cos he's the Tiger and sucks up to the Chief Steward he thinks he's the cat's fuckin' whiskers. I wouldn't be surprised if he drops us in the shit for forgetting to strap up the coffee things.'

As it happened Danny Meeks had done nothing of the sort, prompting Steve to wonder if the Captain's personal steward was the victim of unwarranted prejudice. When all was said and done, the poor little sod could hardly be blamed for his physical architecture; although there was no denying that bowing and scraping to the Chief Steward wasn't the cleverest way to win friends and influence people. 'Looks like Danny kept his mouth shut after all,' said Steve, as he dried up the last of the coffee cups.

'Yeah - this time,' answered Peter, as he wiped excess water from the drainer. 'But don't let that fool you. He'll blow the gaff on one or the other of us sooner or later - you can bet your life on it.'

Steve pressed on with the job, pondering Peter's assessment of Danny until the Tiger was banished from his thoughts as the luncheon gong echoed around the alleyways. Within minutes he was busy at the sink. He was the one with the dishcloth; and every so often he mopped his brow on the sleeve of his pee-jacket - until he dispensed with the jacket altogether and carried on working in his T-shirt. 'Strewth!' he exclaimed, sweeping another bead of moisture from his eyebrows. 'What the hell's it gonna to be like in the tropics.'

'This is nothing,' cast Archie over his shoulder, as he poured a measure of custard over a generous helping of treacle pudding. 'It'll be at least thirty - maybe forty degrees warmer than this in the Red Sea and the Indian Ocean. And another thing you have to remember is, luncheon only consists of four courses. From this evening onwards, when we serve dinner instead of high tea, there'll be five to contend with, along with the additional strapping-up.'

'Not to worry,' rejoined Peter, shuffling and drying a fistful of dinner plates in direct contravention of his training, 'you'll think nothing of it in the morning. It'll be just another part of the workload and you'll accept like everything else.'

'I hope you're right,' answered Steve, tugging at his saturated T-shirt. I'll have to get changed after lunch.'

'You'll be changing several times a day once we've passed through the Suez Canal,' quipped the Second Steward; and then, on a more serious note, he added. 'Still - there's one job you won't have to do this lunchtime.'

'What's that?' asked Steve, wondering if there was a sting in the tail.

'Empty the rosie,' came the reply. 'They towed the barge away half-an-hour ago, so it'll have to wait until we're clear of the river.'

There followed a quieter interlude as the flow of soiled tableware eased, and during which Peter chanced a speculative question. 'What do you want us to do this afternoon?' he asked, glancing at his watch as if impatient to be somewhere else.

'Well, you'll have to turn to for afternoon tea,' replied Sec, 'but until then you can do as you please. After that, I'll find you a job until dinner.'

This was precisely what Peter had been angling for. 'Thanks, Sec,' he answered, cheerily; and nudging Steve, he continued. 'Come on, let's square this lot away, grab some grub and then we can get out on deck.'

Steve was zipping up his wind-cheater when they arrived on the after well-deck deck to find the *Alice Springs* already several feet from the quayside, her tugs laying smoke as their screws churned a path through the water.

The boys kept clear of the poop, having been warned that should a towing spring part it was capable of snaking aboard and causing them serious injury. Instead, they stood to one side as a group of deckies, under the watchful eye of the Second Officer, coiled the mooring lines that until recently had secured the *Alice Springs* to her bollards. Way up for'ard, another gang, under the supervision of the Chief Officer, was carrying out similar work as closer to hand the gangway was lashed to its brackets. Meanwhile, overseeing proceedings from the bridge-wings were the Captain and the Third Officer who, in company with a river pilot, were liaising with the other officers by telephone.

Then, without rhyme or reason, Steve felt emotionally crushed. A lump had grown large in his throat and his eyes became moist at a blast from the *Alice Springs'* siren. They were sentiments he knew only too well, like those he'd experienced when, with its whistle screaming, one of his beloved steam locomotives had come galloping past in charge of an express train. But he was no longer an excited spectator but part of the action, and although not directly involved he felt at one with the ratings who were. Swallowing the blockage and blinking profusely, he croaked, 'How long before we're out in the river?'

'About three-quarters of an hour,' replied Peter, lighting up a Senior Service and pocketing his lighter. 'Once in the lock it's a matter of biding our time until we're down to the outside level. But it shouldn't take long - it usually depends on the tide.'

They watched in silence as they passed Ellerman's *City of Madras* at number three shed, before crossing the mouth of the channel leading to the Royal Albert and Royal Victoria Docks, and to the Royal Albert Dock Basin. As they slid beneath the elevated arms of the bridge carrying Woolwich Manor Way a contingent of pedestrians waited; and behind them a stream of traffic, including a 101 bus on its way to the Woolwich Free Ferry, all seemingly frustrated at having their journeys impeded. They waved to the crowd in the street, few of whom responded, considering the passing flotilla a hindrance at best and at worst an exasperating nuisance. However, a couple of girls on the upper deck of the 101 showed greater enthusiasm, laughing and waving, knowing full well that flirting from a distance was harmless. 'Nearly into the lock,' said Peter, nipping the tip of his Senior Service and throwing the dog-end overboard. 'Another half hour and we'll be out in the river and then it'll be full steam ahead for Australia.'

Eventually, to the accompaniment of some impatient engine revving from the road traffic, the *Alice Springs,* with her tugs nestling snugly beside her, lay tethered to the walls of the lock. With the bridge reopened the disgruntled motorists roared on their way in a cloud of dust and exhaust fumes. Steve craned his neck, hoping for a glimpse of the girls, but the bus had sped on and all he saw was the backs of their heads. His attention returned to the lock where the *Alice Springs* was inching her way down as the lines were adjusted to allow for the fall in water level. Another ten minutes and a graduated marker indicated that their descent had ceased; and Steve noticed that the gates at the outward end were opening to reveal a muddy River Thames flowing past on a slowly ebbing tide. The leading tug tooted and the ship was drawn clear of the lock. The tug at the stern then dug in her heels, swinging the *Alice Springs* through ninety degrees so that she faced the estuary, some forty-odd miles to the east.

'How long does it take to reach the sea?' asked Steve, as he waved to the crew of the *Sun XIV* which had just released the after of the towing springs.

'About four hours if all goes according to plan,' answered Peter, hunching his shoulders against a freshening breeze that had materialized from nowhere now that they were out in the river.

'As long as that, eh?' said Steve, surprised that what seemed such a short distance in his atlas should take so long to negotiate.

'It's all twists and turns,' replied Peter, having previously traversed this stretch of the river, so although not knowing it like the back of his hand he was aware of its basic geography. Pointing to the red and white 'Pilot Aboard' flag flying from the foremast, he continued. 'We'll be following the channel until we're past Southend and the pilot'll be keeping a lookout, so we'll be moving relatively slowly.'

For the next sixty-minutes they observed the flow of water-borne commerce. Most of it was headed upstream: a flatiron collier with a cargo from the Northumberland coalfields for Battersea power station; The United Baltic Corporation's *Baltrover* on her regular run from Gdynia, heading for Hay's Wharf in the Upper Pool, opposite the Tower of London; a General Steam Navigation coaster making for Shadwell Basin; and Blue Star's *Argentina Star*, inward bound for A shed, Royal Victoria Dock at the end of her three-week dash from Buenos Aires.

Shortly after leaving the docks they'd passed the grimy acres of Beckton gas works before encountering the sprawling Ford plant at Dagenham, which covered a far greater area than Steve had ever envisaged. 'I've got a mate works there as an apprentice,' said Peter, as he nodded towards the factory on the Essex bank of the river. 'It was his dad's idea - said he'd be made for life, a steady job and all that shite. He didn't tell him the money was crap and that he'd be bored out of his skull till clocking-off time. I told him to jack it all in and come away to sea but he's scared of upsetting his family. Still, it's his loss - I know where I'd rather be. You can't beat this life - it's far and away better than being cooped-up in a workshop.'

Steve reflected that his own family had been totally supportive when he'd told them of his seafaring ambition. They'd contributed considerably towards the initial cost, and provided last minute encouragement when doubts had surfaced regarding the wisdom of leaving a comfortable home for the unpredictable life of a seaman. He remembered his father's words on the morning of his departure for the Vindi. He'd said, "Go on boy, it'll do you good - It'll make a man of you". He was glad that he'd followed his pioneering instincts and he knew that his parents were proud. He agreed with Peter entirely, and pitied the boy in the factory.

They were now approaching the considerable dock system at Tilbury, and above the sheds they could see the upper works and funnels of a number of passenger liners, nearly all of them belonging to either P&O or the Orient Line, the latter of which the former had recently absorbed. 'Looks like the *'Himalaya's'* in,' said Peter, pointing to the nearest vessel in a line of three, 'and one of the 'Strath' boats as well by the look of it. The one in the distance, the one with the cowled funnel, is probably the *Orcades*. She's due in about now.'

'Might be the *Orsova* or the *Oronsay*,' offered Steve, smugly, knowing that the three Orient liners had similar profiles, and guessing that Peter mightn't know the difference.

'No - she's the *Orcades* all right, replied Peter, grinning like a Cheshire cat.

'How do you know?' queried Steve, suddenly aware that this was more than just a straightforward game of ship recognition. 'They all look the same to me.'

'I read it in Lloyd's List,' laughed Peter, referring to the maritime newspaper that was invariably included among the reading material at the Flying Angel. 'The *Orsova's* in Sydney and won't be home until April, and the *Oronsay* passed through the Panama Canal on Tuesday bound for Fiji and Auckland.'

Shifting over to the starboard side they viewed the town of Gravesend where the Vindi's sister training establishment was sited; although there wasn't a ship, the complex occupying a large swathe of land on the seaward side of the town in close proximity to the river. At one time, prior to the outbreak of war in 1939, the *Vindicatrix* herself had occupied a berth at Gravesend but had been moved to the relative safety of Gloucestershire where, in her rural backwater, she would prove a less obvious target for the Luftwaffe.

A little earlier they'd passed the Merchant Navy's officer cadet training ship *Worcester* at her moorings off Greenhithe. She'd reminded Steve of the pictures he'd seen of the old wooden prison hulks that in Georgian and Victorian times had lined the lower reaches of the river; once-proud men-o-war that had been reduced to punitive purgatory where the inmates were cruelly incarcerated. Many of the convicts would have eventually ended up in the penal colonies of Australia; that's supposing they survived the constant and gratuitous barbarity. But the *Worcester* was far from a Dickensian torture chamber. She was relatively modern and purpose-built of steel, having replaced a wooden-walled vessel of the same name while retaining the appearance of a Napoleonic-era warship.

The more seaward reaches of the Thames were bordered by nothing more stimulating than mile upon mile of desolate marshland. Over on the Essex shore, away in the distance, a train hurried home-bound commuters towards Shoeburyness, but otherwise it was the domain of sea birds and waterfowl. Not being students of wildlife, Steve and Peter belatedly retired to the pantry to strap-up the afternoon tea things - and shortly thereafter the first signs of trouble erupted.

They'd finished the strapping-up and were in the saloon, Steve refilling the cruets while Peter replenished a cutlery drawer that was somehow deficient of teaspoons. It was the uncanny silence and lack of vibration that alerted them. 'Now what's happened?' voiced Peter, slamming the cutlery drawer with such a flourish that the silverware jangled inside. 'Let's go and find out.'

Out on deck they bumped into the Donkeyman who was hastening towards the engine room carrying a bucket and a king-sized spanner. 'What's up, Donks?' asked Steve, with a familiarity that belied the fact that the man was a virtual stranger.

'Nothing much,' answered the engine room petty officer, scurrying past in his grease-stained overalls. 'One of the evaporators is playing up. It shouldn't take long to sort out.'

'This is a fine fuckin' start,' groused Peter, as the Donkeyman disappeared through the engine room hatchway. 'We're not even past Southend and the engines are already playing silly buggers.'

Peter's derision was premature. The words were hardly out of his mouth when the deck trembled, a tower of smoke billowed from the funnel and passage was resumed, as though the ship had merely paused for a breather. For the short duration that she'd been stationary the *Sun XVII* - the tug that had been the forward of the two on their departure from London - had lain alongside should her assistance be called for. The fact that the tug was there at all in no way implied that the *Alice Springs'* engines were still suspect. Escort towage, as it was called, was provided for every vessel over a certain tonnage entering or leaving the river, insurance against emergencies of all sorts. Owing to the presence of the *Sun XVII* there'd been little danger of the ship - not to mention her personnel - becoming an unwanted casualty.

There were no further malfunctions, and as Steve and Peter busied themselves by polishing the saloon brass-work the Essex marshes gradually gave way to a panorama disfigured by the petro-chemical industry, particularly beyond Stanford-le-Hope where the oil refineries and storage tanks of Coryton and Canvey Island dominated the landscape. A boggy wilderness still monopolized the Kentish side of the river but in the faraway distance, where the estuaries of the Thames and Medway merged and finally emptied into the southern narrows of the North Sea, the flares of the massive oil installations on the Isle of Grain blazed fiercely in the gathering gloom.

'Ever been to Southend?' asked Peter, screwing the cap on his tin of Brasso. 'It'll soon be abeam, and it's brilliant when it's all lit up - even in winter.'

'Never,' answered Steve, giving the foyer door-knobs a final buffing before wiping a spilt drop of polish from his shoe, 'but I've been to Clacton and Walton-on-the Naze.'

'They ain't a patch on Southend,' assured Peter, peering through the saloon windows and nodding at a blaze of bright lights in the distance. 'It's the best place in the world on a bank holiday.'

Back in the pantry the task of preparing for dinner was gaining momentum; but thanks to his Vindi training, and the experience he'd gained since joining, Steve was able to work on his own initiative without continually pestering others. Nevertheless, he was still as green as a grasshopper, even though Peter had cautioned that being a first-tripper he'd be a target for all manner of monkey business. This is precisely what happened when Archie, having studied the menu and noticed the options for entrée, instructed, 'Nip down to the galley and collect the jugs for the jugged hare.' Steve, ever willing to be helpful, obliged without thinking twice.

'They're not down here,' advised Norman, staring around the galley to see who else may have been listening. 'The Chief Steward keeps them in his office.'

Steve thought it odd that items for use in the service of food should be kept in other than the pantry or galley, but not being in a position to argue he dashed off in pursuit of the Boss.

'Stop pissing about,' growled the Chief Steward, annoyed at being disturbed in the run-up to what was possibly the most important meal of the voyage. 'And you can tell whoever sent you to stop being so bloody childish.'

Steve was livid - incensed at having made a fool of himself; not only in the presence of the senior catering officer but in front of the entire caboodle. 'I'll give that bloody Archie jugs for jugged hare,' he swore, under his breath as he dashed back down to the pantry. However, as soon as he appeared at the servery everyone just fell about laughing, and in spite of his embarrassment there was little he could do but to join them.

'Never mind, Son,' consoled the Second Steward, as the merriment subsided, 'it wasn't as bad as what happened to the peggy on the *Balclutha*. They sent him in search of some green oil for the starboard navigation lamp. Poor little bugger was pushed from pillar to post for hours on end before they put him out of his misery. At least you didn't have to suffer that kind of torment.'

It was a small mercy, and Steve could have kicked himself for being so easily duped, especially after been forewarned. He forced a sickly grin, but was far from happy as he picked up the rosie, and muttered, 'I'm gonna get rid of this rubbish.'

The rosie was heavy - full to overflowing, and the handle cut into his flesh. He made painful progress; but eventually, after several changes of hand he reached his objective then paused to examine the seascape. The stiffening breeze was a sign of a change in the weather. The stars still sparkled but away to the west the storm clouds were gathering, a harbinger of something less pleasant. After emptying and rinsing the rosie he saw that the garishness of Southend was rapidly receding, as were the red and green navigation beacons that had guided them safely to the sea. There were numerous other lights in the offing, most of it shipping heading to or from the estuary, or lying in the Sea Reach anchorage. But the *Sun XVII* had retired, leaving the *Alice Springs* in the care of her own custodians. A wave slapped the side of the ship sending spray flying high, wide and handsome. Steve tasted brine and felt the heave as his ship met the swell. The jugs and jugged hare were forgotten and his spirits were miraculously restored. It could mean one thing and one thing only. At long last, and without a shadow of a doubt, he could finally, and indisputably, call himself a seaman with all the honesty of either Archie or the Bosun, and not a soul in the world could say otherwise.

5

'What was that you said about a doctor?' asked Steve, as he lay on his bunk and flicked through the pages of the previous week's edition of Picture Post.

'Doctor?' replied Peter, not immediately comprehending but then suddenly realizing who Steve was referring to. 'Oh! You mean our doctor, the one whose daughter everyone's talking about.'

'That's him,' answered Steve, as he tossed the magazine on to the table. 'I didn't know we carried a doctor.'

'We don't as a fully signed-up crew member,' answered Peter. 'This one's what's known as a supernumerary. He's a passenger who travels free to wherever he's going in return for providing health cover for the other passengers and us lot. He's paid a shilling a month in wages but otherwise he's treated just the same as the other bloods. His wife and daughter will have paid the full fare to Australia.'

Steve thought for a moment before proceeding. 'It's good to know we've got a doctor on board, but what about those ships that don't carry passengers, tankers and the like? They can't carry a doctor either - can they?'

'Not likely,' replied Peter, quickly warming to the subject. 'You takes your chance on one of them, and hope that the Second mate or the Chief Steward understand what's written in the medical manual. It's not so bad these days with radio and so on, they can communicate with doctors ashore who can advise them on treatment and suchlike. Even so, I wouldn't fancy having my appendix removed by someone reading from a book, or listening to instructions on the wireless. The big passenger boats are all right - they've got fully-equipped hospitals and surgeons.' Steve was attentive, and was thankful that he'd signed on a ship like the *Alice Springs*. He found it hard to imagine the outcome if a crew member became seriously ill or was injured aboard a poorly provided-for freighter.

'Fancy some music?' asked Peter, who suddenly jumped from his bunk and hauled the biggest portable radio Steve had ever seen from his locker. Standing the set on the table and feeding the aerial cable through the porthole, Peter continued. 'Pete Murray's on Radio Luxembourg on Saturday nights with the latest American Rock 'n' Roll records. It's usually a bloody good show.'

For the next thirty minutes they listened to the likes of Johnny Burnette, The Crickets and Johnny and the Hurricanes as the fluctuating strains of the most popular teenage radio station in Europe wafted across the airwaves; but above them all Steve could hear the creaks and groans as the *Alice Springs* rolled gently, first to port and then to starboard - sometimes a little further than others. 'Do ships always creak? Or is there something wrong with her?' he asked, as the *Alice Springs* slipped gently into another trough before gradually righting herself and tipping in the opposite direction.

'Fuckin' hell!' exclaimed Peter, with a hint of annoyance that his enjoyment of Conway Twitty's latest release had been interrupted by yet another of Steve's interminable queries. 'You're worse than Hughie fuckin' Green. Why can't you just listen to the wireless and stop asking questions. Anyone'd think I was the Encyclopaedia Britannica.' Eventually, with a sigh of resignation he bowed to Steve's inquisitiveness, and answered. 'Of course they creak - they're bound to fuckin' creak. If they didn't fuckin' creak it'd mean they were inflexible and liable to break up - all right? Now shut up and either listen to the music or go to fuckin' sleep. Here - I'll even turn down the volume so it doesn't keep you awake.'

Steve smiled and switched off his light. As much as he enjoyed Rock 'n' Roll music he was just about shattered, so with the incessant creaking for a lullaby, and despite the renderings from the radio, he was soon in the arms of Morpheus.

The pilot was dropped off Dungeness shortly before midnight; then, sometime during the early hours, the ridge of high pressure that had seen such a glorious day for their departure was swept aside by a vigorous Atlantic depression and by morning, the *Alice Springs* was fighting tooth and claw with a gale.

Of all the possible pitfalls associated with seafaring the one that had bothered Steve most was seasickness. His fear was well-founded, and became a reality the following morning, because in addition to the rolling they'd experienced the previous evening the *Alice Springs* was now performing a passable impression of a see-saw. The initial hour or so was pretty straightforward. He performed his scrub-out as usual without feeling unduly perturbed; it was breakfast that triggered the change. The rolling was easy to manage; but pitching was a totally different matter, and allied to the former, thus creating a corkscrewing motion - and the sight of a trayful of greasy bacon emerging from the elevator - caused Steve to make an undignified bolt for the toilet.

The ensuing twenty-four hours were the most miserable of Steve's brief existence. There was no question of him sleeping it off; to have done so would have evoked the wrath of the Second Steward who would have turfed him out with the customary bollocking. He just had to accept what the weather threw at them and make the best of his off-duty periods. The rest of the time he spent either working, occupying a toilet cubicle or, when emptying the rosie, hanging over a rail and paying his dues to King Neptune.

In the course of one journey aft he noticed they were being rapidly overhauled by white-painted masterpiece. He recognized her almost immediately, having seen her on several occasions during his childhood holidays. She was non-other than P&O's *Arcadia,* and she was outward bound from Southampton to Australia via Aden, Bombay and Colombo. Steve was completely mesmerized as the *Arcadia* ploughed past in a welter of spume and spindrift, plunging and soaring as though her twenty-nine-thousand gross register tons were as puny as a galvanised bath tub. For a fleeting interval his woes were forgotten as he gazed in awe as man and steel battled the isobars. But as the nausea returned he spewed over the rail, wondering what on earth he was doing, tumbling about in the English Channel, heaving his guts up when he could have been observing the trains from the comfort of a motionless signal box.

During the afternoon they practised the first of the weekly emergency drills, and although the fire drill was thoroughly rehearsed the boat drill was substantially curtailed, with none of the lifeboats being partially lowered as would happen in the more benevolent latitudes. In normal circumstances the entire complement would have assembled for the exercises, excepting those whose duties excused them. But on this occasion the passengers were conspicuous by their absence and the crew were dismissed as soon as the officers had completed a roll-call and ensured that life jackets were correctly knotted.

By the following morning the *Alice Springs* was heading south across the Bay of Biscay and, owing to an unlikely reversal of fortune, Steve's predicament was eased. Sometime during the night the storm had blown itself out, leaving behind a fresh north-westerly breeze and a tangible swell but none of the legendary ferment normally associated with, 'The Bay'. As he climbed from his bunk he found he no longer felt ill but ravenously hungry, as if he hadn't eaten for a week.

'That's more like it,' said Archie, as Steve demolished a round of toast washed down with a hot mug of tea. 'I thought you were going to die yesterday lunchtime.'

'You're not the only one,' replied Steve, as he sliced another hunk of bread from the loaf and slid it beneath the salamander. 'I've never felt so poorly in my life - not even when I was a kid and had either mumps, measles or whooping cough.'

'Well, you're over it now and hopefully it'll never return,' said Archie, refilling Steve's mug from the teapot. 'And don't let anyone tell you they've never been seasick because if they do they're probably lying. Most of us have suffered at some time or other, usually during the early stages of our careers; but you soon get used to it and being thrown all over the place can often be quite entertaining.'

As if on cue Peter rushed into the pantry - late as ever - and seeing Steve tucking into toast and marmalade, he ridiculed. 'That was some exhibition you put on yesterday. Call yourself a seaman? I've never seen anything like it.'

With Archie's words still fresh in his mind Steve's retort had the sting of a whiplash. 'All right clever dick. I suppose you've never been seasick?'

Peter was on the verge of responding when he suddenly

remembered that Archie had a pretty good memory. 'Well - yeah, I have........once, he stammered, suddenly lacking conviction. 'But that was ages ago. I've been thousands of miles since without puking.'

'Well, that's that then,' said Archie, seeing that Peter had been suitably subjugated. 'That makes three of us, so let's stop pissing about and think about starting work.'

Over the following day and a half they passed down the coasts of Spain and Portugal, overhauling a number of slower vessels including a rust-bucket tramp, down to her marks and bound for goodness-knows where. A survivor of two world wars she was one of a number of this type of ship that was still in existence, roaming the oceans as their tight-fisted owners squeezed every last farthing from their barnacled hulls rather than invest in more up-to-date tonnage. Owing to age and wartime losses few of them flew the Red Ensign, although there plenty of British registered ships still afloat that had been built in the 'twenties' and 'thirties'. And so it was that on the fourth afternoon out, with lunch out of the way and with the Bosun for company, Steve sat on the hatch cover immediately forward of the accommodation, comparing the age-weary tramp with the *Arcadia* which was now way ahead of them on her way to Australia. 'I don't think I'd fancy going to sea in one of those,' he said, wrinkling his nose and nodding in the direction of the geriatric, 'she doesn't look particularly seaworthy.'

'Maybe she is, maybe she isn't - you never can tell,' mused the Bosun, as he tamped a large wad of tobacco into his pipe. 'If she isn't it's probably because she hasn't been properly looked after. Most of them were built to last, mainly in British yards using rivets and thick steel plate, not welded together like some of the newer ships. 'But there again,' he qualified, suddenly recalling something he shouldn't have forgotten. 'What about the Liberty ships that the Yanks churned out in the war? They were only welded together but there are still plenty of them knocking about. Our company's even got one - the *Korumburra* - and don't forget the old *Lilac Hill*. Although she wasn't a Liberty ship she was well over thirty years old. It all depends on the owners. If a ship's well-cared for there's no reason why she shouldn't stay afloat and plod along faithfully for yonks.'

'Mmmmm,' murmured Steve, hardly convinced. 'I still think I'd rather sail on the *Arcadia* - although the *Alice Springs* is all right,' he added, generally happy with his lot now that he no longer felt seasick.

'I'll tell you what,' said the Bosun, turning his back to the breeze in order to light his pipe. 'You'll see a darn sight more of the world on a cargo boat than you ever will on a passenger ship. Oh........they're all right - New York, Hong Kong, Sydney and all the other fleshpots, but they never go to the real out-of-the-way places like the tramp steamers do. Take that old-timer for instance,' he said, waving his pipe at the antiquated scrapyard that was no longer abeam but was rapidly falling astern. 'For all we know she's probably bound for Rosario, miles up the Paraná river with a cargo of coal for the Argentine railways - or maybe some steamy West African creek with a load of cement for a construction project. Wherever, you can bet your life that her crew'll see places that the boys on the passenger ships never see.'

Steve conceded that the words made good common sense, realizing that aboard the *Alice Springs* he would see the best - and possibly the worst - of both worlds. He would see fabulous cities and maybe stinking backwaters, as would the men on the tramp steamer. He shivered and turned to the Bosun, saying, 'It isn't as warm as I thought it'd be.'

'You have to remember you're still in the North Atlantic, and it is only February when all's said and done,' replied the Bosun, getting to his feet and stretching. 'But we'll be passing Gibraltar tomorrow and it should slowly warm up from then on.'

The following morning the *Alice Springs* did indeed pass through the Straits of Gibraltar, although the rock itself was intermittently hidden by a succession of passing showers. There was the occasional glimpse of sunshine but if anything the western end of the Mediterranean was even cooler than the North Atlantic; and not only that, the seas weren't as calm as Steve had anticipated - although there was no repeat of his seasickness. He mentioned the weather to Jimmy Craddock when he ventured down to the galley to collect the lunchtime rolls from the bakery. 'It'll soon warm up,' said Jimmy, as he counted out the rolls on a tray. 'By the time we get to Port Said you'll be lying on a hatch cover, sunbathing.'

'I certainly hope so,' said Steve, as he made to move off. But then, almost as a postscript, he added. 'Can I cadge couple of cigarettes? I smoked the last of mine before breakfast.'

Jimmy looked bemused. 'The Second Steward held a cigarette issue the day after we sailed,' he advised. 'Didn't you bother to get any?'

'In my condition I couldn't have cared less about smoking,' replied Steve, ruefully, remembering how awful he'd felt while the rest of the crew were queuing for their tobacco. 'I even considered quitting altogether.'

'A couple of ciggys aren't going to last you very long,' said Jimmy, weighing up how many he could spare. 'I'll tell you what, I can let you have a packet of State Express until the next issue. If you ask Archie and Peter they'll probably do the same, but you'll have to stretch 'em out. It'll be another ten days before Sec reopens the bond locker for cigarettes.'

'Thanks, Jimmy,' said Steve, with an air of relief as he followed the galley boy to his cabin where the packet of State Express duly materialized. 'I shan't forget to repay you.'

As Jimmy had predicted Archie and Peter proved equally as generous; although Steve was uncertain how his pals would react when, following the next cigarette issue, he offered them Rothmans rather than the brands they preferred.

It took a full five days to cross the Mediterranean from Gibraltar to the Suez Canal, and early on the third of these they sighted the island of Malta, although it was mostly a blur beneath a blanket of low-lying cloud. As far as Steve was concerned the fact that the island was barely visible didn't matter, it was somewhere else to write home about. He'd started his letter off the coast of Portugal, relating the various happenings - including the seasickness - insofar as they currently existed, and although there was relatively little to report he'd already completed three pages. He'd leave the envelope unsealed until the following afternoon in case of any further developments, before posting it in the mail box at the end of the working alleyway, ready for collection in Egypt.

All things considered, with the exception of the initial bout of seasickness and the various shenanigans, Steve was on top of his job.

He got along with his mates and he generally wasn't interfered with. It was only on the ninth morning out, as he set about servicing the Junior Radio Officer's cabin, that things took a turn for the worse - and the crew were in no way to blame.

He was cleaning the washbasin and mirror when he suddenly spotted a gaping hole in the centre of his top-right incisor. A chunk of enamel, about twice the size of a pinhead, was missing, probably swallowed along with his breakfast. Maybe that sliver of bone in one of his rashers of bacon had in fact been part of his tooth. The discovery caused considerable alarm, because until their arrival at Adelaide there seemed little hope of getting it repaired. But then he remembered the doctor. He was only too aware that the *Alice Springs* carried nothing in the way of dental equipment, but perhaps the supernumerary medic could fashion a temporary filling. Sick parade - or whatever it was called in civvy-street - was due to be held at ten-thirty. In the meantime he'd carry on working, cursing the fact that had the tooth broken sooner he could have had it attended to in London.

The consultation period, which was held in the ship's hospital, comprised three casualties; Steve and the Senior Radio Officer, both of whom required dental treatment, and a deckie who'd trodden on a rusty nail while walking about in his stockinged feet and ended up with a septic toe. The deckie was treated first before he hobbled away, his injured toe hidden beneath a magnesium-sulphate dressing and a voluminous layer of bandage. The Senior 'Sparks', who was suffering from toothache, was told to paint the surrounding gum with oil of cloves while Steve, whose broken tooth the doctor was unable to repair, was advised to avoid biting on it if at all possible in order to prevent further damage. In both instances it was suggested they visit a dentist in Aden, even though Port Said was the next port of call. It appeared their stay at the Egyptian port might only be brief, whereas they'd be anchored at Aden for ages while the *Alice Springs* replenished her bunkers. This would allow ample time for a visit to a dentist ashore.

Sparks was far from impressed. 'I bet the bastard'd be ashore soon enough at Port Said if it was his tooth that was playing up, he complained, in a broad Glasgow accent, when they were out of earshot of the surgery. 'This bloody stuff better work,' he grumbled, staring at the tiny bottle of oil of cloves, 'otherwise I'll be back in there to sort that bloody quack out.' Steve took a more sanguine view, believing that although it would be difficult to avoid biting on his broken tooth, a visit to a dentist in Aden was eminently preferable to awaiting their arrival at Adelaide.

In the early afternoon of the following day the *Alice Springs* arrived in the outer harbour at Port Said, dropping anchor among twenty or more other vessels awaiting transit of the Suez Canal. As had been forecast the weather was warm and Steve, along with Peter and Jimmy, leant on a rail in the after well- deck, soaking up the sun and basking in the thrill of his first ever overseas landfall.

There was so much to see that Steve stood utterly motionless - lost for words at what to his eyes at least was an exotic wonderland. Egypt was where east met west, and in the hazy distance he could see the domes and minarets atop the mosques and municipal buildings. The surrounding water was alive with craft of all shapes and sizes, from massive oil tankers to Arab dhows, motor launches; and the ubiquitous bum boats, moving from ship to ship as the boatmen sought their water-borne livelihood. One launch in particular seemed to be making straight for the *Alice Springs*, and on swinging to make her approach to the recently lowered accommodation ladder, Steve could see that seated at the stern was a man wearing a light tropical suit and a Panama hat, a briefcase cradled in his lap. 'Looks like the Agent,' said Jimmy, as the launch bobbed alongside, allowing the suited passenger to jump on to the ladder and begin his ascent to the accommodation area. 'We should get a mail issue soon.'

'You two might,' grumbled Peter. 'I won't.'

'That's your fault as much as anyone else's,' replied Steve, who was confident that at least two of the letters in the Agent's briefcase were for him. 'You don't bother writing to others - why should they write to you?'

'Humph!' scoffed Peter, before clearing his throat and spitting in the vicinity of a bum boat. 'I've already told you that my family couldn't care less, and that my mates are only interested when I arrive on their doorsteps with my pay-off. Who else can I write to?'

'What about girlfriends?' asked Jimmy, knowing that the fairer sex were often a pushover when it came to corresponding with globe-trotting seamen. 'Surely a good-looking fellow like you has a girlfriend hidden away somewhere?'

'Bullshitter,' replied Peter, giving Jimmy a sidelong glance accompanied by a twisted grin. 'No - seriously though. I've never known a girl long enough to get really friendly. Here today and gone tomorrow, that's me........although,' he added wistfully, 'I suppose I could always write to Maureen.'

'Who's Maureen?' prompted Steve, suddenly becoming interested and sensing an opportunity to turn the tables on Peter who until recently had held the upper hand in their leg-pulling stakes. 'This is the first time you've spoken about her. I bet she's someone you've been messing around with for ages but were too embarrassed to talk about.'

'Not on your life,' replied Peter, in mock indignation. 'She's the barmaid in our local boozer. She's no oil painting mind you, and we've never been out together, but when the evenings are quiet we spend the time chatting and she's always a pretty good listener.'

'There you are then,' said Jimmy, assuming the role of a Dutch uncle. 'Why not drop her a line and see where it gets you? You've nothing to lose. It's too late to do anything about it now but if you send her a letter from Aden there might be a reply waiting at Adelaide.'

'Yeah, I might just do that,' said Peter, thoughtfully, expecting some comment from Steve whose self-assurance was growing with each passing minute, but whose attention had inexplicably strayed and who seemed engrossed in the business of the anchorage.

In fact, Steve was congratulating himself, because he knew that he'd scored yet another small point to add to the one he'd picked up on the morning following his seasickness. He knew there'd be more to come but at least he was getting his own back, and his tormentors would know that far from being a doormat he was a more than capable adversary.

As the afternoon progressed the anchorage filled with arrivals from as far afield as North America, northern Europe, the Black Sea as well as the encircling Mediterranean. Steve's attention was drawn to one large vessel in particular, and he pointed her out to his friends.

Partly hidden in the haze her features were indistinct, but she was obviously a tanker and was conspicuous owing to her size. 'I can't be sure,' said Jimmy, using the flat of his hand as a sunshade, 'but she looks like the *British Queen*.'

'Yeah,' agreed Peter, barely hesitating. 'She's the *British Queen*, no doubt about it. She passed us in the Gulf of Aden last September. Brand new she is. Fifty-thousand tons - the biggest tanker in the world.'

Steve knew all about the *British Queen*, having read about the BP flagship in a recent issue of a nautical magazine. She was one of a new breed of tanker that was to revolutionise the distribution of oil. Oil tankers had been growing in capacity for decades, but the *British Queen* was a new departure, one that would see such an explosion in magnitude that within just a very few years vessels of a quarter of a million tons or more would be commonplace rather than the exception. While the *British Queen* and her contemporaries were still able to use the Suez Canal, thanks to their colossal proportions the supertankers - as they were to become known - would have to make the longer journey between the Middle-Eastern oilfields and the European refineries via South Africa and the Cape of Good Hope.

The *British Queen* may have afforded a spellbinding topic of conversation, but she was swept from the limelight by loud whoops of laughter intermingled with some agonizing howls. Over on the starboard side of the ship, surrounded by deckies and engine room ratings stood Sean Cassidy, a gigantic Liverpool fireman who was renowned for his drunkenness and usefulness in any kind of punch-up. Cassidy stood with his abdomen thrust against the rails, and no explanation was needed as to what was causing the uproar. Steve and his pals were about to take a closer look when the Donkeyman pushed into the crowd and ordered Cassidy to his cabin. The Donkeyman was closely followed by the Mate who demanded to know what was happening. 'It's Cassidy, Chief,' said the Donkeyman, wiping his brow with a handful of cotton waste. 'He's been and pissed in a bum boat - and the wog's gone fuckin' berserk.'

The Mate was livid. The last thing the owners of the *Alice Springs* needed was trouble with the Port Said harbour authorities, and trouble there would be if the boatman decided to pursue the issue. Leaning over the rail he began reasoning with the native, not over the cost of any prospective purchase but on the subject of compensation. By this time the mob had begun to disperse, so the boys sidled up and peered down into the bum boat. There, surrounded by sodden merchandise, stood a dark-skinned figure clad in a beige jellaba that reached almost down to his ankles. The man was highly agitated, but thanks to the Chief Officer's diplomacy - and his ability to speak Arabic - had ceased wailing and had commenced negotiating a suitable sum for the damage.

'I bet the bugger's asking for twice as much as it's worth,' commented Peter, showing scant regard for the fact the man was surely entitled to something extra for the indignity of being urinated upon, and for the fact that much of his stock had been ruined.

'He'll probably get it as well,' said Jimmy, who'd heard of similar things happening on previous occasions. 'But the company won't be footing the bill and nor will the Mate for that matter - but Cassidy certainly will.'

Eventually, agreement was reached and the Chief Officer hauled up the boatman's basket. He placed a roll of bank notes in the bottom and then lowered it back down to the bum boat. The eager recipient quickly counted the cash before waving a hand to signify that the transaction had been satisfactorily completed. The Mate then turned and headed into the engine room ratings' quarters, looking for Cassidy to inform him that behaviour such as his wouldn't be tolerated, and that he should report to the Captain at nine o'clock the following morning to face the consequences.

With the excitement over Steve and his mates perused the items in the remaining bum boats. Some of the wares were undoubtedly attractive, but Steve would hang on to his money until he could examine the goods more closely. He had to admit that despite the astronomical asking price the ornately-carved camel stools were tempting; but then there was the problem of storage, not to mention the hassle of transporting it home on the voyage's completion. Jimmy bought an imitation Rolex while Peter splashed out on one of the notorious 'Blue' books which, along with others, would eventually be seen by the entire crew although their purchase was supposedly forbidden. Steve had heard about the books containing pages of degrading pornography, but was surprised to learn that they gained their name not from their erotic contents, but from the colour of the featureless cover.

The Second Steward toured the ship towards sundown, distributing the aforementioned mail. Steve took the letters he'd been expecting, one from his immediate family and the other from his grandmother, stuffing them into his hip pocket where they'd remain until later that evening. He'd catch up on the news from home in the comfort of his cabin but in the meantime there was the small matter of dinner to attend to, not to mention all the other little side-jobs.

It transpired that the *Alice Springs* would be joining a convoy to transit the canal in the early hours of the following morning, in which case there would have been ample time for Steve and the 'Sparky' to have made the journey to a dentist. However, those charged with organizing such excursions presumably knew best and the situation remained as originally planned, that they should keep the appointment in Aden.

6

Last but one in a thirty-long column, the *Alice Springs* crept stealthily past the world-famous lighthouse and the illuminated, 'Johnny Walker' Scotch Whisky advertisement that overlooked the waterway's entrance. Immediately ahead, the brightly-lit Dutch liner *Johan van Oldenbarnevelt* made stately progress into the advancing aurora while astern, the convoy's whipper-in, a decrepit Liberian tanker, was one of that growing family of vessels flying a flag of convenience, enabling their owners to evade the superior standards of ship management that were becoming increasingly common among the more responsible maritime nations.

The decks of the *Alice Springs* formed the perfect viewpoint, and were the next best option to actually walking the streets with a guide book. Steve was up before dawn, bright-eyed and brimming with excitement, scanning the landscape on either side in search of the wonders of Egypt. He knew there were no pyramids or sphinxes in this neck of the woods, but as far as he was concerned it was all virgin territory and he resolved not to miss so much as a grain of sand in the relatively featureless but vitally strategic canal zone. The city of Port Said was still asleep as the convoy slid silently past, the soft lap of water the only sound as urbanization was replaced by wilderness. Initially there was little to see; but daylight revealed a scattering of palm trees and a railway line following the western shores of the canal, while on the opposite bank the Sinai desert sprawled endlessly over the sand dunes.

In the first flush of dawn the desert appeared barren and dark, but from Steve's perspective it evoked memories of the Bible classes in the Methodist Sunday School at home. He recalled the book of Exodus; how Pharaoh's daughter had found the infant Moses hidden among the bulrushes; how an angel had appeared to Moses in the flames of a burning bush; and how Moses had led the Children of Israel to the Promised Land with the sea allowing them unhindered passage. He suddenly realized that everything he remembered could possibly have happened within shouting distance of his present vantage point, and the thought caused an involuntary shiver.

Although not a committed Christian he found it supremely humbling and his reflections remained with Moses and the Israelites; until, that is, the *Alice Springs* passed the dusty settlement of El Qantara where his reverie was abruptly spoilt. He'd been serving the engineers on the eight till twelve their seven-bell breakfasts, and was gazing from the duty mess porthole as the town came bustling to life. Suddenly, he was poked rudely between the shoulder blades, and Danny Meeks rasped, hoarsely, 'This isn't a bloody Cook's Tour you know. If Sec finds you loafing about he'll tear you a strip off.'

'Sorry, Danny,' apologized Steve, startled but thankful it was the Tiger who'd caught him napping rather than the Second Steward. 'I just got carried away.'

'I'd get back to the pantry smartish if I were you,' advised Danny, glancing at his watch. 'It'll be breakfast time soon and there's no one to load up the hot-press.'

Steve belatedly awoke to the fact that he hadn't been loafing at all but had been waiting on the duty engineers. And not only that, but the engineers had only that minute finished eating, and he hadn't yet squared away the covers.

'Hey! Hang about, Danny,' countered Steve, annoyed at having allowed himself to be unfairly reprimanded. 'I've still got to tidy up here - I can't be in both places at once. Where have Archie and Peter got to?'

'Archie's collecting trays from the sheds, and Peter's bloody skiving I shouldn't wonder,' replied Danny, disappearing into the alleyway. 'That's all the lazy sod's fit for.'

Collecting up his tray and waiter's cloth Steve hurried back to the pantry; it was nearly a quarter to eight and there ought to be someone in attendance to load up the hot-press, even if it was only a boy.

Sure enough, the pantry was empty, although cups and saucers piled high in the sink were evidence that Archie had returned with at

71

least some of his trays and although he was cutting it fine, had probably gone to fetch others. As for Peter; there was no telling what he was up to - and the Second Steward seldom showed up until needed.

It proved to be a hectic five minutes. Steve was filling the sink when there came a buzz from the galley, indicating that the food was ready and that whoever was manning the pantry should mobilize the elevator. A couple of minutes later, with the food safely in the press, he was strapping up the accumulated crockery when a deckie appeared in the doorway, and requested, 'Can you rustle up a couple of breakfasts for the canal pilots? They're complaining that they haven't been fed.'

Steve acquiesced, exchanging pleasantries with the deckie while loading a portion of almost everything on the menu on to a pair of dinner plates. 'There, that should keep them happy,' he proclaimed, placing the breakfasts on a tray along with serviettes, condiments and cutlery. 'They'll not be complaining after that.'

Shoving the door open with his shoulder the deckie proceeded on his way while Steve carried on with the strap-up. Almost immediately Peter burst in, followed by Archie with the remaining trays. Peter's excuse was that he'd knocked over his bucket while scrubbing out the officers' alleyway and had needed to mop up the water, whereas Archie had simply got "all behind" and had been trying his best to catch up. Whatever, no harm had been done and with breakfast ready to be served it was just a matter of waiting until the gong rang out and the stewards arrived with their orders.

At three minutes to eight precisely all hell broke loose in the wheelhouse. Archie opened the pantry door and a cacophony of Arab resentment could be heard echoing around the alleyways. For the second consecutive day it appeared someone had ruffled the natives. Archie looked totally bemused; it seemed as much a mystery to him as it did to everyone else. The row was getting louder by the second and showed little sign of abating. Steve's curiosity predominated. He stepped outside to investigate at the very instant the Second Steward arrived at the foot of an adjacent companionway carrying the two recently constituted breakfasts. 'What's all the fuss about, Sec?' he enquired, pointing a finger in the general direction of the hubbub. 'It sounds like a right old shemozzle.'

'Shemozzle's hardly the word for it,' answered Sec, who held out the plates, and demanded. 'Are you responsible for this?'

'Responsible for what?' asked Steve, scratching his head like a ninny.

'You stupid bastard,' growled the Second Steward, who seemed in imminent danger of fragmenting. 'You put bacon on their plates, that's what. No wonder they've gone fuckin' nuts. Christ almighty - didn't they teach you anything at school?'

Steve's bewilderment deepened. He shook his head, and mumbled, 'I don't know what you're talking about.'

Sec heaved a sigh of despair. 'It's simple, Son,' he articulated, showing signs of conciliation as he laid the plates on the worktop. 'Moslems and pig meat are totally incompatible - they wouldn't touch it if they were starving. It's all to do with their religion, and if you insult their religion they're likely to do you a mischief.'

Steve was mortified. To think that his error could have led to personal injury or maybe even worse was horrifying. He eventually discovered his voice, asking gloomily, 'What happens now?'

'Well, the Third Mate's doing his best to placate them,' replied Sec, pessimistically, while stripping the plates of the bacon, 'then we'll re-present them with their breakfasts. Fingers crossed, they'll quieten down with a plateful of grub beneath their kaftans.'

Steve certainly hoped so, and as the Second Steward departed on another attempt to serve the pilots their breakfasts he turned to Archie and Peter for solace; but rather than commiseration they responded with unrestrained laughter. Donald and Keith stuck their heads through the servery and joined in the frivolity while behind them, even Danny Meeks wore a grin. And then it dawned; he'd been set up, and had fallen for it, hook, line and sinker. 'You rotten bastards,' he stormed, his face like a scarlet football. 'Call yourselves mates? Someone could've died because of you lot.'

'All right, calm down,' said Archie, placing a soothing hand on Steve's shoulder. 'It was only a lark and despite what Sec said there was little danger of anyone getting butchered. All right, the coloured gentlemen might be a little light fingered but they wouldn't knife anyone. The Third Mate'll explain that it was all an innocent balls-up and that'll be an end to it.'

Steve was in no mood to be mollified. He swore and stalked off into the alleyway, almost felling the Second Steward who was returning to the pantry having successfully served the pilots their breakfasts. In his present frame of mind he could have flattened anyone - even the Captain - and not given tuppence. But the Second Steward, annoyed at being trampled on by an embittered catering boy was having none of it. 'Hey! What the hell do you think you're playing at?' he bellowed, grabbing hold of a handrail. 'Show some respect to your seniors.'

'It's them in there y'wanna have a go at,' blustered Steve, breathing heavily and nodding in the direction of the pantry. 'They knew I'd screw up if I was left on my own. They did it on purpose.'

'Yeah, all right, steady on,' replied the Second Steward, raising his hands in an effort to restore some sort of order to a disposition that was rapidly disintegrating. He gave Steve a second to compose himself before continuing in a friendly but matter-of-fact fashion. 'I guessed what had happened, but losing your temper isn't going to help things - and just remember this. You're the new kid on this trip, but someone else'll be in your shoes next time around and you'll be dishing it out. Now then, get back in there and for Christ's sake try and act normal because otherwise it'll be hell at mealtimes.'

The lecture was telling; Steve had been an absolute dope. Peter had warned him on numerous occasions that being a first-tripper would make him a foil for all manner of silliness but it had stubbornly refused to sink in. He vowed there and then that in the event of any future skylarking he'd adopt a 'water off a duck's back' attitude. Ultimately, he reasoned, there'd be little point in them continually baiting him if he declined to react. He decided to adopt as brave a face possible, and square up to his mates with all the dignity he could muster.

It wasn't quite as fraught as he'd feared. On his return to the pantry his erstwhile tormentors behaved as if nothing had happened. There was no animosity, and although there were no apologies it brought a satisfactory conclusion to a piece of stupidity that had threatened to undermine what had been up till then, a rewardingly cordial relationship.

Later, with time to themselves, Steve and Peter stretched out on the hatch cover immediately forward of the accommodation area, studying the passing landscape and enjoying the Egyptian sunshine. The late-morning shadows were noticeably shorter than a week previously while the mercury was substantially higher. 'Warming up,' declared Steve, closing his eyes and lounging back on his elbows. 'I might even go sunbathing later.'

'Fair enough,' replied Peter, who already had a tan as a result of his previous trips through the tropics, 'so long as you don't get sunburnt. That's what happened to the galley boy on the *Toowoomba*, and he had the book thrown at him.'

'How come?' asked Steve, sitting up and eyeing a cluster of men in the distance who seemed to be maintaining the canal bank.

'Silly bugger sat out in the sun without a shirt on,' answered Peter, following Steve's example in reclining back on his elbows. 'This was in the middle of the Indian Ocean, mind you. He was peeling spuds at the time. Said he wanted a decent bronzy to show off to his mates back in Cleethorpes. Well, according to all reports by the time he'd finished he looked like the proverbial lobster. He couldn't work - reckoned it was too bloody painful. Anyway, he was fined a day's pay for being an idiot, and had to forfeit another day's pay for not working. If you want to go bronzying then little and often's the answer. You'll have just as good a tan in the end.'

Steve thought of the galley boy and shuddered. He certainly wanted a healthy suntan, but had no intention of allowing himself to be incinerated.

Throughout their conversation Steve had been scrutinizing the knot of canal-side labourers, and with the *Alice Springs* rapidly drawing abeam he could see that they were scantily dressed and were toiling with picks and shovels. Then, with his eyes popping, he saw that they were shackled together, and that one of their number who stood apart from the others carried a rifle.

'Chain gang,' said Peter, rising to his feet and ambling over to the starboard rail for a closer look at the fettered convicts. 'Hard labour, that's what jailbirds can expect in this part of the world - and they'll still be at it in another three months when the temperature's over a hundred.'

'Surely not,' said Steve, feeling a pang of sympathy for his fellow men, regardless of the fact they were criminals. 'It must be bad enough as it is and we're hardly into the eighties. I wonder what they did to deserve that?'

'Probably insulted the President,' replied Peter, cynically, showing scant respect for the Egyptian head of state. 'If they were guilty of anything really serious they'd have either been shot on the spot or had their hands chopped off.'

Steve was unsure if his friend was telling the truth or merely taking a swipe at what was generally perceived as a tinpot Arab dictatorship. However, he later discovered from his mentor, the Bosun, that in some parts of the Middle East extreme punishments were an everyday fact of life, and that summary decapitation was generally the penalty for murder, thieves did indeed have their hands chopped off while death by stoning awaited any female found guilty of committing adultery. But the Bosun also confirmed that Egypt was one of the more moderate and enlightened Arab nations, despite the vitriol spat at it by an acrimonious British Establishment in the wake of the 'fifties' Suez debacle. In view of the Bosun's comments the chain gang could probably think themselves lucky.

Whatever, the convicts were swiftly forgotten as Steve heard a sound that was emotively familiar - albeit in the midst of a desert. He peered in the direction of the gathering crescendo as the sky became blackened astern. A whistle screamed - and out of the haze roared the Port Said to Suez express, passengers swarming like locusts, both outside the train and within.

It was all so very concise. The grossly overcrowded apparition was history in the blink of an eye, with only a vortex of dust to show for its passing. But to Steve it had been classic theatre, with all the drama of a Warner Brothers blockbuster. 'Did you see that?' he cried, as life on the canal bank returned to normal, and the unfortunate chain gang resumed their exertions as though the pageant had never existed.

'It was only a fuckin' train,' observed Peter, with as much enthusiasm as a rain-saturated sheepdog. 'Anyone'd think a flying saucer had just landed by the way you're carryin' on.'

'I know it was only a train,' replied Steve, mildly irritated that such a glorious spectacle should be so flippantly disregarded. 'But wasn't it superb? And what about all those people hanging on the outside? It's a wonder they don't fall off.'

'Some of them probably do,' said Peter, swatting at a fly that was trying to infiltrate one of his eye sockets. 'But the train's the only way some of them are ever going to get anywhere, and a lot of them travel on the outside because it's cooler than riding inside.'

It was a valid enough point, thought Steve, as Peter flattened the fly with his flip-flop; but was it worth risking your neck for a few degrees reduction in temperature? He concluded that walking was preferable to chancing ones arm on a swaying foot-board, where the odds on survival seemed considerably lower than those of the canal-side chain gang.

'I wondered if we'd see the Gulley Gulley Man,' said Peter, as they made their way back to the pantry. 'This is the third time I've been through the canal and I haven't seen him so far.'

'Who's the Gulley Gulley Man?' asked Steve, pinching his cigarette out and sliding the partly smoked stub into its packet; he would normally have tucked it behind his ear but those kind of habits were frowned upon in areas where food was prepared.

'Some kind of conjurer - so I've heard,' replied Peter, holding the pantry door open. 'They say he can pull chickens out of thin air before making them disappear - but it sounds like a load of old bollocks.'

'What's a load of old bollocks?' enquired Archie, who was noisily sharpening a carving knife on a gleaming steel.

'The Gulley Gulley Man,' answered Peter, wiping a dirty finger mark from the door of the refrigerator. 'I've never seen him - and I don't believe that old cobblers about the chickens either.'

'Oh! He exists all right,' replied Archie, testing the knife on a cold joint of beef. 'I've seen him dozens of times - but you're right in one respect, he's a crap conjurer. It's all waffle. He jabbers away nineteen to the dozen and while you're trying to decipher what he's talking about he's hiding the chickens beneath his jellaba.'

'Why do they allow him aboard then?' asked Steve, puzzled as to why an imposter should be afforded the hospitality of a genuine magician.

'Because it's entertainment,' replied Archie, popping a morsel of beef into his mouth. 'It's a diversion for the passengers and crew, and if the bloke can make a few bob into the bargain then what the hell.' Steve suddenly found himself wishing the Gulley Gulley Man was on board, so he could judge for himself whether the man was a charlatan or otherwise; but it seemed he was elsewhere, perhaps on the *Johan van Oldenbarnevelt*, where his capers might be more readily appreciated.

Shortly before lunch the *Alice Springs* passed the teeming city of Ismâ'lîya, where urchins frolicked in the filthy streets and beggars squatted in alleys - and where sensible people kept their wallets and purses buttoned safely in an inside pocket. Steve was desperate for at least a glimpse of the city, and he dashed outside on the pretext that he'd left his lighter on the hatch cover and needed to retrieve it before anyone else discovered it. The gut-churning stench as he arrived on deck was stifling. A cocktail of sewage, garbage and sweating humanity, it stunk like a farmyard manure heap. His initial instinct was to bury his nose in his sleeve but the reaction was futile. He had to accept that these were the smells of the east, and were par for the course in places like Ismâ'lîya where modern sanitation was unheard of. In that fleeting interlude before lunch he witnessed both opulence and poverty, with the latter overwhelmingly prevalent.

Back at the pantry, news had filtered down that the procession of ships would anchor in the Great Bitter Lake to allow the passage of a northbound convoy. 'It looks as though we'll be there for a couple of hours,' announced Donald, who'd picked up the news on the grapevine. 'But they reckon we'll be clear of the canal before nightfall.'

'Well, that's a relief,' said Archie, as the lunchtime gong echoed around the alleyways. 'I never feel safe with all these foreign chappies roaming about - especially after dark.' 'Why's that then?' asked Steve, wondering at the difference between a handful of officially sanctioned Egyptians and the crew of the *Alice Springs'*.

'I'll tell you,' chirped Peter, cheekily, before Archie had chance to reply. 'It's because he's afraid one of those guys'll creep up on him in the middle of the night and sully his reputation.'

'Saucy get!' snorted Archie, aiming a soggy dishcloth at Peter's head. 'It's nothing of the sort as well you know. It's just that they're partial to thieving, and that's liable to happen when you're sleeping - and you don't need your door locked in these temperatures.'

'That's true,' replied Steve, suddenly concerned for his own belongings, even though it was daylight. 'I hadn't thought about that.'

'It's OK,' said Peter, reading his room-mate's thoughts while dodging the airborne dishcloth. 'I locked the door on my way out this morning. Everything's as safe as houses.'

'By early afternoon the *Alice Springs* lay at anchor in the Great Bitter Lake. Some of the crew had planned to go swimming, but with the lake being little cleaner than a cesspit the Captain had wisely ruled otherwise. 'No bathing in the lake,' announced the Second Steward, swiping an Eccles cake from a tray of tabnabs. 'Old Man's orders. He doesn't want anyone either drowning or picking up dysentery, so if you're caught going over the side it'll be your lookout.'

'Right,' affirmed Steve, an extremely poor swimmer who never strayed out of his depth.

'Sure,' answered Peter, a capable swimmer who knew sufficient about the lake's poor water quality to risk getting even his toenails wet.

'That reminds me,' said Steve, as the stewards dispersed to their various recreational activities. 'Does anyone know what happened to Sean Cassidy? He was due in front of the Captain this morning.'

'Haven't you heard?' replied Peter, surprised that Steve didn't know. 'Apart from the logging he was fined a couple of days pay plus twenty quid's-worth of compensation. It was an expensive piss if you ask me.'

'Serves him right,' observed Archie, who had no time at all for the rougher element. 'If people like him can't behave themselves they deserve what's coming to them.'

'Let that be a lesson to you, Steve,' cautioned the Second Steward. 'Cassidy'll be lucky not to get a DR in his book after that little episode - and if I'm any judge of character he'll be in even deeper trouble before this trip's over.'

With the early part of the afternoon to themselves the boys headed up to the poop where an awning had been rigged around the after deck house. Here they found Jimmy Craddock, legs outstretched, reclining against the accommodation bulkhead. 'DR? That's 'Decline to Report', isn't it?' asked Steve, as he sat down on the deck and removed his T-shirt.

'Yeah,' replied Peter, slipping off his singlet and folding it into a wafer-thin pillow. 'But generally speaking you'll only get a DR if you're crap at your job or have a lousy disciplinary record. Most of us'll get VGs, meaning 'Very Good', so it'll only be people like Sean Cassidy who'll have anything to worry about.'

'He won't worry,' chipped in Jimmy. 'He's too thick-skinned to worry about anything as trivial as a DR.'

Steve felt mightily relieved. Since earlier that morning he'd been secretly fretting that his breakfast-time blunder may have jeopardized his chances of a clean discharge. A DR in his discharge book could easily spell disaster for a first-tripper, all but scuppering his chances of gaining future seafaring employment. It now seemed his fears had been groundless.

A good thirty-minutes elapsed before the northbound convoy eventually emerged from the southern section of the canal, and it was another hour before it finally cleared the lake in the direction of Ismâ'lîya. The cavalcade had included several British vessels including Port Line's *Port Vindex* and the Hain Steamship Company's *Trevelyan*; while sandwiched in the centre of the convoy were a couple of homeward-bound Royal Navy minesweepers.

With the northbound convoy clear of the southern section of the canal its southbound counterpart reformed and moved slowly in the direction of Suez. 'Another hour or so and we should be passing the French hospital,' observed Jimmy, as he made to return to the galley. 'It's the only sign of civilization between here and Port Tewfiq.'

'French hospital?' quizzed Steve. 'In the middle of a desert? Funny place to have a hospital.'

'Well, that's where it is,' rejoined Peter, slipping his crumpled singlet over his shoulders. 'It's nothing special, it's just that from now on, apart from the hospital, there's almost nothing but sand until we're clear of the canal - no towns, no palm trees........no nothing.' And so it transpired; nothing but sand from there to eternity, with only shimmering mirages to relieve the monotony.

The Suez Canal is approximately a hundred miles long with the shorter section being to the south of the Great Bitter lake. The hospital, administered by the sisters of a French religious order, lay on the starboard side about an hour's steaming from the lake, and appeared more akin to a residential-come-nursing home for sick and disabled children than a conventional hospital. Clearly excited by yet another parade of shipping the children, most of them running or walking but with a few in wheelchairs and arms, came flocking to the surrounding fence to wave to the passing convoy. Patently well cared for, the youngsters were overjoyed when the passengers and seamen reciprocated.

'Just as well that place exists,' commented a deckhand, poignantly, as Steve studied the faces beyond the chain-links. 'Otherwise the poor little buggers'd probably be either dead or begging on the streets of Cairo.

7

With the sun sinking slowly in the west, the *Alice Springs* passed out of the Suez Canal, past Port Tewfiq and into the Gulf of Suez. This narrow ribbon of water at the head of the Red Sea formed one of the busiest shipping routes in the world, with oil tankers being in the ascendant: thus, the Gulf of Suez had earnt itself the nickname, 'Tanker Alley'. Most of the tankers heading northwards were deeply laden, and were bound for refineries in the Mediterranean, northern Europe and the eastern seaboards of both the United States and Canada, their cargoes having been loaded at terminals in the Persian Gulf or on the Red Sea coast of Saudi Arabia. Most of them flew the colours of the big multinationals such as: Shell, BP, Esso, Caltex and Texaco. Of the remainder, several belonged to the British-based, Lowland Tanker Corporation, and were managed by Common Brothers of Newcastle-upon-Tyne. The Lowland vessels were on time charter to BP and carried similar funnel colours to those of the charterer, but with the BP symbol set in a tartan band. Another variation was that the names of the Lowland ships all began with the prefix, 'Border', for example: *Border Regiment* and *Border Sentinel*, whereas the names of those owned and operated directly by the parent company all commenced with the prefix, 'British'.

Whatever the earlier troubles with the *Alice Springs'* engines they'd behaved impeccably since that brief aberration in the Thames; and on leaving the canal she showed a remarkable turn of speed as she proceeded to overhaul almost every ship in her convoy, with the sole exception of the *Johan van Oldenbarnevelt* which was soon a dot on the skyline. The *Alice Springs'* next port of call would be Aden – essentially for bunkers, but where Steve could hopefully have his damaged front tooth restored to its original condition.

'Weird, isn't it?' remarked Steve, out of the blue, as the three junior catering ratings took a late-evening stroll along the *Alice Springs'* fore-deck as their ship forged purposefully southward in the direction of the Gulf of Aden and the Horn of Africa.

'What is?' queried Jimmy, not having the foggiest what Steve was talking about.

'Being able to see in the dark on a moonless night with only the running lights on,' answered Steve, describing what to his way of thinking was something extraordinary. 'By my reckoning we ought to have bumped into or tripped over all sorts of things - you know, winches, hatch-coamings, ring-bolts, and so on, but we haven't because we can see them almost as if it was daylight.'

'Oh! I see what you're getting at,' replied Jimmy, shifting his gaze to the heavens as he sat himself down on number three hatch cover and lit up a State Express. 'Well, there's no mystery attached to that. It's starlight - pure and simple.'

Steve could hardly believe his ears, suspecting another leg pull; but gazing skywards he was amazed at the brilliance as millions of stars formed a twinkling ceiling across the entire celestial hemisphere, like sequins on a sable ball-gown.

'It's owing to the dry desert air,' added Peter, taking up the topic as he too studied the cosmos with the intensity of a budding astronomer, 'and because there's no light pollution out here like there is in the towns and cities.'

The following morning both Steve and Peter received a ticking off from the Chief Steward, after one of the engineers on the eight till twelve complained that the crusts hadn't been removed from the sandwiches left for the night watches. It was a matter of culinary etiquette that crusts were always removed from toast and sandwiches, especially if they were to be served to officers and passengers. But the boys had decided - without consultation - that the engineers and officers on night duty needed greater sustenance than that afforded by the traditional teatime sandwiches, so had left them with the crusts intact. When all was said and done, back at the 'Vindi' the crusts had formed a substantial proportion of their diet. 'Miserable bastard,' moaned Peter, following the Chief Steward's departure. 'Anyone'd think the engineers were bloody royalty instead of uniformed grease monkeys.' Another practice that was abruptly halted was that of filling the smaller teapots from their own enamel pot after the Second Mate had protested at the absence of leaves in his pot.

Over the following two-and-a-half days the *Alice Springs* headed steadily south towards the Bäb-al-Mändab, the narrow strait linking the Red Sea with the Gulf of Aden, an arm of the Indian Ocean. The pages of Steve's atlas had taught him that Saudi Arabia occupied by far the longest stretch of coastline on the western shores of the Arabian Peninsular, while Egypt, Sudan and Ethiopia shared the African coast; but as they neared the southern portal of the Red Sea, far away to the south-east loomed the mysterious mountains of Yemen, a secretive land of Bedouin and camels - the legendary Empty Quarter - of which almost everyone, excepting the nomads who lived there, knew nothing. Ethiopia crept into sight as land enveloped the *Alice Springs* from both port and starboard; and the sun-scorched landscapes of two opposing continents quivered in the shimmering heat.

The desolate mountains exuded foreboding and menace, evoking scenes from the recently-released Kenneth Moore film, 'North-West Frontier'. Steve could visualise hoards of shifty-eyed tribesmen, observing the *Alice Springs* from their perches - and a flash of light? The sun's rays reflected by a mirror? A signal from one hilltop to another? Steve's imagination was weaving all manner of unlikely scenarios, so he cleared his head and returned to cleaning out the refrigerator, where the only threat was posed by a touch of frostbite.

Further south still, in the sun-baked nether regions of the Red Sea, the *Alice Springs* passed a series of brooding and mountainous islands. No more than variously-sized outcrops of rock the islands bore weird and mystical names, such as: The Kamaran Islands, Zuqua, Zubair Islands and Great Hanish, and all appeared uninhabited; although it was rumoured that they were occasionally occupied by soldiers from both Yemen and Ethiopia as part of a long-festering dispute over sovereignty. 'The Gates of Hell', remarked Peter, mopping his brow as he peered at the rocks through their cabin porthole, 'that's what they call those islands - and they know what they're talking about. You might think this heat's unbearable, but this is nothing compared with the temperatures in the Indian Ocean.'

Sailing through the Bäb-al-Mändab into the Gulf of Aden was indeed like quitting an oven for a blast furnace, and Steve was thankful for his ample reserves of socks, T-shirts and underwear. He perspired constantly. Fortunately, dhobying dried within minutes, so that even those with a more modest wardrobe could change their clothing as frequently as needed.

With the small French colony of Djibouti now rapidly disappearing to starboard, the *Alice Springs* headed north-eastwards towards the tiny British Protectorate of Aden, itself almost encircled by the huge empty desert of Yemen. The Protectorate was only a few hours steaming from the Bäb-al-Mändab, so that on the morning of the fourteenth day out, the *Alice Springs* dropped anchor off Steamer Point, where a number of other vessels were already replenishing their fuel supplies. No shore leave was granted; but the Agent came aboard as soon as the accommodation ladder was down, carrying - among other things - another consignment of mail. Hot on the Agent's heels came a BP bunkering barge which ranged alongside, and under the supervision of the Second Engineer was soon pumping oil into their depleted bunkers.

The ubiquitous bum boats were soon in attendance, with some of the natives being allowed on board to display their wares on the hatch covers. Others bobbed alongside, the boats overflowing with a wide array of souvenirs, consumer goods and clothing. Steve was wary of buying anything from a distance, so he ignored the boats and from his supply of sterling made several purchases from the hatch covers. He would have dearly loved one of the leather-bound transistor radios that were straight from the factories of Japan, but no amount of haggling made the asking price remotely affordable. It was probably as well, as buying electrical items from itinerant salesmen was frequently a gamble, and if the radio had later malfunctioned he'd have cursed the bum boat jockey from the Gulf of Aden to Adelaide. He ultimately settled for a pair of flip-flops, an ornamental music-box for his mum and a white, nylon short-sleeved shirt.

Notwithstanding that Aden was a bunkering port the water was remarkably clear, and despite the presence of some sinister-looking marine life there was plenty of underwater amusement. 'You throw coin, mister – me fetchie,' was a cry that resounded from a boatload of ebullient mudlarks. Seamen and passengers obliged, disposing of pennies and ha'pennies, fascinated as the coins spiralled down before being swooped upon by the triumphant youngsters who shot to the surface, jubilantly brandishing their trophies.

For most of the morning Steve had been awaiting news of when he and the Senior Radio Officer would be proceeding ashore to the dentist. He was assuming that the proposed appointment hadn't been forgotten; although he was virtually certain that the no-nonsense Sparks, whose toothache had become almost unbearable, wouldn't have allowed that to happen. Then, just before lunch, as he was placing serving utensils into an assortment of trays and dixies, the Second Steward tapped him on the shoulder, and said, 'Be ready and dressed to go ashore as soon as you've finished eating. A launch is coming alongside to collect you and the Sparky at two.'

'What about money?' asked Steve, suddenly wondering if he had sufficient to pay the dentist.

'You don't have to worry about money,' called Sec, as he made his way round to the saloon with an armful of clean serviettes. 'The Company'll take care of that.'

'Well, that's a relief,' breathed Steve, sliding a slice into a tray of Cod Mornay. 'I forgot all about paying the dentist when I bought that music box and so on.'

'Most British shipping companies are pretty good about things like that,' mumbled Peter, as he gnawed the end off a thumbnail. 'Mind you, I don't fancy being in your shoes, going to the dentists' in this hole.'

For the first time since the discovery of his broken tooth the alarm bells began clanging. Steve had been so preoccupied with getting the tooth reconditioned that he'd completely overlooked the possibility that an Arab dental surgery might not be so salubrious as Mr McEwan's in the High Street at home. Images of butcher's shops and slaughterhouses bodied forth, and he began wondering if it might be more prudent to cancel the appointment and make do until the *Alice Springs* reached Adelaide. 'Have you ever been to a dentist in places like Aden?' he asked Archie, who'd arrived at the pantry and was busily filling water jugs for the tables. Steve was acutely aware that Peter was only scaremongering, but sought reassurance that his immediate outlook wouldn't be as painful as implied.

'Yes, a couple of times', replied the Bedroom Steward, indicating a narrow hiatus between his upper-right eye tooth and the molars. 'I had this one out in Havana, and I had a cavity filled in Mombasa. Didn't bother me a bit - either of them. The surgeries were a bit more primitive than at home but otherwise........You don't want to take any notice of Peter. He'd shit himself if he had to visit a dentist wherever it was.'

At two o'clock precisely, Steve, having cleaned his teeth and changed into shore-going clothes, was standing at the head of the accommodation ladder with the Senior Radio Officer as a launch ventured out from the shore. He was wearing his new nylon shirt; not the wisest of choices, as with the mercury nudging a hundred the impermeable fabric was clinging to his skin like a limpet. Still, with the launch on its way he'd just have to grin and put up with it. As the launch drew alongside he and Sparks descended the ladder and stepped over the gunnel, and were soon heading for a flight of steps in the granite-faced wall of the harbour.

The stairway formed the gateway to a mysterious and obsolescent world. On reaching the top Steve scanned the immediate neighbourhood, guessing that this must be the Crater district of Aden. He noted, gloomily, that the area looked far more dilapidated than it had done from a distance. It had been an all-too familiar illusion, a case of a false impression created by the tightly-packed whitewashed buildings reflecting the brilliant sunlight. A battered Vauxhall taxi, its engine rattling like a jar of marbles, was already waiting, and as Steve and his companion slid into the passenger seats the bearded and turbaned driver stood smartly on the accelerator before the Sparky had even got the door shut.

The journey had all the ingredients of a Mack Sennett car chase as the Vauxhall tore through the streets, smashing the wing mirror off another vehicle and clipping a lorry, before screeching to a halt in a cloud of dust outside a hovel resembling a cow shed. Indicating that the driver should wait, Sparks led the way into the dimly-lit, single-storey building where they found there were no other patients, and where they were greeted by a beaming Chinaman. They were motioned to a ramshackle bench whilst Steve, sweating more profusely than ever, eyed his surroundings with mounting dismay. His spirits plummeted at sight of the filthy, tobacco-stained walls; the antiquated chair; a handful of dental instruments; a filing cabinet and a spindly table on which stood a bowlful of yellowing teeth. He glanced hurriedly at Sparks, and was on the verge of bolting for the door when the Chinaman asked politely, and in perfect English, 'Right - which of you is going first?'

Sparks didn't budge, as if his aching tooth had somehow been miraculously cured; so Steve, although being the junior - and in an absolute funk - took the bit between his teeth believing the sooner it was done with the better.

'What can I do for you'? asked the Chinaman, donning a blood-spattered apron.

Steve, who, if he'd been a Catholic would have been fiddling with his rosary and praying as zealously as the Pope, stammered, 'C-c-can you please fill this hole in my tooth?'

'Off course,' replied the dentist, wiping a small hand-held mirror on his apron. 'Just sit back and relax and I'll have it fixed for you in no time.'

Sit back and relax? What a ridiculous statement, thought Steve, grasping the arms of the chair, mouth open wide, expecting a local anaesthetic. But instead of administering a gum-numbing injection the dentist began burrowing away with an ancient, treadle-operated contraption as ardently as a British utility worker who was drilling a hole in the tarmac. Steve gripped the chair more tightly, afraid should the drill touch a nerve. But amazingly the process was painless; and as the drilling continued he gradually unwound, convinced there was little to fear. The archaic equipment made leisurely progress but the drilling eventually ceased. The dentist then tamped a filling of some sort into the cavity and Steve rinsed the debris from his mouth.

'There - all finished,' chirruped the Chinaman, replacing his instruments in a jar of cloudy disinfectant, an unfortunate example of Middle-Eastern sterilization. 'Avoid biting on it for a couple of hours and you shouldn't have any more trouble.'

Steve was both physically and mentally drained. He thanked the dentist and slumped on to the bench while Sparky stepped up to the chair. Sparks' ordeal lasted less than a minute, for he too received no anaesthetic. In no time at all his bothersome molar clattered into the bowl and he joined Steve on the bench to recover.

'Just a little paperwork to complete,' said the dentist, withdrawing a form from the filing cabinet and removing the top from a Biro. He made a few notes on the form before presenting it to Sparks, saying, 'Just sign at the bottom there and we're almost finished.' Then, like a bolt from the blue, he turned to Steve, and demanded, 'That'll be five shillings, please.'

It was like a smack between the eyes with a pole-axe. 'Five shillings?' cried Steve, jumping to his feet in protest. 'But I've no money - and anyway, I was told that the company'd pay.'

'The company only pay for extractions,' answered the Chinaman, his hitherto almost permanent grin slowly evaporating. 'All other treatments have to be paid for by the patient.'

Steve was dumbstruck, and panic ensued as he envisaged the dentist inviting him back to the chair to have his tooth removed, thus guaranteeing his payment.

Sparks played the role of a saint. 'Put it down as an extraction,' he suggested, with the authority befitting of an officer. 'No one'll know so long as he keeps his mouth shut.'

'That all right with you?' asked the Chinaman, withdrawing another form from the filing cabinet as Steve eagerly nodded his assent. You could bet your life it was all right, and Steve felt immensely relieved as he grabbed the Biro from the dentist. He scribbled his name on the form, and thanking the dentist profusely he followed Sparks out into the dazzling sunlight where he all but collapsed in a heap. 'Thanks Sparks,' he offered, with all the sincerity that the Senior Radio Officer's mediation merited.

'Don't worry about it, Son,' said Sparks, responding to Steve's appreciativeness with a dismissive wave of the hand. 'So long as the bastard gets his money he won't worry where it comes from.'

'Easy-peasy,' lied Steve, when Peter enquired how he'd fared at the dentist's. 'Didn't feel a thing – not even without an anaesthetic.' At least that bit was true, and Steve had no intention of revealing the full extent of his jitters only to become the butt of a further spate of ridicule.

A few minutes later, whilst passing the Third Engineer's cabin, he noticed the door ajar and that the room was unexpectedly occupied. He knew that the Third was on duty so he inched the door open and startled a coal-black native who was busily rifling a suitcase. Steve wasn't a coward but neither was he particularly brave, so his reaction was purely instinctive. 'What the hell do you think you're doing?' he bawled, making a grab for the interloper. The would-be plunderer, caught completely unawares, made good his escape by bundling Steve over and scampering off down the alleyway. Steve picked himself up and dusted himself down. He wasn't hurt, and although he hadn't been able to detain the intruder he was almost certain he'd fled empty handed. Nevertheless, he had a quick look around, just to make sure that nothing obvious had been taken, before closing the suitcase and securing the cabin behind him. He then reported the incident to the Second Steward who in turn sent a message to the engine room informing the Third of the intrusion.

'Well done, Kiddo,' said the Third Engineer, poking his head around the pantry door on completion of the twelve-till-four. 'That's the first time I've ever forgotten to lock my cabin - and I'll make sure it's the last. 'Thanks to you the bastard didn't get anything, but he probably would've if you hadn't rumbled him.' Steve felt on top of the world. As he was belatedly beginning to accept, all the leg pulling and horseplay were an irrelevance - an irritating sideshow. It was moments like this, when his value was openly appreciated, that really carried weight.

That evening, after darkness had fallen and the air had become cooler, Steve and his pals sat on the hatch cover in the after well-deck, listening to the British forces radio station on Peter's wireless. Some of the other lads had switched on their newly-acquired transistors, and were likewise tuned into the station which was transmitting from a hilltop just a stones-throw away from the harbour. Broadcasting primarily to the British garrison and their families, the network carried an assortment of programmes ranging from record requests to news bulletins; and for what it was worth - the weather forecast.

The *Alice Springs,* having completed her bunkering, sailed from

Aden around midnight. Yemen still lay to the north; but to starboard Djibuti had given way to Somalia, the coastline extending eastwards to the Horn of Africa before sweeping away south through Kenya, Tanzania, Mozambique and South Africa, all the way down to the Cape of Good Hope, more than two-and-a half-thousand miles distant. Their next port of call would be Adelaide, the principal port and capital of South Australia - assuming they actually arrived there.

On Sundays, the inspection was performed by the Captain in the company of the Chief Steward and the doctor, but on weekdays it was delegated to the Mate and Second Steward who were also accompanied by the physician. And so it was that at around eleven o'clock, as Steve was drying the coffee cups, this trio of worthies looked into the pantry in the course of their daily ritual. The Mate was efficient and respected, but he was also ruthless and thorough. He had a nose for dirt, shining his torch into the deepest recesses: within the refrigerator, elevator and hot-press - beneath the salamander and coffee percolator, and into the hidden corners of both the deck and bulkheads. He even ran his fingers along the door-tops and overheads but as usual found nothing to complain of. Steve may have been a first-tripper, but both he and Peter were meticulous and were seldom found wanting in the realms of cleanliness and hygiene.

If Steve thought the troubles surrounding his damaged front tooth were behind him he was mistaken. Apparently satisfied that all was as it should be the Mate and Second Steward departed; but the doctor hesitated, turned, and enquired, 'You're the lad who had a tooth out yesterday, aren't you? I'd better take a look, just to make sure that it's healing.' Steve felt utterly deflated. There was he thinking the company had met the cost of his filling with no questions asked, then along comes this guy with his spanner. Steve hadn't a hope of bluffing his way out of this one so he simply opened his mouth, hoping the medic would guess what had happened and forget it. The doctor examined the perfectly filled cavity for several seconds before smiling, and remarking, 'Hmmm........He seems to have made a pretty good job of it.' And without further comment, he turned on his heel and headed off into the alleyway.

8

It happened somewhere south of Socotra, that exotically-named island that lies in the north-western corner of the Indian Ocean, some three hundred miles from Somalia. Steve was wiping out the elevator when he first became aware of the silence. The reason was obvious. In an ominous sequel to the breakdown in the River Thames more than a fortnight earlier the engines had suffered a relapse, only this time it was far more serious. The turbines were briefly restarted but immediately stalled, and it soon became clear that the *Alice Springs* would be going nowhere in the foreseeable future.

'We're buggered good and proper this time,' complained Peter, when he returned from aft having emptied the rosie. 'If it's as bad as it sounds we'll be here till bloody Christmas.'

'Oh! And who says so?' asked Steve, wondering how his mate could have gleaned such information so readily.

'One of the fireman,' replied Peter, dropping the rosie noisily in its corner of the pantry. 'Fuckin' sea waters got into the boilers again. They reckon it'll take ages to fix this time.'

'What if they can't fix it?' enquired Steve, who was not at all sure of the procedures involved. 'Won't they radio for a tug?'

'A fuckin' tug?' answered Peter, incredulously. 'The company wouldn't go to that expense, not if they can help it - they'll just leave it to our own engineers. I suppose if the worse comes to the worse they might nurse her along to a shipyard somewhere - but a fuckin' tug? You must be fuckin' jokin'.'

In accordance with international maritime regulations, the signal for, 'Vessel not under command', was hoisted at the *Alice Springs'* masthead. Comprising two black balls aligned one above the other, the warning would be perpetuated by a pair of red lights after nightfall.

As an indication of the evolving crisis the flow of fresh water was unexpectedly curtailed. It was quickly re-established, but only temporarily, and it soon became clear that the commodity would have to be rationed. It was down to the fact that with the boilers and evaporators being interdependent the evaporators were also inactive, so water conservation was imperative.

In the run-up to mealtimes sufficient fresh water had to be drawn to meet all cooking, drinking and dhobying requirements, with all suitable containers being utilized. For the remainder of the time the only water available was seawater so consequently, with the likes of Palmolive and Camay being useless, salt-water soap was substituted. Even then, personal cleanliness couldn't be guaranteed because with the generators being intermittently out of commission the showers were also inoperative. The power supply problems meant that sanitation was another casualty, even though it was customary to flush the toilets with seawater.

Dhobying in seawater was inadvisable as not only would the fabric eventually rot but salt-laden clothing worn next to the skin could result in salt-water sores. However, that difficulty was overcome thanks to the limited amount of fresh water that was available. Before turning in Steve crammed as much gear as possible into his scrub-out bucket before stirring in a sprinkling of Surf. It was then left to soak overnight before being rinsed and pegged out in the morning.

The stewards were fortunate in that there were sufficient buckets for everyone, but the deck and engine room boys had to make do with whatever was handy. Empty oil and grease drums that would normally have been jettisoned were cleaned and exploited while in the galley, pots and pans proved practical alternatives to buckets.

On a more positive note, the Carpenter knocked up a timber-framed, canvas-lined swimming pool that was topped-up with seawater whenever the pumps were operational. It was a pretty rickety affair that was in need of constant repair but it served its purpose and prevailed for the extent of the emergency. Located on the starboard side immediately forward of the superstructure the pool was in constant demand, with the hour prior to mealtimes being exclusively reserved for the passengers.

'I wonder if the doctor's daughter wears a bikini?' mused Peter from a saloon window, standing on tiptoe and peering down at the fore-deck for a view of the pool on the morning following the breakdown.

'I wouldn't know,' answered Steve, as he headed for the duty mess with the engineers' seven-bell breakfasts. 'And anyway, you're not going to see much from there. It's the probable reason they situated the pool where it is - to prevent people like you from rubber-necking.'

With no headway to create a breeze and in the absence of forced ventilation it was unbearable down in the engine room where several of the men suffered heatstroke. They were immediately evacuated and compelled to lie down in the shade, the doctor prescribing revitalizing drinks and salt tablets. He eventually advised that salt tablets be made freely available, with the engine room and galley taking precedence.

The sea took on the semblance of molten glass as the *Alice Springs* drifted aimlessly in what was locally known as 'Jilal', the harshest season of the year. The temperature hovered in the low hundreds Fahrenheit but they carried on as normal - or as normally as they could in the circumstances. The passengers lounged in the shade but there was no such relief for the crew. Perspiration was the greatest annoyance, especially for the cooks and stewards. Not only was it uncomfortable and physically debilitating but it dripped on to anything and everything, including into the food if precautions weren't adequately taken. For this very reason additional towels were issued - not for the men's well-being, but purely in the interests of hygiene.

In common with other crew members Steve and Peter had forsaken their cabin and taken to sleeping in the open, in their case on the hatch cover immediately adjacent to the swimming pool. It wasn't the most comfortable of beds and with morning came backache; and the realization that a hatch cover was a pretty poor substitute for a mattress. Nevertheless, they persisted and on subsequent nights they suffered only a niggling stiffness, which was far less onerous than tossing and turning in a sweatbox.

Steve could have murdered a beer, but along with the other boys was denied alcohol owing to his junior status. Meanwhile, their senior counterparts were permitted two cans per day of either beer or lager which was sold during afternoon smoke-ho. In view of the exceptional circumstances it had been hoped that the Chief Steward would sanction additional allowances, but true to his reputation he flatly refused and two cans was the number adhered to. Another bone of contention was that while ratings were restricted to a defined allocation of beer and tobacco, officers and engineers could purchase whatever they wished, including wines and spirits, so long as their accounts were in credit; such were the privileges enjoyed by the officer classes compared with those of their subordinates.

On the third afternoon of the breakdown, in conjunction with the daily beer distribution, the Second Steward oversaw the second of the fortnightly cigarette issues; a couple of days later than scheduled owing to a paperwork discrepancy. Steve purchased two-hundred Rothmans, his account being debited twelve-shillings and sixpence in payment. Shortly thereafter he cleared his debts by handing a packet each to his benefactors.

A ship's grapevine was generally an ultra-reliable information source, conveying snippets of news and gossip with remarkable alacrity; and that's more or less what happened on the sixth afternoon of the breakdown, although on this occasion the accuracy was doubtful. Danny Meeks stuck his head through the servery hatchway, and proclaimed, 'It looks like we'll soon be moving. I was clearing the Captain's table and overheard him talking with the Chief Engineer.'

'Oh! And what were they saying?' queried Archie, who was making up a jug of lemonade.

'It looks like we'll be diverting to Colombo - for permanent repairs and to take on supplies of fresh water,' said Danny, smugly, knowing that as Captain's Tiger he was probably in a better position than most to learn what was happening when important decisions were taken.

'I'll believe it when it happens,' interrupted the Second Steward, with the air of someone who'd heard it all previously, and would wait for the eventual outcome. 'I can't see the company throwing money around on a shipyard job if our own blokes can fix it.'

'Nor me,' rejoined Archie who at sixty years of age had a wealth of experience to draw on. 'Before the war I was on an old tramp called the *Coriander* when she broke down in the Pacific, midway between Ecuador and Java. We lay there a month while the engineers repaired a broken cylinder head. The tanks were virtually empty so we caught rainwater in tarpaulins and buckets. As it was we were down to the last few inches before we eventually shifted. No, I can't see us going to Colombo - not in the short term at any rate.'

'I'm only telling you what I heard,' answered Danny, indignantly, peeved at having his privileged information questioned when in his opinion, he of all people should be believed. 'I'll keep it to myself another time.'

'Please yourself,' replied the Second Steward, casting a wink at everyone else in the pantry as Danny disappeared from the servery. 'But we should know for sure pretty soon.'

In fact, it happened to be one of those very few instances when the grapevine failed, leaving Danny looking decidedly silly. It effectively made him an even more dangerous adversary for Steve and Peter if they were thought to have overstepped the mark. On one occasion he reported Peter to the Chief Steward after spotting him smoking while servicing the Senior Deck Cadet's cabin, and he reprimanded Steve after finding fingerprints on a silver milk jug when he could have easily removed them himself.

'I'll swing for that bastard one day,' complained Peter, after receiving a dressing down from the Chief Steward. 'I'll tip him over the side one dark night when no one's watching, you see if I don't.'

'And a fat lot of good that'll do you,' replied Steve, almost certain that the threat was idle and simply a product of frustration.

'That's right,' cut in Archie, whose glance in Peter's direction carried more than a hint of admonishment. 'You need to watch your tongue my lad. If anyone hears you talking like that, and Danny did mysteriously disappear, you'd be the principal suspect.'

'Maybe, replied Peter, who knew that the warning made sense but conveniently ignored it, 'but he still needs teaching a lesson.'

As it turned out, Danny's intelligence concerning the proposed diversion to Colombo hadn't been entirely flawed. Rather, it was his eagerness to impart it that had been his bugbear. If he'd listened more closely to the conversation between the Captain and Chief Engineer he'd have learnt that a diversion to Colombo would only be considered as a last resort, and that the Chief Engineer had every confidence in his own staff resolving the problem - and that is precisely what happened.

Late one evening, after eight days adrift, the *Alice Springs* suddenly stirred. Exclamations of delight and ripples of applause were heard as ball vents began pumping refrigerated air into cabins and workplaces, while fresh water initially gurgled but then flowed freely from taps and shower-heads. Steve was leaning on the taffrail with Jimmy Craddock when the ocean foamed and the engines burst into life. 'Thank Christ for that,' said Jimmy, whose workplace in the galley had been almost as torrid as the engine room. 'To tell you the truth, the novelty was beginning to wear thin.'

For a nail-biting interval fingers were crossed in the hope that those whose spirits had been unexpectedly raised weren't being unduly deceived. But as the *Alice Springs* moved at first cautiously, but then more purposefully, a wave of renewed optimism swept around decks and alleyways.

The engine room staff excepted, the lads in the galley probably had greater reason for complaint than anyone. For the entire duration of the breakdown they'd provided three meals a day for everyone, without an utterance or show of dissent. The old adages about, 'Sweating over a hot stove', while, 'Standing the heat of the kitchen', had never sounded more appropriate.

For a short while at least, no one could be entirely sure that they weren't diverting to Colombo, but on this occasion the grapevine flourished and it soon became clear that it was, 'Full steam ahead', for Adelaide. 'Pity in a way,' said Steve, as he and Jimmy descended the ladder to the after well-deck. 'I quite fancied a month in Ceylon.'

'Never mind,' consoled Jimmy, who was only happy to be moving. 'So long as the engines keep running we should be in Adelaide in another two weeks, and there'll be plenty of shore leave for everyone.'

In the early hours of the following morning Steve was inexplicably aroused. What on earth caused that? he wondered, as he sat up and gathered his senses, listening to the surrounding noises. Had the subconscious detected some out-of-the-ordinary sound or movement? If so then there was no repetition; and he could tell from the reassuring rumble that the engines were still turning over. Peter still snored in his bunk but there was nothing unusual in that; and then - it hit him like a smack on the jaw. In approximately twenty-four hours, assuming there were no further disruptions, the *Alice Springs* would be crossing the zero meridian, and what had disturbed him was a dream about the potential initiation ceremonies. He'd heard all sorts of stories associated with 'crossing the line', most of them involving either tar and feathers, flour and glue or a multitude of other gooey substances. Understandably, none of them really appealed but there was little he could do as a deterrent. There was no hiding the fact that this would be his pioneering crossing of the equator, so the best he could do was to hope it would be overlooked.

In the event he needn't have worried. The *Alice Springs* crossed smoothly into the southern hemisphere while he escaped totally unscathed. Not so fortunate were the passengers, not least the voluptuous doctor's daughter who, while all but exploding from her tight-fitting swimsuit, was seated in a chair and 'shaved' with a large wooden razor before being 'rinsed' with a bucket of seawater. Steve began wondering if all the practical jokes he'd already endured had served as his personal baptism. He later learnt that as far as crew were concerned such rituals were seldom practised aboard freighters, but formed an essential part of ship-board entertainment for the passengers.

The passage from Aden to Adelaide was memorable not only for the warm sunny days but also for the ocean's emptiness, with other shipping in particular being notable for its apparent non-existence. Even during the breakdown, when the *Alice Springs* had sweltered across some of the Indian Ocean's busiest trade routes, it had seemed that the only vessel anywhere was their own. It had evoked a weird sensation of separatism, as if they were drifting through a parallel universe and that they were totally cut off from reality. Of course, that wasn't the case; there was other shipping out there, somewhere, but far enough away for those aboard the *Alice Springs* to feel completely isolated and forgotten.

But for those with eyes in their heads, and despite the fact that they were far from the nearest landmass, there was some remarkable natural phenomena. One afternoon, during his leisure interval, Steve wandered for'ard and spent some time with the fo'c'sle-head lookout. It was a fascinating interlude, especially when the seaman on duty beckoned him to the bulwark. As they peered over the bow a school of porpoises cavorted to and fro as if playing a bizarre game of chicken. They seemed oblivious of the risks, like sky-diving parachutists, participating purely for the thrill.

On another occasion, as he was polishing the saloon windows, he became enthralled by what could best be described as an oceanic extravaganza. Suddenly, realizing that he couldn't miss such a heaven-sent opportunity, he dashed to his cabin and grabbed the small 'Brownie' box camera his grandmother had given him for his eleventh birthday, intending to record for posterity the most magnificent seascape he'd ever laid eyes on. The view from the wave tops was truly breathtaking as an endless procession of mountainous seas marched relentlessly between the horizons. Steve was wondering if they might be in for a cyclone, but that was only speculation and the Carpenter put him to the wise.

'No, Son', informed the chippy, waving an arm that seemed to embrace all four points of the compass, 'This is an ocean swell, and it's the aftermath of a tropical storm. In fact, it causes the surf in places like Hawaii and California - even down at Newquay in Cornwall.' It was an incredible explanation but one that so clearly made sense. Whatever, it was a never-to-be-forgotten spectacle and Mother Nature at her stupendous best. As an anticlimax, when Steve returned to his cabin to deposit his camera he discovered that the film had already been exposed, and that the photograph he thought he'd recorded was only imprinted in his mind.

As March drew to a close Steve caught his first ever glimpse of Australia. He was unsure of the exact location, but a glance at his atlas suggested it was somewhere in the vicinity of Cape Leeuin, the continent's south-western extremity. By this time the temperatures had fallen to more acceptable levels but still compared favourably with those of a good English summer.

It was another four days before their eventual arrival at Port

Adelaide, and during that period they crossed the Great Australian Bight, one of the stormiest sea areas south of the equator. It was while crossing this turbulent stretch of water that a Wandering Albatross was sighted. One of the natural world's most versatile flying machines it soared in their wake for hours, feeding on the waste that dropped into the sea whenever a rosie was emptied.

Then, late one afternoon, thirty-four days after leaving London, the *Alice Springs* passed into the lee of Kangaroo Island, a natural storm barrier and breakwater off the mouth of the Gulf of St Vincent. The following morning she steamed up the Port Adelaide River and tied up at McLaren Parade, immediately astern of the Shaw-Savill liner *Suevic.* Soon after breakfast a handful of passengers disembarked, their voyages safely completed despite the mechanical complications. The remaining seven, three bound for Melbourne and four for Sydney, would stick with the ship rather than brave the overland pitfalls.

As Steve cleared the duty mess table his attention was drawn to the porthole, and an outward-bound, dust-covered ore carrier. The other ship's name was *Iron King* and she flew the colours of the BHP - The Broken Hill Proprietary Company - final confirmation that the *Alice Springs* had finally arrived in the land of her namesake.

9

The great windjammers, immortalized by the likes of Alan Villiers and John Masefield, had last spread their canvas in revenue-earning service during the 1930s, but that didn't mean that commercial sail was as extinct as the Dodo and Mammoth. Traditional sailing barges still plied between London and smaller ports around the Thames estuary, while junks were a familiar sight in the harbours of Hong-Kong and China. Correspondingly, as the *Iron King* cleared the Port Adelaide River, a trading ketch cast off from the wharf opposite, bound, Steve was told, for Whyalla. Like the junks of Hong-Kong and the barges back home she was evidence that wind-driven freighters were still viable assets as coastal and short-sea traders.

Shore leave had been granted from the moment of the *Alice Springs* arrival, although few were able to take immediate advantage owing to their hours and work patterns. Therefore it was early afternoon before Steve and his pals, having subbed from their wages, were able to leave the ship and make their way into Port Adelaide.

On reaching the quayside Steve was totally unprepared for the absence of movement. When working at sea, even in the calmest of conditions, the placement of one's feet becomes different; and as can be imagined, the more violent the motion the greater the difficulty in standing. Even with the ship alongside the decks aren't completely horizontal so walking with a 'roll' becomes normal. 'It's a matter of regaining your land-legs,' said Jimmy, 'but you'll soon get used to it - it happens to all of us at some time.'

'You'll probably be staggering back to the ship anyway if we stop for a drink,' joked Peter, who clearly intended spending at least some of his time and money sampling the amber nectar.

'You can go drinking if you want but I'm going to take a few photographs,' said Steve, who through talking to others in the *Alice Spring's* crew had learnt that Adelaide, the state capital of South Australia, was a smart modern city of beautiful parks, fashionable department stores and tree-lined boulevards, whereas Port Adelaide was an out-port some six miles north-west of the capital and not at all like the city it served.

Any photographs would be priceless, for the scene that greeted them as they left the port was exceptional. It was like a set from a Hollywood western but without the horses. The streets were virtually deserted, and but for a handful of cars and the odd pick-up truck - or 'ute,' as they were termed in Australia - they could easily have been in Tombstone, Arizona, shortly before the Gunfight at the OK Corral.

'Fuckin' 'ell!' exclaimed Peter, who, along with Steve and Jimmy was staring about him in amazement. 'I should have brought a six-shooter - in case we bump into the Clantons.'

Although both Peter and Jimmy had visited Australia on previous occasions neither had been to Port Adelaide, and all three of the boys were spellbound. As he'd intended, Steve bought a film from the nearest drug store and began snapping away, determined that on this occasion at least he'd preserve a photographic record for his family.

Port Adelaide, although whimsically attractive, was no metropolis, so after strolling around town for an hour and exploring just about everywhere of interest, without confronting either Doc Holliday, Wyatt Earp – or any of the Clanton gang for that matter, they decided a beer was in order.

The hotel at the crossroads was a classic example of a mid-to-late nineteenth-century watering hole that owed its existence to the sailorman. It wasn't the most comfortable pub in the world but it served its purpose and at least it was clean and hospitable. Considering it was four o'clock in the afternoon the place was reasonably well patronized - and would soon be bursting at the seams. The barman welcomed the boys with a friendly, 'G'day, lads. I guess you're all over twenty-one - so what can I get you?'

'Three schooners of lager, please,' answered Jimmy, reaching in his pocket for some money as the barman filled three tapering glasses that fizzed like bicarbonate of soda. Back in the United Kingdom a pint of bitter would have been drawn through the familiar hand-pump, but here, on the edge of the outback, a 'gun' at the end of a hosepipe was the accepted method.

In fact, Steve couldn't help making the comparison with the way fuel was delivered at a filling station. 'I thought for a moment he was going to serve us a gallon of petrol,' he quipped, as they made for a table near a window.

'It's nearly all served like that out here,' replied Jimmy, drawing up a chair and plonking his froth-covered glass on the table, 'unless you buy it in bottles. Then it's even gassier than this.'

'When we get to New Zealand we'll be able to buy it in gallon and half-gallon jugs,' added Peter, slurping the head from his schooner. 'Then when you're empty you just top up your glass from the jug.' Steve buried his nose in his lager, and pondered just how different things were in the colonies.

The passing reference to their ages had been mildly disturbing. Neither of his mates had mentioned that in Australia you had to be twenty-one in order to legally purchase alcohol, and apart from that solitary remark the barman hadn't seemed worried so he assumed it had simply been meant as a reminder. 'They don't usually bother you in seaport towns,' reassured Jimmy, when Steve broached the topic of age. 'Mind you, I don't know how we'd fare in some of the posher joints in the city centres,' he added, gazing into his glass and apparently counting the bubbles, 'but in places like this you've no worries.'

In view of the fact that dinner was still to be served, not to mention the teatime strap-up, they lingered longer in the pub than they should have. In that respect they were in exemplary company as almost every off-duty crew member was grabbing the chance of a 'sundowner'. This was owing to the seemingly archaic law that in those days the pubs shut at 6.00pm in South Australia, and unless they resorted to the sometimes dodgy expedient of, 'sly grogging', it'd be the last drink they'd get until tomorrow. 'What's sly grogging?' queried Steve, who'd never previously heard the expression.

'It's when you go around to the back door of a pub after closing time, give the required number of knocks and keep your fingers crossed,' replied Jimmy, who confessed to having tried it on a couple of occasions, once successfully - and with a kick up the backside on the other. 'The trick is to know the pubs - and the correct number of knocks,' continued Jimmy, with the air of an expert in these matters. 'If you're lucky and they let you in you'll probably be there all night - and don't be surprised if you have half the local police force for company.'

'That's fuckin' typical of them bastards,' added Peter, who clearly had no time at all for the constabulary. 'I was in a hotel in Wellington last November. It was well after closing time when they knocked on the door. They were in there till fuckin' midnight, bragging about how they'd raided a pub down the road for serving after hours. I s'pose the landlord had refused them a drink at some time or other and they decided to teach him a lesson - fuckin' bastards.'

'Whatever, we'd better get going,' said Jimmy glancing at his watch while draining the last of his lager, 'and anyway, you won't be able to move in here come five o'clock when the rush starts.'

As they ambled back to the ship, Steve revealed that on arrival at Port Adelaide he'd received another two letters from his family. It appeared that his parents and grandmother were well, and that his brother, his imagination having been fired be Steve's recent travels, had declared that he too intended becoming a seafarer. Steve went on to enquire if either of his pals had received mail.

'Yeah, I got one from my mum,' replied Jimmy, whose father was a distant memory, but whose mother was her son's best friend. 'She reckons the weather's been lousy. How about you, Peter. Did you get anything?' Peter stayed silent, but looked vaguely troubled as he stared at his feet and kicked a pebble into a clump of stinging nettles. Jimmy glanced at Steve, frowning as he re-posed the question.

'Yeah, all right, I heard you the first time,' answered Peter at length, his suntan glowing with scarlet as he strove to conceal his embarrassment. 'I got one.'

'Who was that from, then?' pressed Steve, suspiciously, suspecting Peter was hiding a secret.

'It was from Maureen, if you must know,' confessed Peter, bashfully, as though it was something to be ashamed of.

'You must have written to her in the first place,' said Jimmy, almost accusingly, 'otherwise, she wouldn't have known where you were.'

'Well, what of it? replied Peter, feeling disgruntled at what he considered an unwarranted intrusion into his private life. 'I dropped her a line from Aden as it happens, just like you suggested - not that it's any of your business.'

'No, not at all,' answered Jimmy,' hurriedly, not wanting to alienate his friend who was showing signs of throwing a tantrum. 'I just wondered how she got the Adelaide address, that's all.'

'Good for you,' rejoined Steve,' anxious to neutralize a potential quarrel. 'Keep it up and it's my guess she'll carry on writing. She must be interested otherwise she wouldn't have replied.'

'Yeah........well. You know me,' mumbled Peter, a sheepish grin lightening his features.

'Well, it's your,' choice responded Steve, resignedly, clearly deciding that the subject of communication between Peter and his newly-acquired barmaid pen friend had run its distance. 'But It'll be no use you moaning about not getting any mail if you're not prepared to do your bit.'

The following afternoon the boys took a stroll down to the Port Adelaide yacht haven. Laying to the seaward end of the docks the marina was home to the Port Adelaide sailing club, the craft on view ranging from sailing boats of all shapes and sizes through fishing vessels to luxury cabin cruisers that in many parts of the world would have been the preserve of millionaire playboys or the well-heeled business community.

Even in those days Australia's everyday affluence was obvious, indicating the growing gulf in the standard of living between ordinary Australians and the British. No one that Steve knew owned a boat, not even a rubber inflatable; and he came from what his contemporaries would consider a comfortably-off family. It was the subject of discussion as they studied the craft in the haven - until they stumbled upon a dinghy that was tethered to a peg on the foreshore.

Given that the weather was fine and that the South Australian autumn had yet to materialize the beach was completely deserted, and apart from the tugging and jingling of boats at their moorings it was as peaceful as a country churchyard. 'Probably because it's a weekday,' surmised Jimmy, staring at the picketed dinghy. 'Chances are you won't be able to move around here come Saturday.' And then, grinning mischievously, he proposed, 'Let's go for a row. There's no-one watching so no-one'll be any the wiser.'

'Yeah, why not,' agreed Peter, who never saw the danger in anything involving a spot of risk taking. 'We could take a closer look at some of those floating gin palaces.'

'What if we get caught?' protested Steve, with the cautionary note of someone who'd never been in serious trouble and habitually baulked at law breaking. 'Oughtn't we to ask permission first?'

'Who is there to ask?' enquired Jimmy, staring around and spreading his arms in emphasis. 'It's not as if we'll be stealing the bloody thing - we'll be bringing it back afterwards.'

'That's right,' joined in Peter, openly frustrated at what he correctly perceived as Steve's inbred aversion to wrongdoing. 'You're too bloody windy, that's your trouble.'

'Okay, okay, I'll come,' consented Steve, reluctantly, not wishing to play the spoilsport. 'But don't blame me if the law turns up while we're out there on the water.'

Contrary to Steve's better judgement Jimmy cast the rope from its peg and they scrambled aboard, with Peter in the bow, Steve at the stern while Jimmy took charge of the oars. Steve was on tenterhooks as the dinghy nosed out from the beach and he scanned the shoreline, concerned should there be any witnesses. However, fifteen minutes elapsed and with no apparent onlookers he slowly relaxed and began wondering if Peter was right, that he was over cautious and too tensed up to enjoy himself. This creeping sense of security was the probable reason why all three of them nearly had kittens as a voice echoed over the water. 'Hey! What the hell do you think you're playing at?'

It landed in the boat like a bombshell, and the boys looked in all directions, seeking the inquisitor's whereabouts. It was Steve who spotted him first, an ape of a man, shaking a fist from a fishing boat's wheelhouse. They'd passed the fishing boat only seconds earlier but hadn't seen anyone. He must have been out of sight, either in the wheelhouse or below the bulwark, and the element of surprise was complete. Jimmy was first to react. 'We're not doing any harm,' he called, nervously. 'We found this dinghy on the beach and decided to go for a row. We'll take it back afterwards.'

The gorilla considered his response, before replying, 'Well, just make sure that you do, because if you don't, and it's damaged, I'll report you to the owner and he'll have your goolies for golf balls.'

'Yeah, sure,' answered Jimmy, waving a hand in acknowledgement. 'We'll take good care of it, don't you worry.' As Jimmy resumed rowing, relieved at the leniency of the let-off, Steve waved his thanks; but the fisherman remained vigilant, his eyes on the dinghy, returning to his chores only when it slipped behind a yacht.

As Steve had feared, Peter soon tired of being a passenger and asked if he could take over the oars. Jimmy declined, proclaiming, 'No chance. I saw your efforts on that boating lake in New Plymouth last trip. You made a right hash of it. You're not fit to be in charge of a pedalo.'

'I can row as well as you can,' argued Peter, casting a scornful glance at the galley boy, 'give me those oars and I'll show you.' Peter made to stand up and the dinghy lurched ominously.

'Sit down!' snapped Jimmy, angrily. 'If you turn the boat over we'll be in deep shit and you'll be the one who's to blame.' But Peter was all fired up, and made a lunge for the oars which fell from Jimmy's grasp as he attempted to fend off his assailant.

'Stop buggering about, you two,' remonstrated Steve, gripping the gunnels as the boat swayed dangerously, 'or you'll tip the bloody thing over.' Steve may as well have been talking to a telegraph pole for all the notice that was taken. Peter and Jimmy carried on wrestling - with the oars and with each other - and it came as no surprise when at the height of the struggle the boat capsized spilling the three of them into the water. 'You........stupid........bastards,' spluttered Steve, expelling mouthfuls of seawater as he struggled to stay afloat, his spectacles perched precariously on the end of his nose. 'Now look what you've done.'

'Aw! Don't be such a fuckin' old woman,' gasped Peter, wiping a strand of seaweed from his mouth. 'There's no harm done. We'll right the boat and no-one'll know any different.'

'What fuckin' boat?' exclaimed Jimmy, staring around in dismay. 'The fuckin' things gone.' All three of them scoured the immediate vicinity while treading water, in Steve's case with increasing difficulty. Sure enough, the dinghy had completely vanished, leaving only the oars afloat, and even they were drifting away on the current.

'It must have fuckin' sunk,' said Peter, stating the obvious. 'We'd better dive down to see if we can find it.' Even the usually imperturbable Peter was showing signs of becoming agitated but credit where credit was due, he did seem prepared to do something towards recovering the situation.

'Yeah, come on,' agreed Jimmy. 'It can't have gone far - the water's clear so it shouldn't be too hard to find.'

'You can if you like,' answered Steve, with little enthusiasm, 'But I'm not very good at this swimming lark - I only got a fifteen-yard certificate at school. You sunk the bloody thing - so you find it.' And with that, he struck out for the shore.

Five minutes and fifty yards later Steve lay prone on the beach, completely exhausted and gasping like a broken-winded camel. But despite his distress he sensed a strange triumphalism, as if he'd achieved a milestone - and in one way he had. It was the furthest he'd swum in his life, and not withstanding the cause of his accomplishment he felt suitably proud - as he'd every right to. In due course, having regained his breath, he rolled on to his back and gazed out over the marina, searching for some indication that all was well with his mates and the dinghy. Initially there was no sign of life; not of his friends, nor of the recalcitrant rowing boat. As the minutes ticked by he began to fret for their safety; but then, from behind a cabin cruiser on the far side of the marina the dinghy emerged, with Peter in the stern and Jimmy pulling gently on the oars.

'We found it easily enough,' declared Jimmy, as after a few minutes he and Peter hauled the dinghy up on to the beach and looped the mooring line over its peg, their clothes steaming freely in the sun. 'The hardest bit was dragging it to the surface and emptying the water out.'

'That's right,' chipped in Peter, who with the situation retrieved was back to his cavalier self. 'Piece of piss, really. We decided to row all the way round so that everything seemed normal, just in case the guy on the fishing boat was watching.' It had clearly escaped Peter that if the fisherman had indeed been keeping a lookout he might have wondered what had happened to the third member of the rowing boat's crew. As the lads wandered back to the ship, their shirts drying on their backs but with trousers sagging heavily from their hips, Steve made it clear that as far as he was concerned their boating days were over, and in the event of any further aquatics he'd be a 'windy' spectator.

On their penultimate evening in port Steve and his friends, accompanied by Davy the baker, caught a train into Adelaide, intending to exhibit their prowess at the city's ice-rink. Both Jimmy and Davy, the tartan emblazoned in their accents, had declared themselves proficient ice-skaters, which in Davy's case had even extended to him being a valued member of the ice-hockey team back in Elgin. Steve, on the other hand, had never skated on ice in his life but at school had been a competent roller-skater and he assumed, quite naively, that ice-skating would be as equally straightforward. For his part, Peter kept quiet, leading Steve to believe that he too was an ice-skating novice.

Steve had been correct in his assumption that Peter was an absolute beginner, but that was the only comparison. Peter took to the ice like a duck to water whereas he, a self-proclaimed roller-skating specialist, struggled to stay upright let alone make any sort of progress. Eventually, after managing a single circuit, and with bruises all over his backside and elbows, he decided to call it a day. He spent the remainder of the evening in the company of some girls while his shipmates carved patterns on the ice.

It evolved that the girls were from the British migrant community, and were temporarily housed in a transit camp located mid-way between Adelaide and the port. Steve learnt that the camp was provided for those European migrants, including the 'Ten Pound Poms' as they were disparagingly referred to by certain Australians, who arrived in the country on assisted passages with no immediate accommodation or employment prospects. The first priority on their arrival was to find work for the male contingent, who would live in hostels closer to their jobs while permanent accommodation was arranged. It was the probable reason, the girls believed, for the camp containing more women and children than men; and also, why they spent most of their evenings at the ice-rink, hoping to socialize with boys.

It appeared that the transit camp was fully self-contained and comprised dwelling units, shops, laundry facilities, a cinema, a dance hall where record hops were held almost every night of the week, and a comprehensively-equipped playground for the kids. That isn't bad, thought Steve, for families arriving in a strange country, jobless and with nowhere to live; and it did at least provide more than adequate shelter until the newcomers were properly rehoused. 'Any chance of me and my pals being invited to the record hop?' asked Steve, nodding towards the ice-rink where Davy in particular was displaying his skills with panache. 'Tomorrow's our last night in Adelaide and it would finish our visit off nicely.'

'Nah,' said the taller of the two girls, a redhead called Valerie who hailed from West Bromwich and who spoke with a Black-Country whine. 'Security on the gate's pretty tight - you wouldn't get in........unless,' she suggested, coyly, while turning to her companion and giggling, 'we managed to make a hole in the fence.'

And that's exactly what happened. The following evening Steve and his mates, along with Davy and John the butcher, headed for the camp and made straight for the perimeter fence. Valerie had been as good as her word, and the lads found an opening that was more than sufficient to crawl through. Once inside they were accepted as recently-arrived immigrants and completed their visit to Adelaide by jiving until they were exhausted, the girls queuing up for the rare opportunity of dancing with a male partner. That was with the notable exception of Steve, who couldn't dance for toffee and was confined to the sidelines after trampling the toes of a blonde.

The stop-over in Adelaide left Steve with a maelstrom of emotions. The fooling about in the yacht haven had been the most alarming. What if there'd been sharks in the water? He'd heard that the creatures occasionally swam into the more brackish waters upstream, and if the rumours were true and there had been man-eaters in the area while Jimmy and Peter were playing silly buggers, God only knows the possible outcome. On a lighter note, Port Adelaide itself possessed an idiosyncratic charm, certainly worth recording and the film in his camera would prove it. On the other hand the ice-skating episode had been a failure, at least where he was

110

concerned, although it hadn't been a total disaster. It had led to a night out at the migrant camp, and although he personally had been something of a pariah and they'd caused a breach of security, the worst that could have happened was for them to have been unceremoniously ejected. He eventually concluded that all things considered his first experience of Australia had been positive, and as the *Alice Springs* steamed out of the Port Adelaide River he was eagerly anticipating their arrival in Melbourne, the principal port and capital of the state of Victoria.

As they sat eating their dinner on the evening of their departure from Adelaide, Archie revealed that Sean Cassidy and a deckie called Roger Oates were adrift, the ship having sailed without them. It seemed that alcohol had been the principal instigator. In Cassidy's case he'd thumped a hotel barman who'd tried to eject him at closing time, sparking a brawl involving other drinkers and the small number of staff on the premises. The police had been summoned and a full-scale riot had developed, in the course of which Cassidy had smashed a chair over the head of a sergeant, rendering him senseless. The police had ultimately gained control and along with the other belligerents the big Liverpudlian had been hauled off to gaol and incarcerated. Clobbering the copper had been his downfall. But for that he may well have escaped with a fine. As it was, he faced the possibility of a lengthy prison sentence - once the Port Adelaide police had finished with him. Roger Oates, on the other hand, was as meek and mild as they come but was hopeless when under the influence. He'd simply staggered into the street and been hit by a truck, ending up in hospital with a fractured leg, severe concussion and a hangover. Given that the truck was a laden six-wheeler he could consider himself lucky at not ending up in the mortuary.

'Serves Cassidy right,' observed Archie, sniffing and tossing his head. 'I never had time for the brute anyway - he's nothing but a great big oaf. It's a shame about Roger, though.'

'You fancy Roger, then?' asked Peter, his eyes twinkling.

'Of course not,' replied Archie,' stiffly, pretending resentment. 'It's just that apart from when he's drunk he's quiet and refined, not like that ruffian Cassidy.'

Danny Meeks, who usually ate his meals in silence, smirked

lewdly, and uttered, 'Archie likes 'em quiet and refined, don't you, Archie?'

Archie turned a deaf ear to the comment. As far as he was concerned Danny's opinions of anything were worthless, were only designed to offend and were best ignored. Give him the cold shoulder and he would slither back under his rock. Danny took the hint, and with a self-conscious glance around the table, carried on eating. 'No', resumed Archie, as if Danny didn't exist. 'Cassidy and the likes give us all a bad name. As far as I'm concerned we're well rid of him.'

As it happened, neither Archie nor anyone else aboard the *Alice Springs* realized that they hadn't seen the last of Sean Cassidy.

10

As an aid to navigation the *Alice Springs* trailed a piece of equipment called a log-line which was securely attached to the taffrail. At the trailing end of the line a small propeller-like device revolved as the vessel proceeded, the rate of revolution dependant on the speed of the ship. The information gathered was relayed, via the line, to the shipboard end where a dial indicator registered the speed, along with the distance covered since the previous reading. The service speed of the *Alice Springs* was a nominal sixteen knots, a shade over eighteen miles per hour, so the average day's sailing should have been in the region of four-hundred and forty-five miles. However, given her proven galloping propensities, and provided conditions were favourable, she was more than capable of covering five-hundred miles in a day.

The *Alice Springs* arrived off Melbourne at ten the following morning, having covered the six hundred miles from Port Adelaide in the remarkable time of just twenty-nine hours precisely. Most of the crew had been hoping she would berth in either the upriver docks or in the River Yarra itself, close to the centre of commerce. To their frustration, they learnt that she would be tying up at one of the piers at Port Melbourne, which would entail either a pricey taxi ride or a train journey into the city.

Port Melbourne, like Port Adelaide, was what was known as an out-port, serving the city without the inconvenience and expense of negotiating, rivers, canals and locks, etc., which could add considerably to the berthing costs. The *Alice Springs'* owners were doubtless happy with the arrangement, and after having time to deliberate many of the crew would feel likewise. 'One thing', said Peter, as he removed some cutlery from a silver dip and began polishing it with a linen duster, 'we won't have far to go for a bevy. We can just pop along to Smoky Joe's on the pierhead. It's only a few minutes' walk.'

'You been here before, then?' asked Steve, putting the finishing shine to a sugar basin and placing it on a tray with some others.

'Yeah, last trip,' replied Peter, untying the pantry cloth from around his waist and adding it to a pile for the laundry. Trouble is, this is another of those places where the pubs shut at six, so we've got to make hay while the sun shines.'

'I'm going to give the booze a miss if you don't mind,' said Steve, to Peter's obvious amazement. 'I'm going to try and get into the city this afternoon - for a look around,' and then, more pointedly. 'The only thing is, I'm not going to have much time to spare.'

Peter was quick to latch on, remembering he owed Steve a favour after the latter had covered for him in London. 'Tell you what, I'll come back and strap up the afternoon tea things if it makes things any easier. That'll give you an extra hour, so long as you remember that it's high tea at five rather than dinner at six-thirty.'

'Thanks - I won't forget,' answered Steve, as he burnished the crest on a cake fork. 'I hear there's a railway station just up the road and I can get a train into Melbourne from there.'

'That's right,' said Peter, gathering up the pile of pantry cloths and heading for the working alleyway. 'It's only a ten-minute ride into Flinders Street then you're right in the heart of the city. Oh! And by the way. Jimmy and me were thinking about going to Luna Park tonight if you want to come along. It'll be better than tramping the streets.'

As it was, with lunch out of the way and before anyone went anywhere, six-weeks accumulation of soiled linen had to be sent to a laundry ashore as the ship had no facilities of her own. This entailed a dozen or more fully-laden and cumbersome laundry bags being manhandled on to the quayside from where they were transported away to be processed. Owing to the number of staff involved it was a chore that was swiftly accomplished, and it didn't interfere with their plans.

With the following three hours at his disposal Steve, smartly dressed in his white nylon shirt and flannels, was soon ashore and stepping briskly in the direction of the station which was adequately signposted and which he found without too much difficulty. Surprisingly, he discovered a British-style branch-line terminus, complete with booking-hall, waiting-room and platform. At shortly after two in the afternoon, in common with most British branch-lines, passengers were in short supply so having purchased his ticket to Flinders Street he had a coach to himself as he boarded a waiting electric train.

Steve's knowledge of Australia in general may have been limited, but thanks to his extensive collection of railway literature he knew something of its permanent way. Nevertheless, he was surprised at the train's antiquity, for although it was an electric train it must have been sixty years old and reminiscent of early America. There was a sense of *déjà vu,* and as at Port Adelaide there was that eerie feeling of being part of the old 'Wild West'.

As the train pulled out the ticket inspector informed him that the rolling stock had originally been built at the turn of the century for steam haulage, and that when the line was electrified some twenty years later, rather than discard what were otherwise perfectly serviceable coaches, they were simply fitted with electric traction motors and returned to the task they were meant for. Just for good measure, the inspector also added that the branch from Port Melbourne to Flinders Street was the oldest stretch of railway in Australia, and had been constructed to cope with the increasing number of migrants arriving at the nearby port from Britain and continental Europe.

Flinders Street station, the busiest in Australia and host for predominantly suburban traffic, covered an enormous area and was an architectural *tour de force*. The imposing façade with its lofty clock tower, domed entrance with an array of clock faces displaying the next fifteen scheduled departures, was as impressive as any in Europe, and the network of tracks and crossovers seemed every bit as complicated as the junction at Clapham in London. Steve roamed the station for several minutes, learning its geography and consulting the timetables, before heading for the concourse and stepping down into the street.

He was making for Spencer Street, home to Melbourne's other

major railway station; and realizing that he needed to be on the other side of the road he dodged between the traffic, only to be collared by a policeman. 'What's your game then, Mate?' demanded the cop, unbuttoning his tunic's breast pocket and removing his notebook, intending to book Steve for whatever. Steve stared blankly at the uniform, utterly bewildered and wondering what the officer was getting at. 'You realize you just crossed the street without using the crossing?' the policeman continued, seemingly puzzled at Steve's lack of comprehension of what he considered a perfectly straightforward question.

Slowly, the penny dropped, and Steve cottoned on that jaywalking must be an indictable offence in Victoria, if not in the whole of Australia. Becoming increasingly flustered he eventually blurted, 'I'm sorry, officer. I've only just arrived from England and didn't know any different.'

Ignorance of the law was usually no excuse but the copper proved a pretty decent fellow. He gave Steve an almighty rollicking in front of scores of onlookers, telling him that he could easily have been killed or seriously injured before warning him that any future jaywalking would be punished. He then returned the notebook to his pocket before wishing him a pleasant stay in Melbourne, leaving him to reflect on an extremely providential let-off. Steve gazed blushingly at the audience; but although he felt completely humiliated at having received a severe dressing down in full view of the passing public, he was enormously relieved at not having a court case to answer.

Spencer Street station, in addition to catering for suburban traffic, was also the Melbourne terminus for interstate services to and from both Sydney and Adelaide. However, long distance rail travel in Australia could be something of an ordeal, even for the most seasoned adventurer. The reason for this was that for the most part, the various state railway systems had been laid to differing gauges, creating a travellers' nightmare. On the positive side it was possible to journey between Melbourne and Adelaide without changing trains, both Victoria and South Australia having opted for 5ft 3ins as the gauge for their networks, but if you were travelling between Melbourne and Sydney then the situation became complex. The railways of New South Wales had been laid to the standard gauge of

4ft 8½ins and at best, this could involve a train having to change its wheel sets when crossing from one state to another. At worst, it entailed the irksome process of passengers having to alight at the border before continuing their journey on a different train altogether. The situation was further complicated by the fact that the railways of both Queensland and Western Australia had been built to a gauge of just 3ft 6ins, which not only rendered through travel impossible but made high-speed running impractical. However, as Steve was to discover, plans were afoot to unify the gauges in Australia and standard gauge trains would soon be speeding between Melbourne and Sydney; while later on still the classic streamliner, the 'Indian Pacific', would commence running between Sydney and Perth, a distance of some two thousand miles, all on standard gauge track.

As Steve made his way back to Flinders Street station - using pedestrian crossings whenever appropriate - and on the return train journey to the port, he reflected on Melbourne's stylish opulence with its bustling commercial heart and for the most part, prosperous suburban streets. The fashionable bungalows dotting the residential districts, far from being exclusive retreats for the wealthy, were mostly the homes of the working community, many of whom were immigrants who would have stood little chance of owning such a property had they remained in their countries of origin. It was highly likely that many had spent time in a migrant camp on their arrival in Australia, similar to the one at Adelaide, and if that was the case then the initial upheaval and inconvenience had certainly been worth the endeavour.

Steve's first impressions were that Melbourne was characteristically British, but in fact it proved thoroughly cosmopolitan. Although English was the spoken language the Aussie accents were peppered with a wealth of European dialects, with Greek being more prominent than most. What he could say with all honesty was that whatever their derivation the people he'd come into contact with had been both helpful and considerate - and in that analysis he had to include the policeman who'd apprehended him for jaywalking.

In contrast with most recent meals high tea was a comparative walkover. It was over in no time at all and with the evening in prospect Steve joined Jimmy and Peter for a trip to St Kilda and Luna Park, where 'Sheilas' were high on their agenda. Archie had gone to visit a long-lost brother who'd emigrated to Australia in the years following the war and who lived in the Melbourne suburb of Northcote, while the rest of the catering crowd, the Chief Steward and Ted excepted, had headed into the city, maybe to the mission or pictures or perhaps to try their luck at sly grogging.

The weather was fair as the boys headed along Beaconsfield Parade to St Kilda, and this was reflected in their clothing. They were dressed in their shore-going best, which in Jimmy's case comprised a pair of crocodile shoes and a hand-made suit that he'd bought in Hong Kong whilst a kitchen boy on P&O's *Cathy*. Each had been made to measure and had been delivered on the day it was ordered. The entire outfit had cost just fifteen pounds of which the suit had accounted for ten. Peter sported a pair of tight denim jeans, a black leather jacket and winkle-pickers, while Steve was wearing the same set of clothes that he'd ventured ashore in earlier.

The seaside suburb of St Kilda, a magnet for holidaymakers in the summer months, lay within easy walking distance, and it wasn't long before they were among the masses thronging the palm-lined esplanade with its penny-arcades, hamburger stands and ice cream parlours. Steve hadn't seen crowds like this since that bank-holiday excursion to Skegness the previous summer, when he'd met that girl from Nottingham and they'd spent the entire day feeding coins into slot-machines without winning so much as a gob-stopper. St Kilda's sea-front was typically vibrant and it was easy to appreciate its attractiveness; but once again it gave a false impression and on delving back a few streets it was clear that the area's history had been more illustrious.

In the earlier years of the century the district had been home to the gentry, evidenced by many of the elegant houses that still graced the various neighbourhoods, but which had long since been converted into smaller and more economical dwelling units. In more recent times the area had also earned the unwelcome reputation of being a haven for pimps and prostitutes whose activities were decidedly unsubtle. But like it or not, and as with many of its British counterparts, St Kilda offered just about everything that the majority

118

of younger people sought from life; namely, a thoroughly good time and the company of the opposite sex. Luna Park, the principal attraction, was an extensive funfair that occupied a sizeable chunk of the foreshore, and was entered through a turreted portal styled as the face of a huge laughing clown.

Shoving their way through the crush the boys tried their luck at a variety of side shows with only limited success. At an air-rifle range Jimmy was rewarded with a teddy bear for downing the required number of targets, while at a coconut-shy they each scored a succession of hits while failing to unseat a coconut. 'They're probably glued into the cups,' snorted Peter, as he stalked away in disgust. 'You'd need to lever them out with a crowbar - cheatin' bastards. Come on, let's have a go on the rides.'

Steve and Jimmy were well aware that the balls were only lightweight and that a particular knack was needed in order to dislodge a coconut, but they took it in their stride and tagged after Peter whose attention had been drawn to the ghost train. Sixpence bought a two-minute ride in the dark accompanied by some wailing banshees; a grinning skeleton that had somehow managed to retain its eyeballs; the occasional glimpse of a hunchback or hobgoblin; a headless Anne Boleyn-like character that let rip with a blood-curdling scream before the entire swindle was rounded off with a faceful of synthetic cobwebs. The journey was over almost before it had begun and as they climbed from the car, Steve couldn't help thinking that in retrospect, the coconut-shy had provided far better value for money.

Nevertheless, the ghost train was to play a pivotal role in what for Steve at least was to become the most unforgettable factor of his personal association with St Kilda - and it had nothing to do with the unearthly. In fact, it was romance, for as they made to move off another car drew up and out stepped three pretty, young women, seemingly frightened to death while trembling with laughter and excitement.

It could have been a problematic few seconds, for there was just no telling how the girls might react in a first-time face-to-face encounter. Steve recalled a similar confrontation in his final months at school, albeit in a one-to-one situation when, on spotting Steve

119

ogling her, a glamorous but notorious local beauty had spat, 'What the fuckin' hell are you staring at - never seen a pair of tits before? Here, have a closer look,' and with that the girl, who was certainly well endowed, had unbuttoned her blouse and waved a two-fingered rebuke before leaving Steve in a state of shock and embarrassment.

However, on this occasion the reception was different - and the boys didn't have to lift a finger. The girls, after huddling together and sniggering, walked self-confidently over, and the eldest of them asked, 'You blokes looking for a date?'

It was the most brazen approach and should have been a warning but the boys were smitten and beguiled. Still, whatever the caveat the chemistry seemed to be working and within minutes of the extraordinary introduction the six of them had matched up in pairs and were strolling around with the closeness of life-long sweethearts. Jimmy presented his partner with the teddy bear that he'd won with the air-rifle, while even Peter stopped grumbling about how everything was a rip-off and spent his money more freely than anyone. It emerged that the girls were sisters although there was an obvious disparity in their ages. For whatever reason the younger siblings, who were clearly teenagers, had paired off with Jimmy and Peter whilst the older girl, who was plainly well into her twenties and whose name was Carol, had favoured Steve, perhaps considering him the more mature of the three although in truth he was marginally the younger.

The sisters proved excellent company; notwithstanding that they were spendthrifts who regarded the boys as their personal cashiers and blew away their money like dust. But there were no complaints - not even from Peter - because before parting they arranged a meeting for the following evening, and although this initial assignation culminated in nothing more sensual than a peck on the cheek, tomorrow might bring something more wanton.

Steve was hooked on Carol from the outset; perhaps the 'older woman' syndrome in retrospect. Earlier relationships with the fairer sex had been transient, platonic affairs, but he felt sure that with Carol it was different. She was certainly smart and good-looking, thoroughly good company and she'd latched on to Steve without a second glance at either Peter or Jimmy. She was maybe more pushy than previous girlfriends, and there was that obvious difference in their ages; but by and large it seemed a match made in heaven and he was convinced that the feeling was mutual. If there was a fault it was her profligate tendencies, but he could live with that and he determined to enjoy Carol's friendship to the utmost - or at least within the bounds of his pocket.

Sometime around the following midday the *Oriana,* the Orient Line's spanking new flagship, tied up at the berth opposite, dwarfing the *Alice Springs* and from late afternoon onwards obliterating the sunlight as if a gigantic parasol had been erected on the intervening quayside. As her mooring lines were secured and her gangways lowered the *Oriana's* rails were thronged with passengers, maybe searching for loved ones and thrilled at the prospect of a family reunion, while others would be apprehensive, feeling lonely and perhaps dubious as to whether or not their decision to emigrate had been a wise one. Many would be met by friends or relatives and whisked off to a warm reception while the remainder, whose first night in Melbourne might be as guests of the Australian Government, awaited the instructions of immigration officers before collecting their belongings and heading for lives a long way removed from those they were used to. Steve was resolute that if he was ever to emigrate it would be on the basis that he had a home and employment already waiting, and not be left wandering around on the quayside, relying on his hosts to provide a roof over his head and a self-sufficient means of support.

At seven-thirty precisely Steve and his pals descended the *Alice Springs'* gangway and set off for St Kilda, armed with the sisters' address on a small scrap of notepaper. It had been agreed the previous evening that they should meet at the girls' home in Norris Street, from where it was a straightforward tram ride into the city. An evening at the cinema followed by supper was one option that had been discussed, although there was no telling as to the eventual outcome.

Norris Street materialized as a drab-looking avenue flanked by modest - and in some cases shabby - timber-built bungalows that were a far distant cry from the properties that Steve had come to accept as the norm in residential Australia. Okay, this was clearly an older part of the city, but that was no excuse for the neighbourhood's air of dilapidation. The boys looked at each other, wondering if they'd correctly followed the directions, and not strayed into some hidden-away slum locality. Jimmy scanned the crumpled piece of notepaper. Forty-two Norris Street, St Kilda, were the only words scribbled on it, and Norris Street was the name on the sign attached to a lamp-post on the corner of the street they were standing in. 'Yup, this is it all right,' said Jimmy, thrusting the slip of paper back into his pocket, 'and it looks like number forty-two's down here on the right somewhere.'

They carried on walking, counting off the numbers until they arrived at number forty-two which was probably the most ramshackle of all. Faded green paint was peeling from its walls and one of the side windows was boarded. The garden was overgrown and the surrounding fence would have been a suitable candidate for a bonfire. The garden gate hung wonkily from its hinges, and opened on to a crazy-paving pathway that was dotted with dog excrement in various stages of decay. At the far end of the path a rusting, wire fly screen concealed the front entrance that was set back into a darkened lobby. 'Fuckin' 'ell!' exclaimed Peter, staring at Steve in amazement. 'Surely they don't live in this dump.'

'Well, we'll soon find out,' responded Steve, as he gently eased open the gate, careful should it fall off its hinges completely. 'If they don't, I don't know where we're going to find them.'

They ambled up the path, sidestepping the faeces, until they arrived at the fly screen where they hesitated, wondering who'd make the next move. Eventually, it was Jimmy who turned and pulled open the screen before tapping gently on the hardboard-panelled door. They stood and waited. Thirty seconds elapsed and no-one answered so Jimmy tapped harder. His head became suddenly inclined. 'There's someone in there,' he declared, using his hand as an ear-trumpet, 'I can hear them moving about.' They stood back, waiting for the door to be opened, and when it was they got the shock of their lives.

The door was inched ajar by a grubby, unshaven middle-aged fellow dressed in stained shorts and singlet who glanced furtively up and down the street before beckoning the boys inside. Peter drew Steve to one side and made a whispered enquiry. 'Who's the fuckin' scruff-bag?' he asked, throwing a glance over Jimmy's shoulder at their unexpected host who'd retreated back into the hallway. 'They didn't say nothing about him.' Steve shrugged and followed his pals over the threshold. He was as much in the dark as they were - and enlightenment would shake him to the core.

'Now then you blokes,' said the guy in the shorts and singlet once the boys were inside and the door closed behind them. 'I don't mind you comin' round here to see the kids but keep the noise down. We don't pay no rent, we just live here and don't want to upset the neighbours - okay?' The lads simply nodded, wondering what was going to come next. Their attention was drawn by a noise at the end of the hall; the two teenagers had appeared from a room to one side, a pair of snotty-nosed toddlers clinging to their skirt hems. The fellow in shorts pushed past them and into the room, slamming the door shut behind him.

Steve looked around at the décor - such as it existed. Wallpaper hung in shreds from the walls and cobwebs festooned the ceiling. The uncarpeted floor was littered with debris, and a mangy, whippet-like creature cowered at the end of the hallway, as if frightened to encroach any further. There was no sign of Carol; but as if reading his thoughts one of the younger girls said, 'It's all right. She's in the bathroom bathing the baby. You can go in if you like - she won't mind.'

The bathroom opened off the hallway to Steve's right, and for the first time he heard the sound of a child whimpering, and of water sloshing to and fro. He tapped on the door and turned the handle, opening the door just far enough to reveal a bedraggled-looking Carol on hands and knees beside the bath, rinsing lather from the body of an infant. 'Oh! Hello,' she said, rising to her feet, cradling the baby in one arm while sweeping a lock of hair from her forehead with the other. 'I guess you've met my old man. Well, don't worry about him. His bark's worse than his bite and he doesn't give a damn what I get up to. I'll be finished hear in a jiffy. I've just got to dry the ankle biter, put on a dab of make-up then we can get going.'

You could have flattened Steve with a snowflake. For several seconds he stood rooted, just gazing at Carol as the enormity of the situation sunk in. It was little wonder that the attractive, mature and self-assured woman from the previous evening had appeared older than the other girls because it was guaranteed inevitable, for she wasn't their sister at all - she was their mother. But even that disturbing discovery didn't explain the intrinsic squalor that the woman and her family dwelt in compared with their public persona. Jekyll and Hyde probably wasn't the precise term to describe the inhabitants of number forty-two Norris Street, St Kilda, but there was clearly a double-sidedness to Carol and her spurious 'sisters'.

Whatever Steve's feelings for Carol they were swept into the gutter by the rapidly unfolding scenario. For one thing, there was no way he was going out on the town with a married woman, even if it was with the consent of her husband - if indeed he was her husband - and secondly, how many others had preceded Steve without his inhibitions and probity. But the most sickening thing as far as he was concerned was the woman's imperviousness. It beggared belief that she'd invited he and his friends to her home in the full knowledge that all would be revealed on the doorstep; while expecting them to meet in this filthy hole without exhibiting either a hint of shame or without provoking some kind of adverse reaction took first and second prizes for arrogance. Steve turned on his heel, and ignoring Peter and Jimmy stalked out of the house and down the garden path, skidding on some dog mess as he went.

Steve stood at the edge of the pavement, scraping the muck from his shoe on kerb-stone as Jimmy and Peter joined him. How on earth could I have got it so wrong? he thought, weighing the situation as it existed against the one that he'd previously perceived. They'd looked so presentable, had even spoken nicely, while Carol herself had seemed highly respectable. Rather late in the day it also dawned that the girls were freeloaders, painting the town at the expense of short-sighted blockheads. Jimmy stood with his hands in his pockets, staring back at the bungalow. 'You know, when we met up we didn't ask a thing about their backgrounds,' he offered, as if by doing so they might have been better prepared.

'It wouldn't have made any difference,' said Peter, inspecting the soles of his shoes to make sure he hadn't trodden in anything. 'They'd probably have told us a load of bollocks and we'd have turned up anyway.'

Steve finally spoke. 'I can't believe people live like that - and to think she was married and I didn't know..................' The sentence tailed off as words failed him and he lapsed into another spell of silence. Eventually, he asked, 'Did they say anything when you walked out?'

'Not a dicky bird,' replied Peter, who was first to see the funnier side of things and was grinning like a Littlewoods winner. 'Probably happens all the time and they're used to it. They're probably thinking we're the weirdoes.'

'I'm not a weirdo,' protested Jimmy, with an offended air of superiority, before declaring. 'I'm generally not too fussy where women are concerned - but after seeing the state of that place I wouldn't touch any of 'em with a bargepole.'

'What are we going to do now, then?' asked Steve, who seemed to have regained his equanimity. 'It's too early to go back to the ship - and I don't fancy hanging around here, not with Carol and her brood in the neighbourhood.'

'We might as well catch a tram into the city and go to the pictures,' answered Peter, motioning to the nearby tram stop. 'That's what we'd most likely have done anyway - and The Magnificent Seven's showing at the Embassy.'

'Well, that settles it,' said Jimmy, setting off in the direction of the tram stop. 'The trams run every ten minutes so we'll be in plenty of time for the second house.' So that's what they did, enjoying a thoroughly entertaining evening as Yul Brynner, Steve McQueen and the other mercenaries annihilated a bunch of Mexican bandits, before the boys rounded things off with coffee and buns in a café. They chatted and laughed about the goings-on in Norris Street, and wondered if Carol and her daughters were back on the prowl, spinning a yarn to some other mugs.

'Seems you had a lucky escape,' reproved Sec, over breakfast the following morning. 'That's what you get for wasting your money on women- and there's no telling how many other blokes had been sniffing around before you three turned up. And another thing - for all you know they were poxed up to the eyeballs and then where would you have been?' Steve polished off his bacon and eggs, reflecting on the doctor's lecture back at the Vindi, and on what the

Second Steward had told him in the Royal Oak on the evening of Archie's birthday. In light of the warnings he really should have known better, and thought himself lucky that his star-crossed liaison with Carol had resolved itself with no undesirable side effects.

The remainder of their free time in Melbourne was spent at places like Smoky Joe's, mixing with the crews of other British ships, and sometimes drinking a great deal more than they ought to. They attended a dance at the Flying Angel where they were befriended by the mission superintendent's daughter who invited them, along with several of her own friends, to her home in South Yarra where they dined on sandwiches and coke while listening to the latest releases on a state-of-the-art Dansette auto-changer.

For their entire time on the Australian coast Peter's wireless was tuned into one or other of the local radio stations, many of which transmitted a diet of pop music that was frequently interrupted by jazzy advertisements and promotions. A band that featured prominently was a home-grown instrumental outfit called The Thunderbirds. The Thunderbirds, completely unknown back in Britain, played Rock 'n' Roll music similar to that of the American group, The Champs, whose hit record 'Tequila' had already topped the charts almost everywhere in the English-speaking world. Steve became hooked on The Thunderbirds' latest offering on which the twanging guitars were complimented by a honking, tenor sax.

One afternoon, as Steve and his mates were making for Smoky Joe's, they stumbled on a pair of seamen who were drunkenly staring at the patch of water that the *Oriana* had only recently vacated. 'Where's the fuckin' ship?' slurred one of them of no one in particular, while clinging to his mate like a limpet.

'She sailed half an hour ago,' volunteered Steve, trying to be helpful, but knowing the information would be of only limited value to the pair who were now in fact stranded.

'Ah, well, never mind,' said the other inebriate, turning and tripping over his feet as he fought to stay upright. 'There'll be another one along in a fortnight - the *Orcades* is only a couple of weeks behind us.' And without further palaver they staggered off in the direction of Smoky Joe's, seemingly unconcerned that they'd rendered themselves temporarily homeless.

Apart from the evening at Luna Park the boys spent little of their time at the seaside. This was despite Melbourne and its locality playing host to some excellent beaches which were easily the equal of Bondi and Manley at Sydney. Extending away south of the city lay the Mornington Peninsular, and every summer weekend thousands of trippers crowded into cars, trains and buses and headed for the coast, and mile upon mile of some of the most glorious sands in Australia.

Unfortunately, there was also a sinister side to the southern Australian coastline, and while the beaches made safe and expansive playgrounds there were also cliff-hardened stretches where the seas were whipped on by the 'Roaring Forties', hurricane-force winds that had total disregard for seamen and the vessels they sailed in. These were the northern fringes of the legendary storm track, where the iron-tempered shore was an infamous maritime necropolis. Although most of the casualties had occurred at a time when barques and barquentines were at the mercy of the vast Southern Ocean, the rusting wreckage of steamers and motor ships lay among the rotting remains of clipper ships and schooners, along with the bones of their crewmen. Thankfully, in the latter half of the twentieth century, highly-advanced navigational aids along with more powerful and reliable engines decreed that calamities such as these were for the most part historic, although given the dangers inherent with seafaring nothing could be taken for granted.

Twenty-four hours after the *Oriana's* departure the *Alice Springs* slipped her own moorings, heading out into the Bass Strait, the unpredictable stretch of water separating the state of Victoria from Tasmania. She was on passage to Sydney, one of the most glamorous cities in the world and the capital of New South Wales. Shortly before sailing the catering staff had been handed the unenviable chore of hauling aboard the bags of clean linen that had been returned from the laundry ashore. It was a hard but essential task that was all part and parcel of seeing the world without paying. The work had been heavy and exhausting, the more so given that in the absence of an available derrick the bags had had to be carried, leaving them gasping for breath while their muscles were stretched to the limit. However, the job was completed and hardly anyone complained- for the very good reason that New South Wales was a more civilised state where the pubs had more sociable opening hours.

11

Any new landfall for the seafarer is inevitably enshrouded with mystery, provokes high expectation and is frequently laced with intrigue; although intellectual preparedness for such an event can be almost if not totally impossible. Travelogues, tourist brochures, geographical publications and hear-say may all instil a modicum of awareness; but nothing short of an actual arrival can stir the innermost-senses quite so dramatically as watching a skyline rise out of the ocean or loom through the early-morning mist. Cape Town, Hong-Kong and Rio all rate highly on an impressive list of destinations; but the water-borne approach to Sydney also falls into this category and as Steve was to discover, was nothing short of superb.

Sydney Harbour itself is actually the innermost sanctum of a vast natural haven more properly as Port Jackson, the complete sheet of water being accessed from the Tasman Sea via a pair of promontories known as Sydney Heads which open into the island-studded refuge. The enclosure's entire shoreline is punctuated by coves and inlets so that if Botany Bay is included, the sea is easily accessed from even the most landward parts of the city.

It was after the *Alice Springs* had negotiated Sydney Heads that Steve, having gobbled his breakfast and left his tea to go cold, hurried on deck in the hope of photographing Sydney Harbour Bridge. The trouble was he didn't know where to aim his camera. Out on the after well-deck he could see nothing resembling the world-famous landmark either ahead or astern nor to port or starboard. In fact, there was nothing akin to a bridge of any description in any direction. Instead, he found the *Alice Springs* encircled by pleasure craft and merchant ships, heading hither and thither or - given that it was a Sunday - riding lazily and appropriately at anchor. He looked frantically around, fearful that a golden opportunity had been wasted. 'Where's the harbour bridge?' he asked, directing his question at the Bosun who was making his way aft with a tin of red lead and a paint roller. 'I haven't missed it, have I?'

'No, Son,' replied the Cornishman, eyeing Steve's Brownie and pointing to a spit of land away to starboard and about a mile ahead of their present location. 'It's around and beyond that headland. We won't be there for at least another half hour, so if I were you I'd get as much of my work done as possible and nip out here again later. We'll be tying up at Glebe Island which is way beyond the bridge, so you should get a reasonable photo whichever way you look at it.'

Steve offered his thanks and hurried back to the pantry where Peter was already cleaning down. 'Thought you'd gone walkabout,' said the other boy, cheekily, as Steve filled a bucket and stirred in some soda and soap.

'No, I just wanted to make sure I got a photo of the bridge,' replied Steve, ignoring the jibe as he grabbed a stiff-bristled broom and began scrubbing with the verve of a dynamo. 'The Bosun reckons we'll be tying up at Glebe Island, on the far side of the bridge - but I'd rather snap it from this side, with the sun behind me so the picture isn't spoilt by the glare.' And so it was. The pantry was squared away and they raced on deck, mingling with others who were sampling the view while the bridge was still way in the distance.

A couple of tugs took up station as the *Alice Springs* slid up the fairway, the ferryboats and pleasure craft plying the harbour taking evasive measures while remaining close enough for their passengers to wave and be waved to. The pilot had boarded much earlier, before breakfast, and his red and white flag was fluttering from the signal halyards, below the Australian 'courtesy' flag but above the house flag of the Australasian and Pacific Steam Navigation Company. The quarantine flag was notably absent, that requirement having been satisfied back at Port Adelaide.

They slipped past the Naval Base at Garden Island, the water sparkling in the sunlight as those who weren't saddled with military commitments set about enjoying the Sabbath. The bridge was drawing closer, and the crescent-shaped icon loomed large in the viewfinder as Steve took aim with his Brownie. He snapped repeatedly away, replacing the film before turning his attention to Circular Quay, another important location which was all but overshadowed by the 'Coat-hanger'.

In Steve's opinion Circular Quay was a misnomer because for one thing it wasn't circular and for another, it consisted of numerous piers and jetties. Whatever, it was a bustling transport exchange, even on a Sunday, and it basked in the loveliest of settings. The 'Quay' played host to many of the liners that arrived frequently from all over Europe, and was the point of disembarkation for thousands of migrants who Settled in New South Wales in the years following the Second World War. One of those liners, Sitmar Line's *Castel Felice,* lay alongside, having disgorged the hordes she'd transported from Southampton and ports on the European mainland.

Commuters and tourists could also be found at Circular Quay, as in addition to being an international arrival and departure point it doubled as a hub for the city's excursion and ferryboat services. With regard to the bridge, which carried a triumvirate of road, rail and pedestrian traffic: it had its origins in the unlikely landscape of north-eastern England, where a miniature prototype spanned the river at Newcastle-upon-Tyne. As the *Alice Springs* passed beneath the steelwork and Circular Quay became hidden, Peter remarked, enigmatically, 'Don't look now but guess who's lurking behind you.'

Steve turned around, and was initially puzzled - but then saw what Peter was referring to. Nestling just beyond the bridge on the opposite shore from Circular Quay stood the face of a huge laughing clown, mouth agape like some abominable technicolour shark. It too was the entrance to Luna Park, Sydney's equivalent to and a veritable copy of its Melbourne namesake at St Kilda. 'Humphh!' snorted Steve, turning his back on the visage. 'I won't be going there in a hurry.'

'Oi! You two,' breathed a voice at Steve's elbow, as he leant on the rail, peering at P&O's *Strathnaver* which lay alongside one of the wharves at Pyrmont.

'Oh, it's you, Danny,' said Peter, leaning back so as to see around Steve's shoulders. 'I wondered what the smell was.'

131

'Ha ha, very funny,' replied Danny Meeks, with a crafty leer, 'but you'll be laughing on the other side of your face when Sec catches up with you. He's bloody livid back there - wondering why the leftover food hasn't been sent back to the galley.'

'Sod it,' flustered Steve, lowering his camera and forgetting the photo he was about to take of the *Strathnaver,* 'it completely slipped my mind. I'd better go and see about it now.'

'I wouldn't worry on that score,' replied Danny, who was staring at the city's skyline and clearly enjoying his mischief making. 'Sec's been and done it himself - and he wasn't too pleased at having to do your job while you're loafing here in the sun.'

'Knowing you I bet you dropped us in it, you little shit,' blurted Peter, who plainly didn't care who overheard. You'll get your comeuppance one of these days, you see if you don't.'

'Forget it, Peter,' cautioned Steve, fearful of the potential for fisticuffs. 'I'll go and have a word - see if I can't smooth things over.' And without waiting to see whether or not Danny got clobbered he disappeared into the superstructure.

'Hey, Sec,' called Steve, as he spotted the Second Steward at the far end of the working alleyway. 'Sorry about the breakfast leftovers. I intended sending them back to the galley as soon as I'd photographed the bridge, but Danny said you'd already done it.'

'That's right,' answered the leading hand, disapprovingly, leaving Steve in little doubt there was more to follow. 'You might think you're on a world cruise but your main purpose aboard here is to work -and don't you forget it. If you want to go taking photographs then do it in your own time, not in the company's - okay?'

'Yeah, sure,' replied Steve, turning and heading towards the pantry. And then as an afterthought, just to reassure Sec that any perceived negligence was just a blip, he added. 'Peter's' already started on his cabins, and I'm just off to do mine.'

'Then just make sure you do them properly,' answered Sec, his tone cautioning against a rushed makeover, just to make up for lost time. 'There'll still be a morning inspection, even though we'll be docking shortly.'

Cabin routine could be extremely demanding, especially on the mornings when a change of bed linen was due - as was scheduled to happen each Sunday. He had to collect the fresh linen before making up the bunks; clean washbasins, mirrors and brass-work; empty ashtrays and waste-paper baskets; dust the furniture and brush rugs and carpets before scrubbing those areas of deck that weren't carpeted. As the ship carried no such refinements as a vacuum cleaner all rugs and carpets had to be swept manually, adding more precious minutes to an already overcrowded timetable. Finally, all the soiled linen had to be returned to the appropriate locker to await its turn at a laundry. There could be no loitering, not with two cabins to service and coffee to be served between breakfast and the daily inspection.

Steve was putting the finishing touches to the Junior Radio officer's cabin when he heard the familiar sounds that hinted that berthing was imminent. The vibration from the engines became more pronounced, suggesting 'half astern' had been ordered, to reduce the *Alice Springs'* headway. There were shouts, and the sounds of whistles being blown on the quayside; and as Steve glanced out of the porthole he could see warehouses and forklift trucks, and men gathering hold of the lines that had already been thrown from the ship. He perspired freely as he hurried to accomplish his chores, not in a slip-shod fashion but to a standard fit for inspection. Despite the recent reprimand he was as anxious as ever to witness proceedings ashore, and had already decided that as soon as he was able he'd empty the rosie, on the dump that the Bosun had told him was located at the rear of the warehouses.

As soon as the accommodation ladder had grounded the agent scrambled aboard carrying orders for the skipper and another consignment of mail. And then, surprisingly, considering it was a Sunday, a technician from the Post Office arrived to install a telephone. In most ports a telephone was rigged as soon as a ship was alongside, the handset usually being positioned in a sheltered location near the gangway. Intended primarily to facilitate ship's business the apparatus was available to all, perhaps to ring for a taxi or maybe fix a date with a girl. Whatever, there was often a queue for the telephone and just for good measure, the calls were paid for by the company.

The bin wasn't full but it provided Steve with the ideal excuse to slip ashore while in theory not resorting to negligence. Not only that, he reasonably calculated, but if the rosie became overloaded it would difficult to convey to the dump, which was a good hundred yards from the ship. With the *Alice Springs* now securely alongside the mooring party had evaporated, and being a Sunday the quayside was eerily deserted, with not a soul to disturb the seabirds that with the exception of Steve formed the only sign of life on Glebe Island.

The journey ashore with the rosie was accompanied by the usual swearing, about the idiot who'd dreamt up the silly wire handle. It hadn't occurred to either he or Peter that the regular and often painful exercise of emptying the rosie could be tempered by the simple expedient of wrapping the handle in a pantry cloth. Notwithstanding, he eventually arrived at the tip and disposed of the rubbish, and was rinsing the bin at a standpipe when a car rumbled over the concrete. The vehicle, a large beige Holden containing two passengers, drew up beside him, and as soon as it was stationary the near-side window was wound down and a voice echoed out, 'Coooeee! Steve. Hello.'

Steve spun around in amazement, for the voice belonged to none other than Sylvia Hough, an old family friend who along with her husband, Harry, the Holden's driver, had only recently emigrated from Chelmsford. The Houghs had arrived in Sydney the previous April, having sailed from Tilbury as 'Ten Pound Poms' aboard P&O's *Stratheden,* only weeks after a heart-wrenching parting from Steve and his kin back in Essex. Aware that their friends were emigrating, Steve's father had driven his family to Chelmsford for a farewell get-together, knowing it would be a bitter-sweet gathering.

The unlikely catalyst for the upheaval had been the Houghs three-year-old son, Simon, who'd suffered chronically from asthma and was forever in and out of hospital. Medical advice eventually suggested that the drier, much warmer atmosphere of Australia would be more beneficial to the boy's well-being than the damp, chilly climate of England, hence the decision to emigrate. Sadly, poor Simon died before the dream of a new life could be realized. But his parents had stood by their plans and now, here they were on Glebe Island, having learnt of Steve's imminent arrival from his family whom they'd kept in touch with via airmail.

Steve was still trying to come to terms with the situation when

Sylvia leapt from the Holden, threw her arms around his neck and planted a big sloppy kiss on his cheek. Harry, meanwhile, walked round from the driver's side and greeted him with a warm, friendly handshake. 'We've come to take you out for the day,' gushed Sylvia, her eyes twinkling gleefully in the sunlight. 'Show you the sights - you know, the city and perhaps the Blue Mountains.'

It was happening all too quickly for Steve who although delighted just held up his hands and cried, 'Whoa!' He shook his head, waiting for whatever came next. But when it became clear that the Houghs were waiting for what Steve had to say, he continued. 'Wow, what a lovely surprise - and so good to see you. But I can't come anywhere today - well, not for the time being at any rate.' He went on to explain. 'You see, I have to work, even on Sundays, and won't be free until six o'clock at the earliest. But I'll tell you what,' he added, trying his best to alleviate what was bound to be a huge disappointment. 'If you leave me your address I'll come out to see you this evening, then we can catch up with the news.'

Sylvia looked decidedly downcast as her plans disintegrated, but Harry was more up-beat and knowing. 'We'll come and fetch you if you like,' he said, eagerly. 'It's no trouble - won't take twenty minutes.'

'No, really,' protested Steve, who didn't want to be a burden and had sniffed out the chance of a train ride. 'You save your petrol, and I'll be out there as soon as I've finished work - honest.'

'Fair enough,' said Harry, turning and walking back to the driver's side of the car. 'I'll be looking out for you. Any idea what time?'

'Seven-thirtyish I should imagine,' answered Steve, accepting a scrap of paper with an address scribbled on it from Sylvia who was back to her cheerful self now that a watered-down alternative to a day's sightseeing had been formulated. 'But don't worry if I'm late - I'll be there whatever.' And with that, Sylvia clambered back into the front passenger seat, Harry put his foot on the accelerator and the car disappeared whence it came.

An evening at the Houghs was something that Steve hadn't bargained for, but he was suddenly looking forward to the trip out to the suburb of Kogarah where, with the proceeds from the sale of their house in Chelmsford, his friends had invested in a mini-market with living accommodation attached. From all accounts the venture was a roaring success - hence the new car, a luxury that had been out of the question in their homeland. As Steve ambled back to the ship he was already making plans, wondering which of the city centre railway stations was most handily placed for his journey to Kogarah.

'Town Hall or Wynyard Street are your best bet,' advised Archie, who seemed to have relatives and friends all over Australia. 'I've a pal living out near Botany Bay and I'm going there this evening. Kogarah's on the same route so we may as well travel together. Mind you, we'd better take a taxi into town because either of those stations are a fair old walk from Glebe Island.'

'Suits me,' answered Steve, who felt happier now that he'd the offer of an experienced travelling companion; not that the prospect of making his own way out to Kogarah had bothered him. 'I'll ring for a taxi,' he said, cheekily, 'and you can foot the bill for the fare.'

The journey out towards Botany Bay from the subterranean depths of Town Hall station was a delight, especially from Circular Quay onwards where the train ran mostly on the surface. Through the lofty, glass walls of Circular Quay station Steve had a grandstand view of the wharves and teasing glimpses of the harbour. He also noted that the berth that had played host to the *Castel Felice* earlier that morning was now occupied by the Greek liner *Patris*, which until recently had been the *Bloemfontein Castle*. 'I did a couple of trips on her a few years ago,' commented Archie, nodding at the former Union-Castle vessel laying comfortably alongside the terminal. 'Fantastic voyages, all around Africa - Mombasa, Dar-es-Salaam, Laurenco Marques and down towards Cape Town, then back up the west coast via the Canary Islands and Madeira, and the passengers tipped like millionaires. I made nearly as much in tips as I did in wages. Now she spends her days on the emigrant run, sailing between Piraeus and Sydney.'

The train hurried on, through some of Sydney's most affluent suburbs. Well-spaced houses and bungalows, some with swimming pools and others with sun decks flashed by the windows, leaving Steve wondering where on earth the money had come from to buy such properties. What a far cry from Great Britain, he thought, where most people still lived in rented accommodation, and not very good rented accommodation in many cases. In fact, he reflected, living conditions in some parts of the country were downright criminal and not much improved from the Victorian era. Still, there were doubtless some areas of Sydney that were seedy and run down, he reasoned, thinking back to Melbourne and the ill-fated outing to St Kilda and the decrepit bungalow in Norris Street. He smiled inwardly, and wondered if Carol and her daughters were still sponging and if that was the case, how many others had been fleeced.

Archie left Steve at Arncliffe, after advising that Kogarah was only two or three stops further on. The doors slid shut and he waved cheerily from the platform as the train moved off while Steve raised a hand in acknowledgement.

Ten minutes later and Steve was standing in the street at Kogarah, wondering which way to turn. The scrap of paper given to him by Sylvia carried an address but no directions. They'd been conveyed orally back on Glebe Island and amid all the surprise and confusion had flown away with the seagulls. The only option was to ask, so he approached an elderly lady who was walking her dog, and enquired, 'Can you direct me to the Express Mini-Market? I'm told it's not far from the station.'

The lady, who was a good foot shorter than Steve, gazed up into his eyes as her pet, a Jack Russell terrier, cocked its leg against a lamppost. 'No worries, Son,' she replied, breezily, pointing away to her right as Steve kept an eye on the terrier, just in case it decided to pee up his leg instead of the lamppost. 'Just turn left at that corner and you'll find the mini-market on the other side of the street.'

'Fine,' said Steve, taking a step back as the dog sniffed his ankles. 'Thanks a bundle,' and without waiting to see what the jack Russell did next he turned and set off towards the corner. Meanwhile the lady dragged her pet in the opposite direction, to the next in a succession of lampposts.

Two minutes, that's all it took Steve to find the Express Mini-Market; and there was Harry, standing just inside the door, keeping a lookout just as he'd promised. As Steve crossed the road Harry slipped the bolt and ushered him in, closing the door and shepherding him towards the rear of the store where another door led to the living quarters. 'Just go straight through,' said Harry, picking a tin each of

137

peas and carrots from a shelf as he followed Steve down the aisle, 'Sylvia's in there watching television. You can help me get the dinner ready if you like.' Another cooked meal was the last thing Steve needed. He'd eaten three already that day and another would be asking for trouble. However, having already put the damper on the plans for a sightseeing tour he thought better of refusing and agreed to help Harry in the kitchen.

Steve inched open the door to the sitting room and there in an armchair sat Sylvia, eyes glued intently to the television. He opened his mouth to speak but was stopped in his tracks as she raised a finger to her lips, and hissed, 'Shhhh! It'll soon be finished.' Steve wondered what was so absorbing until she pointed to the set in the corner then all became clear - she was engrossed in Coronation Street. It appeared that Ena Sharples, Albert Tatlock, Elsie Tanner and the rest of Wetherfield were as popular in this part of the world as they were in the United Kingdom, at least in the eyes of the British community, although it was anyone's guess what the natives thought of it.

Steve carried on through to the kitchen while Harry followed closely behind. 'Likes her Coronation Street,' said Harry, turning down the gas on one of the cooker rings to prevent a pan of potatoes boiling over. 'She's settled in pretty well considering, what with Simon and all that, but still likes to keep tabs on the Old Country. Only natural, I suppose.'

Steve agreed. The Houghs had suffered traumatically, first with Simon's illness and then his passing - then there was all the upheaval of emigrating. But now, he mused, it all seemed to have clicked into place and he said as much.

'Yeah, not going too badly at all,' acknowledged Harry as he opened the tin of peas. 'The business is doing well, we love the climate, and the standard of living and quality of life over here is everything we could have wished for. It's just such a bloody shame that poor little Simon's not here to enjoy it.' Harry's eyes moistened and he lapsed into silence, clearly contemplating what might have been. There was little if anything Steve could say so he busied himself at the sink, a task he was comfortably familiar with.

Success stories like the Houghs' seemed to abound in Australia, at least for those willing to commit. Over the years it seemed very few people had thrown in the towel complaining that they couldn't make a go of things; and of those that did jack it in a minimum of sifting usually revealed that it wasn't the country at fault but the migrants themselves, unable - or unwilling - to adapt to an alternate lifestyle.

They were joined for dinner by Sylvia's brother, Tim, who'd emigrated some fifteen years previously and was a serving officer in the Australian army, having completed his training in one of the British guard's regiments. He and Steve were complete strangers but became immediate buddies, and what might have been a prosaic few hours evolved as a thoroughly enjoyable evening. Dinner was served, drinks were poured and the photograph albums had the dust blown from them; not so much that they could wallow in nostalgia but to gaze at the faces of those far away whom the Houghs may well have seen the last of. Steve recognised several of those in the photos, not least his mum, dad and brother who along with himself had been photographed during that final get-together in Chelmsford. News was exchanged and conversation engaged in, and before Steve knew it was almost a quarter to twelve. 'Hey! Look at the time!' he exclaimed, jumping to his feet and rummaging through his pockets for the return portion of his ticket. 'The last train of the day leaves at midnight so I'd better be getting a shift on.'

'You don't have to worry about the train,' said Tim, setting his empty wine glass on the table and wiping his mouth on his serviette. 'I'll be driving back to camp in a few minutes time and I'll be passing quite close to Glebe Island. I can drop you off on the way.' Steve was more than grateful, especially as it would save him either the cost of a taxi, or a walk from the station to the ship.

'Thanks........Tim,' he offered, suppressing a hiccup while struggling into his jacket. 'It'll either save my legs or a good chunk of money.'

Steve felt bloated. The roast lamb dinner that Harry had prepared had been his fourth cooked meal in a day - not to mention afternoon tea - so little wonder he felt like an over-inflated inner-tube. On the other hand, the sherry trifle had slid down easily and had helped quell the indigestion that had threatened to put a cap on the soirée. Whatever, and regardless of what many would have regarded as

gluttony, he smiled, thanked Sylvia and Harry for their kindness -
and accepted the large bar of chocolate that Sylvia proffered as they
walked through the store and on to the forecourt where Tim's
Volkswagen 'Beetle' was waiting.

Bidding farewell proved decidedly more complicated than the
morning meeting on the quayside. Steve was inexplicably tongue-
tied while Sylvia was fighting back tears. The *Alice Springs* would be
in Sydney for another two days but he knew very well that on this
trip at least he'd see no more of the Houghs. For one thing they had a
business to run and for another, he wanted to see more of the city - to
spend some time with his mates and work permitting, visit the
beaches at Bondi and Manley. He gave Sylvia a hug and was
rewarded with another wet kiss, while Harry gripped his hand and
wished him well on his travels. For his part, Steve promised he'd
write to his parents, assuring them that their friends were well and
enjoying their Australian adventure. He made a mental note not to
mention that in his opinion the Houghs were unlikely to return home,
and that if they wanted to see each other again then his own family
would have to make the trip to Australia.

Apart from the cleaning gangs the streets were deserted as they
hurried though the brightly-lit city, passing *en route* through the
suburb of Mascot and past the rapidly expanding Kingsford-Smith
International Airport. Although few people knew it, the airport was to
eventually supersede both Pyrmont and Circular Quay as Sydney's
principal international gateway; and even at this juncture, an
occasional glance at the sky would have revealed the ever-growing
number of jet aircraft that would ultimately render the great ocean
liners redundant.

The Beetle swung off the main road and on to Glebe Island, past
transit sheds and other vessels before drawing to a halt at the foot of
the *Alice Springs'* gangway. Steve hauled himself out of the front
passenger seat, thanking Tim for the lift and wishing him a safe
journey home.

The day had been long, and as soon as the Beetle roared off he
climbed wearily aboard, dead on his feet and clearly in need of his
bed. Under normal circumstances he'd have made straight for his
bunk; but tonight wasn't to be normal, for on turning the corner into

the working alleyway he stumbled over the sozzled Chief Cook who was lying flat on his back in a stupefying self-imposed coma.

Ted enjoyed a drink like everyone else but seldom if ever got plastered. That said, when he did become sloshed he made a thoroughly good job of it and tonight he'd attained a gold medal. On his way up town he'd called at several watering holes, had spent an hour in the Wynyard Hotel before fetching up at the Ritz where he'd bumped into a chum off the *Suffolk*. They'd drank themselves silly while 'swinging the lamp', had been unceremoniously ejected and ended up sharing a taxi. Ted had been dropped off first, had negotiated the accommodation ladder safely enough but had collapsed in a heap in the working alleyway where he lay until Steve tripped over him.

Steve scratched his head, wondering how he was going to manoeuvre Ted to the relative safety of his cabin. He looked hopefully around, seeking out help; but the ship seemed abandoned, with only the hum of the auxiliaries to hint that someone was up and about, even if they were in the engine room. It appeared that everyone else was either still ashore or asleep, prompting Steve to consider rousing one of the cooks or stewards; but no one, he concluded, would thank him for waking them at the middle of the night for the benefit of a drunken tosspot. Therefore, in the absence of available assistance, he decided he'd manage on his own.

Although Ted was of only average height, maybe five-feet-nine in his socks, he was as round as a Christmas pudding and tipped the scales at seventeen stones; so, however Steve approached it, getting the cook to his cabin wouldn't be a simple assignment. Trying to coax him to his feet proved utterly futile and was greeted with a slurred, 'Fuck off and leave me alone.' It was an option that was becoming increasingly attractive, but Steve knew in his heart that he wouldn't have slept soundly knowing that Ted was out there in the alleyway, a danger to himself and to those who could easily fall over him.

It was a scene that Laurel and Hardy would have been proud of, but it was the only thing Steve could come up with. By passing his hands beneath Ted's armpits and clasping them together he began dragging him along, stopping every few feet for a rest. As Sod's Law would have it, Ted's accommodation was at the very far end of the alleyway, making the task a great deal more arduous than it could have been. Nevertheless, Steve was adamant that he wouldn't give in and after a ten-minute slog, punctuated by bouts of swearing, he finally achieved his objective. He opened the cabin door and with a supreme effort bundled Ted over the threshold. By this time he was sweating profusely. There wasn't a snowball's chance in hell of hoisting the cook into his bunk, and he wasn't going to rupture himself trying, so he resorted to the only alternative. He stuffed a pillow beneath his head before covering his torso with a blanket. Then, as an afterthought, having remembered a caveat in a St John's Ambulance Brigade instruction manual, he rolled him on to his side so that in the event of him being sick there was little danger of him choking on the vomit. With his muscles quivering Steve stood back to examine his handiwork. He'd done his best, so satisfied that Ted was as comfortable as he reasonably could be he closed the door and laboriously made for his own bed.

Steve's first thought in the morning was to check that Ted was still breathing; but on opening the cook's cabin door he saw that the room was empty, the only signs of life being a crumpled blue suit strewn carelessly over the bunkboard, a shirt and tie hanging on the inner door handle and some shoes and socks on the sofa. Puzzled, Steve hurried down to the galley where he found Ted already incumbent, leaning on his favourite corner of the work surface, puffing on a Player with no obvious hangover and apparently never feeling better. 'You all right, Ted?' he enquired, his forehead furrowed in amazement. 'Christ, you were in a hell of a state. I had the Devil's own job shifting you out of the alleyway.'

'Oh! It was you, was it?' answered Ted, exhaling a stream of tobacco smoke and wafting it away with a menu card. 'Well, you might have taken my clothes off. My suit looks as if it's been through a mangle.'

Steve was astonished at the ingratitude, but quickly recovered, retorting, 'You ungrateful old sod. Think yourself lucky I didn't leave you lying where I found you - that's what most people would have done.' And spinning on his heel he stalked from the galley, missing the smile that had lit up Ted's face like a lantern.

Steve and his pals never did get to visit the beaches at Bondi or

Manley, but they saw plenty more of the city, especially the bars that abounded in King's Cross and Paddington. Steve also found time to get his hair cut, his first encounter with a hairdresser since he'd visited the barber's shop in Woolwich. Like almost everyone else on board they subbed from their wages to fund their exploits, comfortable in the knowledge that the Chief Steward, for all his other faults, would allow them only what they could afford so that they always had money to fall back on.

Any hope of an ongoing peaceful existence was quashed shortly before their scheduled departure from Sydney. The day had been largely uneventful. The Post Office engineer had called to disconnect the telephone; the deck crew had begun replacing the hatch covers, leaving the derricks in the raised position, ready for use on arrival at Brisbane; and the hum from the engine room was more pronounced as a whisper of steam curled lazily around the funnel. The catering staff were squaring away after lunch, so with an hour to go before sailing time Steve headed ashore with the rosie, to empty it one last time on the tip at the rear of the warehouses. He was on his way back when out of the blue a police car sped by while close on its heels was an ambulance. He wondered who the law had come to arrest and who might be the unfortunate casualty, but it transpired there were no such emergencies. In fact, it was a jolly sight worse.

His eyes were on stalks as several policemen emerged from the squad car, while handcuffed to one of them was none other than Sean Cassidy, the Liverpudlian fireman who'd spent the past couple of weeks languishing in Port Adelaide gaol. What Cassidy got up to was his business so long as it didn't bother others; but during his absence the ship had been generally quiet and the hope had been that they'd seen the last of the troublesome Scouse. Unfortunately, the Port Adelaide police had also seen enough of Sean Cassidy, hence him being handed over to the New South Wales Constabulary who were equally keen to be shot of him. Whatever, Cassidy was back and his battered features bore testament to a frightful pummelling, either at the hands of his fellow inmates or more likely from vengeful police officers.

As Cassidy was being hustled up the gangway, the doors of the ambulance swung open and out tumbled Roger Oates, his lower right leg sheathed in plaster. Plainly, the staff at Port Adelaide hospital had reasoned that they'd done all they could for the Englishman and, not wanting one of their valuable beds monopolized by a dipsomaniac who seemed able to conjure up booze from almost any source, even when hospitalized, had packed him off back where he came from. And so it was that as the ambulance crew supported him up the gangway, he gripped a carrier bag containing his meagre belongings in one hand, and a bottle of Penfold's in the other.

After being disciplined by the Captain - the obvious logging, loss of wages for the time spent in prison and a fine to suit the misdoing - Cassidy would resume his duties in the engine room, although it would doubtless be his ultimate spell in the service of the Australasian and Pacific.

Even though the *Alice Springs* was an oil-fired steamer, the very nature of their work demanded that her firemen be hardened. However, this didn't mean they were all drunken ruffians with disfigured noses, busted knuckles and a string of criminal convictions. In fact, although every man Jack of them was a copious beer-drinker they were generally hard working and amiable; and, despite not having to shovel huge amounts of coal in sky-rocketing temperatures, still endured incredibly difficult working conditions. Steve recalled seeing several of them emerging from the engine room following a stint of tube cleaning during the stopover at Melbourne. They were as black as the Ace of Spades and it would surely have taken hours of showering and scrubbing to remove the deposits. Assuming that much of this muck must also have been inhaled and ingested, their prodigious intake of alcohol could probably be justified as a means of decarbonization.

Roger Oates, the sailor who'd survived an inebriated showdown with a lorry on the streets of Port Adelaide, would play no further part in the voyage, his broken right leg an impediment to any useful employment. The Bosun suggested he help earn his keep by assisting Jimmy Craddock in the galley, peeling potatoes and so forth, a task he could perform sitting down; but Ted was having none of it, saying that Roger would be far more trouble than he was worth.

The penny-pinching Chief Steward was another who wasn't best pleased at Roger's second coming. As far as he was concerned the disabled deckie would be just another drain on the catering budget, the more so considering that if Cassidy had remained in gaol and Roger in hospital then a healthy surplus might have accumulated on the *Alice Springs'* balance sheet.

12

As the *Alice Springs* slipped beneath the harbour bridge, it was announced that another port had been added to her schedule. On their way up the coast to Brisbane they were to call at Newcastle, New South Wales, to offload the police Land Rovers that for reasons best known to the forces of law and order hadn't been landed in Sydney. Steve was cock-a-hoop as Newcastle was off the beaten track - one of the more unglamorous ports where colliers and ore carriers were more likely to be found at the quaysides. But to him it was unexpected and different - perhaps even one of those backwaters that the Bosun had spoken of during their discussion about tramps.

'You needn't get too excited,' unveiled Archie, over dinner, thinking back to the days of the Great Depression when any kind of seafaring employment was grabbed at whatever your *forte*. 'Newcastle's a dirty old place, all heavy industry - coal, steel, shipbuilding and the like. You won't find me going ashore there I can tell you. And anyway, it's only a few hours steaming so we'll probably have arrived and departed before you turn to in the morning.' Steve felt a sense of disentitlement because filthy or not, shore leave was a cherished component of the seafarers' calling, and you couldn't honestly boast of having been to a place if you hadn't actually set foot in it.

In the event, although they arrived overnight it would be lunchtime before they could sail as no night shift had been engaged by the port authority. The trouble was, owing to the short duration of their stay no shore leave was granted which in itself caused some bitter resentment. Still, it was out of Steve's hands; but he was able to join Peter and Archie in the minutes following inspection at the after end of the now empty passenger accommodation, casting

146

disapproving eyes at the grimy and unsightly portscape.

An industrial city and the second largest in New South Wales, Newcastle had prospered on the back of a coal producing industry that saw the commodity widely exported. The fact that the coal was mined locally encouraged related industries to become inseparably established, iron and steel in the form of BHP being the most prominent with the raw material arriving in the company's own vessels and the finished product representing a sizeable chunk of Australia's overseas earnings.

On a brighter note, the *Alice Springs* wouldn't be taking aboard coal for which the crew could think themselves lucky for as Archie enlightened, it was a lousy cargo to both load and transport. He went on to elaborate that the dust permeated every nook and cranny, despite a crew's efforts to prevent it. It collected in the folds of your skin and the fabric of your clothes; and by penetrating every closed door and porthole, even into lockers and living-quarters, forming a velvety, black film on surfaces that hadn't been protected. Once at sea the ship had be thoroughly hosed down, the dust turning to sludge as it was finally flushed through the scuppers. But even then, a cargo of coal could still cause havoc as it was liable to spontaneous combustion. In such instances the crew had to fight the conflagration with the only means at their disposal, by playing hoses into the hold containing the burning cargo. Whether or not they were able to extinguish the fire would be a matter of chance but provided the hatch covers weren't destroyed, allowing the flames unfettered access to oxygen, they might have been able to contain it. 'I should know,' said Archie, eyeing a huge cloud of coal dust rising from the holds of a freighter at the opposite quayside. 'I was once on a coal-burning tramp called the *Cherrywood* when the bunkers ignited. The crew did their best to put it out but it just stubbornly smouldered. Luckily we were only a couple of days from Madras and arrived with a ten-degree list. They had to discharge the coal while it was still alight before the bunkers were pumped dry of water. Then it was into a shipyard for repairs.' Steve absorbed Archie's words and reflected on that conflab with the Bosun a couple of months earlier as they'd passed down the Portuguese coast. Tramp ship life might have its attractions, exotic ports of call and so on, but it clearly wasn't all milk

147

and honey as Archie had so eloquently outlined.

'Christ, Archie,' cheeked Peter, who clearly intended a wind-up. 'You must have been on every old scow in the world. Is there anything you haven't seen or done?'

'You don't have to be saucy,' replied Archie, not rising to the bait but determined to teach Peter that smart-arses aren't always as clever as they think they are. 'You have to remember that I've been at sea over forty years now - through the Great Depression as well as the Second World War. During the depression I took any job going. Sometimes I was the only steward on a leaking old rust-bucket and believe you me, we went to some pretty out-of-the-way places and saw some awful going's-on. During the war I worked on the liners, the 'Queens', and such, while they were trooping, so luckily I didn't get torpedoed. After the war, when world trade picked up and work became plentiful, I had the pick of the berths. Catering Superintendents called me by my Christian name and knew I was good at my job. That's how you accumulate knowledge and respect, young Peter - through years of effort and experience, and by listening to those who know better, not by extracting the Michael.' And with that final checkmate, Archie, flounced off in sham, limp-wristed indignation.

'Well, that's put you in your place,' said Steve, with a hint of amusement as Peter squirmed uncomfortably against the rail.

'Yeah, well,' said Peter, as he turned and headed off in the direction of the pantry. 'That's as maybe but I can't be too upset about that. I've got other things to worry about.'

Steve wondered what those other things might be, having suspected that even discounting the recent bout of banter with Archie, Peter hadn't been quite his chipper self. Then, suddenly, he had an inkling. 'You heard anything from Maureen since we left Adelaide?' he asked, almost certain that his cabin-mate's gloominess was somehow related.

'That's the trouble,' replied Peter, confirming Steve's suspicions as he opened the door to an internal alleyway and stepped over the coaming. 'I got one before we left Sydney - but I don't suppose I'll be getting any more.'

'Why's that?' enquired Steve, as the door closed behind him and he followed his mate down the alleyway.

'Found another bloke, ain't she?' replied Peter, casting the remark over his shoulder as he stepped around Donald who was on his hands and knees, removing a coffee-stain from a carpet. 'Says they want to go steady, and didn't think it would be right if she was writing to me while the two of them were courting.'

'Well, that is a shame,' answered Steve, with heartfelt sincerity. 'I honestly thought that you'd cracked it. Still,' he offered, while knowing it would be of only minimal solace, 'if nothing else, it shows that if you're willing to write to people they're likely to return the compliment - and anyway,' he consoled, 'there are plenty more fish in the sea.'

'I suppose so,' said Peter, resignedly. But then, as if a magician had pulled a rabbit from a hat, his face lit up, and he continued, 'I'm going to get well and truly pissed in Brisbane, to drown my sorrows,' and as he rubbed his hands gleefully together, he added. 'And next week we'll be in New Zealand.'

Peter wasn't the only crew member to get the cold shoulder while the *Alice Springs* was in Sydney, a fact that became apparent in the most hilarious but threatening of fashions. Steve was dusting the panelling at the forward end of the saloon when he glanced out of a window and saw Jimmy Craddock race on to the starboard side of the forward well-deck - closely pursued by a cabbage, half a dozen onions and a cauliflower. The cabbage missed Jimmy by a whisker, one of the onions hit him between the shoulder blades and the cauliflower shattered against the winch drum behind which the galley boy had taken refuge. As Steve gazed down from his vantage point, Norman, the Second Cook, stomped ponderously into the picture, a swede in his right hand and a vicious-looking knife in his left. It was clear that he sought Jimmy's blood and that Jimmy was in fear of his life. Jimmy searched frantically around, seeking the optimum escape route. To head on up to the fo'c'sle would only make matters worse; he'd be cornered like a rat in a trap and at the Second Cook's mercy. It was clear that he would have to find his way aft, into the accommodation and then lock himself away in his cabin. As Steve looked helplessly on Jimmy made his move. He was younger and more agile than Norman, so he darted between a pair of hatch covers to the port side of the ship then made a dash for the superstructure. Norman threw the swede which missed by a mile, clunking against the adjacent bulkhead as Jimmy disappeared through the door. Steve dropped his duster and hurried down to the cabin which Jimmy shared with the sailors' peggy, although he hadn't a clue what he'd do when he got there. There was no sign of Norman as Steve arrived in the working alleyway where he rapped urgently on Jimmy's cabin door. 'Open up, Jimmy' he called, wondering if his friend was safely inside. It's me, Steve. I've come to see if you're OK.'

The was no immediate response and Steve wondered if Jimmy might have hidden elsewhere; then, slowly, the door handle turned and Jimmy's frightened face appeared in the crack between the door and the door-post. 'Cor, am I glad to see you, said the galley boy, swinging the door open wide.' I thought the mad sod was gonna to kill me.'

'What was that all about?' demanded Steve, closing and locking the door behind him, jamming a chair beneath the handle as an additional layer of security.

'Well,' began Jimmy, before launching into an explanation that had all the ingredients of a music-hall joke that had Steve doubled up and in stitches. 'Just before we left Sydney, Norman got a letter from his missus telling him he was a waste of space and that she was clearing off with a travelling salesman. Norm was fuming. He evidently smashed up his cabin, went ashore on the piss and when he got back at two in the morning, wandered through the officers' and engineers' quarters, banging on the cabin doors, and shouting, "Wake up you bastards". The Second Mate and the Third Engineer managed to quieten him down and turn him into his bunk. Then in the morning, after he'd slept it off, he was sent to the bridge where he was logged and fined a day's pay for the trouble.'

'So, where do you come into all this? 'enquired Steve, eager to get to the bottom of Jimmy's involvement in the matter.

'Well,' continued Jimmy, who seemed more self assured than he had done a few minutes earlier. 'A little while ago, Norman was still mouthing off about how he was going to wring his wife's neck and castrate the travelling salesman, so I said, "You'll have to catch them first, you old bugger", and with that he just went bananas, started

150

chucking vegetables around and chased me out of the galley.'

'Hmm, I don't suppose it was the wisest thing to have said given his state of mind,' answered Steve, who still thought the episode extremely funny. 'But if I were you I'd lie low for a while to let him get over it and then go on bended knee and apologise. Norman always seems a decent enough bloke to me so it's my guess that so long as you don't make matters worse he'll be receptive.'

'Yeah, I suppose so,' replied Jimmy who now appeared happier. 'But I'm going to stay out of his way till I'm sure.'

'Probably the best thing to do,' agreed Steve, inching open the cabin door and scanning the alleyway to make sure that the coast was clear. 'Anyway, he's not out here so it's ten to one he's back in the galley. Whatever, take care - and I'll catch up with you later.'

As Steve headed back to the saloon he glanced warily around every corner, just to ensure that Norman wasn't still roaming the ship in search of Jimmy. As it happened he needn't have worried because as the Second Steward advised over lunch, on returning to the galley poor old Norman had collapsed in tears, the events of the past couple of days being more than he could handle. Jimmy had indeed approached Norman as Steve had counselled and the cook had slung an arm over his shoulder in a gesture of reconciliation. 'Even so,' confided Jimmy, when Steve bumped into him later, 'he scared the shit out of me good and proper.'

Brisbane, the state capital of Queensland, lies a short distance south of the twenty-seventh parallel, roughly two hundred miles from the Tropic of Capricorn; and this was reflected not only in the sub-tropical climate which even in the Australian autumn was noticeably warm and sticky, but also in the luxuriant vegetation lining the banks of the Brisbane River. As the *Alice Springs* made her approach, Steve took time to peer into the undergrowth which he understood formed the ideal habitat for the snakes and crocodiles that were said to inhabit the coastal areas of large swathes of northern Australia.

'We're too far south to see any of those,' replied the Lamp Trimmer, when Steve asked about the probability of seeing the reptiles. 'You're more likely to catch those up in Arnhem Land, or around the Gulf of Carpentaria where there are far fewer people to disturb them.'

Steve was a mite disappointed, although if the truth be told he'd be scared to death if confronted by anything more frightening than a spider. Nonetheless, there was plenty of other wildlife in the jungle, most noticeably the colourful avi-fauna of which there were numerous and alien varieties, all with their own unique birdsong. 'I wonder what species they are?' said Steve, gesturing towards the treetops which were alive with sound and fluttering activity.'

'Buggered if I know,' replied the Lamp Trimmer, who clearly had little interest in the topic and was simply content to lean on the rail and watch the world go by, 'I'm a seaman, not an ornithologist. Birds are like dogs to me. As far as I'm concerned all dogs are mongrels and all birds are shitehawks - I can't tell the one from the other.' Steve smiled, and had to admit that even back home he'd be pushed to distinguish between starlings, blackbirds and thrushes, so in that respect the Lampy was in pretty good company.

It was mid afternoon when the *Alice Springs* tied up at her riverside berth, in the heart of the city and where according to Queensland law the pubs remained open till ten. 'It's an easy evening meal tonight, lads,' said the Second Steward, as the pantry came alive in preparation for afternoon tea. 'Cauliflower-cheese for starters with apricot pudding to follow.'

'What, no second choice?' queried Steve, who wasn't really a lover of cauliflower and wasn't too fussed about apricots. 'There's usually an option.'

'Not tonight there isn't,' replied Sec, brandishing a make-shift menu. 'There's an electrical problem in the galley and part of the stove's out of action. Whatever, there shouldn't be a great deal of work involved so the sooner we get cleaned down the sooner we'll all get ashore. And remember, we're only here for a couple of days so make the most of it, but don't go getting into trouble.'

'You don't have to worry about us, Sec,' said Peter, as he made to leave the pantry for the engineer's lounge carrying a tray crammed with crockery, cake and tea-making silverware. 'We'll probably do some sightseeing then go for a drink later on. Oh! By the way,' he added, turning and facing the Second Steward, balancing the tray on his left forearm while his right hand acted as a stabilizer. 'Will we be able to sub? I'm nearly skint and could do with another few bob.'

'The Chief Steward said no,' replied Sec, as he slipped the menu cards into their folders, having pinned one to the pantry notice board. 'He reckons that as it's only a two-day stay it wasn't worth ordering more Australian currency, so you'll have to make do with what you've got.'

'You shouldn't have squandered it all in Sydney,' said Danny Meeks, self-righteously, as he headed off with the Captain's tray laden along with the tea-making accoutrements, a generously proportioned vanilla slice, 'you should have saved some for a rainy day.'

'Piss off, arsehole,' snapped Peter, as Danny disappeared along the alleyway, heading for the internal bridge companionway and the Captain's day room. 'I wasn't talking to you.'

'That's enough of that,' cautioned Sec, wagging a finger under Peter's nose. 'I know he's a pain in the bum but you should ignore him. He only does it to annoy you.'

'I know,' replied Peter, glaring after the departing Danny. 'It's just that he's such a gungy bastard - and a creepy one too. Just look at the size of the piece of cake he put on the Old Man's tray - and there's another thing. I don't like the way he splits on Steve and me to either you or the Boss if we don't do just as he thinks we should.' He was about to launch into a further tirade but spotted Steve shaking his head, a warning not to overstep the mark. The Second Steward smiled, knowing that although Peter losing his rag wasn't going to improve the chemistry between Danny and himself, he'd merely been stating a fact.

'Don't worry about money,' called Steve, as Peter headed off with his tray. 'I can lend you a few bob until we get to Nelson.' Peter briefly loosened his hold on the tray and waved an appreciative hand, feeling fractionally less grumpy now that his pent-up animosity had been partially relieved - if only until the next disagreement.

When Steve and his pals went ashore that evening they were joined by Norman and John. Before leaving the ship, Norman had been at pains to point out that although he'd be taking a drink there'd be no repetition of his behaviour in Sydney which he assured them was quite out of character. Suitably appeased, the five of them strolled through the streets of what could aptly be described as the quaintest state capital in Australia.

Brisbane exuded a relaxed timelessness, as if it was jogging along at the same old pace as it had done a hundred years earlier. Life, it seemed, was measured in days not minutes, the city itself being noticeably more laid-back than either Adelaide or Melbourne, and - with the exception of the temperature - far less sizzling than Sydney. The parks and gardens were both verdant and colourful, while the architecture betrayed an enduring colonial affluence. His companions had all been to Brisbane previously so perhaps took everything for granted, but to Steve it was a brand new horizon and another example of Australia's diversity and wealth.

They walked for a good sixty minutes, covering a sizeable area of the commercial district and part of a residential suburb, until Norman began complaining, 'My feet are killing me. I've got a bloody great corn on my little toe and it's playing up something rotten. I need a rest, and anyway -isn't it time for a noggin?'

John agreed. 'I'm game. I'm as dry as a Saudi off-licence. A schooner would slip down a treat.'

'Where do you reckon on going?' asked Norman, who, while perching on a near-by wall, had removed a shoe and was busily massaging his toe.

'What about the Wharfies' Club,' suggested John, indicating back towards the waterfront. 'It's not very far and they sometimes lay on entertainment.'

'Suits me,' answered Norman, replacing and relacing his shoe. 'It's only half-a-mile from where we're tied up, and if we don't feel like walking back to the ship we can always take a taxi.' And so they set off; and as if some fairy-godmother had sprinkled her stardust, Norman's troublesome corn seemed to have been miraculously cured as he strode purposefully in the direction of the Wharfies' Club.

In Britain, dockworkers were generally known as either dockers or stevedores, while in the United States they were longshoremen; but in Australia and New Zealand they were referred to as wharfies, and in many of the ports they had their own social clubs where visiting seamen were also made welcome - if only for the additional income.

Brisbane Wharfies' Club was just such an establishment, a typical working-man's institution where the atmosphere, although naturally noisy and high-spirited, was for the most part hospitable and friendly. It was teeming with drinkers when Steve and his pals arrived, and headed for a table that had just become vacant and which was located in the opposite corner to the entrance, close to the bar and an emergency exit. As usual, most of those present were either port workers or seamen, the former still in their working attire and downing a 'quickie' before setting off home to their suppers. As they'd steamed up the Brisbane River Steve had noted Shaw-Savill's *Runic*, P&O's *Aden* and Blue Star's *Fremantle Star*; and there were others moored further upstream that were too far away to identify. Whatever, it was fair to assume that their crews would be out and about, and that at least some of them would be slaking their thirsts in the Wharfie's Club.

As Steve sipped his beer he thought how refreshing it was that so many people from varying backgrounds could socialize in such close-knit harmony, especially when some dockside hostelries were notoriously boisterous - fight-a-night pothouses for want of a more colourful description. As he glanced around the room he saw there seemed little threat to this affable state of affairs save for a lone pickled wharfie who the management were obviously aware of but whom most patrons chose to ignore. The man, who'd apparently been suspended from work after belting a foreman, was just about legless, was swaying and spilling his beer while mumbling obscenities that amid all the hubbub were largely incoherent. However, to those who listened closely it was clear that he was taking a swipe at the seafarers who in his opinion were a bunch of good-for-nothing interlopers. Steve couldn't help wondering why the bar staff didn't eject him, or at least caution him as to his behaviour; but they didn't appear bothered, and Steve hoped fervently that the club's clientèle would feel likewise.

They must have been on their fourth schooner of ale, and Norman was as good as his word. He enjoyed a drink as did the rest of them, but he wasn't an habitual drunkard and apart from the occasional grievance was usually mild-mannered and disciplined. Tonight he was his familiar, convivial self, although it had been agreed among the others that the breakdown of his marriage was a taboo topic for

155

fear of upsetting the scales. All things considered an enjoyable enough evening seemed in prospect - until all hell broke loose, and it had nothing to do with Norman.

The half-empty bottle of Castlemaine missed Peter's ear by a whisker. It cleared every other potential obstacle, human and otherwise, before pole-axing the outspoken wharfie. He collapsed in a heap, spitting out teeth while the remains of his mouth blossomed like a pulverized strawberry. Blood began seeping, and the previously amiable atmosphere became suddenly hushed and electric. Then, as if roused from their apathy by a thunderclap, several of his previously unconcerned workmates rushed to his aid while others sought the source of the missile. They didn't have too far to look, for leaning on a table some thirty feet from the bar, his eyes smouldering like recently-fired pistols, stood Sean Cassidy, surrounded by his engine room cronies. There must have been half-a-dozen of them all told, all built like Tarzan and each in the mood for a roughhouse.

Sean may have had Irish ancestry but he was Liverpool - and therefore British - through and through, and no lippy wharfie was going to denigrate either he or his fellow countrymen. Someone smashed a bottle over his head but might just as well have flicked him with a duster. Sean turned, hoisted his assailant as if lifting a sack of King Edwards, and lobbed him into the onrushing mob. They toppled like ninepins; but it was purely a catalyst for the entire assemblage to become embroiled in a brawl of titanic proportions, with wharfie setting upon seaman and conversely. Chairs and bottles flew in all directions, indiscriminately, seeking a target combatant or otherwise. Eyes became blackened, ear lobes were shredded while lips and noses exploded like burst tomatoes, with blood staining furniture and clothing. A full-length mirror lining the rear of the bar metamorphosed into a billion fragments of crystal, courtesy of a soda syphon that that had been hurled at a terrified barman who took split-second evasive action and saved himself a trip to the undertakers. In his scramble to flee the mêlée Steve shot under the table; and for some bizarre reason he suddenly recalled the sight that had confronted him at Port Adelaide. If the town had resembled Tombstone, Arizona in the minutes leading up to the 'Gunfight at the OK Corral', then the happenings in the Wharfie's Club mirrored a

156

scene from 'Rio Bravo', and he couldn't help thinking that the appearance of John Wayne, Dean Martin and Ricky Nelson would have been greeted with rapturous applause. Whatever, it was a frightening state of affairs and escape became an urgent priority.

Steve and his pals hadn't come ashore for a fight, and they'd no intention of becoming embroiled in one; so this was where the emergency exit close to where they were seated fulfilled its intended purpose. The bar staff may well have been lax in turning a deaf ear to the ill-judged comments that had ignited the flare-up, but were quick enough in summoning the police when it detonated. And so it was that as the first khaki-clad officers stormed into the building through the front entrance, Steve and his companions slipped stealthily out of the rear.

'Christ, that was too close for comfort,' remarked Norman, removing a sliver of glass from his hair as he tumbled out into the street.

'Whew! Not half,' agreed John, who'd witnessed many a free-for-all during his years at sea but nothing quite so violent as that now taking place in the Wharfies' club. Steve and the other two youngsters, who'd also joined him under the table, were visibly rattled and put quite a few yards between themselves and the club while Norman and John showed remarkable composure. Eventually, John, being one of the two senior members of the party and therefore shouldering a degree of responsibility for the boys, enquired, 'Are you three okay?'

'Yeah, sure - no worries,' replied Jimmy, without a great deal of conviction. 'Just a spot of blood on my shirt - but I don't know whose.'

Peter, who'd come so close to being clobbered by the projectile that had precipitated the riot, displayed his customary devil-may-care bravura while sounding far from convincing. 'That was nothing,' he boasted, although the words carried a noticeable quiver. 'I've seen bigger punch-ups in our local.'

'How about you, Steve?' asked Norman, smiling at Peter's bravado. 'Are you all in one piece? You're looking as white as a sheet.'

'Fine,' replied Steve, whose heart was racing and whose breath came in short, frequent gasps. He squatted down on his haunches and gazed up at Norman. 'I was frightened something like that was going to happen. I didn't know Sean and his mates were sitting behind us otherwise I'd have suggested leaving earlier.'

Peter, who was rapidly reverting to his combative self, tossed his head in the direction of the Wharfies' Club, and cried. 'What? And lose out on that little rumpus? I wouldn't have missed it for the world.'

'You're welcome to it,' countered Jimmy, who'd spat on his handkerchief and was rubbing vigorously at the bloodstain. 'I've seen ructions like that back in Glasgow and I can tell you, they're not a pretty sight, especially when the razors are flashing.'

By this time several more vanloads of police had arrived at the front of the Wharfies' Club along with a number of ambulances. The din from inside the club had by this time subsided as the police laid about them with truncheons. The first of the arrested antagonists were escorted to the waiting police vehicles, while those who needed medical attention were whisked away to the hospital. Steve felt sure that somewhere among the former would be Sean Cassidy and his gang; and sure enough there was Sean, struggling for all he was worth, as half-a-dozen no-nonsense coppers bundled him into a Black Maria.

'My guess is that we really have seen the back of him after that little humdinger,' observed Norman, as the shaken but otherwise unharmed quintet turned and set course for the docks.

'Maybe,' mused John, who didn't sound at all convinced that they'd finally seen the last of their ship's principal hoodlum. 'But he seems to have an uncanny knack of worming his way out of the tightest corners, and I wouldn't be at all surprised if he turns up on the quayside tomorrow.'

Steve and Peter fell into their bunks as soon as they reached their cabin; but with Peter soon snoring his head off Steve lay awake, unable to sleep, not only owing to the racket that Peter was making but because he couldn't forget the fight at the 'Wharfies'. He either tossed and turned or merely stared at the deckhead before eventually drifting into that drowsy no-man's-land between sleeplessness and slumber. And then, suddenly, he was wide awake and aware of an

158

unexpected presence. There'd been a knock at the door and two silhouettes, one tall and slim the other short and round, stood side-by-side in the doorway, framed by the light from the alleyway. A torch flickered on and was directed first at Peter and then at Steve, dazzling the latter who propped himself up on an elbow, and demanded, ' Who the hell are you?'

This in turn prompted the cabin light to be switched on to reveal the lanky Third Mate and his associate who was pumpkin-shaped and bald, and who was scowling like a dispossessed bulldog. Steve heard a mumbled, 'Recognize anyone?' The 'Halloween-lantern' peered first at Steve and then at the sleeping Peter, before shaking his head and waddling out into the alleyway. The officer switched off the light and pulled the door to, whispering as he went, 'Sorry to have disturbed you, Lad.' A second or two later Steve heard a knock at the cabin shared by Jimmy and the peggy. It appeared that the same question was asked only this time there was greater deliberation before Steve heard the light switch 'click' off, followed by the now familiar knock at the adjoining cabin. Steve lay back in his bunk, wondering what had initiated this latest happening.

The sailors' peggy on any ship was the most junior of the deck ratings and was in all probability making his seafaring debut. As well as learning the fundamentals of becoming a seaman it was also his job to clean, fetch and carry for his messmates, which was the most likely reason for him being the only member of the deck department to be accommodated in the working alleyway. Other companies may have made different berthing arrangements, but that was the set-up in the Australasian and Pacific Steam Navigation Company.

Peggy was in all respects the deck department's dogs-body, collecting meals from the galley and provisions from the stores. He'd clean the cafeteria-like mess room and alleyways, heads and showers; and woe betide him if the tea and coffee wasn't made when the deckies on day work knocked off for 'smoke-ho'. His duties also extended to servicing the deck petty officers accommodation, in addition to which he'd serve them their meals at their table. On many ships the peggy would also perform these duties for the engine room ratings and petty officers whose mess rooms and accommodation were adjacent to those of the deck department, although arrangements might vary from ship to ship and doubtless from company to company.

On joining the *Alice Springs* Steve had wondered why this seemingly most put-upon of deck boys was routinely referred to as, 'Peggy'. The Bosun had enlightened him - well, as near as damn it given any number of founts for the sobriquet, although the most likely had its origins in sailing ship days as the Bosun had so logically explained. It seemed that if a seaman became incapacitated through the loss of a leg rendering him incapable of climbing aloft, work would be found for him at deck level; cleaning, helping the cook or running errands for the Captain and officers. As it was almost certain that the missing limb would have been substituted by a wooden replacement he'd jargonistically be referred to as 'Peg-leg,' which as the years rolled on had gradually been corrupted to, 'Peggy'; although of course the modern-day peggy was as fit and adaptable as every other functioning crew-member.

Morning brought the solution to this latest enigma which wasn't such a mystery after all. Steve was collecting provisions from the store room next to the galley when Jimmy poked his head around the corner, and with a beckoning finger, hissed, 'A word with you if you've got a minute.'

Steve nodded, and straightened the assortment of tea, coffee and cocoa, sugar and a variety of jams and marmalades that had accumulated on his tray, agreeing with Sec that he'd need to return for the cereals, pickles and fruit. He hurried up to the pantry and unloaded his tray, informing Archie that there was more to collect, before dashing back down for the Weetabix, Branston and prunes. He then sidled into the galley where Jimmy was peeling potatoes. 'Okay,' said Steve, leaning back on a bulkhead and balancing his tray on his forearms. 'You wanted to see me about something?'

'Yeah,' said Jimmy, who didn't look up but carried on scraping with his peeler. 'That little disturbance last night, when the Third Mate came around with that other bloke. Well, the roly-poly fellow was a taxi driver, and they were looking for some guys who'd skipped off without paying their fare. Anyway, it seems that Peggy was involved but because it was dark the driver couldn't positively identify him.'

'So, what happened?' pressed Steve, who was eager to learn the full story.

'Well,' continued Jimmy, who was digging away at an eye in a potato as if he was prospecting for gold. 'Peggy had been ashore with three of the other deckies - that big AB from Manchester, Billy I think his name is - and a couple of EDHs, Anyway they took a taxi back to the ship, but what Peggy didn't know was that the other three were gonna play a prank on him.'

'Yeah, so - and then what happened?' cajoled Steve, who by this time was fully absorbed in the tale and wanted to get to the bottom of it.

'All right, let the dog see the rabbit,' protested Jimmy, annoyed that Steve's interruption had prevented him completing his narrative with the desired fluency. 'If you let me finish I'll tell you. What happened was this. It seems that all of them were skint, so Billy left the other three in the taxi while he supposedly came aboard for some money. When he never returned one of the EDHs said that he'd go and see where Billy had got to, but he did a bunk just like Billy. That left Peggy and the other EDH sitting in the cab on their own. Lo and behold - and the driver still hadn't cottoned on - the remaining EDH did exactly the same as the other two. Of course, by this time poor old Peggy's on his lonesome. Anyway, and you're never going to believe this, Peggy's shitting himself by this time but still tells the taxi driver to hang about while he gets some money as it looked like the other three had beat it - and you know what? The silly bloody driver lets him do it. In the meantime, Peggy's come aboard to see if he can locate the other three and finds them tucked up in their bunks - so he does the same. That's when the driver comes to his senses and realizes he's been taken to the cleaners.'

'Rotten bastards,' said Steve, only too aware that he'd been the victim of his own share of practical jokes, but nothing quite so dirty as this. 'Did the taxi driver get his money?'

'I suppose so,' answered Jimmy, who was poking the point of his peeler deep into the innards of a potato to remove yet another eye, 'but with the driver not being able to identify anyone they got away with it. The Third Mate probably paid him and he'll claim the money from the company.'

'Peggy didn't split on the other three, then?' asked Steve, half hoping the answer would be in the affirmative but knowing in his heart that it wouldn't.

'Course not,' answered Jimmy, examining the potato before tossing it into a milk churn along with the others. 'They'd have made his life a misery if he had.'

That afternoon Steve went ashore on his own. He strolled around the city that had seemed so inviting the previous evening but had provided the setting for a battle royal and the arrest - yet again - of Sean Cassidy. Wandering through the streets he wondered if Sean would be released into the custody of the *Alice Springs* Captain for if nothing else, the unruly fireman was gradually becoming a folk hero, at least where the crew were concerned even if he was a headache for the officers. Opinions were changing, and Steve couldn't help thinking that it'd be a gross injustice if Sean was detained, for extreme as it may have been, he and his colleagues had only been reacting to incitement.

But there was obviously even-handedness somewhere, for shortly before sunset, as the *Alice Springs* made ready for her crossing to New Zealand, a police car drew up on the quayside. It was precisely as John had predicted. Out stepped the irrepressible Sean, handcuffed to an officer who inserted a key and released his rumbustious prisoner. Steve, who found himself studying the scene with quiet satisfaction, glanced sidelong and saw that both Peter and Jimmy were smiling, proof that he wouldn't have been the only one to have felt disappointed if the free-spirited fireman had been left rotting in an Australian gaol.

For all that Australia had to offer there was scarcely a soul among them who wasn't eagerly anticipating their New Zealand landfall; and although he couldn't pinpoint the reason, Steve too had fallen victim to the enchantress. There was a tangible buzz in the air as with three farewell blasts on her siren the *Alice Springs* slipped silently down the Brisbane River. She was heading for the harbour at Nelson, a diminutive port on the northern shores of the South Island and an emerald in the New Zealand crown.

13

It may have seemed callous but most of the catering staff couldn't have cared less when Danny Meeks was taken ill in the middle of the Tasman Sea, miles from anywhere and the nearest medical assistance. The doctor and his family had left the *Alice Springs* back in Sydney, so it was left to the Second Mate and Chief Steward to consult the ship's medical manual in an attempt to identify the ailment. After scrutinizing the relevant pages neither could agree a diagnosis. The Second Mate thought Danny might be suffering a kidney infection while the Chief Steward felt sure it was an enlarged prostate. But whatever, the Captain's Tiger was unable to pee so with seven hundred miles still to go before they reached Nelson his immediate prospects were unpromising.

'Make sure he takes plenty of fluids,' whooped Peter, who seemed positively elated on learning of the Tiger's condition.

'Don't be so nasty,' rebuked Steve, who was shocked at Peter's rejoicing, even if it was common knowledge that the relationship between his pal and the Captain's personal steward was decidedly chilly. 'You wouldn't like it if people said things like that about you if you were in Danny's position.'

'Well........he's been asking for it all trip,' countered Peter, who even more than Steve had been a target for Danny's sneakiness. 'I told you he'd get his comeuppance one day so I guess this is it - and I had nothing to do with it.'

The Second Steward seemed more concerned with who'd fill the void created by Danny's indisposition than by the Tiger's well-being. In the end he opted to appoint Keith, the senior and most competent of the remaining ASs, as the stand-in Tiger until Danny was pronounced fit to resume; assuming of course that he made a speedy recovery and that there was little likelihood of a relapse. 'Meanwhile,' he announced, addressing Steve and Peter, 'one of you two will have to wait at table in the saloon, and I'll rearrange the roster so that all the cabins are serviced and that the other side jobs are attended to.'

'Fuckin' 'ell,' stormed Peter, untying the pantry cloth from around his waist and throwing it into the sink. 'We've got enough to do here at mealtimes as it is without having to do the AS's work as well. Who's going to cover for us in the pantry? The fuckin' Chief Steward?'

'There'll be no arguments,' retaliated Sec, who wasn't at all impressed by Peter's outburst. 'I've told you what's going to happen so it's up to you how you go about it. You can take it in turns if you like - I don't care just so long as the job gets done. We'll be in New Zealand in another two days and half the crew'll be ashore at mealtimes, so the chances are you'll have sod-all to do when it comes to it.'

'I haven't got a white jacket,' protested Peter, sullenly, not at all keen on changing his work routine if it could be avoided, 'so I can't wait at table even if I wanted to.'

'I'll lend you one of mine,' volunteered Steve, eager that he shouldn't have to shoulder the burden of waiting at table alone. 'I've got two in my locker that I brought from the Vindi, just in case they were needed.'

'I'll leave you two to sort things out between yourselves, then,' said Sec, who'd explained his position and expected his orders to be adhered to. 'Just so long as one of you is in that saloon at lunchtime.'

'Thanks for nothing,' scowled Peter, aiming the remark at Steve as Sec slipped out of the pantry. 'I hate waiting at table. I had to do it last trip after one of the ASs sprained his ankle. The Second Engineer got a spoonful of mashed potato down his jacket and I knocked the Senior Cadet's coffee over. They went fuckin' bananas,' he added, picking his dripping pantry cloth out of the sink and wringing it out on the deck.

'Well, you heard what Sec said,' retorted Steve, intent on standing his ground. 'And I don't see why I should do it all on my own. If it makes you feel any better I'll do lunch and we can take it in turns from then on. That's fair, isn't it?'

'I suppose so, answered Peter, sulkily, as he mopped up the inconsiderately-spilt water. 'But I just hope Danny soon gets better. I don't want to be lumbered with this little lark for goodness-knows how long.'

Steve smiled inwardly at the abrupt change in attitude; but felt suddenly apprehensive at the prospect of serving in the saloon, even though he knew it would happen sooner or later as he scaled the ladder of promotion. In twelve months time he'll have celebrated his eighteenth birthday, will hopefully have earned his rating and graduated to the position of Assistant Steward. In theory his pay will more than double overnight, although in reality it wouldn't actually happen until he next signed on following his birthday. But all that was way into the future and depended on him staying the course as a seafarer. In the meantime he couldn't help thinking that Peter should have been automatically detailed to cover in the saloon as he was the senior of the two catering boys and should therefore have been expected to assume the additional responsibility. He voiced as much to Archie over morning coffee, and added a few of his reservations about waiting at table. 'I'm not very good at silver service - and how am I going to cope with serving soup from a tureen when the ship's rolling all over the place?' he fretted, remembering how he'd been all fingers and thumbs when trying his hand with serving spoon and fork at the Vindi. 'What happens if I spill something in someone's lap?'

'You won't,' comforted Archie, emphatically, fully understanding Steve's diffidence. 'If you don't feel happy about using the serving spoon and fork together just use them separately until you become more proficient. No one's going to mind - this isn't First Class on the *Queen Mary* you know. And as for serving the soup, just wait until you're perfectly balanced before ladling it on to the plate. This sort of thing happens all the time, catering boys having to deputize for stewards for some reason or other. And not only that, if you get a little experience under your belt before you get your rating you'll be a ready-made waiter when the time comes.'

Steve felt happier following his chat with Archie. He knew the Bedroom Steward would be keeping an eye on him from the servery, ready to offer advice, and he was pretty certain that Donald and Keith would be equally helpful. He wasn't the least bit worried about the extra scrub-out he'd been saddled with - he'd just have to work a bit harder; it was simply the thought of some terrible catastrophe in the saloon that haunted him. Still, the die was cast so he proceeded to his cabin and took the pair of white jackets from his locker, draping one over Peter's bunk as he examined the other for creases. Fortunately, he and his mate were of similar physique so there should be no excuses as regards fit. In fact, both jackets were somewhat on the large side so would hang sloppily whoever was wearing them. Back at the Vindi size had been determined by an instructor making an educated guess rather than using a tape measure, and very few items of apparel had fitted ideally. Steve recalled that even the beret bearing the badge of the National Sea Training School had left a crimson weal where the hat-band had clung to his forehead.

At bang on twelve-thirty Steve took his place in the saloon, looking extremely smart in a crisp, white jacket that was buttoned to the collar, even if the sleeves were over-long. His polished, black shoes sparkled beneath the fluorescent lighting, and his navy, serge trousers had creases fore and aft as sharp as if they'd recently been pressed. In terms of appearance no one would have known he was a novice and his confidence was accordingly bolstered.

Steve had been assigned two of the smaller tables, both of which were occupied by officers he was acquainted with, including the Senior and Junior Radio Officers; so although he wasn't exactly on Christian name terms with his charges he did at least know who he was dealing with. And so it was that he headed first for the Sparkys' table, handing each of those seated a menu card; and from that moment on he sailed through the meal as though he'd been a steward since childhood. Showing good common sense he wasn't over ambitious, using the serving-spoon and fork individually as Archie had counselled. Absolutely nothing was spilt, and the only flaw in his ministration came right at the end of the meal and away from the tables when he fumbled a packet of cream crackers. It wasn't the disaster he'd dreaded, and simply necessitated opening another packet and kicking the crumbs of his mishap beneath the dumb waiter and out of sight until later.

He was positively beaming as he took his seat in the saloon for his own meal, and try as he might he just couldn't conceal his elation.

'Didn't do too badly, did I?' he quizzed, glancing around as the topside catering staff tucked into their lunches. 'Apart from dropping those biscuits I thought I did pretty well.'

Keith was of the same opinion and Archie nodded in agreement. 'I was keeping tabs on you from the servery,' he affirmed, from beneath raised eyebrows. 'As far as I could see you didn't put a foot out of place.'

'Except for dropping that packet of cream crackers,' chided Sec, although it was accepted he was in fact joking. 'And don't forget to sweep those crumbs up after you've eaten. Then you'd better come down to the stores to fetch another packet, otherwise there'll be none for later.'

Through all of this Peter sat eating in silence, knowing that in a few hours time it would be his turn to wear a white jacket. He knew that Steve had excelled, and recalled his own clumsy efforts of the previous trip, fearing a repeat performance. In view of Steve's lunchtime success he considered asking him if he'd mind waiting at table indefinitely but thought better of it. If Steve could acquit himself then so could he, and he vowed quietly to equal his cabin mate's achievement. In the event Peter also prevailed, and such was their mutual triumph that the boys began vying for the privilege of waiting, taking the view that it was far more rewarding than slaving at the sink, up to their armpits in soapsuds.

In light of Danny's worsening condition the Skipper consulted the Chief Engineer to ask if a few extra knots could be squeezed from the *Alice Springs'* engines. The Chief and his men responded, with the result that the remaining seven hundred miles were reeled off in an amazing thirty-five hours. That particular gallop must have represented something of a record for a run-of-the-mill cargo liner, even for the *Alice Springs*, a vessel renowned for her sprinting.

On arrival at Nelson it was essential that Danny be admitted to hospital as quickly as possible, and thanks to the wizardry of radio an ambulance was already waiting. The tortured form of the Captain's Tiger was rushed ashore as soon as the ship was alongside and even those such as Peter, who'd previously had little sympathy, were wishing him a speedy recovery. 'He must have a bladder like a barrage-balloon,' said Peter, as Danny disappeared into the ambulance. 'It's bad enough when you're bustin' for a pee after a couple of pints so he must be in absolute agony.' For all his belated contrition, Peter was aware of an enormous weight being lifted from his shoulders, a feeling shared by others who'd wished Danny well but were hoping he wouldn't return.

They were berthed on the outer face of the Main Wharf, the only wharf in the port that was capable of accommodating a vessel of the *Alice Springs'* dimensions. The inner faces were frequented by the coastal traders of the Union Steamship Company and also provided shelter for the fishing fleet. Ahead of the *Alice Springs* was a tanker-handling facility from where petroleum products were pumped ashore to the associated tank farm, while astern, on land reclaimed from the sea, work was progressing on additional wharfage, part of an expansion plan to cope with a burgeoning traffic in forest products and fruit.

The miniature port of Nelson was extremely ambitious and what it lacked in mechanised sophistication was compensated for by graft and innovation. They were at it from the word go, as cases of apples and pears were winched on to the ship and thereon into the holds. Meanwhile, an armada of forklifts was transferring palletized goods from the cool stores as truckloads of produce were rolling into the port from the surrounding countryside. In the absence of adequate storage space this motorised conveyor was extremely effective, and loading continued until the street lamps twinkled in the twilight.

When Steve noted the wharfies' work rate he couldn't help but compare it with that of their British equivalents. He had to admit that those in London had seemed reasonably industrious; but he clearly remembered how on one occasion a procession of dockers, each wheeling a sack barrow laden with merchandise, had come to a halt while one of them retied a shoelace. None of those following made an effort to overtake and so keeping the cavalcade moving. Then there were the times when a queue of lorries at the dock gates was turned away in the late afternoon and told to return the following morning as work for the day was suspended; and it seemed that every other week a BBC news bulletin or newspaper article was reporting strike action at either Liverpool or London, seemingly for the most trivial of grievances. All this disruption was causing some shipowners to seek alternative wharfage, at some of the smaller ports such as Parkstone and Newhaven, where industrial relations were less volatile and deadlines more likely to be met. Superficially, and despite the frequent upheavals, it probably seemed to seaman and docker alike that the traditional seaports were perennial; but those with a crystal ball would know otherwise, and the omens were there for anyone able to recognize them.

Beyond the port the compact but delightful city of Nelson nestled agreeably beneath the surrounding mountains. On an overcast day the peaks would be obscured by cloud, but that seldom happened for Nelson enjoyed the enviable reputation of being the sunniest city in New Zealand. The climate was warm and the countryside fertile, ideal for the fruit-growing industry; so situated as it was at the head of Tasman Bay, with its glorious beaches and magnificent scenery, the setting was a pastoral Shangri-La.

With no passengers to cater for and most of the crew ashore from late afternoon onwards, the Chief Steward unexpectedly decreed that whenever they were in port, and provided a fair and workable shift system was adopted, the catering staff could have every other afternoon off. It was an arrangement that was to remain in place for as long as they were trading on the coast and was greeted with utter astonishment. It was so out of character that Peter just didn't believe it. 'Whatever's come over him?' he questioned, when Sec relayed the news over lunch. 'It didn't happen last trip - there must be a catch to it somewhere.'

'Not as far as I know,' replied Sec, who couldn't honestly provide a motive for the Boss's benevolence. 'You'll still be getting paid, so the only thing I can think of is that he's no intention of replacing Danny, and that this is some kind of recompense for the extra duties you've been landed with. That doesn't mean you'll be cutting corners in order to get the job done more quickly,' he cautioned. 'There'll still be inspection each morning, and if you slip up at your work you can kiss goodbye to your additional leisure time.' They all knew a gift horse when they saw it, and none of those present had the slightest intention of blowing it, each of them determined to toil that little bit harder in order to secure this unexpected windfall. In fact, the catering staff became the envy of the deck and engine room departments, none of whom enjoyed such generosity. The only supplementary idleness that they could look forward to was that that was taken unofficially - and ultimately paid for following the inevitable interview with the Captain.

Back in the mid-twentieth century New Zealand was deemed as being ultra-conservative, much as Britain had been thirty years earlier but even more neolithic in some ways. It allegedly closed at 6.00pm every weekday and didn't open at all on the Sabbath, and while that may have been a slight exaggeration it proved largely a matter of fact. Whatever, it was certainly true of the watering holes so any drinking had to be engaged in accordingly and forgotten altogether on Sundays.

Evenings ashore meant alternative sources of amusement, and this is where know-how was important. As Jimmy had conveyed back in London, the 'Kiwi' girls were easily attracted by young British seamen, especially those sporting the aforementioned Old Spice and Wranglers. Whether or not they were wearing the necessary attire and fragrance was never fully established, but several of the crew formed relationships with Nelson girls with some becoming seriously attached. It may have been pure coincidence but none of the women whom Steve came into contact with showed the slightest bit of interest in him. It may have had something to do with him wearing grey flannel trousers rather than the desired brand of denims and toiletry. On reflection he could have worn the black and white pin-striped jeans that he'd bought in a sale with money he'd been given for his birthday, but they remained on their hanger as despite their initial appeal, he now thought them overly flamboyant. Therefore, in the absence of female company he spent his evenings exploring, and finding his feet in the land known to the Maori as, Aotearoa - The Land of the Long White Cloud.

What he discovered was a utopian idyll, with a quality of life that no longer existed in urban areas of his own country. Devoid of haste and impatience, it reflected a contentment that more often than not could nowadays be found in only the more rural of British communities. It was a pleasure to just stroll through the streets, to be acknowledged politely, to be treated courteously and not be in fear of the traffic. That said, although the roads were virtually deserted almost every family had access to mechanised transport of some sort, notwithstanding that the handful of cars that were to be seen appeared dated. This was owing to newly-produced vehicles having to be imported at the buyers expense as there was no indigenous motor industry. It resulted in most models being of the second-hand variety, many of them Holdens that had been shipped across from Australia.

Television was for the most part non-existent, although it was in its infancy in the larger centres of population such as Wellington and Auckland. Nevertheless, this particular deficiency didn't seem to bother anyone with most people engineering their own amusement; maybe frequenting the cinema or practising what was rapidly becoming - at least in homes where there was a television set - the obsolete art of conversation. In a nutshell, the Dominion, with the exception of the obviously superior living standards and a more vigorous economy, was comparable with the 'Mother Country' of the '30s' - with the added advantage of the most comprehensive and longest established welfare state in the world.

Although New Zealand had adopted an assisted immigration policy similar to that of Australia, the Kiwis appeared more selective in their choice of invited guest than their neighbours, whose prime concern was that immigrants were healthy and industrious. New Zealand, by contrast, was looking for tradesmen whose skills could be tailored for the future, engineers especially being in great demand although those with experience in a wide range of occupations might also be considered for acceptance.

For Steve, the *Alice Springs'* sojourn in Nelson marked the beginning of an enduring love affair, not with any of the city's womenfolk but with this delightful country as a whole. He was wooed by the lack of urgency, the friendliness, the beautiful scenery, the crystal-clear air; and being slightly claustrophobic, the glorious wide open spaces. He was in his element, the only drawback being the archaic licensing laws; although a coded tap on a pub's back door would often be handsomely rewarded.

It goes without saying that the seafaring life by its very nature is impermanent. In this respect the *Alice Springs'* and her crew were typical and after seven days in Nelson their sojourn in port was complete. Romantic liaisons were victims of this transience, and although Steve hadn't formed any such relationship there were plenty of others who had. Jimmy, for instance, had become intimately involved with a hairdresser, and had expressed the desire of forsaking the *Alice Springs* and setting up home with his girlfriend. By taking such action he would effectively be jumping ship, or 'skinning out', to use the jargon of the mess-room. Despite Peter's thoughtless encouragement Steve had attempted to dissuade him, arguing that he'd probably end up being arrested and ultimately deported DBS (Distressed British Seaman), not to mention the associated penalties. However, the galley boy wasn't to be swayed and in the minutes leading up to their departure time, Jimmy was nowhere to be found.

Ted and Norman were furious. No spuds had been peeled for either lunch or dinner, the sink was overflowing and the galley rosie was humming like a municipal rubbish tip. 'I'll kill the little bastard when I get hold of him,' growled Ted, frustrated at having to rearrange the galley's working routine. 'He gets every other afternoon off and he still isn't satisfied.'

'If what the pantry boys tell me is anything to go by you'll be lucky to see him again,' offered Norman, taking hold of the rosie and heading for the galley exit. 'They reckon he's fallen in love and is staying behind with his sweetheart.'

'Hrrmph,' snorted Ted, who'd heard similar stories a thousand times. 'I'll believe it when it happens. I wouldn't mind betting he'll be back on board - if not before we leave Nelson then long before we sail from New Zealand.' Norman wondered if Ted was being over optimistic or if Jimmy was indeed gone for good. In the meantime he humped the rosie over the coaming and headed for the shore-side dump, while Davy and John began peeling a sack of potatoes.

Ted would never have claimed to be psychic but he had reams of experience; and sure enough, as sailing time arrived and the ship began moving, the cry went up, 'Hey! Here comes Jimmy.' Sure enough, as heads swivelled round and eyes became trained, there was Jimmy, tearing hell-for-leather along the dock road as if being chased by a lion.

In desperate situations a crew became a tightly-knit brotherhood, regardless of whether they were deck, engine room or catering. They could generally be relied upon to come to the aid of a shipmate in need and that's exactly what happened in Jimmy's case. By this stage of proceedings most of the mooring lines were free and were being reeled in by the winches. However, using commendable initiative, one of the winchmen, awake to the galley boy's predicament, ceased winding on his line, simultaneously calling for Jimmy to grab hold of the rope, place a foot in the loop and to hang on for all he was worth. Jimmy did precisely as bade and quickly became airborne. By this time the *Alice Springs* was several feet from the quayside and Jimmy hit the hull with a thud. It was a jarring impact, as if he'd been involved in a head-on collision with a truck, but he somehow clung on to the rope. The winding-in operation resumed, Jimmy was hauled over the rail; and with a hurried word of gratitude, and regardless of the fact he was dressed in his shore-going best, rushed into the galley and reclaimed the tasks he'd neglected.

Both Steve and Peter hurried in pursuit, but skidded to a halt on hearing Ted administering the riot act - the bollocking of a lifetime as Jimmy later described it. They thought better of hanging about, wary of Ted's disposition, considering it prudent to allow the atmosphere to cool, knowing they'd learn soon enough the reason for Jimmy's conversion.

'So, what caused you to change your mind?' asked Steve, when he and Peter at last had Jimmy to themselves.

'Silly bitch went and told her old man, didn't she?' replied the galley boy, who was peeling potatoes at such a rate of knots that there was a danger of his peeler overheating. 'Silly old duffer threatened to kill me if I didn't fuck off and stop playing around with his daughter.'

'At least you won't have to suffer the consequences if you've put her in the family way,' chirped Peter, accentuating the positives as always rather than sympathizing. 'By the time she finds out you'll be half way across the Pacific.'

'I wouldn't have minded,' replied Jimmy, wistfully, his thoughts drifting back to what might have been if she hadn't spilt the beans to her dad. 'She was an absolute cracker - a bit dippy, mind you, but it was as though we were made for each other. I reckon the two of us could have been really happy together.'

There followed a general discussion on the pros and cons, given similar situations, of whether jumping ship was a practical means of achieving one's objective. Each viewed the subject differently. As expected, Peter's response was rash and ill-considered; Steve thought it irresponsible, whatever the circumstances, preferring instead to proceed through recognized channels; while Jimmy deemed it worth chancing if the end justified the action and you didn't get caught and deported. Jimmy also disclosed that Ted's chastisement was his only punishment, and that he considered himself extremely fortunate in not ending up with a fine.

14

It was late in the day as the *Alice Springs* headed north from Nelson, towards the Marlborough Sounds and the myriad of islands that made this corner of New Zealand so exquisite. Later, under cover of darkness, she'd swing east - and then south, to navigate the stormy Cook Strait before passing down the Pacific coast of the South Island towards Lyttleton and the Banks Peninsular. The peninsular constitutes the northern extremity of the Canterbury Bight which extends all the way down to Dunedin over two hundred miles further south, and as its name suggests the waters of the bight lap the shores of the Canterbury Plains. Approximately ninety miles south of the Banks Peninsular, overlooking the delightfully-named Caroline Bay, the busy industrial town of Timaru sat amid undulating countryside that contrasted starkly with the surrounding flatlands. The timing couldn't have been better. The *Alice Springs* tied up on a Friday afternoon, and by seven o'clock was almost deserted as the crew piled ashore in their droves.

Protected from the Pacific swell by a pair of extended breakwaters, the artificial port of Timaru had been constructed in the 1870s following a series of shipwrecks on the foreshore. It comprised two separate piers, each capable of accommodating an ocean-going freighter on either face, while additional wharfage, including tanker-handling provision, was available along the inner walls of the breakwaters. As at Nelson the local fishing fleet was adequately catered for, as were those who exploited the waters for recreational pursuits.

In addition to being a prominent seaport Timaru had also evolved into a thriving holiday resort. Over the years, one of the safest beaches on the east coast of the South Island had formed against one of the breakwaters so in effect, creation of the port had served two purposes. With its backdrop of gently ascending cliffs the beach was highly popular with holidaymakers, as was the sound shell where open-air entertainment was provided on warm summer evenings and at weekends.

Following the initial exodus, Steve found himself waiting around for Jimmy Craddock, Peter having decided to 'go it alone' in the hope that by operating solo he'd click more easily with the females. From the courtship perspective Steve wasn't unduly worried. If it happened, it happened and if it didn't, it didn't, and there was always the cinema to fall back on. Anyway, Steve had got his hands full trying to convince Jimmy that moping about was pointless, and that he should pull himself together and accept that his love-affair with the hairdresser was over, a certainty her father had made sure of. In Steve's view the best thing Jimmy could do was to get out on the town and if nothing else, perhaps spend the evening at the pictures. Eventually Steve had prevailed, although Jimmy was far from persuaded.

It may have been early autumn but the evening was mild, and the boys were suitably attired as they ambled away from the harbour and across the Dunedin to Christchurch railway. In a rush of bravado Steve had finally opted for the black and white pin-striped jeans to complement his white shirt and slip-ons, while Jimmy, who was usually tastefully dressed, was more raggedly clothed in grubby dungarees, a faded blue T-shirt and plimsolls. Neither was wearing Old Spice. It was far too expensive for Steve's modest budget and Jimmy had clearly lost interest. 'Women are nothing but bloody trouble,' he'd grumbled, remembering how the *Alice Springs* had almost sailed without him, and his subsequent tongue-lashing. 'I'm going to forget about birds and stick to the beer from now on.' Steve was initially sceptical, but on noting his companion's scruffy appearance began wondering if the sentiment was real.

The sun, which in the southern hemisphere passes to the north as it crosses the heavens, had slipped beneath the horizon, leaving Timaru and its seafront bathed in artificial light which illuminated the cliff-tops and in some of the more exposed locations even filtered down to the beach. Waves could be heard beating on the sands; and even this late in the day youngsters were frolicking in the surf, their squeals of laughter echoing up through the darkness. The sounds of juvenile jollity reminded Steve of his own seaside summer holidays, and of the role they'd played in bringing him half way around the world to New Zealand. So much had happened in such a short space of time that it was difficult to accept that everything he'd seen and experienced since joining the *Vindicatrix* was indisputably real and not just an impossible dream. It seemed out of this world; and he was only jolted back to reality when he and Jimmy ventured out on the cliffs from where there was a bird's-eye view of the port.

If Steve was honest he'll have admitted that it wasn't so much the sight of the floodlit *Alice Springs* that had broken his reverie as that of two pretty girls, eating fish and chip suppers while occupying a bench on the cliff-top. Dressed in high-heeled shoes, pretty summer frocks and cardigans, they were obviously aware of a presence for after glancing coyly over their shoulders they giggled and carried on eating, concentrating on some fantasy landmark as if Steve and Jimmy were transparent. Jimmy had also become galvanized, the Nelson hairdresser completely forgotten - as was the sweeping indictment that girls were more trouble than they were worth.

The reaction from the bench had been encouraging, but in the absence of any ready-prepared approach strategy the boys' response was unpolished. After mumbling between themselves, something along the lines of, 'Shall we? - Shan't we?' they sauntered over and without a hint of subtlety, Steve blurted, 'Hi! I'm Steve and this is Jimmy. Is there room on the bench for us?'

Jimmy rolled his eyes in despair, believing the introduction would have been better handled had it been left in his more capable hands. But Steve was a good-looking lad, and what he lacked in tact was more than compensated for by charm. After faking initial surprise the girls reciprocated, creating space on the bench and inviting the boys to sit down. It transpired that their names were Maxine and Claire, Maxine coming from a nearby township while her cousin, Claire, was on holiday from her home in the North Island. Maxine, bespectacled with shoulder-length brown hair was slightly shorter and thicker set than her brunette cousin who was willowy and tall and carried her plastered right arm in a sling. 'What happened to you,

177

then?' asked Jimmy, sitting himself down, clearly showing a preference for the slimmer of the two girls.

'Oh! Nothing much,' answered the raven-haired Claire, who'd clearly taken a shine to Jimmy despite his vagabond appearance. 'I fell off my horse and busted my collar bone. It happened last month so it ought to be just about mended.'

Steve had never understood the old adage that, 'Men seldom make passes at girls who wear glasses', since he'd frequently found bespectacled women extremely attractive - and Maxine was far and away the most fetching he'd ever set eyes on. It seemed the consummate pairing, for Steve and Maxine appeared drawn to each other as if by some magical lodestone, as if the meeting had been preordained and that their destinies were inexorably bound. The fact that Steve was wearing his own glasses didn't immediately register, but may also have helped seal the bond.

They soon became intricately involved, getting to know each other and bringing to light their respective backgrounds. Maxine, it emerged, came from the country town of Manoao, about six miles north of Timaru, where among other things her family were the proprietors of a general store, her father also being an accomplished motor mechanic whose services were widely sought after. Along with her parents there was a kid sister called Holly who, like younger siblings everywhere, was tolerated rather than cherished. Steve told Maxine about his own home, about his parents and brother and about England in general. He pointed out his ship in the harbour and spoke of his fledgling career as a seafarer; and she confided how she longed to sail away, to all the wonderful places that Steve had talked about, along with others besides.

So engrossed were they - not only in conversation but with each other - that the evening evaporated, and it was only when Claire interrupted to say that she and Maxine ought to be moving in order to catch the last bus that they realized their hands were entwined. Steve let Maxine's hand slip; but as they made their way to the bus station Maxine slid her arm through his, suggesting they meet again the following evening at the bench overlooking the bay. Steve was exultant. There was a warmth to this girl which radiated to his very innards, and although he made no attempt at kissing her he readily agreed to the rendezvous. With the bus waiting to leave the girls climbed aboard, and waved happily from a window as it growled on to the highway and roared away into the night, the sound of its engine clearly audible long after its tail lights had vanished.

Strangely enough, Steve had developed an appetite for a fish and chip supper, even though he'd always considered the fish and chip shop to be uniquely British, a corner-shop preserve that wasn't to be found in the world's wider reaches. However, that clearly wasn't the case and as they followed their noses the mouth-watering aroma of frying fish and potatoes became ever more tantalizing, until they rounded a corner and there stood the hallowed establishment, lights ablaze with a queue forming outside the door. The boys soon discovered that the ordering and serving of fish and chips in New Zealand was markedly different to that with which they were accustomed, for although the chips were identical the fish were alien, with a portion comprising several small fillets. However, it wasn't so much the composition of their meal that caught their attention as the delivery, for rather than being shovelled on to a sheet of greaseproof and bundled in grubby newsprint it was neatly parcelled in snow-white wrapping paper, an embarrassing testament to British shortcomings when it came to presentation and hygiene.

During the days that followed Steve and Maxine became all but inseparable, idling away their time either on the beach, in coffee bars or at the cinema; but the pinnacle of their association - as it had thus far escalated - came when Maxine invited Steve and Jimmy to dinner, to meet her family and to sample Manoao hospitality. They arranged a date, and straight after lunch on the appointed afternoon Steve headed off for the bus station, brimming with the joys that had so enriched his being since that initial ham-fisted encounter. The feeling was sublime, as the relationship between he and Maxine had by this time exceeded friendship, was verging on devotion and veering towards something more intimate.

Unfortunately, Jimmy had to work, the other galley staff refusing to cover in retribution for his misdeed in Nelson. He knew he had only himself to blame, so he'd make his own way to Manoao as his situation dictated. Meanwhile Steve hurried on, totally ignoring Andrew Weir's *Cedarbank* and Federal's *Essex*, both of which occupied neighbouring quaysides. His thoughts were firmly focussed on Manoao, the general store and a girl who lived there with her family.

Being early afternoon the bus was only lightly loaded, so after paying his fare Steve chose a seat near the front with an unrestricted view of the road. At two o'clock precisely the driver engaged gear and placed his foot on the accelerator, taking them clear of the town and on to the expanse of the Canterbury Plains. The road was of only a single carriageway but was as straight as a die and seldom deviated from the linear. He concluded that this uniformity was the probable reason why he found the journey disappointingly dull, with no significant landmarks, although he was amazed at the dearth of traffic on what was the South Island's principal highway. Apart from the occasional jalopy rattling in the opposite direction the road was empty, with not so much as a cyclist to break the monotony. Back in the United Kingdom the roads were becoming increasingly clogged with all manner of traffic, including an increasing number of goods vehicles, a problem that almost everyone complained of but one that politicians routinely ignored.

Every so often they crossed a stream or river, carrying the melt-waters from the Southern Alps that on the clearest of days could be discerned away to the west but which today were hidden by haze. Intermittently the otherwise featureless landscape was punctuated by a remote homestead, linked to the road by an unsealed track at the entrance to which stood a mailbox on a post, evidence that somewhere out in the wilds lived a family like Steve's, but with a conspicuously alternative life-style.

Twenty minutes after leaving Timaru the bus ran into the scattered outskirts of Manoao, and shortly thereafter deposited its sprinkling of passengers. Even at this hour of the afternoon the town seemed deserted, as if the population had suddenly upped-sticks and absconded. It was as well that Maxine had given him directions as there was no-one to ask and he would have been lost if he hadn't been pre-advised. After taking his bearings he was reasonably sure of his whereabouts so he began walking, as certain as he could be that his orientation was correct. However, it always pays to play safe, and when he spotted an elderly fellow lounging on the veranda of what proclaimed to be the 'Shearers Hotel' he enquired as to the store's location. The man beckoned him into the street, his extended left arm and forefinger making a passable imitation of a signpost. 'See that sycamore tree about a hundred yards away, right on the edge of the pavement? Well, the store you're looking for is just beyond that. You can't miss it - not with all those old motor cars dumped outside.' Steve remembered how Maxine's dad was something of a nifty mechanic, so after offering his thanks he carried on walking, now confident of the store's proximity.

As Steve neared the sycamore tree he was suddenly aware of his earlier self-assurance being steadily eroded, eaten away by something he hadn't previously considered. Maxine had told him virtually everything there was to know about her family; but that wasn't quite the same as him actually knowing them, and he found the prospect more daunting than he'd imagined. He wondered how he'd be received, and how her parents would react to their daughter becoming involved with that most unreliable specimen of humanity, a seaman. He could scarcely complain if they objected for when all was said and done, his occupation was nomadic, and the last thing they'd want would be for her feelings to be hurt, or her reputation to be irreparably damaged.

Passing the sycamore tree the store wasn't immediately obvious; but suddenly there it was, of timber construction and of a single storey, standing back from the street with a Studebaker, a couple of old Fords and a Holden laying out front, in various stages of repair. Steve stopped, smoothed his hair while straightening his tie, and drew himself up to full height. He'd made an effort, opting for a collar and tie to accompany his black and white pin-striped jeans. He'd done his best - it now rested in the lap of the gods.

In the event his fears proved groundless. As he entered the store he was greeted by Maxine who ushered him through to the living quarters where he was introduced to her parents, a cheerful couple who welcomed him as a friend and not as an absolute stranger. They insisted he call them by their Christian names rather than Mr and Mrs, Frank and Margaret sounding far less formal and stuffy. They offered him tea while asking about he and his family, without once referring to the relationship between himself and Maxine. He relaxed, sipping his tea as the conversation flowed, confident of the impression he'd created. They made no mention of his calling's unpredictable nature so were perhaps unaware of just how close the ties between he and Maxine had become. Whatever, he accepted the situation as it was, grateful for the kindly reception and determined to make the most of what was a potentially memorable occasion. After an initial, 'Hello,' Claire was content with her own company until Jimmy's arrival; and of Maxine's kid sister, Holly, there wasn't so much as a murmur, suggesting the rapport between she and Maxine wasn't quite as fraught as he'd imagined - or that she wasn't yet home from school.

The inaugural pleasantries over, Maxine took Steve on a guided tour of Manoao, arms interlinked and heads together, totally wrapped-up in each other. He discovered that it wasn't a ghost town after all, meeting several of Maxine's friends and acquaintances, nearly all of whom greeted Steve as if he was a film star. Maxine had to explain that very few foreigners ever visited the more rural parts of New Zealand, and that black and white pin-striped jeans along with stylish slip-on shoes were even more of a rarity; that's why he was being lauded as a celebrity rather than a seaman. They stepped into an ice-cream parlour and bought cornets before dallying in a park, giggling and furiously licking their ice-cream before it melted. And then, Steve suddenly noticed that Maxine had fallen silent and that her expression had darkened. 'What's the matter?' he enquired, concerned in case he'd spoken out of turn.

'Oh! Nothing much,' she answered, turning towards Steve and kissing him lightly on the lips, her frown being replaced by a smile. 'Probably just the thought that by the time we get back Holly'll be home. Nothing that I can't handle.'

'That's not all though, is it?' answered Steve, stopping and staring at Maxine. 'Come on, out with it, what's really bothering you?'

She suddenly burst into tears, sobbing, 'You'll be leaving on Saturday and I might never see you again.'

Steve felt his own eyes moisten. It was something he too had been fretting over but had pushed to the back of his mind. Now it was out in the open and there was no point hiding his feelings. 'I know,' he gushed, sweeping Maxine into his arms. 'It's been worrying me too. But then I thought, these ships are out here every few months so perhaps I'll be back again by the spring - and anyway, we can always write to each other in the meantime.' He had to concede that his words sounded hollow, and would be of little comfort to Maxine who was dabbing at her eyes with his handkerchief; but he didn't know what else to say. After allowing Maxine a moment to compose herself they headed unhurriedly back to the store, Steve adding, trying to sound cheerful, 'Anyway, we've still got another three days together so let's make the most of them and who knows, something might turn up.' Maxine lifted her eyes and managed another limp smile; but Steve was only too aware that she wasn't convinced by his forced optimism and to be truthful, neither was he.

As Maxine had predicted, by the time they arrived back at the store Holly was home - and what a right little madam was she. Wherever Maxine and Steve went Holly went too, depriving them of their valuable privacy. She trailed them indoors and out, despite Maxine's pleas that she go play with her friends or listen to her records in her bedroom. Eventually, Steve's patience snapped; and although it wasn't his place to do so he turned on Holly, telling her to make herself scarce or he'd give her backside a good tanning. Holly reacted like a vixen. 'Who the hell do you think you're talking to?' she rasped, raising two fingers and looking Steve straight in the eye. 'If you're not bloody careful I'll bloody-well ruin your future.' She then turned and stomped off, on to the forecourt where some of her playmates were waiting.

'Sorry about that,' apologised Maxine, who was clearly embarrassed by her sister's outburst. 'But she's been a handful since she was knee high to a possum, and she's only twelve years old now.'

As Maxine had hinted, there was nothing refined about Holly who had a tongue like a whip and could use it with devastating cruelty. But Steve's rebuke had hit home and henceforth, except while they were at dinner, the odious kid sister was generally nowhere to be seen.

Claire's afternoon was completed when Jimmy turned up at around five, sooner than expected as he shouldn't have been finished until six. 'How did you fiddle that?' asked Steve, as Jimmy took his place at the dining table, between Holly and Claire while Maxine and

Margaret served dinner.

'Easy,' replied Jimmy, unfurling a paper serviette and tucking it untidily into his collar. 'Ted got so cheesed-off with me mooching about that he told me to clear off and that he'd finish the strap-up and scrub-out.'

The meal was eaten in light-hearted fashion, with Steve and Jimmy relating tales from home and about the *Alice Springs*, whilst the boys were regaled with stories of life in Manoao, and how Maxine's family came to be in New Zealand in the first place. It emerged that Margaret was a fourth-generation Kiwi, one set of her great-grandparents being known to have arrived aboard a sailing ship in the late 1870's, the voyage from south Wales having taken more than four months to complete. They'd originally settled in the North Island, in the countryside around New Plymouth where they'd raised sheep and cattle. They'd moved south to take advantage of the latter stages of the South Island gold rush, around the Clutha River, but when the gold fizzled out they'd taken root in Manoao, establishing the store that Frank and Margaret now ran. Frank's lineage was more straightforward. He was a descendant of a British military family that had stayed on following the earliest days of colonization. He'd met Margaret while working on a nearby farm and they'd married in the late nineteen-thirties. He'd learnt his trade as a mechanic while serving in the New Zealand army; had been wounded whilst fighting at Tobruk; had been repatriated and now here they all were, the family having apparently prospered in their forebears' adopted country.

With dinner out of the way Steve and Jimmy offered to wash up but their offer was politely declined. 'There's no need,' answered Maxine, pointing to a pair of stainless-steel sinks, both full to the brim, one with steaming hot water the other with soapsuds and china. 'We just rinse everything off, load it into this basket and then dunk it in the sink of hot water. It'll be sparkling clean and dry as a bone in a jiffy.' The British Merchant Navy prided itself in standards of cleanliness and hygiene that were supposedly second to none, but Steve had never seen anything like this. It certainly set him thinking about their own practices, and although they didn't have two sinks at their disposal they could at least change the water more often. It was something he'd have to remember whenever he saw grease on the soapsuds.

Claire and Jimmy were soon conspicuously absent, probably seeking their own solitude, whilst Steve and Maxine took a stroll in the meadow-like garden - but only after Maxine had skipped round to the front of the store and grabbed a blanket from the rear of the Studebaker. At the lower end of the garden, which was at least fifty yards long and dotted with shrubbery, ran a fast-flowing stream, the entire area bounded by tall waving trees which rustled in the warm evening breeze. Once again it was uncharacteristically mild; but it was early yet and Maxine carried her ubiquitous cardigan, in case it was cool later on. The moon hadn't yet risen, but there was just enough light for them to pick their way down to stream where they spread the blanket, beneath the trees and in a handily-placed thicket of undergrowth.

Romantic eloquence and Steve made uncomfortable bed-fellows, but with Maxine it was different and telling her how much he loved her came as simply as reciting his tables, although it was said with tenderness and affection. They embraced, whispering sweet nothings, their voices barely audible as the breeze stirred the trees and the stream babbled playfully past. It felt suddenly cool, causing them to instinctively snuggle closer together. The effect was electrifying, as if a switch had been thrown, their bodies reacting and their desire for each other becoming irresistible. They needed no prompting; it seemed perfectly natural and before they knew it their limbs were entwined and in blissful fulfilment they crossed that magical threshold between teenage innocence and adulthood, a milestone in the odyssey of life. It had been remarkable, not only for its spontaneity but also its brevity - although neither of them cared about that. They kissed passionately, hugging each other, exhausted and perspiring but laughing with joy and excitement. Steve had hoped it would happen and he suspected that Maxine had planned it from the very beginning. If that was the case he was thankful for he'd have never had the courage to have forced the issue for himself. Eventually, her breathing having resumed its normal smooth rhythm, Maxine whispered, 'That was my first time, Steve. You know that, don't you?'

185

Steve had wondered but it didn't really matter. The important thing was that she'd chosen to do it with him. He nuzzled closer, burying his face in her hair. 'Mine too,' he murmured. 'Mine too.'

'Come on,' said Maxine, at length, pushing herself up on an elbow and scanning the near-by shrubbery. 'We'd better get back before Mum and Dad get suspicious - and just in case that bloody sister of mine is lurking out there in the bushes.' Steve had never previously heard Maxine swear, but he knew very well what she meant. They stood and straightened their clothes, laughing nervously like kids who'd narrowly escaped being caught while stealing from a sweet jar. Maxine slipped her cardigan over her shoulders while Steve folded the blanket and held it in the crook of his arm. Then, hand in hand they ambled slowly back to the store, trying their best to appear natural, as if they'd merely been out for a stroll. They disposed of the blanket in the Studebaker; and then, drawing deep breaths they passed through the lobby and into the warmth of the sitting room where Frank and Margaret sat reading.

'Hello,' said Maxine, nonchalantly, removing her cardigan and draping it over a chair while Steve perched on the sofa and began flicking through the pages of a magazine. 'It's beginning to feel nippy out there so we thought we'd better come in.'

'I'll make some cocoa,' offered Margaret, rising to her feet and sidling out of the sitting room. 'It'll warm you up - and I don't suppose the other two will say no to a cup either. Have you any idea where they've got to?'

'Haven't a clue,' replied Maxine, joining her mother in the kitchen. 'They went off on their own earlier on.'

Then, as if on cue, voices could be heard in the lobby and in walked Jimmy and Claire. 'Hello there, you two,' said Steve, glancing up and laying his magazine on the coffee table. 'Been anywhere special?'

'Not really,' replied Jimmy, taking a seat next to Steve while Claire went off to the bathroom. 'Mostly wandering around town - we must have covered every inch of Manoao. 'How about you?' he added, turning and staring at Steve.

'Oh! Nothing much,' answered Steve, striving to sound casual while trying desperately to avoid Jimmy's gaze. 'Just been loafing in the garden.' Steve missed the gleam in Jimmy's eye but was beginning to feel decidedly uneasy; but that was before salvation arrived from a totally unexpected quarter.

'Either of you two go angling?' asked Frank, removing his spectacles and laying his newspaper in a rack. 'The trout and salmon fishing around here is superb.'

'N-n-never,' stuttered Steve, grateful for the change of subject. 'I've never held a fishing rod in my life.'

'The only fishing that I've ever done is from the beach at Ardrossan in Ayrshire,' answered Jimmy, recalling his childhood in Glasgow. 'We used to take day-trips down the Clyde, and me and my mates had these hand-held lines that we baited and threw into the sea. I can't remember catching anything, though.'

'Pity about that,' said Frank, sounding mildly disappointed that neither of his guests appeared the least bit interested in his favourite pastime. 'But if you ever come this way again remind me to take you angling. I can guarantee you some of the finest fish in New Zealand.'

'Cocoa's up,' announced Maxine, entering the room and placing a tray holding half-a-dozen mugs of the steaming beverage on the coffee table. 'Sugar's in the basin if you want it.' Maxine had already taken a mug of cocoa to Holly's room where her sister lay reading, and where she'd hopefully remain until bedtime.

Perversely, Steve's first thought on seeing the cocoa was of the thick, brown liquid dished up at supper time back at the Vindi. In view of the evening's events he found the analogy amusing. He glanced up at Maxine who was lazily stirring sugar into her cocoa, miles away and clearly in a world of her own. She looked positively radiant. Her eyes were sparkling and her cheeks bloomed like roses in spring. He loved her dearly and he knew without doubt she loved him - and he also knew that this particular mug of cocoa hadn't been laced with bromide.

Jimmy glanced down at his watch, clearly concerned at the time. 'You know, we'd better get moving. Any idea what time the last bus goes?' he asked of no-one in particular.

'That went ages ago,' said Margaret, handing round a plateful of ginger biscuits. 'But don't worry. Frank said he'd run you back in the van when you're ready.' Steve could have happily stayed where he was, but agreed with Jimmy that they ought to be making a move, especially now that Frank had offered them a lift, and that it would be almost midnight before he was back in Manoao.

The 'van' turned out to be not so much a commercial runabout as some fantastic fairy-tale charabanc that served as the family's conveyance. It was an old pre-war Morris that Frank had lovingly rebuilt using salvaged spare parts and others that he'd made up from scratch. Steve had never ridden in anything quite so eccentric, nor so expertly engineered. The motor had been reconditioned; a four-speed gearbox had replaced the earlier more primitive three-speed version; and thanks to a self-devised system of pneumatic suspension the unlikely concoction ran as smoothly as a brand new Rolls-Royce. To complete the ensemble seats had been fitted throughout, creating a sort of windowless omnibus that from the exterior looked just like the original. It was the product of an ingenious mind, and as Frank's virtually home-made prodigy pulled on to the highway, with its creator and Margaret in the front and the teenagers canoodling in the back, Steve couldn't help thinking that as the proprietor of a general store his talents were criminally wasted.

It had probably been the happiest day of Steve's life - Maxine's too come to that, but as it drew to a close the earlier ecstasy had given way to a hollowness with which Steve was too readily familiar. He was experiencing that dreadful sensation he'd invariably felt as a child, when the holidays were at an end and it was time to pack up and go home. He'd always been reluctant to leave the seaside - and he didn't want to leave Maxine now. He recalled how the *Alice Springs* had broken down in the middle of the Indian Ocean, and he hoped desperately that some other calamity would befall her before Saturday; maybe an electrical fault or a propulsion defect, it didn't matter what so long as it prevented them sailing. He knew that such an event was unlikely, but by a strange coincidence he was beginning to think the unthinkable. An embryonic brainwave was gradually taking shape in his mind, and although he wouldn't yet mention it to Maxine he was coming to the conclusion that it was the only practical solution.

By comparison with seaports in Britain, where it was virtually impossible to gain unauthorised access to the quaysides, it seemed that here in New Zealand it was open house where no-one gave a fig who you were. And so it was that Frank was able to steer his van across the railway tracks and on to the brightly-lit wharf, to the very foot of the *Alice Springs'* accommodation ladder, with no-one to question his motives.

The youngsters tumbled out through the back while Margaret and Frank remained seated, Frank keeping the engine ticking over as Steve sauntered round to the front. Margaret opened the passenger window and Steve thanked them both for their kindness, expressing the hope that it wouldn't be too long before he was back in Manoao. Unexpectedly, Margaret leaned out and gave him a 'peck' on the cheek while Frank stretched across, offering his hand, proof that in their eyes at least that Steve was a jolly good sport. How, he wondered, might they have reacted if they'd known of the fireworks that had taken place in their garden only a few hours earlier? He turned and took hold of Maxine, holding her tightly, feeling her warmth and response. They kissed tenderly before Maxine disentangled herself, saying, 'We'd better be off - Holly's at home on her own. See you on the cliff-top tomorrow.' She stroked Steve's face as she climbed into the van and seemed about to speak but didn't say anything. She didn't have to - her eyes said it for her. Frank revved the engine and the Morris moved off, the girls waving frantically until they were way out of sight.

The boys stood staring, long after the van had disappeared, leaving only the hum of the auxiliaries on the nearby ships to punctuate the silence. Eventually, they turned and faced one another; and with his eyes glinting, Jimmy demanded. 'You did, didn't you?'

Steve feigned puzzlement. 'Did what?' he replied, stepping on the platform at the foot of the accommodation ladder and taking a hold of the side ropes.

'You know, you and Maxine,' pressed Jimmy, suggesting he wouldn't take 'no' for an answer. 'You did, didn't you?

'None of your business, Matey,' defended Steve, fondly remembering the earlier delights as he took the ladder three steps at a time. 'None of your bloody business.'

As always on entering the accommodation, Steve became instantly aware of that mysterious smell that seemed to permeate almost every area of their living quarters. He'd initially noticed it on his very first morning on board. It could hardly be described as a fragrance although it was far from unpleasant and had a comfortable shipboard redolence. Its origins had proved an enigma, the nearest and most plausible cause having been suggested by Archie. He'd identified it as a cocktail of engine oil, cleaning materials and food; although he'd hastened to add that for whatever reason, the odour was peculiar to cargo ships.

What was also becoming familiar was the impression that half the female population of Canterbury was treating the *Alice Springs* as a lodging house. A number of cabins were out of bounds to their rightful occupants, other crew members having claimed them in order that they and their girlfriends could enjoy their lovemaking in private. However, such niceties weren't always observed, with some rooms being occupied by two or maybe three couples whose activities could only be guessed at.

Thankfully, Peter had remembered to lock up before going ashore and Steve's key turned in the lock. Not so fortunate was Jimmy whose door had been locked from inside. 'Fuckin' Peggy,' cursed Jimmy, aiming a kick at his cabin door. 'He's either forgotten to lock up and someone else is using it, or he's in there with a bird and doesn't want anyone disturbing them.'

Jimmy received his answer almost immediately, in the form of a shouted, 'Fuck off,' followed by muffled laughter and giggling.

'That's fuckin' Peggy in there - the bastard. I'll give him fuck off,' swore Jimmy, aiming another hefty swing at the door, 'I'll murder him when I get hold of him.'

Steve took the view that murder wouldn't provide an immediate answer to Jimmy's predicament, and proposed that the galley boy temper his feelings and sleep on the small settee in his own cabin, leaving his differences with Peggy until morning. As things were, Jimmy was unwittingly playing the part of Jack Lemon in that wonderfully frustrating movie, 'The Apartment', but instead of walking the pavements in the rain, waiting for his flat to become vacant, Jimmy would be pacing the alleyways, with little chance of reprisal until dawn.

Steve could see the real picture now, why New Zealand was such a popular destination among British seaman; and he knew exactly what Peter had meant, when he'd said, "You'll find out when you get there". It wasn't so much the beautiful scenery and wide-open spaces that were the attraction - although they certainly played their part - as the 'comforts' afforded by a certain faction of the female population, and none of them had to be paid for.

With an ever-growing number of these women actually living on board he wondered if they enjoyed any sort of a home life, or if they had any homes to go to. It may have been that they hadn't, as in some instances they actually hung around on the quaysides awaiting an incoming ship - any ship - and generally speaking they didn't have too long to wait. Once they were on board there were some amusing instances, such as a deckie here or a fireman there, sidling up to the galley or pantry, and whispering, 'Is there any spare grub for my girlfriend?'

The following morning Steve was awakened by the strains of a bugle call, and for an awful instant he imagined himself back at the Vindi as reveille was sounded by the bugler. He propped himself up on an elbow and peered over his bunkboard. Peter's bunk hadn't been slept in and Jimmy was snoring his head off, blissfully undisturbed by the din. The mystery of the bugle call was speedily resolved by a glance through the open porthole, for there at an adjacent wharf, having arrived overnight, lay the New Zealand Shipping Company's cadet training-vessel *Otaio*, a ten-and-a-half-thousand-ton cargo liner that doubled as a seagoing college. The company's deck and engine-room apprentices were being rudely awakened from their slumbers, and the bugler had ensured that everyone else sleeping within ear-shot was also wakefully aroused.

Much of the cargo loaded at Timaru arrived at the port by rail, hauled by impressive steam locomotives with melodious chime whistles that echoed across town and sent Steve into raptures of joy. He'd seen pictures of the machines on previous occasions, most improbably on Will's cigarette cards; but these were the 'beasts in the flesh', close enough to touch and to feel the warmth of their breath. The cargo they transported was typical of the era and comprised meat, dairy produce and animal by-products, mainly from the surrounding countryside. More of the same plus a variety of fruit

191

awaited the *Alice Springs* up in Napier, the ultimate port on her visit to New Zealand, where she'd remain for close on a month.

Over breakfast, Peter could hardly stop talking, salivating over a misspent night aboard Shaw-Savill's *Doric*, where a party had been raging, until the *Otaio's* bugler had reminded the revellers that there was work to be done and that life on the New Zealand coast did have the occasional down side. It emerged that he'd spent the early part of the evening in his own cabin, with an absolute 'dazzler' before the pair of them had left for the *Doric*. 'Only seventeen, she was,' enthused Peter, as he swept up the remnants of a carelessly dropped saucer. 'And talk about firing on all cylinders - I was just about knackered by midnight. Still, never mind. We're going back again tonight, 'cos someone's organizing another party. I'll be well and truly buggered by tomorrow.'

'Mucky little tyke,' interrupted Archie, who'd been listening to Peter's comments with an ill-concealed air of distaste. 'You'll end up with a dose before this trip's over, you see if you don't - and don't say you haven't been warned.'

'Well, it's better than shaggin' arse,' countered Peter, crudely, instinctively ducking to avoid the anticipated backhander. 'There's nothing more disgusting than that.'

However, Archie refused to be baited. His homosexuality may have been an open secret but he didn't flaunt it and as far as most people knew he was the only homosexual on board. 'Well, it's your funeral, not mine,' he answered, resignedly, knowing that trying to re-edify Peter was pointless. 'At least I stick to the same partners, not like you and some other blokes, messing around with all those different women. It's no wonder the Albert Dock Hospital does a roaring trade in penicillin injections.'

Peter had no regard for what he considered the bedroom steward's hypocrisy, simply pulling a face behind Archie's back and neatly switching the subject. 'I noticed the peggy had a fat lip when I collected the stores this morning. I wonder what he did to earn that?' Steve knew very well how the peggy had earnt his fat lip, and it seemed that Jimmy had been as good as his word.

Over the ensuing three days Steve's rationality was seriously challenged as he pondered the options available. To be honest, they were paltry at best. He didn't want to leave Timaru - and by definition, Maxine - but what alternatives were there short of jumping ship and hiding out, hoping he wouldn't be discovered? What a difference a week makes, he thought, remembering Jimmy's tribulations in Nelson, where the galley boy had all but skinned out and probably would have done if it hadn't been for the hairdresser's father. Unbelievably, Steve had been considering this very same stunt in the back of Frank's van on the evening of his trip to Manoao, regardless of the fact that only seven days earlier he'd considered such action irresponsible. He belatedly mentioned it to Maxine who despite her innermost yearnings was more level headed.

'You can't,' she said, as they exchanged photographs on the Friday evening, prior to the *Alice Springs'* departure. 'I'd love you to be able to stay but where would you live? If Mum and Dad were to put you up at our place and the law got wind of it we'd all be in trouble, you for deserting your ship and us for harbouring an illegal immigrant. No! We'll just have to accept things as they are and hope things work out for the best. As you say, you might easily be back here by springtime. Of course,' she continued, holding Steve's hand and looking him squarely in the eye, 'You could always emigrate and make things legal. It'll probably take ages but it'll be worth the wait in the long run.'

It was such a simple remedy that Steve was left wondering why he hadn't thought of it in the first place. 'Your right!' he exclaimed, sitting bolt upright, and instantly brightening at the prospect of becoming a legitimate immigrant. 'I can set the ball rolling as soon as we get home - and you never know, I might even qualify for an assisted passage. Maxine, you're a marvel - why didn't I think of that?'

'Because you're a man,' she replied, teasingly, holding Steve's hands and kissing him gently on the forehead. They always go off half-cocked without thinking things through. 'I'll miss you in the meantime, though, she whispered, snuggling closer to Steve who was already racking his brains as to which of London's underground stations was closest to the New Zealand High Commission. 'But I can wait if you can.'

15

As the *Alice Springs* prepared for sea on Saturday morning Steve felt decidedly less gloomy, owing to the flourishing ambition to emigrate and become a New Zealand national. He'd completely ditched the idea of jumping ship as after a fitful night's sleep he now fully accepted that Maxine's was a common-sense solution. It wouldn't be fair to embroil her family, and the chances of him evading the law and avoiding deportation were slim. He'd heard of some who'd succeeded, had wrong-footed the police, found employment and accommodation and eventually settled in this glorious country; but there were plenty who hadn't, had spent time in jail and had been repatriated DBS. Much as he adored Maxine, and would have remained in Timaru at the drop of a hat given official sanction, he'd become resigned to a lengthy migration process that if all went according to plan would ultimately yield its rewards.

Maxine had made up her mind that she wouldn't be at the port to see Steve off and had said so the previous evening; not because she didn't want to be there, but because she was afraid that if she broke down in tears he might forget everything they'd spoken of and do something utterly stupid. For want of a better alternative she'd busy herself at home, helping her mum while awaiting a phone call from Napier.

Nevertheless, a sizeable crowd had gathered, the majority of them girls, some of whom, in light of the *Alice Springs'* departure, were now temporarily homeless. There must have been at least twenty of them, some sobbing their hearts out while others showed obvious restraint. Whatever, most of them were waving and shouting as the ship slipped her moorings. Peter's 'dazzler' was there, kicking up a racket along with the rest of them while Peter waved morosely from the porthole. From Steve's point of view the scene on the quayside had all the ingredients of a best-selling romance, of lovers being permanently separated. But in light of the girls' promiscuity he couldn't help wondering just how much of this outpouring was sham and how much was truly sincere, an ambivalence propagated as they cleared the breakwaters and passed the inbound *Papanui*, which would be occupying the berth the *Alice Springs* had only recently vacated.

That evening there was a terrific slanging match between Donald Dunne and the Chief Steward, concerning alleged misconduct by the Ulsterman. As was often the case the argument revolved around drink. It didn't help that the Chief and Donald were incompatible, the former being resolutely abstinent while Donald was a thorough-going soak. It was a ding-dong of a squabble although the outcome was never in doubt. In the event, Donald hadn't a leg to stand on seeing that he'd spent the previous day's lunchtime in the bar of the Royal Hotel instead of waiting at table as he should have. He was ultimately logged, had to forfeit half a day's pay for the time not worked and was fined a day's pay for the crime.

The run up to Napier on the east coast of the North Island took longer than Steve had expected, and it was Monday morning before the *Alice Springs* tied up in the company of Shaw-Savill's *Canopic*, and Port Line's *Port Montreal* which had recently arrived from Japan. Steve had worked through the weekend in a daze, his mind set on nothing but Maxine, and he was eagerly awaiting the installation of the telephone so that he could speak with the girl in Manoao.

Napier's modern and well-equipped port was the product of a ruinous earthquake that in 1931 had destroyed much of Hawke's Bay and its hinterland. The city itself had been devastated, not only by the quake but also by the ensuing conflagration. Casualties had been high with over two-hundred and fifty fatalities; but given the scale of destruction it was perhaps surprising that the death toll hadn't been exceeded. With the rubble removed and the infrastructure restored, the city had been rebuilt in the Art Deco style of the times but with a restriction on the number of storeys, a sensible precaution given the area's unstable geology. The concept was captivating, so that in harmony with the small number of second-hand vehicles on the streets the place had the feel of the 'Thirties'.

Perversely, the upheaval had created a ready-made harbour where previously none had existed. In layout it was similar to that at Timaru, its wharves being protected from the worst of the swell by a curving breakwater. Even so, with the wind in the east and a sea running, every vessel alongside had to slip its moorings and head for the anchorage until the waves subsided, avoiding damage to both ships and quaysides.

After what seemed an age the phone was connected and Steve hurried along to ring Maxine. He wasn't the first in the queue as the Lamp-trimmer had beaten him to it. The petty officer was also ringing a girlfriend, to inform her that he was back in Napier after a six-month absence and ready to take up the reins. As Steve waited patiently it became patently clear that not all was as Lampy had wished. After a heated exchange he slammed down the receiver, complaining, 'Fuckin' women - they ain't worth a candle. She's only been an' married a fuckin' sheep-shearer from Rotorua, ain't she?' As the Lamp-trimmer stomped moodily off, muttering something about there being plenty more where she came from, Steve smiled and picked up the receiver, asking the operator to connect him to the number printed on a carefully-folded slip of notepaper.

In a way it was a wasted call for Margaret answered the phone, explaining that Maxine and Frank were collecting supplies for the store and wouldn't be home until lunchtime. However, she assured Steve that Maxine was fine despite missing him, and suggested he ring again later. Following a few words of light conversation Steve confirmed that he'd certainly ring back and passed on his love to Maxine, adding that he was missing her greatly and that she'd hardly been out of his thoughts.

Steve had the afternoon off, and he spent some of the time with John and Norman in the Crown Hotel which was just along the road from the port. Being unable to speak with Maxine had been a minor setback, but one that all being well he'd shortly be able to rectify. Until then, he'd enjoy a few beers and dream of the girl in the photograph. He wasn't planning to go ashore that evening as the pubs would be shut; but not only that, he'd become so accustomed to having Maxine around that to go anywhere without her would to his way of thinking represent some kind of betrayal, as if he was out and about and enjoying himself while she was left idling at home. So, he'd stay on the ship and catch up with his letter writing that just recently he'd rather neglected.

But that was before John had spoken. 'I'm going to see a girlfriend tonight,' announced the butcher, taking a Woodbine from its packet and tamping the butt on the table. 'Either of you blokes fancy coming along? It's nothing special - just a few drinks to celebrate her birthday. There'll be plenty of others there too.'

'Sure,' replied Norman, without hesitation, stubbing out the remains of his roll-up in the ashtray. 'I've got nothing spoiling.'

'I don't know. I've got a phone call to make and it might take some time,' explained Steve, who was longing for that chinwag with Maxine. 'What time do you intend leaving?'

'About seven-thirty - eight o'clock, something like that,' affirmed John, lighting his Woodbine 'windy-deck fashion', even in the calm of the bar-room. 'It doesn't really matter.'

'OK then, I'll come along too,' declared Steve, waveringly and after some deliberation, believing Maxine wouldn't object over something so innocuous as a drink. 'Who else is going?'

'Just the three of us at present,' answered John, tapping the ash from his cigarette. 'But if Peter and Jimmy - or anyone else for that matter - want to join us there won't be any problem. The girl's a brick, and it's usually the more the merrier in her book.'

The telephone was in great demand and it was almost seven-thirty before Steve eventually lifted the receiver, asking the operator to connect him to the number on his notepaper. Even then he wouldn't be able to spend the amount of time chatting with Maxine as he'd wished as the queue for the phone had been long and there were others still waiting. As it was they spent several minutes making small talk, relating how much they loved each other and how they longed for each other's company - until the Second Fridge Engineer tapped him on the shoulder, and rebuked, 'Come on, youngster, there's several more of us here wanting to use the phone, and the way you're carrying on we'll be here till bloody midnight.'

Steve raised a hand in apology, hurriedly repeating to Maxine how much he loved her and promising he'd ring again later. Then, as an afterthought he read out the ship's telephone number, warning her that the phone was in more or less constant use and might well be engaged if she rang. He finished by blowing a kiss into the receiver before reuniting it with its handset.

In the event, it was the five who'd gone ashore together in Brisbane who set off for the party, striding along Marine Parade, a broad promenade with an avenue of pine trees on one side and a beach of dark, volcanic sand on the other. Nearer the city centre the seafront embraced many of the features of a British coastal resort, including ice-cream kiosks, cafés, a roller-skating rink, well-tended gardens and amusements. As at Timaru there was a sound shell, while on the beach sat an ancient locomotive that had been cosmetically refurbished and mounted as a museum exhibit; although given its location it more generally saw use as a plaything. All these attractions made Napier's seafront a credit to this once flattened but thoughtfully reconstituted city.

John's beloved lived in a pink-painted bungalow on the outskirts, a half-hour walk from the beach. Her name was Kate and she was as bubbly as a glass of lemonade. She couldn't sit still, and was forever jumping up to brew coffee or to change the 45s on her Dansette. She was a stone overweight, wore decorative horn-rimmed spectacles, and jeans so tight that every contour of her backside was maximized. The jean's tightness was the probable reason for the horizontal zip-fastener in their hindquarters. But for that she'd never have got into or out of them, although it made them look thoroughly grotesque. Steve had never seen anything like them and nor, he suspected, had John. On one occasion, when their host was deemed out of earshot, John leaned over, and said, 'Don't she look bloody awful in those things. What the hell does she think she looks like? It seems like I'll have to have a word.' It provoked a bout of sniggering, prompting Kate to poke her head around the door and query the reason for the laughter. 'Oh, nothing much,' replied John, trying his best to sound nonchalant while formulating a little white lie. 'Just one of Peter's dirty jokes.'

The party was typical of Kiwi social gatherings, with masses of people, plenty of beer, wine and soft drinks not to mention coffee and tea. As for more solid sustenance: the tables were loaded with far

198

more food than could ever be reasonably eaten. That said, Kate had invited so many guests that as the evening wore on the bungalow became so overcrowded that it was virtually impossible to move. At one stage the crush became so intense that it spilled into the garden while a queue even formed for the loo. Then out of the blue there was a kerfuffle, and Kate was seen bundling a scruffy-looking individual along the hallway and out through the open front door. Given the man's appearance Steve instinctively assumed he was a gatecrasher, but it wasn't quite so innocent. 'What was all that about?' asked John, as Kate made her way back indoors.

'Caught him peeing in the wash-basin - dirty bastard,' complained Kate, brushing her hands together as if to rid them of Bubonic Plague. 'He's not getting away with that in my house.'

Happily, the Hawke's Bay area enjoyed a Mediterranean climate with the evenings staying humid and mild. This was just such a night and even with the doors and windows wide open, other guests coming and going, all of them generating heat, it became uncomfortably warm in the bungalow. As good as the party had been that was the principal reason why just before midnight the boys from the *Alice Springs* politely excused themselves and left.

'She won't take the huff, will she?' asked Norman, closing the garden gate behind him. 'You know, us leaving early and so on.'

'Nah,' replied John, dismissively, leading the way along the pavement. 'She's as good as gold that one. Never known her get upset about anything. Anyway, I'll be out here on my own tomorrow and me and her will be well away. After tonight I'll probably be sleeping at Kate's until sailing day so if any of you have need of a cabin, just help yourselves.'

John, along with Ted, Norman and Davy, was what was known as a leading hand, meaning that in view of his tradesman's credentials he was entitled to a few extra privileges, which included a single-berth cabin. The only other members of the catering staff so treated were the Chief and Second Stewards, with the rest of them having to share. It was an arrangement that varied between companies while a vessel's age was a factor. On Port Line's newer ships, for example, every member of crew with the exception of boy ratings, enjoyed the luxury of single-berth facilities; whereas in the 'Glory Hole' on some of the older passenger liners, Royal Mail's 'Highland' class ships, for instance, fourteen to a cabin had been commonplace. In this respect the Australasian and Pacific Steam Navigation Company was somewhere middle of the road - a good deal better than some but not quite as commendable as others. Whatever, and although he couldn't speak for the rest of them, Steve felt certain that he wouldn't have a need of John's cabin.

Their route back to the port bisected a glorious sub-tropical garden, the scent-laden air indicating that even this late in the season Mother Nature was still bountifully active. There were shrubs and trees that Steve had never seen or heard of, and thanks to the tree-filtered light from the street lamps the flowers were a kaleidoscope of colour. It was the ideal spot for a rest, especially for Norman whose little toe was again causing trouble. 'I really need to see a chiropodist,' he moaned, sitting down on a bench and unlacing his shoe while John sniffed the fragrance of some roses.

'Then why don't you see one?' enquired Steve, sitting on the grass beside Peter and Jimmy, having just relieved himself in the bushes.

'Because it'll bloody cost me, that's why,' answered Norman, who by this time had removed his shoe and was busily massaging his foot. 'I'll just have to wait until we get home and get it fixed on the NHS.'

'You could have had it seen to in Aden,' said Peter, collecting a handful of leaves and allowing them to fall through his fingers. 'I remember this bloke coming aboard with his guaranteed corn cure. It was something like a drinking straw placed upright on top of the corn and sealed at the bottom with chewing gum. He then just sucked out the air, sealed the straw at the top and twenty minutes later the corn lifted out with the straw - well, at least I think it did. One of the fireman was having it done but I didn't see the end result.'

'I'm not having no bloody Arab messing about with my feet,' protested Norman, who by this time had his sock off and was picking at the corn with a fingernail. 'No telling what I might pick up. Might even get gangrene and end up having my foot off.'

'Well, seeing as how we're not going home via Aden it doesn't matter anyway,' replied Peter, sifting another handful of leaves. 'I just thought I'd mention it, that's all.'

Norman was on the verge of telling Peter he could have saved his breath when another voice interrupted, this one belonging to a stranger. 'Hello, what are you lot doing out here at this time of night when most law-abiding folk are in bed.'

All five simultaneously looked up to find a young police constable looming over them, his white, British-style helmet yet another indication that up here in the North Island it was still to all intents summer. 'Just taking a break while our mate here rests his feet,' answered John, nodding at Norman who seemed not the least perturbed by the officer's appearance. 'We're on our way back to our ship. Been to a birthday party a few streets away - and his corn's playing up.'

The policeman considered John's reply. Eventually he removed his helmet, pointed to the bench, and replied, 'OK, shove up a bit. I might as well join you for a few minutes.'

The ensuing exchanges were more of a question and answer session, with the friends supplying most of the answers. The constable seemed genial enough but the interrogation just intensified. 'What are your names? What ship are you off? Where have you been? What's your next port of call?' And so it went on until Jimmy, becoming tired of the inquisition, took umbrage.

'Look, we're not doing any harm,' he protested, sitting suddenly erect, his hands anchored firmly to the ground. 'We're not robbers or bandits or anything like that. It's just like John said, we're on our way back to the ship and just stopped for a rest - all right?'

Peter was about to add his two-pennyworth but was dissuaded by a sharp kick on the ankle from Steve, just as the policeman replaced his helmet, with the words, 'Fair enough - but don't be hanging around here all night otherwise people will be wondering what you're up to.' And with a pleasant, 'Goodnight,' he arose from the bench and sauntered off into the trees.

'What was the kick for?' demanded Peter, ruefully, rubbing his ankle as Steve climbed to his feet and brushed leaves from the seat of his trousers.

'To prevent you making a balls of things,' answered Steve, reproachfully, dusting his hands together before sliding them into his pockets. 'We didn't need you putting your foot in it after Jimmy's little outburst - and anyway, the copper was only doing his job.'

'Aw - bollocks,' snarled Peter, pushing himself upright and aiming a kick at the pile of leaves he'd assembled. 'I told you before - they're all bastards. Nice as pie one minute and booking you for bugger all the next. I wouldn't trust any of 'em as far as I could throw 'em.' And with a dismissive wave of the hand he mooched sulkily into the street, followed some thirty seconds later by the others.

'He's certainly got a chip on his shoulder where the police are concerned,' declared Norman, who having re-laced his shoe was hobbling in pursuit of his shipmates. 'He must have crossed swords with them somewhere along the line to bear that kind of malice.'

'After what he told me about his upbringing I wouldn't be at all surprised,' voiced Steve, sotto voce, with Peter still some way ahead.

'He has,' whispered Jimmy, pressing a finger to his lips, suggesting that what he was about to tell them had been imparted in confidence and should be kept strictly to themselves. 'He told me last trip after the law raided that pub in Wellington.' Jimmy went on to elaborate, keeping an eye on Peter should he stop for his pals to catch up. 'It happened early last year. Some lads had been smashing windows around his estate and the cops collared Peter, even though he had nothing to do with it. I suppose with his background he was an easy target. He got charged and finished up in front of the magistrates while the real culprits were never arrested. I think he'd have got probation at the very least, but when they heard about his seafaring ambitions they let him off provided he signed up immediately. That's how he ended up at the Vindi. He's never regretted going to sea,' added Jimmy, as an afterthought. 'But he's never forgiven the fuzz for framing him.'

'That's as maybe,' said John, philosophically, fully understanding where Jimmy was coming from but seeing the broader picture. 'But he can't go through life with a cob on just because of a couple of bent rozzers. They're not all like that - and I agree with Steve. That bloke back there was well within his rights asking them questions. For all he knew we might have been burglars on our way to a job, and,' he added, aiming his following remark at Jimmy. 'You could have buggered the entire evening up by having a go at him.'

Jimmy was on the verge of pointing out that if they had been burglars they were hardly going to admit it when he noticed that

202

Peter had paused while the stragglers slowly caught up. Instead, he just followed on in silence, largely content that he'd satisfactorily explained the situation, and that it would go no further.

Arriving back at the *Alice Springs* they discovered that in their absence the milkman had called and deposited a churn of fresh milk on the quayside. In those days, and for whatever reason, fresh milk wasn't frozen, so it was generally the case that as supplies became exhausted the canned variety was substituted. However, since their arrival at Adelaide, and fresh milk had again become readily available, the tins had been shelved until such time as they were needed. As had happened in London and at each port in Australia and New Zealand the milk had been delivered daily, and while it usually arrived in cartons, at Napier it turned up in churns.

'Can you give us a hand to lift this into the handling room?' asked Jimmy, explaining to Steve that it was impossible to shift single handed. 'There's twelve gallons of the stuff in here, and it's delivered by a farmer each evening.' Shifting the milk into the handling room would be a necessary undertaking for the duration of their stay in Napier, the farmer collecting the empty churn whenever he delivered a full one.

The following afternoon Steve attempted to ring Maxine, but her phone was engaged and when he tried again later the apparatus on the ship wasn't functioning. A hastily scrawled notice hinted that it might be repaired by the morning. Steve couldn't help feeling that their attempts to stay in touch were blighted. Nevertheless, he resolved not to give in and would try again tomorrow - assuming the phone had been mended.

Later, with the pantry squared away and no other appointments in his diary, Steve joined his pals for an evening at the fabled Top Hat, Napier's principal dance venue and a popular meeting place among teenagers. To say that he was apathetic would be an understatement. His thoughts were still centred on Maxine and he just wasn't interested in dancing. The trip out to Kate's had been different. It had only involved a few drinks and some gramophone records, and while other women had been present there'd been no form of physical contact. He wanted desperately for his relationship with Maxine to succeed, and to his way of thinking any kind of infidelity wouldn't seem appropriate, no matter how innocent his actions. Not only that, but as the blonde at the migrant camp had discovered, Steve was no ace on the dance floor. He had two left feet, no sense of rhythm and was as accomplished as he was on an ice rink. He'd gone along with his friends after they'd finally persuaded him that an evening ashore would be preferable to brooding on board.

Both Steve and Peter were smartly but casually dressed whereas Jimmy was more formally attired, as if he'd been invited to a wedding. 'Overdoing it a bit, aren't you?' teased Peter, playfully, tugging the flap at the back of Jimmy's jacket, as they walked along Marine Parade. 'You'll probably be the only one wearing a 'whistle'.'

'You can scoff,' replied Jimmy, with the certainty of an experienced hand in dance hall etiquette. 'But it's my guess that the girls will be better influenced by a collar and tie than scruffy old T-shirt and jeans. Anyway, we'll soon find out - and see who gets the quickest result.'

'I'm not scruffy - and this isn't a T-shirt,' protested Peter, resenting the knock to his pride. 'All right, I'm not wearing a tie but I'm as presentable as you are.'

Steve reflected that Jimmy's was a pertinent point. He remembered his afternoon walk around Manoao with Maxine, and how her friends had drooled over his black and white pin-striped jeans; and he hadn't forgotten the collar and tie that he'd worn to influence Maxine's parents. On this occasion he was wearing an open-neck shirt - but there again, he wasn't setting out to impress.

The Top Hat materialized as another of those delightful Art Deco masterpieces that Napier was renowned for, with just a hint of Spanish flair in its architecture. The actual ballroom occupied the upper storey, and as the boys approached the building they could hear Rock 'n' Roll music emanating from the upstairs windows.

The lads joined the queue for the box office; but as Peter made to pay a burly doorkeeper threw an arm across the doorway, and declared, 'Sorry, no neck-tie, no admittance - I'm afraid it's the rules of the house.'

'What rules - I can't see no rules,' challenged Peter, glancing up and around, loath to comply with some invisible regulation that appeared to have been plucked from thin air.

'Those rules,' indicated the doorman, stepping aside and pointing to a printed notice in the box office window, stating that admission would be refused to anyone not wearing a tie or suitable footwear. 'And don't get shirty with me. It's not my fault. I don't make the rules - I only make sure they're adhered to.'

Jimmy, spotting the potential for a scuffle, hurriedly drew Peter aside. 'Look, it's no use losing your temper because you don't like the rules. That'll get you into trouble quicker than anything. Now listen here - this is what we'll do.' Jimmy went on to explain that he'd enter first and once inside he'd take off his tie and drop it from a first-floor window. Either Steve or Peter could catch it, knot it around his own neck and repeat the exercise until all three were safely inside. 'Works like a dream every time,' assured Jimmy, turning towards the box office on his own, leaving the other two staring at the upstairs windows. And work like a dream it did. Steve caught the tie and did precisely as Jimmy had instructed. He had no trouble gaining admittance, and by the time Peter had knotted the tie around his neck and re-presented himself at the box office the doorkeeper was heatedly engaged in another argument, so he would probably have sailed through anyway.

The Top Hat's resident musicians were a loud and exciting group called The Contacts, a five-piece combo that like The Thunderbirds in Australia, featured saxophone, drums and guitars. There was a heavy emphasis on instrumental output - Steve's favourite - although vocals weren't totally neglected. The driving rhythms were certainly infectious, and a couple of belters from The Contacts, reputedly the North Island's premier rockers, were sufficient to convince Steve that coming along to the dance hall, no matter how unwillingly, had indeed been a good idea.

Jimmy definitely had his finger on the pulse when it came to working the dance halls and as he'd so rightly predicted, the women were suitable impressed. He grinned at Peter and Steve, as much as to say, 'I told you so', as girls of all shapes and sizes clamoured for his attention, as if he was some kind of deity. That said, Steve and Peter weren't completely ignored, with two of the more attractive specimens showing more than a passing interest.

'I like your trousers,' said the more striking of the two, cheekily grasping a handful of Steve's pin-striped jeans. 'We don't often see anything like that in this part of the world.'

'So I understand,' answered Steve, blushingly, not accustomed to having his more intimate clothing handled so familiarly by an out-and-out stranger. 'They are rather out of the ordinary.'

The girl stood tall and was firmly built without being overweight while her face was a dusky jewel, an oval with a soft, brown sheen. This, along with her jet-black hair, revealed more than a hint of the Maori, and she was as stunning as a native princess. 'My name's Glenda,' she announced, proudly, shouting to be heard above The Contact's version of Duane Eddy's, 'Peter Gunn'. 'What's yours?'

'Steve,' he replied, a little perturbed by the girl's assertiveness, and by the piercing brown eyes that bored into his without blinking. 'I'm off one of the ships in the harbour,' he added, shyly, trying his best not to stifle the exchanges. 'This place is fantastic.'

'Best place in Hawkes Bay,' proclaimed Glenda, as the lights dipped and The Contacts slowed the tempo with a smoochy rendition of Frankie Avalon's, 'Why'. And then, before Steve knew what was happening she'd grabbed his hand and was dragging him on to the dance floor, saying, 'Come on - let's dance. We can talk as we move around the floor.'

'I can't dance,' protested Steve, loudly, trying desperately to resist, fearful of humiliating himself - and of causing the girl serious injury.

'Rubbish,' cried Glenda, who was clearly not interested in negatives. 'Anyone can dance, it's easy - look, I'll show you,' and placing Steve's hands in all the right places, she continued. 'I'll lead and you follow. You'll soon get the hang of it.'

Unfortunately for Glenda, Steve didn't get the hang of it and within no time at all they were back in their seats, Glenda with her shoes off and gently caressing her toes as Steve mumbled, apologetically, 'I did try to warn you, but you wouldn't listen.'

Glenda, sadder and wiser and replacing her shoes, answered, 'Don't worry about it, I've had my toes trodden on before now.' Then with a rueful smile, she added. 'But you really are the most hopeless dancer.'

'He's bloody hopeless at everything,' chipped in Peter, whose ears had been flapping and who never seemed to miss a chance of poking fun at Steve when in the company of others. 'He can't dance, can't skate and can hardly swim - and he can't take a practical joke.'

'Bugger off!' snarled Steve, angry at Peter's uncalled-for intervention. 'Who asked for your opinion? At least I don't get ratty every time I see a copper.'

This time it was Peter's turn to take offence, and as The Contacts launched into a rousing arrangement of Elvis' 'King Creole', he grabbed Linda, his partner, and strutted on to the dance floor with a curt, 'Arsehole,' while simultaneously waving two fingers.

'That wasn't necessary,' said Glenda, as Peter and Linda were swallowed by the throng. 'Is he always as crude and outspoken as that?'

'Quite often,' answered Steve, glossing over what was after all only a minor altercation. 'But he's all right really - he just comes from a rough part of town.' And while it was fresh in his mind, he added, 'Oh! And sorry about my language. I don't usually swear in front of ladies.'

As the evening slipped by, Glenda was frequently invited to dance by other boys and she duly obliged, but always made her way back to Steve. If Steve had found conversation awkward in the early stages of their acquaintance it was a short-lived impediment and they were soon chatting away nineteen-to-the-dozen, most probably owing to Glenda's easy-going personality. It emerged that both she and Linda were student nurses at Napier hospital and in the final year of their training. Linda, of whom Steve had seen little owing to she and Peter spending most of their time dancing, hailed from Auckland, while Glenda was a native of Russell, a township in the Bay of Islands, way up beyond Whangarei. From Glenda's portrayal it seemed that The Bay of Islands was the most fabulous place on earth and Steve was keen to learn more. 'It sounds beautiful,' he observed, offering Glenda a cigarette which she politely refused. 'You must miss it, being so far away from home.'

'Yes, I do miss it - and it is absolutely gorgeous, but I try and get back as often as possible,' replied Glenda, a distant look in her eyes. 'It's so peaceful, and the scenery's out of this world. But there again,' she added, brightly, raising her palms and motioning at the band and dancers - and the ballroom in general, 'there's nothing like the Top

Hat in Russell, and there's a lot more going on in Napier than there is up north so all in all, I'm as happy as a sandboy down here.'

Steve had to agree that the Top Hat did indeed have a lot going for it. It was certainly the liveliest rendezvous that he and his pals had discovered since arriving in New Zealand, with the only missing ingredient, he fancied, being a licensed bar. But that was only a minor inconvenience and all things considered it was the ideal venue........with the cautionary qualification that the longer he remained there, the greater his attraction to Glenda. He viewed this with a certain unease, wondering what Maxine would have thought. But on the other hand, he reasoned, just talking to someone wasn't being unfaithful, so thereafter he was simply content just to relax and enjoy Glenda's company.

But as everyone knows, affairs of the heart have an uncanny knack of steamrollering out of control, and as Tuesday drew to a close and The Contacts played the gathering out into the night with a blistering interpretation of Johnnie & the Hurricanes', 'Farewell Farewell', Steve involuntarily bumbled, 'Can I walk you back to the nurses home?' It was out before he could prevent it, but there was nothing he could do about it now.

Glenda briefly considered the invitation before smiling sweetly, and replying, 'Better not. Matron's not keen on boys hanging about the home so the least seen the better. Anyway, I'll be walking back with Linda so I'll be OK.' Then, as they stepped out into the street, she brushed Steve's cheek with a kiss, saying, 'It's been nice meeting you - and we'll be back again on Saturday so I might see you then?' And with a cheery, 'Goodnight,' she linked arms with Linda and they mingled with the home-going crowds.

Jimmy had been lost in the swirl for most of the evening, having been appropriated the moment he arrived. Nonetheless, and despite his preoccupation, he'd clearly kept tabs on his mates. 'You pulled yourself a cracker there, Steve,' said the galley boy, as the pals dawdled back to the port, the scent from the pine trees hanging heavy in the moist evening air, 'and judging by the gleam in her eyes I reckon you're in for some excitement.'

'I very much doubt it,' replied Steve, recalling the apparent rebuff as they'd left the dance hall. 'She wouldn't even let me walk her back to the nurses home so I can't see her agreeing to a date. And anyway,' he continued, hoping to disassociate himself from any kind of hankering after Glenda, 'to tell you the truth I'm not really interested.' But Jimmy had witnessed the kiss and he smiled to himself in the shadows, knowing full well that Glenda had been stirred – and that Steve was denying the obvious.

Jimmy remarked that Peter and Linda also seemed to have struck a chord to which Peter spiritedly agreed. 'Yeah, she's really nice,' he enthused, rubbing his hands together with undisguised exhilaration. 'She's genuine class, not like that 'bit of rough' I was knocking about with in Timaru.' This time both Steve and Jimmy stared at their friend in amazement, left speechless by Peter's conversion. The previous week the 'bit of rough' in Timaru had been an absolute knockout.

Back on board, with the milk safely in the handling room, Steve returned to his cabin to find the lights extinguished and Peter driving pigs to market. He, on the other hand, was wide awake and he took to his bunk fully clothed, unable to sleep, suffering a crisis of conscience. He was deeply in love with Maxine, and he'd ring her tomorrow provided the phone was working. But she was no longer monopolizing his thoughts, and to his consternation he found himself thinking more and more about Glenda, and less and less about Maxine.

To Steve's delight, the following morning the telephone was indeed working, and during his coffee break he and Maxine were able to chat to their hearts' content. Maxine, he learnt, had had a blazing row with Holly over possession of a lipstick which Holly had claimed as her own, despite being scarcely old enough to wear it, while Steve told Maxine about Napier, a city she'd never visited but was planning to sometime in the future. They nattered about a whole host of things, mostly chit-chat, and before ringing off they reaffirmed their commitment, with Steve, carefully but guiltily, avoiding any reference to Glenda.

Back in the pantry, Steve discovered that the *Alice Springs* was to slip her moorings and proceed to sea, allowing another of the company's vessels, The *Temuka*, to come alongside to load cargo. The *Temuka* had in fact arrived overnight and was biding her time in

209

the anchorage. The *Alice Springs'* deck crew were hastily replacing her hatch covers and the wisp of steam from her funnel indicated that the engine room was ready. According to the Second Steward it would only be a temporary transposition, as the *Temuka* had only to load a deck cargo of wool before sailing for Bristol and Glasgow. The *Alice Springs*, he assured, should be back alongside again by Friday. This final snippet of information was vital. Steve may have only recently declared his undying love for Maxine, but he was itching to spend Saturday evening at the dance hall, where he hoped to re-establish himself with Glenda.

Soon after lunch, with the telephone disconnected and the mooring lines released, the *Alice Springs* steamed slowly out to the anchorage, passing as she did the in-bound *Temuka*, a smaller vessel and one that was powered by diesel.

As in every other New Zealand port, Napier's wharves were seldom empty of shipping with most of those present being British. During the course of her stay the *Alice Springs* was joined by - among others - New Zealand Shipping Co's *Hauraki* and *Hurunui*, Ellerman's *City of Poona*, Port Line's *Port Launceston*, Federal's *Cornwall*, Shaw-Savill's *Cymric*, Blue Star's *Rockhampton Star*, and Trinder-Anderson's *Ashburton*, a smart but elderly tramp that was well into the second half of a two-year engagement trading around and across the Pacific.

An unofficial record of the vessels that had visited Napier in the years following the earthquake adorned the bluffs that the disaster had created. Given their steepness the men responsible must have braved life and limb to daub their ship's name for posterity. Those lacking the courage to go rock climbing, or who could find insufficient space on the sandstone, painted the name of their ship on the face of the wharf it was moored to. Leaving one's calling card in this fashion wasn't just peculiar to Napier. This form of graffiti could be found scrawled or painted on quaysides from Yokohama to Yalta, and while in some quarters it was viewed as vandalism it did at least serve a purpose, and nothing was ever done to erase it.

'Still, it isn't as bad as what happened to a Yankee ship in the Royal Victoria Dock a few years ago,' said Keith, as the *Alice Springs* swung around her anchor to face the incoming tide. 'She was the *American Gunner*, and a few of her crew got into a punch-up with some British lads in The Connaught. When they turned to in the morning they found someone had crept aboard during the night, climbed over the taffrail and painted the letters EAR on the end of *'Gunner'*, so that it read *'American Gunner*ear'. They suspected the culprit was off Royal Mail's *Drina*, but as far as I'm aware no one was ever apprehended.'

Forty-Eight hours in the anchorage deprived the crew of their shore leave but enabled alternative pursuits. Some darned their socks or caught up with their dhobying while several of the deckies went fishing, although none possessed a fishing-rod or line. Still, they were nothing if not resourceful and in no time at all had twisted the prongs of a dinner fork into a claw, attached it to a line that was in turn lashed tightly to the taffrail. Having baited their creation with thinly-cut slices of pork, they tossed it into the sea and settled to a game of dominoes.

Steve, who'd elected to spend part of his afternoon bronzying, viewed the goings-on with scepticism. What on earth would Frank have made of it, he wondered, what with him being an experienced angler. He'd have probably been laughing his socks off, he concluded, as the line hung limply and the deckies carried on with their game. And then, to his astonishment, the line became taught and the men began hauling it in, hand over hand until a gleaming, shark-like creature lay thrashing on deck, and the fork was removed from its jaws. 'Tope,' said the Bosun, who'd sidled up next to Steve and who was equally engrossed in the proceedings. 'Or dogfish........or rock salmon to you and me when we're in the fish shop.' Steve and the Bosun looked on as several more of the dark, slender, creatures were landed, given a sharp tap on the head with a hammer and consigned to a pile that would eventually end up on their dinner plates.

As if on cue, John strode past with a tray. He collected the fish; and as he meandered back to the galley, he declared, 'Fish and Chips for lunch tomorrow, lads, and seeing as how it'll mean another few quid off the catering budget the Boss'll be as happy as Larry.'

New Zealand's abundant and hungry wildlife was fully evident, for while the *Alice Springs'* amateur fishermen were industriously landing their catch a family of penguins appeared and frolicked around the fishing line, at the same time hoping for a meal. The penguins were a welcome and entertaining diversion; but on their second afternoon at anchor the catering boys were faced with a more odious animal, and one that wasn't quite so amusing.

Steve and Peter were squaring away after lunch, and were both looking forward to another spell of sunbathing when Jimmy dashed into the pantry, panting, 'There's a problem up at the potato locker - you'd better come and give me a hand.'

The potato locker was a large, white-painted, cage-like affair of timber construction located immediately forward of the after deck house. It was so designed to allow the potatoes access to fresh air and daylight, essential to prevent them becoming spoilt in the tropics and from chitting. 'I can't understand it,' said Jimmy, as the boys hurried aft, each pulling on a pair rubber gloves that Ted had managed to scrounge from the Donkeyman. 'I was up here only this morning and everything was as right as ninepence.'

Steve was puzzled. Surely it couldn't be that bad, he thought, as they climbed the ladder from the after well deck, because when all's said and done, what could possibly go wrong with a spud. But when they arrived at the locker they found that in the space of only a few short hours a month's supply of perfectly edible potatoes had been transformed into a mountain of slush. The reason was readily apparent as the entire locker was crawling with maggots, causing the floor and the surrounding area to assume the qualities of a skid-pan as the slime was trampled underfoot. The eggs must have lain there for months; now they'd hatched and created a quagmire.

Only the uppermost layer of sacks was unspoilt, and even these would have to be sorted to ensure that their contents could be eaten. As for the remainder; it was a case of heaving most of them overboard, while those at the very bottom of the pile that had completely disintegrated were sluiced away into the sea. It was a messy and time-consuming chore that culminated in the entire locker having to be scrubbed and disinfected before the salvaged potatoes could be reinstated. 'Might just be enough to last until we're back alongside,' said Jimmy, as he and Peter hauled the final sack into its rightful place in the locker. 'But the Boss'll go fuckin' berserk when he discovers he's got to order another two ton of potatoes - and that's on top of the additional overtime.'

As predicted, following the *Temuka's* departure for Bristol and Glasgow the *Alice Springs* returned to her moorings. She'd remain in Napier for another three weeks, until her holds were crammed with all manner of foodstuffs bound for the High Streets of Britain. During that time her crew, Steve included, would experience a whole gamut of adventures; most of them pleasant, a few embarrassing or unsavoury, along with the downright criminal.

An example of the latter occurred that very afternoon; and as though it was their constitutional right it was Sean Cassidy and the forlorn Roger Oates who were the villains. Roger's inability to work, along with Sean's couldn't-care-less attitude, meant that as soon as the ship was alongside they were able to take a taxi into town and set up camp in the Criterion Hotel. When they finally emerged some seven hours later they hadn't a penny between them, so without the wherewithal for a taxi and Roger unable to walk, they were desperate for alternative transport.

Left by its unsuspecting owner at the rear of the Criterion it was a gentleman's sit-up-and-beg model - sturdy but without a three-speed. Still, that wouldn't be a problem for Sean who despite being drunk was also enormously strong. And so they set off, with Sean in the saddle and Roger perched precariously on the crossbar, his plastered right leg protruding at ninety degrees, a hazard not only to itself but to everything that stood in its path. They fell off only once, half way along Marine Parade, and lay laughing in the road before dusting each other down and remounting, Sean pedalling gamely but erratically while Roger was blissfully blotto.

Now theft is one thing - and this wretched pair may have thought they'd made the ideal get-away having not been collared at the scene - but compounding the felony by disposing of the evidence was another. Sure enough, a bystander who'd witnessed their capers had reported the matter to the constabulary. The police force set off in pursuit, arriving on the quayside at the very same instant that Sean tossed the bike in the sea. Roger was totally out of it; but as the three policemen approached Sean Cassidy he promptly flattened the first, and was only subdued when the second held him firmly in a headlock while the third clamped his wrists in handcuffs. They were carted away to the cells and appeared in court on the Monday. They were each sentenced to a week's imprisonment and fined fifteen pounds for the theft and disposal of the bicycle, while Sean received an extra fortnight's gaol and was fined an additional twenty pounds for rendering the constable comatose.

'That's definitely got to be the end for Sean Cassidy,' observed Steve, over breakfast on Saturday morning, before knowing the outcome of the impending court proceedings. 'I can't see either of them getting off lightly - especially Sean, not after walloping that copper.'

'I wouldn't bet on it,' replied Archie, staring down his nose while spreading marmalade on to a slice of toast. 'You saw what happened in Brisbane, and after that punch-up in Adelaide. They were glad to get rid of him, so I wouldn't be at all surprised if the same thing happens here.'

'I hope so,' slavered Peter, shovelling a forkful of fried bread and bacon into his mouth between slurps from his mug of tea. 'I'd miss him if he wasn't here - and anyway, It wasn't his fault what happened in Brisbane. That fuckin' wharfie was asking for it.'

'I'm glad you think so,' rebuked Archie, scornfully, fussily brushing crumbs from his shirt-front. 'But I still maintain there's no need for that kind of behaviour whatever the provocation, and the fact that he was drunk is irrelevant. They can lock him up and throw away the key for all I care, horrible lout........and there's another thing, young Peter.'

'What's that?' queried the pantry boy, laying down his knife and fork and slumping back in his chair, simultaneously letting rip with a belch.

'Your table manners are fucking atrocious,' answered Archie, disgustedly, standing and making for the pantry carrying his plate, cup and saucer. 'You'd be more at home in a zoo.'

Peter sat up with a jerk, mouth wide open but dumbstruck while Steve spluttered into his tea. Archie seldom resorted to foul language, but when he did it was totally destructive and Peter had no ready answer.

It wasn't really Peter's morning as before he'd fully recovered the

Second Steward, wearing a deadpan expression, strolled casually into the saloon, and announced, 'There's a girl on the quayside carrying a baby. Says she's looking for someone called Peter Grimble who she met in Wellington last November. Reckons she heard that the *Alice Springs* was back on the coast so she popped up to Napier to see him.'

Peter went as white as a sheet. He leapt from his chair and ran to the only window on the starboard side of the saloon that looked directly down on the quayside. He glanced first to one side and then the other, peeking from either side of the curtains, scanning the entire quayside from the seaward end to the shore. However, he could see no girl, no baby - in fact no anything, save the wharfies who were shifting the cargo. And then he tumbled, realizing that on this occasion it was he who was the victim of a prank. As he sauntered back to the table feeling utterly foolish his shipmates giggled with glee. Mathematics had never been Peter's strong point. If it had he'd have calculated that they'd been in Wellington only six months previously, so if there was a girl on the quayside carrying a baby then the child couldn't possibly have been his.

Tedium was hardly the word for it as Steve pondered the vagaries of time, how it frequently raced away like a rocket while sometimes it weighed like a stone. The latter was the case on this particular Saturday, as he eagerly looked forward to an evening at the dance hall and a hoped-for reunion with Glenda. But, eventually six o'clock rolled around and as soon as he'd eaten and scrubbed-out the pantry he changed into his shore-going best which on this occasion included the requisite tie. It also extended to his wind-cheater jacket as for once there was a nip in the air, perhaps a sign of the encroaching winter.

'I wish I was wearing a woolly,' complained Peter, hunching his shoulders as they hurried along Marine Parade on their way to the dance hall. 'I didn't realize it was quite this chilly.'

'Then slip back and get one,' answered Steve, stopping and indicating back towards the harbour. 'It won't take you long, and we can wait for you at the sound shell.'

'Nah, let's keep going,' replied Peter, with his usual bravado. 'It'll be warm enough in the Top Hat – and anyway, I was thinking.'

'Don't overdo it,' teased Jimmy, winking at Steve in anticipation of his follow-up comment. 'We don't want you suffering a stroke and ruining our Saturday night out.'

'Ha ha, very funny,' sneered Peter, resorting to the customary two fingered salute. 'But seriously, though. It's a bit early to think about going to the Top Hat so why don't we spend half an hour at the skating rink. If nothing else it should warm us up.' So that's what they did - and for once it was Steve who excelled, displaying all the roller-skating artistry that had once made him the envy of his school friends. Jimmy also proved equally as adept on wheels as he had on the Adelaide ice although Peter, whose idea it had been in the first place, came a cropper at least twice and spent most of his time at the rink side. At length, fed up with being humbled, and after studying his watch every few minutes, he shouted, 'Hey! Come on, we'd better get a move on. We don't want to keep the girls waiting.'

'Soon changed your tune, didn't you?' taunted Steve, as he swung in a giant backward arc, coming to a text-book stand beside Peter who looked frozen and utterly dejected. 'Now who's the one who can't skate? I wonder what the girls at the Top Hat will make of that?'

'Yeah........well, I suppose you'll make sure they all know,' grumbled Peter, moodily, as Steve and Jimmy removed their skates and handed them back to the attendant. 'But I reckon that my pair were faulty.'

Both Steve and Jimmy cracked up, finding it hard to believe the excuse. 'Come on, you,' said Steve, throwing a sympathetic arm around Peter's shoulder as they turned and set off for the dance hall. 'You may be hopeless at roller-skating but at least you can dance better than me so that more or less makes us even?'

Saturday night at the Top Hat was always the busiest of the week and it was as well they arrived early. They had no trouble gaining admission, and found seats in almost the same part of the hall that they had done previously, which would hopefully make it easier for the girls to locate them. All this, of course, was assuming that they actually turned up, because as the minutes ticked by and the place rapidly filled there was no sign of either Glenda and Linda. There were no such worries for Jimmy, for as on their previous visit he was soon an irresistible attraction. 'What's he got that we haven't?'

216

whinged Peter, glancing again at his watch and then towards the doorway, fearful of being stood up. 'He's no better looking than us and he's only an average dancer. I just don't understand it.'

'It's probably as he says,' explained Steve, looking anxiously towards the entrance, wondering if Glenda would show. 'If you're wearing the gear and have got the charisma then the girls'll follow. I think the suit's the answer.' A suit was something that Steve had never owned. He wore stylish, slip-on shoes, having detested lace-ups since he'd been old enough to appreciate fashion. His pullovers were colourful and his black and white pin-striped jeans had certainly proved controversial, at least over here in New Zealand; but where girls were concerned, he concluded, a suit would prove a useful acquisition.

'I bet they don't turn up,' moaned Peter, staring again at his watch and then at Steve, as though expecting his friend to work miracles.

However, Steve too was beginning to have doubts, although Glenda had said that they'd be there and he hadn't yet given up hope. 'They've probably been held up,' he offered, with a noticeable lack of conviction. 'I wouldn't be at all surprised if they're already on their way up the stairs.' And then, as if the gods had been listening, there they were, pushing through the crowd, waving and dodging the dancers as they made a beeline for Steve and Peter.

'Sorry we're late,' apologised Glenda, breathlessly, removing her jacket and hanging it around the chair that Steve had reserved for her. 'But we had to work late and didn't get finished till seven.'

'That's right,' agreed Linda, sitting herself down next to Peter while unbuttoning her cardigan. 'This old duffer fell off his bedpan. Christ! You never saw such a mess. It took us ages to clean up, then we had get him back into bed so it was a pretty hectic half hour - then we had to get changed and have tea. Talk about a rush.'

It wasn't long before Peter and Linda took to the dance floor; and it was only then that Steve became aware of his actions. He'd held Glenda's hand without thinking; but more significantly, he noted, she hadn't attempted to resist. He felt suddenly nervous, and began wondering just where their friendship was leading. He'd already puffed his way through three cigarettes and he hadn't been in the place an hour. He kept thinking of Maxine - that was the trouble -

and hoped that she wasn't clairvoyant, knowing just what he was up to. He lit up another Rothman's, inhaling deeply before raising his head and exhaling a stream of smoke towards the ceiling. The nicotine was an instant palliative, and he slowly relaxed as he listened to The Contacts and chatted with Glenda. There was only one interruption, when a guy invited Glenda to dance; but this time she politely refused, explaining that she was with her boyfriend and didn't really feel like dancing.

Glenda was with her boyfriend? It was a second or two before the significance penetrated. He felt suddenly elated - but perfidious, ashamed that he was cheating on Maxine. But he couldn't help it so he sought consolation from the fact that what Maxine didn't know wouldn't hurt her. Of course, he knew it was a poor excuse but it made him feel better; and when all was said and done, just because Glenda wasn't Maxine it didn't mean he shouldn't enjoy himself. It was a possible reason that he readily agreed when Glenda unexpectedly stood up, took her jacket from the chair-back and proposed, 'It's getting too stuffy in here - I need some fresh air. Let's go outside for a walk.'

Steve had to admit that the atmosphere in the Top Hat was verging on the oppressive, not helped, of course, by the amount of cigarette smoke in the air, smoke to which he'd contributed. As they walked down the stairs and into the street the wave of cool air washing over them was at once both refreshing and invigorating. Glenda, whose eyes had been streaming put her hanky away, while Steve breathed deeply, freeing his lungs from the clag. He'd enjoyed a cigarette for as long as he could remember; maybe five Woodbines or four Domino in the early days, provided of course he could afford them. Ten a day was his usual quota since becoming a teenager; four in little over an hour, he chided himself, was downright irresponsible.

As they strolled through the streets, stopping at the occasional shop-front to stare in the window, Steve was more than content just to follow for when all was said and done, Glenda knew the place like the back of her hand whereas he was a virtual stranger. But he then realized that they were straying further and further from the city centre, and it wasn't long before he recognised the sub-tropical gardens where he and his pals had rested whilst returning from

Kate's. And then he noticed that Glenda was making directly for the gardens, and that her pace had quickened so that they were almost at a canter by the time they reached the trees and were hidden from view by the shrubs.

At almost the precise spot where the lads had sat talking to the policeman, Glenda turned, took Steve's head in her hands and kissed him fully on the lips - and then dragged him headlong into the bushes. In no time at all his black and white pin-striped jeans - shorts and all - were around his ankles; and what followed was nothing less than a forty-minute lesson in debauchery. Now then, it may well have been Maxine's first time back in Manoao, but it most certainly wasn't Glenda's here in Napier. She was a carnal craftswoman and Steve, who was still serving his sexual apprenticeship, learnt more in those forty minutes than he'd hitherto gleaned in his life; and it only ceased when from the corner of her eye Glenda spotted a conspicuous white helmet bobbing ominously along beyond the bushes. She went suddenly still, lying prone astride Steve, her dress-front wide open and its hem riding up around her waist, her backside exposed to the treetops. In the very same instant she pressed a finger to her lips, and whispered. 'For Christ's sake keep quiet. There's a bloody copper out there in the street, and if he catches us like this we'll be buggered.'

Steve craned his neck, and answered, dreamily, 'I can't see anyone - you must have imagined it. Let's........'

'Shhh!' hissed Glenda, clamping a hand over Steve's mouth. 'He's out there I tell you, and he's shining his torch into the trees.' And then Steve saw it too, the beam of a flashlight swinging lazily to and fro, probing the depths of the undergrowth. The officer may not have seen anything but might well have heard something for they hadn't been especially discrete, going at it hammer and tongs, oblivious of everything - and of anyone who may have been watching.

Steve went rigid. The beam from the torch was swinging back towards them, and no way could he imagine it not picking them out in the darkness. Fearing the worst, Glenda buried her face in his armpit, almost like a cornered animal believing that by concealing its head it would also be hiding its torso. As if reading her mind, Steve gingerly inched the hem of her dress, which was made of a dark green material, down over her buttocks; a more effective camouflage, he reckoned, than even her brown-tinted skin. And then, just when it seemed certain that they'd be discovered, in all their undignified glory, the torch was extinguished.

They lay there, completely motionless for a good five minutes, breathing as softly as their cramped situation would allow, until Glenda looked slowly up and scanned the vicinity for a sign of the policeman. Eventually, as satisfied as she could be that the coast was clear, she pushed herself on to her knees and then stood up, smoothing and re-buttoning her dress while removing the odd blade of grass. 'I think he's gone,' she said, shakily, picking leaves from her hair with one hand while replacing a shoe with the other. 'Strewth! That was bloody close. We must be the luckiest couple in Napier,' she quipped, nervously, holding a hand out to Steve.

Steve took her hand and hauled himself upright, hitching up his shorts - although it was a trifle too late to be modest. 'You sure he's gone?' he asked, tucking his shirt-tail into his jeans and re-buckling his belt. 'He might be out there waiting for us.'

'It doesn't matter now, does it?' answered Glenda, who was rapidly regaining her composure. 'We're both dressed and decent. If he does happen to be out there, for all he knows we might just have been sitting here talking.'

'Good point,' said Steve, straightening his tie before sliding his windcheater over his shoulders. 'In that case we may as well go back to the dance hall.'

'Not me!' said Glenda, glancing sidelong at Steve, as they ventured cautiously out of the gardens and on to the pavement. 'I'm going back to the nurses home, otherwise everyone'll guess what we've been up to.'

'I suppose you're right,' agreed Steve, reluctantly, a little annoyed that the most exciting night of his life had been foreshortened by a nosey policeman. And then he added, almost as an afterthought and more in hope than anticipation, 'Can I walk you back to the nurses home tonight?'

'Yes, of course you can,' replied Glenda, slipping her arm through Steve's after espying the officer a hundred yards away on the other side of the road and heading in the opposite direction. 'Matron's off for the weekend and you know the old saying, "While the cat's away"........' And so, they wandered off, the only trace of their recent exertions being the flattened grass among the bushes - and Glenda's knickers in the branches of a tree. Later, as they kissed goodnight outside the nurses home, Glenda whispered, 'I'll let you into a secret, Steve. You're not hopeless at everything - and you can tell Peter that from me.'

Steve was in an absolute daze. He just couldn't believe what had happened and he kept pinching his thigh, just to make sure he wasn't dreaming. Every so often he chuckled, tickled pink by the sheer exhilaration. At one juncture, as he was strolling back through the city centre, he was even on the verge of jumping for joy and clicking his heels, but was dissuaded by the sight of a couple on the opposite pavement. They probably though he was barmy as it was, what with him laughing to himself in the dark. If he started leaping all over the place they'd most likely consider him certifiable and call the police, and that would bring an unforgettable evening to a very unsatisfactory conclusion. And then he had a horrible thought.

He'd become so intoxicated with his self-perceived copulatory prowess, propagated by Glenda's own assessment of his performance, that he'd completely forgotten the golden rule concerning sexually transmitted diseases. What if I've picked up a dose? he wondered, suddenly in a spate of alarm. The very idea made him cringe. The prospect of having to visit the Albert Dock Seamen's Hospital for a shot of penicillin was bad enough, but the various horror stories about the instruments supposedly employed in the treatment of such afflictions made his toes curl. In the twinkling of an eye he wished his unforgettable evening was simply a figment of the imagination. The sudden reversion had been spurred by the awful realization that Glenda's libertine skills hadn't been copied from a book but had been acquired during sexual relationships.

In the space of only a few seconds he'd lapsed from feeling on top of the world to being down in the doldrums, almost convinced he'd contracted an infection. All right, he felt well enough physically; but of course, he would, wouldn't he? After all, it had only happened an hour or so ago and would probably take days to emerge. As he trudged miserably on to the quayside he'd become totally disillusioned, the probability that he was still perfectly healthy being lost in a fog of despair.

'What are you looking so glum about?' asked a voice from almost in front of him.

Steve was brought up with a start. It was Jimmy, waiting at the foot of the *Alice Springs'* accommodation ladder for someone to help him with the milk. 'Oh.......nothing,' replied Steve, sounding thoroughly depressed. 'Just thinking about things,' he lied, forcing a smile that Jimmy could see through as if it were a porthole. 'Here, I'll help you shift that into the handling room.'

But Jimmy was in no particular hurry. He knew instinctively that something was wrong and was determined to winkle it out. He'd also noted Steve's dishevelled appearance; the badly-scuffed toes of his normally highly-polished shoes and the grass stains on his pin-striped jeans. 'You been fighting?' he queried, studying his pal by the harsh light of the cluster lamps illuminating the *Alice Springs'* gangway.

'Not at all,' answered Steve, desperate to talk to someone about what was after all a delicate subject, but lacking the confidence to broach it. 'Far from it. Me and Glenda have had a whale of a time - and that's the trouble.' And then it all poured out, and before he could draw breath he was regaling Jimmy with everything that had happened, including the brush with the cop.

'Bloody hell!' exclaimed Jimmy, unable to mask an enormous grin as Steve brought his story to a close. 'I should think you have had a whale of a time. Most blokes spend a lifetime waiting for something like that to happen but it seldom does,' he continued, perplexed by Steve's sullen mood. 'So, why all the gloomy looks? I'd have thought you'd be over the moon.'

'I was,' explained Steve, glad now of someone to talk to, someone who'd listen and not spill the beans to the crew. 'The trouble is, I'm frightened I might have picked up a - you know........'

'What? From Glenda?' challenged Jimmy, astounded, unable to believe that Steve hadn't grasped what to he, Jimmy, was as plain as the nose on his face. 'No way!' he resumed, offering Steve a ciggy before lighting up one for himself. 'Not with her being a nurse and all. She'd know all the signs as well as the remedies, so you know what I think? She's as clean as a saintly old maid.'

'You really think so?' replied Steve, instantly cheered by Jimmy's analysis which, voiced in such matter-of-fact terms, made a great deal of sense. 'You really think I've nothing to worry about?'

'No worries whatsoever,' affirmed Jimmy, whom Steve regarded as being something of an oracle, and whose advice merited all due respect. 'Oh, I know what they teach us at sea school, and what Sec - even Archie, for that matter, keep banging on about,' he continued, tapping the ash from his cigarette, 'but I think it's all a matter of discretion. Now then, if you'd been having it away with a black senhorita from Recife, well, that'd be different. Your 'old man' would probably have dropped off by now and then it'd be, Goodnight Vienna.'

The pair of them chuckled, a little uneasily in Steve's case as he still wasn't totally reassured. But having spoken to Jimmy he at least he felt less jittery and he told himself that he'd just have to keep an eye on things, and hope there were no tell-tale symptoms. Then taking a hold of the churn, he said, 'Come on, let's get this milk into the handling room, otherwise it'll go bloody sour.'

When Steve turned to in the morning he saw that Blue Star's *Gladstone Star* had berthed overnight, adding a splash of colour to her otherwise monochrome surroundings. Her varnished lifeboats contrasted sharply with her white-painted upperworks, while her lilac-grey hull reflected softly in the mill-pond of a harbour. But it was the funnel bearing the Blue Star colours that really caught the eye. Almost everyone agreed that no more beautiful a device had ever graced a merchant ship's funnel. That was one thing about the Blue Star boats, thought Steve, as he busied himself at servicing the first of his cabins - they always looked good; well, most of them did, especially the newer ones with those whopping great colourful smoke stacks. In fact, he wouldn't mind doing a trip on one some time, providing it wasn't of too long a duration. He had to bear in mind that intended visit to New Zealand House. If they were able to help him get back to Maxine on a permanent basis then constant communication would be vital, although he'd have to earn his keep in the meantime. He knew that Blue Star ran a service down to South America - a couple of months at a time. That would suit nicely, he mused, as he put the finishing touches to polishing the brasswork around the porthole. But that was way into the future, and as he packed up his cleaning gear and headed around to the Junior Fourth Engineer's cabin he was only too aware of the pitfalls.

As it happened, his cabin mate's bunk hadn't been slept in. It later emerged that he'd had a blazing row with Linda who'd stormed out of the dance hall leaving Peter playing the role of a wallflower. However, he'd soon become acquainted with another girl - her name had escaped him - and they'd spent the night together in her apartment.

How to spend a Sunday in New Zealand? wondered Steve, who had the afternoon free but didn't know quite what to do. He and Glenda had made no further arrangements owing to the hospital's shift pattern, so after polishing his shoes he decided to go for a walk. He couldn't wear his black and white jeans as they were in soak, so he wore his grey flannel trousers instead. Given the previous evening's ill-treatment his shoes had responded positively to the 'Cheery-Blossom', and it wasn't long before he was stepping out along Marine Parade towards Tennyson Road, intent on an afternoon's exploring.

Napier was a magical city, and as Steve roamed the streets he couldn't help but wonder how gloriously it had risen from the spoil. He'd known nothing about the earthquake until shortly before their arrival, and only knew now because the Bosun had told him. The present harbour, the petty officer had informed him, had actually been created by the quake, throwing up the bluffs at the landward end of the port while leaving a deep-water pool in its wake. The good people of Napier had done the rest and now had a port to be proud of. And then there was that fabulous architecture. Those responsible had certainly grasped the metal, and with incredible foresight had created an Art Deco masterpiece that would someday be a magnet for tourists.

He carried on walking, reaching right to the residential fringes before pausing for a check on the time. It was past four o'clock, and although he was in no particular hurry he would soon be in need of his tea. It wasn't so much that he was hungry, but it would take him the best part of an hour to get back to the ship, then once he'd eaten he'd go and phone Maxine. He turned and retraced his steps, noticing at a crossroads a signpost pointing to the hospital. He was tempted to

224

follow his nose, but he decided against, not knowing if Glenda was working.

It was remarkable how his mood had lightened. The previous evening he'd been fretting that this beautiful girl might have presented him with an unspeakable disease, now here he was, still a mite anxious but also thinking, if it's happened it's happened so why not carry on and enjoy it.

Back on board he went straight to the pantry where Sec was manning the servery and Peter was busy strapping-up, hurrying to get finished and away to the arms of 'what's-her-name'. 'Been anywhere interesting?' asked Peter, grabbing a pantry cloth and giving a handful of desert spoons a cursory wipe before dumping them noisily into a cutlery basket.

'No........just loafing,' replied Steve, taking a plate from the carousel and helping himself to a princely portion of chilli-con-carne and rice. 'I took a walk through town - and, Oh! Yeah! I found a cinema - the Odeon, I think it was, and there's a western on tomorrow so I might slip along after work.'

'Not going out with Glenda, then?' queried Peter, impishly, removing some soiled dishes from the servery hatchway and tossing them into the sink. 'But there, I don't suppose she'd be interested in westerns, would she?'

'Nothing at all to do with it,' answered Steve, sliding a dishful of trifle on to his tray and collecting his cutlery from the basket. 'It's just that we didn't make any more arrangements. She didn't know what shifts she'd be working, but all being well I'll be seeing her at the Top Hat on Saturday.' And before he could be pestered with any more questions he shouldered his way out of the pantry and made his way down to his cabin where he could hopefully enjoy his tea in peace.

As he settled down on the settee he could hear female laughter emanating from the next-door cabin: one of the off-duty stewards - Keith most probably, thought Steve - and his girlfriend, engaged in some afternoon fun. Steve smiled inwardly, his mind's eye vividly focussed on his own recent impropriety, his resolve to phone Maxine involuntarily forced on the shelving. He wondered what was happening next door, visualizing the various contortions and other erotic proceedings evolving beyond the dividing bulkhead.

Something stirred deep in his loins. I wonder what Glenda's doing tonight, he thought, as he forked a piping-hot morsel of chilli-con-carne into his mouth and began eating. It was an issue that became increasingly monopolistic, and the more he dwelt upon it the more he found himself wishing he'd arranged a date with Glenda. The pressure to satisfy his urges was becoming so intense that he'd virtually made up his mind that as soon as he'd finished his tea he'd flick through the telephone directory with the aim of contacting the nurses home – and then came a knock at the door. It was Norman. 'Telephone call for you, Steve,' sang the cook, through the partly opened door. 'I've left the phone off the hook so I wouldn't hang about if I were you, in case someone comes along and replaces it.'

'Cheers, Norman, said Steve,' placing his tray on the table and wiping his mouth with his handkerchief. 'I'll be up there directly.' His heart was pounding as he dashed from the cabin, slamming the door shut behind him. He'd intended ringing Maxine as soon as he'd finished his tea, but Maxine had saved him the bother.

'Hi........Maxine?' he called, grabbing the receiver from where Norman had laid it and speaking in the same smooth flourish. There was a portentous hush. He could hear someone breathing on the other end of the line but there was no reply and he initially suspected a fault. 'Hi........Maxine?' he repeated, this time less loudly and more cautiously, a sense of foreboding trying to warn him that everything wasn't as it should be.

Steve rapped the receiver against the bulkhead, as if giving it a clout would solve any technical problems and he'd be able to speak with Maxine. And then, at long last, a female voice enquired, softly and accusingly, 'Who's Maxine?'

In that one terrible instant Steve cottoned on that he'd made a fundamental and fatal mistake. He'd been so preoccupied with not dropping clangers while talking to Maxine and therefore revealing his relationship with Glenda that he'd forgotten a basic principle - never assume you know who's calling when answering the telephone. Steve was mortified, and wished the deck could swallow him, for the voice on the other end of the line wasn't Maxine's at all - it was Glenda's. Somehow, Glenda had gotten hold of the telephone number that had been allocated to the *Alice Springs* and had contacted Steve with the object of fixing a date. Now, in a fleeting, thoughtless, injudicious moment of carelessness, he'd blown it, lock, stock and ruddy great barrel. He tried desperately to cover his tracks. 'Sorry, Glenda, I thought it was someone else,' he blustered, seeking to recover a situation that was already irretrievable. 'Who's Maxine, did you ask? Oh! No-one special, just someone I met in Timaru. It isn't serious.'

It sounded everything it really was, a load of mendacious waffle, and Glenda wasn't fooled. She could tell by the tone of his voice that he was lying through his teeth and launched into a string of profanities. In fact, the tirade was so intense that Steve had to hold the phone at arm's length so as to avoid being deafened by the decibels. 'And you needn't think you'll be going out with me again,' she finished, before slamming down her receiver with such unrestrained vehemence that Steve felt convinced it had shattered.

Steve was stunned by the outburst. His head was spinning and he needed to regain some stability but unfortunately, the opposite occurred. He became irrationally furious, initially with himself for being so stupid but also with Norman for not being more specific about the person who was making the call. The first of these was perhaps understandable; but to blame Norman into the bargain was both unjust and illogical - but fairness wasn't even on his tick-list. He dashed down to the working alleyway, threw open Norman's cabin door without knocking, and yelled. 'You useless pillock - why didn't you tell me it was Glenda who was calling? You've buggered things up good and proper now.'

Norman, who'd only just finished in the galley and had put his feet up while enjoying a mug of tea, looked round with a start. He immediately guessed what had happened - and then went equally ballistic. 'Don't blame me if you've fucked up your love life,' he bawled, waving Steve out of the room and into the alleyway. 'I don't even know your girlfriends, let alone what their names are. You should've used your loaf before opening your mouth.' And as he slammed the door in Steve's face, almost flattening his nose, he shouted. 'And another time, don't come barging in here without knocking.'

Aiming a brutal kick at Norman's cabin door Steve turned and stormed off, out on to the after well-deck where he lit up a Rothmans and perched fractiously on the edge of the hatch cover. He was seething, and for several seconds remained so; but as so often occurs in fraught situations the tobacco eventually kicked in with a resultant decrease in rancour. He smoked the Rothmans right down to the butt and lit another one straight from the stub. His previously astronomical rate of respiration gradually eased while his blood-pressure moderated, the pounding in his ears slowly diminishing until his anger was under control.

The first thing that struck him was how unreasonably he'd blamed Norman, and he resolved first and foremost that he'd go and apologize. Secondly, as soon as he felt sufficiently composed he'd have to phone Maxine; and thirdly, he'd somehow get a message to Glenda, trying to convince her that she really had nothing to worry about. In this last respect he felt thoroughly deceitful, knowing he was a two-timing schemer. But he couldn't help it, and as much as he adored Maxine he just thrilled to the excitement that Glenda so capably generated.

'Sorry, Norman,' he mumbled, sheepishly, after tapping on the Second Cook's door and inching it open barely wide enough to peep through. 'I just didn't think. It wasn't your fault. It's just that I thought someone else was ringing and........well, you sussed the rest.'

'Come on in,' invited Norman in a conciliatory fashion, motioning for Steve to sit down, a smile creasing his lips as Steve settled nervously on the settee. 'Fancy a drink?' he asked, reaching into his locker and withdrawing a bottle of Lemon Hart that had already had the neck taken out of it. 'A shot of this'll do you the power of good.' Norman poured two generous measures and handed one to Steve before replacing the cap on the bottle. 'Good health,' he toasted, holding his glass aloft before reducing its contents by a half.

'Yeah........cheers,' acknowledged Steve, hesitantly, wondering why Norman was being so sociable when he, Steve, had been expecting a roasting. He took a sip from his glass and wriggled uncomfortably while the cook sat deeply in thought. Eventually, Norman spoke, and Steve was totally unprepared for what followed.

'I suppose I ought to apologise as well,' declared Norman, switching his gaze and staring at Steve as he mulled over how to proceed. 'Not for the misunderstanding over the phone call, mind you,' he eventually continued, swilling the rum around his glass. 'That was your fault, no two ways about it - but I shouldn't have sworn and shovelled you out into the alleyway like that, even though you were out of order.'

'Well, I suppose I asked for it,' replied Steve, feeling a little happier now that for whatever reason Norman seemed to be struggling with his own conscience. 'At the very least I should've knocked before bursting in like that.'

'Yes, you should have,' agreed Norman, before emptying his glass and reaching again for the bottle. 'Trouble is, after you'd gone I got to thinking that your behaviour wasn't so very different from mine when I went after Jimmy for taking the piss - you know, after I got that letter from my missus.'

Steve chuckled, diffidently, remembering the incident as if it was only yesterday. 'You certainly scared the shit out of him that's for sure,' he reminded Norman, not that Norman needed any reminding. 'And I honestly thought that you'd kill him.' Steve took another sip of rum. 'By the way,' he continued, warily and after an appropriate pause. 'Have you heard any more from your wife? Or is it really all over?'

'Haven't heard a squeak,' replied Norman, topping up Steve's glass before replacing the bottle in his locker, 'and I'm not fuckin' worried either. Having thought about it I'll be a fuckin' sight better off without her. I've already had a word with the Boss about cancelling my allotment.'

It was clear that Norman was viewing the matter less freakishly than he had been, but Steve decided not to push the issue. Caution was the safest policy, he concluded, and that it was better to drop the subject than dwell on it. He followed the cook's example and emptied his glass, wincing as the liquor seared his throat. 'Anyway,' he croaked, his eyes streaming as he set his glass on the table. 'Thanks for the drink. I'm going to phone Maxine, then I'm going to try and smooth things over with Glenda - and sorry once again for being nasty.'

'Don't mention it,' answered Norman, draining his own glass before rinsing it out in the washbasin. 'And the best of luck with

Glenda - it sounds like you're going to need it.'

16

Following the blast from Glenda, Steve's hopes of a thaw in relations were only a few degrees above zero, although he'd give it a run for its money. But first things first - and then came a twist in the tale. As he hurried up top to ring Maxine he bumped into the Senior Cadet, a Tasmanian lad of about his own age who lived on the outskirts of Hobart. The apprentice was beaming, and was clearly delighted about something. 'You're looking pleased with yourself, Gary,' observed Steve, pausing halfway up the companionway. 'You just off on a date?'

'Better than that,' answered the trainee officer, as he pushed past Steve on his way to his cabin. 'The Mate's just told me I'm paying off tomorrow, so that I can attend nautical college and finish my exams - but I've got a week's leave in the meantime. I'm just off below to sort a few things out. See you around sometime.' And without further dalliance, the excited teenager hurried on his way, humming some tuneless ditty that vaguely resembled Gene Vincent's, 'I'm Goin' Home'.

'Yeah........see you,' called Steve, as the cadet disappeared into the officer's accommodation to begin packing his suitcase. 'Best of luck.'

It had only been a brief conversation, but the content was sufficient to set another bee buzzing. If Gary can pay of just like that, Steve wondered, why can't I?

'Because I bloody well said so,' stormed the Chief Steward, after Steve had had the temerity to tap on the senior catering officer's door and ask the improbable question. 'He's leaving the ship for a perfectly good reason - to finish his exams and hopefully qualify for his Second Mate's ticket, not to go mooning off with some woman. Now get out of my office and start acting like an adult.'

Steve's second eviction in less than an hour wasn't as galling as it might have been owing to his sights having been set in the basement; but it had been worth the try and he'd have kicked himself if a golden opportunity had gone begging. Now, where's Maxine's telephone number? he ruminated, rummaging about in his trouser pocket for the now dog-eared fragment of paper, as finally he attempted that call.

He could hear the numbers engaging as the operator made the connection, and soon afterwards the buzz of the ring tone. He waited with baited breath, fingers crossed there would be no more foul-ups, although he knew there shouldn't be given the number he was calling. 'Hi........Maxine?' he enquired, as eventually a maidenly voice answered. This time everything went smoothly; and it was as if their separation was only defined by a garden fence rather than half the length of the country. As always the conversation was that of soul mates, and as Steve blew a kiss into the receiver at the end of the call he was in raptures - but he was already speculating as how best to rebuild bridges with Glenda.

His initial instinct was to ask the operator to connect him to the nurses home in the hope that he could speak with Glenda - but then he had a better idea. He would ask if he could speak to Linda, in the hope that she'd play the role of mediator. That way, he reasoned, Glenda wouldn't be able to slam the phone down without giving him chance to explain. By a stroke of good fortune, Linda wasn't working and came to the telephone in the nurses home foyer where she listened to what Steve had to say.

'I'm not sure she'll believe you,' she answered, after hearing what was after all a load of old cobblers, disingenuously laced with contrition. 'But I'll give it a go, and who knows - you might be lucky.'

'Thanks, Linda,' acknowledged Steve, believing that maybe the pendulum might be swinging back in his direction. 'You're a gem.' And then, almost as an afterthought, he added, lamely. 'Is she really mad at me?'

'Mad at you?' cried Linda, having heard what to her ears at least was the most ludicrous question. 'What do you think? After what happened between you two yesterday evening, only for her to discover she'd been playing second fiddle to this Maxine. Of course she's bloody mad at you.' And then, before Steve had chance to defend himself, she continued. 'Still, I'll pass on your message - but if I were you I wouldn't be holding my breath.'

The immediate future was decidedly grey from Steve's perspective. Initially, his hopes had been high that Glenda would believe him, and even if she didn't that she'd maybe forgive him; but the phone remained silent - at least as far as calls for Steve Chapman were concerned, and as the hours became days he became less and less certain that he'd ever see Glenda again.

By Wednesday he'd all but given up hope; but not only that, he'd gotten around to thinking that he wasn't entirely to blame for the stand off. Okay, he hadn't been as straight as he might have been regarding Maxine, but the romp in the sub-tropical gardens had been entirely of Glenda's making; he hadn't forced the issue in any shape or form. In fact, although he'd been a willing and enthusiastic participant he'd been completely unsuspecting as to what the girl had intended. And then there was the fact that she'd obviously discussed their cavorting with Linda, so she'd clearly not displayed an iota of refinement. I bet Linda even knows the colour of my shorts, he told himself, feeling a little aggrieved that Glenda had chosen to discuss their relationship in such apparently specific detail. No, he told himself, I'm not the only one at fault for this little balls-up.

On the Thursday evening every ship in the harbour had to slip its moorings and head for the anchorage, owing to a rising swell rolling in from the Pacific. Some faraway storm was the likely culprit as in sunny Hawkes Bay the weather was fine and the swell apart, the sea was as smooth as a looking glass. Still, what may have played havoc in the Cook Islands, some twelve-hundred miles or more away to the north-east, but delighted surfers both here on the east coast of New Zealand and maybe even in Australia, was now causing disruption at the port of Napier, and an excursion to the anchorage was imperative. Some of the crew were ashore; but it couldn't be helped and it was generally accepted that it wasn't their fault and that they wouldn't mind in the slightest.

'What are you looking so miserable about?' enquired Peter, on the Friday morning as the boys set about laying-up the breakfast tables, Keith and Donald being among those stranded when the ship had moved out to the anchorage. 'Anyone'd think you'd lost a fortune.'

233

Norman excepted, Steve hadn't told anyone about his falling out with Glenda, not even Jimmy, and he was as certain as he could be that the cook hadn't been blabbing his mouth off. So, Peter's probing left him in a difficult position; whether to mention the break-up or to hold his tongue, pretending there was nothing wrong and that he was simply feeling under the weather. After a few seconds deliberation he opted for the former, omitting the finer points and only mentioning that Glenda had inadvertently found out about Maxine.

'Oh what a tangled web we weave...............,' sang Archie, teasingly, having overheard the conversation from the pantry side of the servery. 'That's what you get for being disloyal, dipping your wick into too many jam jars while not remembering who's who. Funny, I never have that sort of trouble'.

'You mean to say that shirt-lifters never get jealous?' taunted Peter, more in mischief than malice. He winked at Steve. 'I bet you lot fight like cat and dog when you find out that someone's been cheating – scratching, hair pulling, spitting, biting, the whole caboodle. I bet your cabins look like battlefields by the time you've finished.'

'Of course it happens,' replied Archie, matter of factly and with an air of superiority. 'I'm simply saying that I don't have your kind of trouble - because I'm not interested in women.'

Steve felt better for the banter and couldn't resist adding his own three-ha'penceworth. 'You've got to be sharp to get one over on Archie,' he commented, addressing Peter specifically, but loud enough for Archie's benefit, 'but I bet he's left some claw marks in his time.'

The first Steve knew of the dripping dishcloth was when it hit him squarely in the nape of the neck, sending water cascading down his shirt collar and across the shoulders of his clean white jacket. 'You dirty bastard, Archie', he complained, feeling thoroughly miffed as he dried the scruff of his neck with his waiters cloth. 'This is the only clean jacket I've got - now look what you've been and done.' In a fit of pique he lofted the dishcloth back through the servery; but Archie ducked and the cloth hit Sec - who just happened to have entered the pantry - slap between the eyes, rendering him temporarily sightless while soaking the front of his jacket.

Sec was livid. Peter made himself scarce while Archie pretended he'd only stooped down to load plates into the hot-press and knew nothing whatsoever about the missile. In the handful of seconds it took this cameo to unfold Steve stood petrified, knowing only too well he was jiggered.

'What the hell d'you think you're playing at?' spluttered Sec, at length, sponging water from his jacket while drying his face on a pantry cloth. 'Don't you think it's time you grew up?'

Steve was about to pin the blame on Archie but thought better of it, making do with a feeble apology. 'Sorry, Sec.' I'd just been wiping down in the saloon and decided to toss the dishcloth into the sink via the servery. It was just plain laziness really - it wasn't aimed deliberately at you.' It was a putrid excuse, and Steve was in little doubt that he wouldn't escape this indiscretion with a plain old-fashioned ticking-off.

'Well, you can say goodbye to your free afternoons,' confirmed Sec, with a look that stated unequivocally that he wasn't prepared to negotiate, 'and just think yourself lucky that it was me who walked in when I did rather than the Boss, otherwise you'd have been for the high jump.'

The sigh of relief was palpable. Steve hadn't escaped retribution, but he'd avoided a trip to the bridge and the dreaded interview with the Captain. 'Thanks, Sec,' he mumbled, with genuine remorse, 'it won't happen again - honest.'

'Just you make sure that it doesn't because if it does, well - you know what'll happen,' answered Sec, as he vacated the pantry to change his jacket. 'I won't be so lenient next time.'

And then Peter piped up. He'd been filling the cereal containers on the opposite side of the saloon; but he was a master at eavesdropping and had no intention of missing a trick if he could help it. 'Hey, Sec,' he called, sniffing out a chance of profiting from Steve's misfortune. 'Seeing as how Steve'll be working, can I have his afternoons off?'

You had to admire his cheek, but the Second Steward left him in little doubt that he would have been better off keeping his mouth shut. 'No you bloody well can't,' he stormed, still clearly incensed. 'Come to think of it, I'm not totally convinced that you weren't

235

involved so just to be even handed, you'll be keeping him company.'

'But Sec,' implored Peter, realizing he'd dropped a clanger. 'I haven't done anything wrong. Why should I have to pay for Steve's lash-ups?'

'Because I'm not sure I believe you,' answered Sec, making it clear that the matter was closed and any further protest was pointless.

'Thanks a bundle,' grumbled Peter, once Sec was out of earshot and he could vent his enmity on Steve. 'You drop yourself in the shit and I have to face the consequences. Some fuckin' mate you turned out to be'

Steve wasn't standing for that. 'Don't blame me,' he retorted, fed up to the teeth, furious with Archie and in no mood to be lectured by Peter. 'If you'd kept your silly trap shut you'd have probably gotten away with it. As far as Sec was concerned you had nothing to do with it - well, not until you started rabbiting on about having the extra time off. That was your own stupid fault.'

'Now then, come along girls,' trilled Archie, clearly enjoying a situation he'd helped to create but had escaped with totally unscathed. 'Stop behaving like a pair of schoolchildren and get on with your work - and you, Steve, don't forget you're serving in the duty mess this morning so you'd better get a move on.'

'Aw! Piss off, Archie,' snapped the boys, in unison, clearly of the opinion that the Bedroom Steward was largely to blame for their woes.

'If you hadn't chucked that dishcloth none of this would have happened,' continued Steve, resolute that Archie would at least get a flea in his ear.

'And none of this would have happened if you hadn't taken the piss out of me in the first place,' reminded Archie, determined not to be trampled on by what he considered a pair of young whipper-snappers. 'And just remember this seeing as how you're the one who mentioned it. You've got to be sharp to get one over on Archie.'

Steve could hardly argue with that, and he regretted letting his mouth get the better of him. As he headed around to the duty mess he resolved to be more careful what he said in future. His tongue, he concluded, was responsible for his clutch of recent troubles.

By early afternoon the swell had subsided sufficiently to allow the port to be reopened. The Captain and owners were happy as time spent idling in the anchorage meant money that wasn't being earned. Then there was the crew. They were delighted as they could resume their free-and-easy lifestyles; although as far as Steve was concerned that wasn't necessarily so, not with Glenda being missing from his radar. In fact, the only miseries who didn't seem bothered whether they were in port or biding their time in the anchorage - although if anything they preferred the latter - were the handful of money-grabbers who welcomed the situation as another source of income: 'More days - more dollars', being a phrase that Steve had heard often, especially from the masochists during the breakdown in the Indian Ocean.

Even the friction between the pantry staff was forgotten; although to be truthful Archie had remained his usual, unflappable self, while Peter didn't seem overly bothered about having his free afternoons confiscated. 'Not much fun mooching about on your own in the daytime, anyway - unless you're out on the piss,' he confided, when Steve made a stumbling apology in an attempt to patch up their differences. 'And anyway,' he announced, like a dog with two tails as they prepared for afternoon tea. 'I'm back with Linda now so I should be well away this evening.'

'You're back with Linda?' queried Steve, who always had difficulty in keeping up with Peter's romantic assignations. 'Since when?'

'Since last Monday night when you were at the pictures,' replied Peter, who clearly regarded his bed-hopping as a matter of routine. 'That other piece of crumpet gave me the elbow so I gave Linda a ring - you know, to try and bury the hatchet, and she agreed.'

'Lucky you,' answered Steve, his thoughts drifting back to the previous Saturday night and the following day's telephone bust-up. 'Has she said anything about me and Glenda?'

'No,' pronounced Peter, sorting out a tray of tabnabs for the officers and engineers while reserving the two largest and creamiest doughnuts for themselves. 'Only that the pair of you had a stinking row over Maxine - but no more than you told me this morning.'

And then, the peggy looked into the pantry. 'Telephone call for you, Steve,' announced the junior deckhand, snatching a doughnut and vanishing in one deft movement.

'Who is it?' called Steve, his pulse-rate in overdrive as he pondered the caller's identity.

'Dunno,' flung the peggy over his shoulder as he slid down the companionway to the working alleyway. 'Just some bird asking for Steve Chapman.'

Steve hurried topside, trying to work out who was calling. Was it Maxine simply keeping in touch? Or was it Glenda, offering to restart their affair? In the end, accepting that it was impossible to know, he just said, 'Hello,' hoping fervently that the voice on the other end of the line could be easily recognised.

As it happened he needn't have worried, as before he had chance to say anything incriminating, the caller declared, 'Hello, Steve. It's me, Glenda. I'm just calling to apologise for bawling you out last Sunday, and not giving you chance to explain. How are you?'

'Oh! Hi, Glenda,' replied Steve, with as much indifference as he could muster without sounding totally disinterested: let her sweat a bit, he thought; make her feel guilty about the way she'd behaved, but don't be pig-headed and overdo it. 'Yeah, I'm fine,' he continued, hoping his apparent lack of enthusiasm wouldn't prove the final nail in their relationship's coffin. 'How about you? Are you keeping well?'

Glenda didn't answer. Instead, she gushed. 'Oh! Steve. I'm so sorry. I've missed you so much. I've been miserable all week. I even tried ringing yesterday evening but the line had been disconnected.'

'Yeah, that's right,' replied Steve, by now accepting that Glenda was serious and that it was time he packed up playing games. 'Every ship in the harbour had to move to the anchorage. It was all pretty short notice - there wasn't time to let anyone know. We only arrived back alongside this afternoon.'

'If I hadn't been so proud and stubborn I'd have rung earlier,' went on Glenda, pressing her case to resume where they'd left off the previous Saturday. 'Linda gave me your message but I just couldn't forget this Maxine. I felt sure there must be something between you, but after I'd had time to think about it I realized it didn't really matter - I just wanted to be with you. Can we go out together again tomorrow? Maybe tonight, even?'

Steve was cock-a-hoop, but he didn't show it. Instead, he

238

responded rather lukewarmly, 'Yeah, that'd be great,' and then, not wishing to sound too apathetic, but at a risk of ruining the effect, he added. 'Tonight would be fine. Where? And at what time?'

Glenda was clearly overjoyed. 'How about in the gardens where we went last Saturday, after we left the Top Hat. At about half past eight - if that's all right.' And then, in that seductive manner of hers, she added. 'It'll be dark by then.'

'Sounds good to me,' replied Steve, by this stage barely able to contain his excitement. 'See you at eight-thirty.' And then, before he could say anything else, the line went dead, leaving him staring at the receiver, wondering at the real reason for Glenda's apparent change of heart.

'I told you last week,' repeated Jimmy, while seated on the hatch cover in the after well-deck after Steve had informed him of his recent difficulties. 'She's clamouring for it, and just can't help it. I'm afraid, Steve,' announced the galley boy, with poker-faced gravity, 'you've got yourself a nymphomaniac - and if I were you I'd make the most of it.'

Steve was dumbfounded. Him knocking about with a nymphomaniac and not being even vaguely aware of it? He had to admit it made sense. Glenda's wealth of experience was a product of regular sexual activity, that much was obvious, but the term 'nymphomaniac' hadn't even entered his head, although it was firmly implanted there now. 'Bloody hell, Jimmy,' he blurted, sliding his fingers to and fro through his hair. 'I'm not sure I can handle this.'

'Oh! And why not?' quizzed Jimmy, before answering the question for himself. 'You handled it well enough last Saturday so why all the sudden anxiety.' And then, switching his gaze to Steve's nether regions, he asked. 'Any sign of the other?'

'Uh! What! Oh! No,' replied Steve, still clearly flustered, 'I've been keeping my eye on it but I haven't noticed anything.'

'Well, there you are, then,' declared Jimmy, reassuringly, drawing a State Express from its packet and firing it up with his Ronson. 'You've nothing to worry about. It seems you've a clean bill of health and just about everything a fellow could wish for, so just get out there and enjoy it.'

Steve wasn't sure; but then he suddenly realized that he could handle Glenda and that Jimmy was right, one twelve-letter word hadn't altered anything. When all was said and done, most of the girls on the coast seemed to be nymphomaniacs, and none of the other blokes seemed bothered. So, this was a new beginning; he'd discovered the new Steve Chapman. Gone was the callow individual who'd joined the *Alice Springs* in the depths of an English winter. The newer model had emerged, and had matured in a New Zealand Summer.

The remaining two weeks in Napier were ephemeral, passing like a burst of sunlight. Steve phoned Maxine and she rang him; but shipboard obligations apart he spent the rest of his time with Glenda, excepting on the occasions when her nursing responsibilities took precedence. Glenda was on top of her game throughout: in the gardens, on the beach, even between the timber piling supporting the piers at the harbour; in fact, just about anywhere she fancied. Even so, Steve never invited her aboard, notwithstanding that John's offer of a vacant cabin held good. If nothing else he was forever protective of his privacy and single cabin or otherwise, he didn't relish their affair becoming a spectator sport, even if it was an open secret.

Towards the end of that fortnight the exertions were taking their toll. Steve felt thoroughly exhausted, even to the extent that it was difficult to rouse him from his slumbers. 'You've been burning the candle at both ends, my lad,' chided Archie, one morning, when Steve stumbled bleary-eyed into the pantry almost five minutes late, looking frazzled and still half asleep.

'Oh no he hasn't,' intervened Peter, eager to paint the truer picture. 'He's been having it off with that Maori nurse - and it's not only been once a night if what I've heard is anything to go by.'

'So what,' snapped Steve, in no mood to be harried by Peter of all people. 'You've been screwing that Linda like nobody's business - and anyway, Glenda isn't a Maori, she's only part Maori.'

'They're all the same lying down,' reminded Peter, not in the least bit ruffled by Steve's prickliness. 'How many times was it last night? Once? Twice? Half-a-dozen?'

'Aw! Bugger off!' snarled Steve, whipping his pantry cloth from the work surface and sending a milk jug flying in the process. 'You're only jealous - not that you've any need to be from what Glenda told me.'

Peter was halted in his tracks. 'You mean, you talk about me and Linda?' he queried, suddenly unsure of his ground.

'Course we do, just like you and Linda talk about me and Glenda,' replied Steve, quickly sensing the upper hand as he stooped to mop up the milk. 'And not only that, but they talk about you and me with the other girls. I bet there's nothing the girls at the nurses' home don't know about the four of us or what we get up to - and you know something else? Glenda even told me that Linda once got a tape measure out and measured..............................'

'Yeah! Yeah! All right,' interrupted Peter, not wanting his vital statistics to be bandied about for the absorption of all and sundry. 'You can spare us the details. It's just that I didn't know that our love lives were such common knowledge - although I ought to have guessed.'

'You should have,' affirmed Steve, now fully awake and ready to divulge another tasty titbit, 'but it's not only us they have over. Glenda even mentioned our very own Second Steward and one of the ward sisters. From what I can gather their antics would make Lady Chatterley's Lover read like a Bunty Annual.'

'What? Sec? Our Sec? You're fuckin' joking,' spluttered Peter, as if he'd been hit with a rock. 'After all he's told us about messin' around with different women. Cheeky bastard - and him a married man too.'

'OK, that's enough,' cautioned Archie, who'd been listening to the conversation with both interest and amusement: he'd already spotted Donald grinning to himself while scrubbing out the saloon, and didn't think it prudent for the second Steward's entanglement to be discussed so openly. 'Whatever you think of the Second Steward he's got a life of his own, the same as you,' continued Archie, softly. 'And anyway, he was only thinking of your welfare, as junior ratings in need of guidance. I suppose it was a case of do as I say, not as I do - and he did it for your own good, although I can see he was wasting his breath.'

'Maybe,' objected Peter, unwilling to let the issue rest. 'But I still think it's a bit of a cheek, him lecturing us while him and this ward sister are going at it like rabbits.'

'You can think what you like,' replied Archie, regarding Peter from beneath arched eyebrows. 'But remember this. The Second Steward's been pretty good to you two, even when you haven't deserved it. OK, he may have stopped your afternoons off after that episode with the dishcloth, but he soon reinstated them when he considered you'd both learnt your lesson.'

'That's true,' conceded Steve, who didn't really give a hoot about Sec's private life, married or otherwise. 'He's usually treated me pretty fairly, apart from the odd bollocking, so live and let live, I say. How about you, Peter?'

'Yeah, I suppose so,' answered Peter, grudgingly, as he emptied the dregs from his teacup. 'But I still reckon he's got a nerve, no matter what you say.'

'Well, now we've agreed on that here's something else for you to get used to,' said Archie, who was preparing a tray for the Chief Steward. 'You'd better make the most of the next couple of days because we'll be sailing on Monday evening. The Second Mate told me a few minutes ago.'

'But that's only the day after tomorrow,' complained a visibly-shocked Peter, who like almost every other member of the Alice Spring's crew had regarded their current situation as somehow semi-permanent. 'I didn't think we were leaving till Wednesday.'

'Change of plan,' expanded Archie, placing a couple of biscuits on a tea-plate which he squeezed between the teapot and sugar basin. 'Loading progressed faster than expected. The deck crew will be squaring away and battening down over the weekend and then on Monday, we'll be taking aboard a deck cargo of wool. The bloods'll be boarding from two o'clock onwards.'

The weeks on the New Zealand coast and the time spent rock-dodging around Australia, mostly with no passengers to worry about, had lulled the catering staff into a make-believe comfort zone, where work was an inconvenience and *'La Dolce Vita'* was the byword. They'd still had their duties to perform, but thanks to the charitable staffing arrangements it had seemed more like a six-week holiday. But being at sea would put a stop to all that and the thought bludgeoned Steve like a brick. He'd noticed the *Alice Springs* settling lower in the water as her cargo was loaded but the implications hadn't registered. 'Bloody hell!' he exclaimed, knotting the pantry cloth around his waist while waiting for his bucket to fill. 'I'd forgotten all about bloody passengers - and working all the hours under the sun. Can't say I'm looking forward to it.'

'Me neither,' groused Peter, as he rummaged through the locker beneath the sink in search of a roll of mutton cloth. 'I think I'll skin out - see if I can't shack up with Linda somewhere, get a job, even. It shouldn't be too difficult.'

'That'd be daft,' admonished Steve, with all the enlightenment of a professional counsellor. 'I thought about the very same thing back in Timaru, about going to live with Maxine and her family in Manoao - but she talked me out of it and we came to a better arrangement. I'm going to the New Zealand High Commission when we get home, see if I can't emigrate, maybe get an assisted passage with Maxine as sponsor. That way I won't get deported, not like most of the blokes who skedaddle and end up getting arrested.'

'Mmmm........I guess you're right,' agreed Peter, who'd found the mutton cloth and was busily slicing a strip off with a carving knife. 'But I can't say I'm looking forward to leaving. I've nothing to go home for.'

How utterly depressing, thought Steve. He too was wishing he could stay in New Zealand, and he remembered how he'd spoken to Maxine about jumping ship and how she'd persuaded him otherwise. No, he didn't want to go home either; but he'd go and bask in the joy of a family reunion, telling them about Maxine and regaling them with some - but not all - of his exploits. And then, once he'd discussed the matter with his parents, he'd go to New Zealand House and initiate the emigration process. 'Why don't you come with me to the High Commission when we get home,' he invited, cheerfully, stirring a handful of soap into his bucket with an enthusiasm that belied his fatigue. 'Who knows, we might even end up emigrating together.'

Archie rolled his eyes in disbelief. It was something else he'd heard time and again and he wondered just how often these boyhood seedlings had ripened. He hoped in Steve's case that they would, because despite his recent philandering he seemed a decent young man who really did love the girl in Manoao. Peter, on the other hand, was a hopeless example who seemed destined to drift with the effluent.

'I see Sean Cassidy's back,' said Donald, when Steve eventually arrived in the saloon having finished his scrub-out. 'Apparently he was let out of gaol yesterday lunchtime. He called at The Crown for a quick one and was back on the ship again by teatime. Said he wouldn't be drinking or going ashore again till London.'

'What! You must be joking,' rubbished Steve, who couldn't see the fireman remaining abstinent indefinitely, not with places like the Panama Canal Zone and Curaçao to contend with. 'I can't see him staying on the wagon, even if he doesn't go ashore.'

'I agree,' answered Donald, who himself had remained remarkably sober since arriving in Napier. 'I'm only saying what he said - not what he's likely to do.'

'What about Roger Oates?' asked Steve, wondering what had happened to the seaman with the broken leg. 'I haven't seen anything of him, and he should have been released over a week ago.'

'He was as far as I know,' replied Donald, spooning jams and marmalades from their jars into their respective dishes, 'but no one's seen hide nor hair of him. Knowing Roger he's probably shacked up with a female alcoholic.'

'Right, listen up you blokes,' called the Second Steward, entering the saloon just as Steve and the other stewards were putting the finishing touches to their table lay-ups. 'I suppose you've all heard that we'll be sailing on Monday. Well, we've a load of clean linen coming aboard straight after breakfast and I want it taken care of right away.' The groans could be heard in the galley. Getting the soiled linen ashore the previous week had been bad enough - humping it aboard again would be bone-wearying. And then, as if he was a mind reader, Sec continued, 'I've had a word with the Bosun and he'll get it hoisted with a winch.'

'Well, that's a relief, sighed Keith, the steward who'd assumed Danny Meeks' responsibilities as Captain's Tiger, and who'd listened to Sec whilst gently massaging his lumber regions. 'My back's been killing me just lately - I must have put it out somehow.' The rest of them sniggered. Keith had in all probability indeed put his back out; and given the scrumptious blonde he'd been knocking about with, just about everyone knew how.

As for Danny Meeks, there was little likelihood of him returning. 'According to the agent he was operated on in Nelson and had a number of bladder stones removed,' advised the Chief Steward, when Sec posed the question after breakfast. 'The operation was a success but he developed complications - nothing life threatening I understand, but sufficient to keep him in hospital. I suppose he'll be repatriated when he's fit to travel.'

'Thank goodness for that,' sighed Peter, who was delighted that his erstwhile tormentor was still immobilized. 'I was afraid they'd discharge him before we left Napier.'

For much of Saturday the deck department was busily engaged in preparing the *Alice Springs* for sea. A whole host of tasks needed attending to, not least the clearance of a month's accumulation of clutter that would otherwise hamper the hatch-sealing process. That took for most of the morning, and it was gone two o'clock before the hatches could be properly secured. Steve had the afternoon off - in fact it was his last afternoon off - but he didn't go ashore. Instead, he stood with Jimmy at the forward rail of the poop, overlooking the after well-deck as a quintet of deckies replaced the hatch covers and tightened down the battens.

Heavy weather could strike without warning, so to prevent the hatches being breached it was essential they were absolutely watertight. This was achieved by a simple yet time-consuming exercise. On a conventional cargo ship a hatch cover took the form of a tarpaulin, stretched over baulks of timber that fitted snugly together on ledges on the inner faces of the hatch coaming. The hatch was secured by hammering wedges into place between the folded edges of the tarpaulin and brackets on the outer walls of the coaming. Finally, heavy steel battens, shackled to deck-mounted ring-bolts, were tightened over the hatch creating a durable, waterproof seal.

'Just like that,' said Jimmy, turning his back to the breeze and lighting a State Express. 'Mind you, I've heard that some of the more modern ships are being fitted with sliding hatch covers that can be operated at the press of a button. If it's true they won't need anywhere near as many deckhands in future and that'll suit the owners no end.'

Steve appreciated the point, and was immediately aware of the wider ramifications. If the deck department needed fewer deckhands then the catering staff would have fewer mouths to feed. 'Won't need so many cooks and stewards, either,' voiced Steve, firing up a Rothman's and slipping his lighter into his pocket. 'Still, no need for us to worry,' he continued, lapsing into a comfortable complacency, 'it'll be years before ships like the *Alice Springs* are done away with.' Steve was most probably right. The *Alice Springs* was only seven years old and the likelihood was that she had another fifteen years ahead of her, but that wasn't necessarily true of more venerable vessels. Older ships like the *Lilac Hill* were already being replaced, in her case by the *Milford Sound* which Jimmy adopted as an example.

'She's bigger than us by three thousand tons,' said Jimmy, who'd clearly been doing his homework, 'but she only carries sixty-six crew whereas we carry seventy-four.'

It was a sobering reminder that they lived in an ever-changing world, prompting Steve to recall that on British Railways his beloved steam locomotives were being rapidly displaced by diesels. No, Jimmy was right. Nothing could be taken for granted, and come another two decades the seafaring life might have altered out of all recognition.

With nothing else on his agenda, Steve sauntered back to his cabin and flicked through a copy of the overseas edition of the Daily Mirror that Peter had retrieved from a waste-basket. The yellow-bound volume comprised a week's publication of the tabloid that was airmailed to wherever it was wanted. Peter had considered it legitimate salvage and it now formed part of their cabin's reading material.

He spent the evening with Glenda, at the Top Hat, where the pair of them chatted and listened to the music before leaving to resume more energetic pastimes. It was past three o'clock when they parted and four before he tumbled into bed.

'Wasn't worth turning in, was it?' teased Peter, having finally roused Steve from his coma. 'Blimey, you were well away. You must have been dreaming of Glenda.'

'Why? What's the time?' queried Steve, rubbing the sleep from his eyes with one hand and propping himself up with the other. 'Is it half-past five already?'

'Half-past five? I should think so,' answered Peter, making his exit, having assured himself that Steve was mobile and unlikely to drift back to sleep. 'It's a quarter past six, and everyone else has turned to.'

Steve scrambled from his bunk and into his dungarees, stepping into his shoes while his socks were stuffed into a pocket. He slipped a T-shirt over his shoulders on his way to the pantry and reported for duty at six-sixteen precisely, a passable parody of a scarecrow. He felt completely shattered but at least he was there, hoping no-one who mattered had missed him.

'What a sight for sore eyes,' tut-tutted Archie, who'd followed Steve into the pantry having already completed his own scrub-out, namely the Chief Steward's office and the adjoining bibby-alleyway. 'It's just as well we are sailing tomorrow - it'll save you a stay in a convalescent home.'

Steve smiled, wryly. He knew he looked like a corpse and didn't need any reminding. 'Tell you what, Archie,' he answered, stifling a yawn as he began filling his bucket. 'It's been a fantastic few weeks but I'm glad it's all over. Glenda's been terrific, but she's just about buggered me up.'

'You don't say,' replied Archie, his voice heavily-laced with pseudo sarcasm, 'no-one would ever have guessed. Still, you're safe in one respect,' he continued, pouring himself a second cup of tea. 'The Second Steward isn't back yet, either.'

Well, that's a relief if nothing else, thought Steve, as he shambled out of the pantry to commence his own scrub-out. All that mattered now was for him to get his skates on and make up the lost fifteen minutes.

By extremely good fortune Steve had turned to just in time, for as he left the pantry and made for the engineers' alleyway he bumped into Sec who appeared equally as dishevelled as he did. 'Good night, Sec?' he asked, involuntarily, as he squeezed gingerly past with his bucket. There was no reply. Instead, the Second Steward paused while knotting his tie wondering what, if anything, Steve knew. Steve carried on, and it wasn't until he was down on his hands and knees with his scrubbing brush that he appreciated his remark's connotation. Initial uncertainty gave way to serenity as he concluded that to keep the fellow guessing would be an advantage rather than a handicap.

'Are you coming down to the harbour to see us off tomorrow?' asked Steve, on Sunday evening, as he and Glenda got hurriedly dressed beneath the trees in the sub-tropical gardens. 'We're sailing at six in the evening.'

'If we can get finished in time we'll both be there,' answered Glenda, snapping a suspender over a stocking top. 'We're due to finish at five so if all goes to plan it shouldn't be a problem. But you know what? I'm going to miss you, Steve - more than you can ever imagine.'

'I'm going to miss you too, Glenda,' replied Steve, slipping his jazzy-patterned pullover over his head before wiping a smear from his spectacles. 'I've never met anyone like you before - ever.' Steve had never uttered anything truer, and he hoped Glenda took it as a compliment rather than as a reference to her sexual virtuosity. For her part Glenda never batted an eyelid, as if she hadn't even noticed the unintended double-entendre. However, Steve had noted that she'd chosen to close their relationship more or less where it had begun, as if she might have developed an emotional attachment to complement the excitement of lovemaking. But he thought it unlikely, and although this beautiful, brown-skinned girl had been a revelation, illuminating his life and finishing what Maxine had started, he knew there was no deep-seated longing.

Sailing day dawned, and like many others among the *Alice Springs* crew Steve was feeling down in the mouth. As had happened so often lately his thoughts drifted back to the close of those childhood holidays. Today he was equally downcast and desperately in need of a lift. He'd always intended phoning Maxine, so to cheer himself up he rang her straight after breakfast. It was mostly the usual small talk, but critically included the agents' addresses in Panama, Curaçao and Dunkirk. They chatted about all manner of things; and then, as if the floodgates had opened, Maxine dissolved into tears. 'Promise you'll come back to me, Steve,' she sobbed, unable to contain herself any longer. 'I love you so much.'

'I Promise - cross my heart,' assured Steve, sensing his own eyes moisten. 'I'll be going to the High Commission as soon as we get back home, and I'll write regularly so that you'll know exactly what's happening. I will be back, Maxine, I promise,' he reiterated, before blowing a farewell kiss into the receiver. 'And remember, there'll never be anyone else.'

As Steve resumed his work in the pantry he reflected on his relationship with Glenda. He knew that he'd never forget her; how could he given their extraordinary affiliation. However, there wasn't that feeling of emptiness that had accompanied his parting from Maxine. They hadn't swapped contact details, nor had he offered her the addresses of the *Alice Springs'* agents. Pointedly she hadn't asked for them, proof it was needed that although he'd be missed in the short term he'd served his purpose and was already one of yesterday's toys.

Throughout the morning layer upon layer of bailed wool was assembled on top of the hatch covers, so that by early afternoon it was being lashed down to secure it from the wrath of the elements. The loading of the deck cargo had a claustrophobic effect, depriving the *Alice Springs* of her wide open spaces and in some instances plunging accommodation areas into darkness. This was especially true of the forward-facing cabins at main deck level and the deck above in the midships section of the ship, where the portholes were literally an arm's-length from the cargo.

During the outward leg of the voyage, particularly through the tropics, the occupants of these cabins had also enjoyed superior ventilation owing to an uninterrupted air-flow. Now, with a mountain of wool only feet from their portholes, this throughput of air was curtailed. Perversely, it was the officers, cadets and engineers who inhabited these cabins that suffered most. By contrast, the working alleyway, home to the catering staff, ran along the starboard side of the ship where, when the cabins were occupied, their doors were invariably 'on the hook'. This favourable situation meant that the rooms were more than adequately ventilated, thanks to an ingenious piece of equipment called a scoop. This device, which vaguely resembled a bottomless coal scuttle, fitted snugly into the open porthole, protruding outboard with the cut-away portion facing forward. The breeze created by the *Alice Springs'* headway was swept up by the scoop and fed into the cabin where the air kept refreshingly cool.

That afternoon, Steve joined Norman and John in The Crown Hotel, their last chance of a drink before sailing. As they sat cradling their beer there was some general conversation, but the principal discussion was of the weeks spent tied up in Napier. 'Where the hell has that month gone?' asked Norman, as he fashioned a roll-up from his tin of Golden Virginia. 'It seems only five minutes ago since we were sitting here talking about Kate's birthday party, now here we are thinking about home.'

'Don't ask me,' replied John, who apart from the spells in the anchorage had spent most of his leisure time at Kate's, 'it doesn't bear thinking about. I'll tell you what, though,' he continued, after taking a draught from his glass. 'Sleeping on board's going to seem strange. Kate's place has been like a second home to me. I'm going to feel like a fish out of water.'

It seemed to Steve that nearly everyone was singing the same ballad. Most of those he'd spoken to recently were going to miss someone or the other, although Norman was a notable exception. 'I've had my fill of women for the time being,' he announced, removing a loose strand of tobacco from the end of his roll-up, 'what with my missus playing up. I'm going to stick to the beer from now on - but only two or three at a time, mind you.' That was fair enough. Since the aberration in Sydney, and during the run up to Brisbane when he'd threatened to annihilate Jimmy, Norman's behaviour had been impeccable. Apart from an infrequent trip to the cinema and the odd afternoon in The Crown he'd seldom ventured ashore except for the rare special occasion, like the evening they'd spent out at Kate's. However, Steve suspected that Norm's wayward spouse was only part of the reason for his self-imposed solitude, the other being the corn that had greatly inhibited his movement.

Many of the *Alice Springs'* crew, duties permitting, had slipped ashore for some eleventh-hour refreshment or some other purpose, although not everyone was quite so fortunate. Archie, for instance, who had a 'friend' he'd been visiting over at Hastings, was one of those adversely affected. While Steve and his pals sat enjoying a drink in The Crown, Archie was busy settling his new crop of passengers into their staterooms. The Second Steward was another who'd had to remain ship-bound, dealing with passengers' enquiries and any last-minute issues over stores. Meanwhile, Peter and Jimmy had gone shopping, in Peter's case to supplement his limited wardrobe while Jimmy sought a gift for his mum. Steve wasn't fussed about shopping, buying only what he needed out of 'slops'. This on-board emporium, that sold everything from working clothes, shirts and underwear to washing powder, toothpaste and boot polish, opened for an hour each week and was manned by either the Chief or Second Stewards.

The term 'slops' had its origins in sailing ship days when destitute seamen, many of whom had been shanghaied, were bundled aboard owning only the clothes they stood up in. Bereft of all personal possessions they would need oilskins, sea boots, bedding and so forth which, with the vessel at sea, could only be bought on the ship. To cater for these requirements the ship's master - often the vessel's owner - kept a chest, for some reason known as a slop chest, that would be stocked with the seafarers' needs. The prices charged were supposedly reasonable; but more often than not were expensive, the money owed being stopped from the purchasers' pay. The system in place aboard British merchant vessels of the nineteen-sixties wasn't dissimilar, although by this time it was funded by the owners and prices were comparable with the High Street.

Back at the harbour, the *Alice Springs* was undergoing a complete transformation. The deck cargo of wool was firmly lashed down and the deckies were clearing away any unwanted items of tackle. High up in the funnel a feather of steam indicated that in the bowels of the ship the boilers had been fired, ready to propel them the twelve-thousand miles back to London. Meanwhile, the topside accommodation area resembled a busy concourse as the fresh troupe of passengers discovered their whereabouts; although that wouldn't be difficult given the *Alice Springs'* modest proportions. Among their number was the regulation supernumerary doctor, this one an unmarried New Zealander who was taking up a post at Freedom Fields Hospital in Plymouth.

When Steve, John and Norman arrived back at the port they found a stack of provisions on the quayside, awaiting transfer to their respective store rooms. 'If you two can manage those cases of butter,' said John, as he hoisted a crate of eggs on to his shoulder, 'I'll get the stewards to help with the rest.'

The cases of butter were heavy but even so, Steve still shifted three to Norman's one as the cook hobbled painfully up the gangway. Keith and Donald mucked in with the remainder, mostly top-up stuff such as tea, a couple of sacks of sugar and some flour. 'We could have had this lot aboard ages ago,' grumbled Donald, lifting the solitary case of strawberry jam that marked the final item on the invoice. 'Trouble was, the Chief Steward had us doing a silver dip - said some of the cutlery was tarnished. Sec was bloody furious. We only did it last week - and what's more, we couldn't get ashore for a drink.'

'If the tight-wad had ordered sufficient a couple of weeks ago none of this would have been necessary,' added Keith, as he followed Steve up the accommodation ladder empty handed. He was warned there were things we were short of but he wouldn't listen.'

'I suppose he hadn't accounted for another two ton of potatoes,' reminded Steve, referring to the plague in the spud locker. That'll have punched a hole in his budget - and pissed him off into the bargain.' They laughed, but it was far from a laughing matter. If the ship was to suffer a breakdown and there were insufficient foodstuffs to see them through the emergency then they'd all be in trouble, none more so than the miserly Chief Steward.

Back in the pantry Steve was soon back in the thick of it, strapping up twice the amount of teatime crockery than he'd become used to. But despite the scramble there were some lighter moments, and when Archie breezed in with yet another tray of soiled chinaware, crooning, 'Once I had a Secret Love,' it was clear he had something to sing about.

'You sound pleased with yourself, Archie,' said Steve, sliding the cups, saucers and tea-plates into the sink. 'You must have got to see that friend of yours over in Hastings after all.'

'He's got himself a new sweetheart,' informed Keith, before Archie had chance to reply. 'He's a winger off one of the passenger liners. Got left behind in Wellington with appendicitis. When he got out of hospital they sent him up to Napier because he didn't fancy going home DBS on another passenger boat. Said it was too much like hard work for a poor, sickly creature like him. He's got Danny's old berth in Archie's cabin - that's the reason for the Doris Day impersonation.'

'Jealousy will get you nowhere,' trilled Archie, looking happier than Steve could remember. 'At least if I play my cards right I'll have someone to snuggle up to at nights over the next five weeks. You lot won't.'

'Hello, boys,' warbled an unfamiliar voice as Archie skipped out of the pantry, not wanting to draw any more attention to himself than was necessary; although he needn't have bothered given the obvious. Steve and Keith spun around to find a medium-height, stockily-built individual beaming at them through the servery, lounging half in and half out of the hatchway. Past middle age, his partly-bald head sported a comb-over haircut and there was a wart on the end of his nose. 'Oh! I've already met you haven't I, Keith? Sorry, Duckie, I should have recognised you from the rear. I'm Sid by the way,' announced the newcomer, for Steve's benefit, studying his fingers, first on one hand and then the other as if searching for some abnormality. 'But you can call me Ruby - everyone else does, and I think it sounds nicer, don't you? I'll be taking the vacant bunk in Archie's cabin. He seems such a sweetie and I'm sure we'll get on together - if you know what I mean. Oh! Bollocks. I've snagged a fingernail - I'll have to go and look out my nail file. Sorry if I go on a bit - see you later.' And as a deathly silence settled over the pantry Ruby toddled off in the direction of the working alleyway, presumably to carry out repairs.

'What the hell was that?' asked Steve, at length, staring at Keith, having finally recovered from the shock. 'I thought it was a bloody cartoon.'

'That, my friend, was the real McCoy,' answered Keith, as he grabbed a pantry cloth and began drying the freshly-washed crocs. 'Come party time and she'll be wearing lipstick and eye-shadow - mutton dressed up as mutton, if you get me. Whatever, Archie's been pretty subdued up till now, but if I'm any judge of character Ruby'll bring him out of his shell. I think we'll be seeing the real Archie from now on, you see if we don't.'

Keith had got it just about taped. Thus far, apart from the occasional female mannerism and girlish outburst Archie hadn't flaunted his sexuality; there'd been little point seeing that up until now he'd been the only homosexual on board. But the situation had changed, as Archie's effervescence clearly demonstrated.

Ruby's arrival brought the catering staff back up to strength, allowing Steve and Peter to concentrate on their own jobs, although waiting at table was a task they'd enjoyed once their initial nervousness had been conquered. Ruby was set to work in the saloon, filling the void left by Danny, although Keith remained the substitute Tiger.

It was past five o'clock and Roger Oates was still absent, so it was assumed he'd jumped ship and the appropriate authorities were notified. However, by a quirk of fate the deck department was also to sail with its full complement owing to the appearance of another DBS. He arrived courtesy of Napier police and was in the process of being deported. He was a scruffy and mysterious character who'd been arrested in some outbuildings at Havelock North following a tip-off from a member of the public.

A native of the Western Isles his name - or so he insisted - was Dingwall Patterson, a refugee - if he was to be believed - from Federal Steam Navigation's *Cambridge*, which had sailed from Napier back in January. It appeared that until yesterday he'd been hiding out in the countryside, living off the land after falling in love with a local girl who'd ditched him once the *Cambridge* had sailed. Rather than hand himself in he'd kept out of sight in the belief that if he stayed out of trouble he'd be allowed to remain as a legitimate immigrant. Steve had heard of such happenings, whereby seamen who'd deserted their ships had successfully applied for New Zealand citizenship, but he'd found it hard to believe given the numbers routinely deported.

'Oh! It happens,' confirmed Donald, when Steve expressed doubts that the Kiwi immigration authorities would even entertain it, 'but you've got to get yourself a sponsor, keep a clean nose and have a means of support before they'll consider it.'

Whatever, as an EDH Dingwall Patterson would make an admirable replacement for Roger Oates and he was allocated the berth that up until then had been Roger's. After a thoroughly good scrub and a change of clothes - donated by other members of the deck department - Dingwall looked as clean and presentable as the rest of them, and nowhere near as sinister as his initial appearance had implied.

Also joining at Napier - although not as a DBS - was a brand new Senior Cadet. This fellow, a Yorkshire lad with an infuriating tic that caused an eyelid to persistently twitch, had arrived overnight from Auckland. He'd been transferred from the *Murchison*, a vessel that could best be described as the company's equivalent of the *Otaio*, although she carried considerably fewer apprentices.

'All ashore who's going ashore,' called one of the junior cadets, as he roamed the alleyways, advising those with no further ship's business that the *Alice Springs* would shortly be sailing. In fact, there were few who needed reminding, the last three to leave before the gangway was raised being a lad from the agent's office and the constables who'd delivered Dingwall from the cells. Down on the quayside the mooring lines were already singled up, the rat guards having been removed a half-hour previously. To complete the picture and witness their departure a substantial crowd had assembled, most of them female, some of whom were now in need of lodgings.

A blast from the siren, along with the now deafening roar from the safety valves, left little doubt that their already tenuous links with New Zealand were about to be severed. 'Come on, Steve,' urged Peter, as Steve hurried to complete a few unfinished chores, leaving as little to do as possible when he returned. 'You can finish that later.'

'Just coming,' answered Steve, sliding a handful of saucers into their rack. 'I've just got to hang up these cups and I'll be right along.'

Two minutes later and Steve stood shoulder to shoulder with Peter, and almost everyone else who wasn't immediately involved with the *Alice Springs'* leave-taking. Jimmy muscled in between Peter and Keith and they all began waving to the girls who were massed on the quayside. Steve searched for Glenda but she wasn't to be seen; and then Peter cried, 'There they are, just coming round the corner of that warehouse.' Sure enough, there were Glenda and Linda, running for all they were worth having just been dropped off by a taxi. As the *Alice Springs* inched slowly away from the quayside

Glenda kicked off her shoes so that she could run more quickly, until she stood right below Steve, shouting and waving although amid all the racket Steve hadn't a clue what she was saying. It didn't matter, everybody was waving and shouting at someone, trying to be heard above everyone else, along with the din from the safety valves. Slowly the gap between ship and shore widened. Inches became feet - yards - a hundred yards, until the *Alice Springs* began swinging towards the harbour entrance and the open Pacific. Those lining the rail fought for the optimum vantage points, waving and calling until those they were waving to were nothing but anonymous dots.

Eventually, some of those on the quayside could be seen drifting away although it was impossible to see who was who. Steve suspected that Glenda was among those who tarried. He was delighted that she'd come down to the harbour; but as the *Alice Springs* set out on the almost six-and-a-half thousand mile run to Panama he couldn't help thinking that she already had an eye on the anchorage - and the Alexander Shipping Company's *Eastbury*, that was awaiting the berth that his own ship had barely relinquished.

So, that was the end of Steve's first ever visit to New Zealand. The previous six weeks had lit up his life in a way that he'd never thought possible. Maxine had been out of this world, a home-spun girl whom Steve loved with every beat of his heart. And then there was Glenda, a straight-from-the-shoulder seductress with no inhibitions and to whom Steve had been the latest in a string. Only now it had all fallen flat. No more romping in the 'enchanted gardens' with Glenda, and no further phone calls to Maxine. But then he realised that not everything was as bleak as it seemed. In only a few weeks' time he'd be at the New Zealand High Commission, planning a permanent return to Manoao and the South-Island girl he adored. He smiled at his mates each in turn, and said, 'What a fabulous country - and now I know what you meant, when you said, "There's nowhere else like it on earth".'

17

'Don't forget the clocks go forward by an hour tonight,' warned the Second Steward, as they sat finishing their dinner in the saloon. 'And another thing - today's Monday, so what with us crossing the International Date Line tonight, tomorrow'll be Monday as well.'

The more experienced hands knew all about crossing the International Date Line and the apparent anomaly, but Steve was one of those who didn't. Still, rather than open his mouth and make a fool of himself he remained silent, knowing he'd learn soon enough the reason for the unexplained oddity.

While the *Alice Springs'* catering staff had reverted to a seagoing routine the deck and engine room departments had resumed the responsibilities of watch-keeping. The watches were of four hours duration followed by eight hours off, some of which would have been taken up by obligatory day-work which added to their overtime earnings. For whatever reason some of the deck crew had no watch-keeping duties and were employed instead on permanent day-work, although still with the mandatory overtime. Steve had long been acquainted with the watches, but not with their enigmatic titles which seemed at odds with the hours they alluded to; and so, with the day's work at an end he was enjoying a smoke at the taffrail as the Bosun embarked on the peculiarities of the watch-keeping system.

'Well, Son, it's like this,' began the Bosun, as he tamped a massive wad of St Bruno into the soot-encrusted pipe that he may well have been smoking since 'The Flood'. 'I know it sounds odd, but the watch from midnight until 0.400 hours is known as the Middle Watch..............................' The Bosun proceeded to reel off the various watches and the hours to which they related, dwelling at length on the mystery of the Dog Watch, the four-hour stint from

257

16.00 till 20.00 that had once comprised two separate watches. 'It goes back to the days of the windjammer,' explained the Bosun, puffing away at his pipe so that it flared like a beacon in the dark, 'when four on and four off were the accepted hours of watch-keeping. By creating a First and Second Dog Watch it effectively rotated the watches, making life less monotonous for the watch-keepers.'

'I see,' said Steve, who had a great regard for those earlier seamen who'd faced danger and hardship without any modern-day comforts. 'All I can say is I'm glad I wasn't around in those days. I can't imagine myself clinging to a spar in the dark, grappling in a storm with a flapping sail, freezing and soaked to the skin while the sails ripped my fingernails out - and I'll tell you another thing. I'd be frightened to death of either being washed overboard or maybe even falling from a mast.'

'A lot of them were and a lot of them did,' stated the Bosun, bluntly, 'but it was all part and parcel of the job. There was many an old lugger set off from Australia with a crew of twenty or more and arrived home with a good many less, so just thank your lucky stars that you're not on an old-fashioned windbag. Anyway, getting back to the watches. The final watch of the twenty-four hour period, the 20.00 till midnight, is called the First Watch - and cock-eyed though it sounds, that completes the watch-keeping day.'

Steve extinguished his Rothmans and picked up the rosie, depositing the dog-end inside. 'Thanks, Bose,' he said, patting the elderly seaman affectionately between the shoulder blades. 'I've often wondered, and - oh! By the way. Seeing as how today's Monday and, and that tonight we'll be crossing the International Date Line, why should tomorrow..............................?'

The day following their departure from Napier marked the beginning of an intense period of activity, not least for the deck department who began toiling away with sanders, chipping-hammers and scrapers, removing any flaking paintwork and corrosion. Once the debris was cleared the ship would be thoroughly hosed down, so that only bare metal and well-established paintwork remained. There'd follow a complete repaint, from top-mast to main deck, including the funnel, samson-posts and derricks. The hull, which for obvious reasons couldn't be painted while the ship was at sea, had received its new paint-job in Napier, courtesy of deckhands working from either a cradle, a raft or from the quayside. By the time they'd finished the *Alice Springs* would be arguably the shiniest vessel on the Pacific and as smart as anything straight off the slipway. Once the exterior had been repainted attention would turn to her innards, this time involving the catering staff, although not in a way they'd have preferred.

It would take seventeen days to cross the Pacific, so Steve had made sure that he'd written to his family beforehand, assuring them he was well and that if all went according to plan he'd be seeing them soon, assuming there were no further hitches. Phoning home with this information would have been out of the question. For one thing, it would have meant booking an expensive call via the operator, there being no such convenience as International Subscriber Trunk Dialling; and for another, in common with most British households of the day his family weren't connected to the telephone.

The early part of the passage was uneventful. The days were pleasant and a gentle swell caused an occasional roll that more often than not went unnoticed. It seemed the mighty Pacific was behaving as impeccably as its name implied until early one afternoon, when the *Alice Springs* was a week out of Napier and making steady progress towards Panama. Orders were issued from the bridge to batten down all moveable objects as during the night they were expecting to pass through an extremely disturbed spell of weather.

Steve had noticed the halo around the sun, and that the wind had turned into the south; although this was hardly perceptible given that the *Alice Springs* was forging steadily on and creating an appreciable breeze of her own. In fact, apart from the hazy sunshine the only sign of the impending turmoil was the increasing number of white horses on the previously mirror-smooth sea.

'Make sure all the cutlery drawers are locked, and that the doors on the dumb waiters are closed before you tick off tonight,' ordered Sec, as he inspected the preparatory work in the saloon and pantry. 'Tell you what, it might be as well if we shoved the breakable things - gravy boats and other non-essential crockery, jam jars, sauce bottles and so on - in the cutlery baskets before stowing them away. That way they shouldn't break loose and get damaged. The cups ought to be okay on their hooks, and the other crockery should be safe enough in the racks and carousel.'

'Don't forget we've only got two cutlery baskets,' advised Keith, as he wedged a handful of surplus ashtrays bearing the company crest into an empty carton, alongside a variety of other items -spare cruets, etc., that wouldn't be needed over dinner. 'There won't be room for everything in the baskets so we'll have to use old cardboard boxes.'

'I'll see what I can find in the stores,' volunteered Sec, as he headed out of the saloon on this latest errand. 'If there isn't anything suitable you'll have to pack everything out with mutton cloth. There's plenty of that in the locker.'

Elsewhere in the saloon, the table-tops were surrounded by fiddles while the tables themselves, along with the dumb waiters, were securely tethered from below. Likewise the chairs, which were chained to the deck from the undersides of the seats, allowing sufficient freedom for them to be used but prohibiting their potential for chaos. In the pantry Steve rigged a fiddle around the top of the hot-press whilst down in the galley the stove was similarly protected. And so it transpired that whether it be in galley, pantry or saloon, even in the living accommodation, every moveable object that wasn't immediately needed was jammed into any nook and cranny in an effort to restrict its mobility. Of course that wasn't the end of the matter for as Steve pointed out, space still had to be found for all those items that would be employed in the service of dinner.

Similar precautions were being taken by the other departments, the deck crowd in particular paying special attention to the deck cargo of wool that while apparently as safe as Fort Knox was further lashed down as an additional measure of insurance. It was exactly the same in the engine room. Although not as exposed as other areas there was still the propensity for mayhem; fifty-gallon oil drums, for example, that could easily become free-ranging battering rams if not effectively hobbled. These were lashed to the nearest suitable fixture to protect not only those working below but also vital items of machinery without which the vessel might be vulnerable.

By early evening the *Alice Springs* and her components were as securely battened-down as they could be, with crew and passengers alike awaiting the inevitable onslaught. For several hours it had seemed the alarm may have been false as there was no dramatic change in the weather; and then, shortly before dinner there was an unannounced lurch, causing Steve to grab a door-post for support. 'Bloody hell!' he exclaimed, relieved that he'd already deposited the soup dixie in the hot-press. 'That was a close one. Two seconds earlier and the minestrone would have gone for a Burton.'

'Well, this is it,' said Archie, as he placed serving spoons and ladles in the assortment of trays and serving dishes. 'We just slipped into a trough, so the sea's coming in from the beam. It looks like it could be a rough-un.'

As if in agreement the *Alice Springs* heeled sharply to port. Simultaneously, she soared startlingly upwards, cresting a wave and tilting to starboard before sliding into an abyss that was far, far deeper than the first. Steve clung to the corner of the hot-press, ignoring the heat that on any other occasion would have forced him to relinquish his grip. 'Isn't this is a bit sudden?' he asked, disturbed by the speed of the onset. 'I didn't expect it to happen this quickly. Are you sure everything's all right?'

'It's commonplace at sea,' reassured Archie, showing not the slightest concern as the ship scaled another giant comber, 'more so than ashore where any deterioration is usually gradual.'

Archie wasn't one to make a fuss about nothing; and when Steve took stock of the situation he saw that the rest of his colleagues seemed equally relaxed, getting on with their jobs with no outward sign of anxiety. He gathered his senses and carried on working, leaving one hand free to grab the nearest support should any such action be necessary.

Peering through the servery hatchway he could see rain and spray already lashing the saloon windows, and intermittently the *Alice Springs'* bows, rising and falling, leaning first to port and then to starboard as she negotiated the mountains of water that sought to overwhelm her. For a fleeting instant he was mesmerised, reminded of that dreadful day nearly four months earlier when he'd felt like death reinvigorated. He was desperate to avoid a repeat; so he ignored the spiralling scenario and focused on filling the sink.

'I wonder how many'll turn up?' queried Peter, as Donald let rip

261

with the gong, summoning those who felt like eating to their dinners.

'I'm not usually a betting girl but not very many by my reckoning,' answered Ruby, who was sprinkling water over the tablecloths, further surety against wholesale ruination of a shipload of crockery and glassware. 'I've just seen one poor biddy spewing her ring up. She won't be eating anything till tomorrow, that's for sure.'

'You go careful, Ruby,' said Archie, uneasiness clouding his features as his recently acquired darling gave his tables a last-minute check. 'One hand for the ship and one for yourself - you know how the saying goes. We don't want you ending up in hospital again, do we, dear?' Steve and Peter were in stitches, and almost piddled themselves when Ruby called over his shoulder.

'Don't you worry about me, Duckie, I'll be as safe as houses. You just look after yourself.'

Ruby had hardly finished speaking when the Senior Cadet barged into the pantry dressed in oilskin and sou'wester, dripping water as if he'd just swum the Channel. 'Just to warn you that we're rigging lifelines out on deck. Nothing to worry about - just a precaution, but I wouldn't venture out unless you have to. This is going to be one hell of a blow - the barometer's dropping faster than Maggie May's knickers.'

'Well, we'll have to go aft at some time,' said Peter, as the cadet disappeared to deliver his message in the engine room, leaving a trail of water in his wake. 'We'll have to empty the rosie for one thing. It'll stink like a sewer if we don't.'

'Then it'll have to stink,' said Archie, contemptuously, suggesting he couldn't care less about a smelly bin if it meant putting lives on the line. 'Better than getting washed overboard when all's said and done.'

'That's right,' agreed Steve, who'd no intention of risking his life for the sake of a binful of rubbish. 'You've got to be bloody crackers to go out there if it isn't called for.'

The preciseness of Ruby's prediction soon became clear, for as the usual parade of off-duty officers and engineers trooped into the saloon for their dinners, most of passengers were absent. Only four of the twelve took their seats and two of those looked decidedly groggy, picking over their food before performing a hasty exit, having fulfilled their objective of at least making a cursory appearance.

'Told you, didn't I,' said Ruby, unloading a trayful of soiled dishes at the servery. 'Haven't got the stomach for it, poor dears. Mind you, those other two, the overweight mother and daughter at the Chief Engineer's table - they're cramming it down as if they haven't been fed for a week. Still, from what I hear they're used to it. They're millionaires. Made their money - or the older one's husband did - out of cosmetics. It seems he sold out to one of the big international conglomerates before popping his clogs and leaving the two of them a fortune. Now they're seeing the world on the proceeds.'

As Ruby tripped off carrying two handsome second-helpings of jam roly-poly and cream in the direction of the Chief Engineer's table, Steve shook his head at the irony. It was a familiar tale. Someone spends a lifetime slogging his guts out then drops off his perch at the very moment he has chance to enjoy it. OK, not all of them were millionaires but the principle was the same, even if the 'proceeds' meant nothing more than a few quid in the bank as a nest egg. He vowed there and then that whatever his financial circumstances he'd live for today and let tomorrow take care of itself. OK, stash some away for a rainy day by all means; but no one lived forever and he couldn't see the point of being the wealthiest corpse in the graveyard.

By seven o'clock the saloon was empty, allowing Steve and his pals to delight in the galley's endeavours. It never ceased to amaze him just what a galley was capable of given that even on the calmest of days there was usually movement of some sort; and on a night like tonight, just on the advent of dinner when they'd run smack into a storm of typhoon proportions, they'd delivered the customary banquet. The pity was, most of the passengers hadn't been able to appreciate it.

'I'm going to have a bloody great chunk of that jam roly-poly,' announced Peter, as he soaked up the gravy from his roast beef and veg with the remainder of his mashed potato. 'There ought to be plenty left seeing as how most of the passengers were missing.'

'I wouldn't bet on it,' answered Sec, wiping his mouth on his serviette before neatly aligning his cutlery. 'Most of the uniforms had second-helpings, and our generously-proportioned lady guests had three.'

'Greedy bitches,' cried Peter, jumping from his seat and scampering to the pantry carrying his empty dinner plate. 'No wonder they're as fat as two London buses.' He returned a few seconds later with a plateful of jam roly-poly topped with a bountiful coating of custard. 'Sorry about this, you blokes,' he apologised, looking as sorry as a cat with two mice, 'but this was all there was left, and it wasn't worth divvying it up as there wouldn't have been enough to go round. Never mind, there's plenty of Black Forest Gateau along with fruit salad and ice-cream so you won't go without.' And without waiting to assess the reaction he set about demolishing his pudding.

'Peter, you just about take the biscuit,' reproved Archie, who wasn't too bothered about the jam roly-poly, preferring instead the fruit salad. 'Those women aren't a patch on you when it comes to greediness. Talk about noses in troughs. I've a good mind to go and fetch my camera, just so you can see how repulsive you look while you're feeding.' Peter's response was to let rip with the customary belch. He couldn't care less what Archie - or anyone else for that matter - thought about his eating habits. The main thing as far as he was concerned was, he'd collared the last of the roly-poly.

Hoping Peter suffered a crippling bout of indigestion his mates began squaring away, leaving the pantry boy slumped in his chair, looking suddenly gruesomely bilious. Meanwhile, the *Alice Springs* threw herself into a frenzy, sometimes laying over on her beam-ends before slowly righting herself and leaning on her opposite flank. Somehow, the stewards kept their feet, stripping the tables and stowing everything away, leaving the saloon as barren as an abandoned warehouse. The tablecloths proved invaluable, being far more effective as packing than mutton cloth. 'They'll be as creased as buggery in the morning,' said Keith, making sure the doors of his dumb waiter were secure before standing back to survey his handiwork, 'but there are plenty of others in the linen locker.'

Steve was clearing away and carrying out similar preventive measures in the pantry, assisted by Archie, Peter having vacated his seat in the saloon for the nearest lavatory. 'Serves him bloody-well right, leaving us to finish off here on our own,' he complained, drying the last of the freshly-washed dixies and inserting it into the hot-press. 'Fat lot of good his dinner did him.'

'It ought to teach him a lesson,' acknowledged Archie, closing the door of the elevator and returning the last of the uneaten food to the galley. 'But I'm afraid it won't. People like him never learn. Still, that's his problem not ours. Now, I'll just take a double check, to make sure nothing's liable to roll around in the middle of the night and get smashed to smithereens, then you can get on with the scrub-out - and forget about that rosie till morning.'

'I will, never fear,' replied Steve, taking care not to overfill his bucket while stirring in a handful of soap. 'You won't catch me out there on a night like this, not after what the Senior Cadet told us.'

'Night night, then - and sleep tight,' said Archie, sweetly, lighting a Kensitas as he left the pantry for a deserved gin and tonic with Ruby. 'Hopefully, this'll blow through by tomorrow.'

'Hope so - G'night,' answered Steve, who was already on hands and knees, steadying his bucket with one hand while scrubbing away with the other. 'And if you see anything of Peter tell him to get a shift on.' In the event it was past eight-thirty when he finally dimmed the lights and vacated the pantry; Peter hadn't shown and the alleyways were eerily deserted.

Steve proceeded gingerly, gripping the handrails on either side until he reached his cabin where he had the most ominous feeling that everything wasn't hunky-dory. There'd been hardly a sound when he left the pantry, yet down here in the working alleyway the savagery of the storm was ear-splitting, as if it was battering away in the midst of his very own living quarters. Slowly, he inched open the door and made to step over the threshold - but that was as far as he got. The door was whipped from his grasp and thrown back against the inner bulkhead while he was blown clean off his feet and across the alleyway, cracking his skull on the handrail. He lay there, stunned, massaging his scalp which felt as if it had been whacked with a rolling-pin. In his stupefied state he wondered what on earth could have happened; and as he slowly came to he reasoned that the only way to find out was to look, only this time with a little more care. Rising groggily to his feet, and gripping the handrail for support, he reached round the door and hesitantly switched on the light. He peeped into his room, shielding his eyes from the blast, and there saw the cause of his headache.

On receiving the order to batten down both he and Peter had stowed away every conceivable object, but had forgotten the scoop in the porthole which was still open wide and assuming the role of a wind tunnel. The scoop itself was buckled out of all recognition; hardly surprising given the strength of the gale - which must have been registering somewhere in the region of eleven on the Beaufort Scale - but there were additional complications. Not only had the scoop formed an ideal conduit for a naturally-generated compressed-air system, but it had also channelled a considerable quantity of rain and seawater into the cabin. The deck was awash, the water swishing to and fro like wavelets lapping on a beach. Peter's bunk was saturated, and the leather settee beneath the open porthole glistened beneath the deckhead light. Thankfully, Steve's bunk, which was situated a good five feet above deck level, had largely escaped so he at least might be sleeping in the dry; but by and large the cabin was a mess, and would require a good hour's remedial attention.

'What's happened here, then?' yelled Jimmy, bellowing to be heard above the bedlam, having ventured outside to investigate after hearing the clatter from next door.

'Forgot the bloody scoop,' bawled Steve, as if any explanation was needed, 'and everything's soaked. Here, give me a hand to shut that porthole.'

Without pausing to discuss the matter they kicked off their shoes and removed their socks, stuffing them deep in their pockets. Then, stooping as low as possible to avoid the jet stream they waded forth, forcing the door shut behind them. Denied an escape route the wind's ferocity was lessened; the roar became considerably muted and if nothing else, they were able to communicate without shouting. On reaching the porthole Steve removed the brass-encircled disc of reinforced glass from its hook while Jimmy wrenched the scoop from the opening, drenching himself in the process. The porthole slammed shut, and as Steve tightened the securing nuts and lowered the dead-light silence prevailed, as if the tumult had never existed.

'Phew! Thanks,' acknowledged Steve, slumping on to the sodden settee, his relief palpable now that the aperture was sealed. 'I'd have gotten wet through on my own.'

'I did,' answered Jimmy, ruefully, indicating his wringing wet jeans and T-shirt. 'The scoop was half full of water.'

With the porthole now secured they concentrated their efforts on the cabin. It was in a sorry state, but by turning to with dustpans, buckets and mops the water was soon cleared and they could focus on drying things out. The dustpans had been Steve's brainwave, and they proved to be thoroughly effective water-scoops, slashing minutes from what had threatened to be a wearisome procedure. Strips of mutton cloth did the rest, drying the deck and furnishings leaving Peter's bunk the only thing waterlogged.

'That's something he can do for himself,' said Jimmy, when Steve suggested knocking up the Second Steward and asking for a change of bedlinen. 'Let him get the bollocking when Sec learns the score. By the way, where is he,' asked Jimmy, wondering where Peter had got to. 'He's the one who ought to be helping.'

Dunno,' replied Steve, as he stepped back into the alleyway to admire their heroics. 'Haven't seen him since dinner. I guess he's still in the heads - heaving his heart up most likely.'

'Mmmm........maybe,' replied Jimmy, accepting the possibility but not sounding totally reassured, 'but you know, if he hasn't shown up after all this time we really ought to go and look for him, just to make sure he's okay.'

Peter wasn't in the toilet as Steve had intimated, nor was he in the pantry or saloon. The galley was locked so he couldn't be in there so where on earth could he have possibly got to? Enquiries at the other cabins proved fruitless, so for every minute that Peter remained missing his friends became increasingly anxious.

'Where the hell is he?' queried Steve, palms uplifted, expecting no answer to what was essentially a rhetorical question.

'Search me,' replied Jimmy, scratching his head while wondering where else to look. 'Unless........! You don't think he's gone out on deck, do you? It's just the kind of thing the silly bugger'd do, especially after being warned not to.'

'It's worth a gander........I suppose,' answered Steve, not too enamoured with the idea of venturing outside on what promised to be a fool's errand with nothing to show for it afterwards. 'But to be truthful, I don't much fancy going out there in this weather, lifelines or no lifelines.'

'We don't have to - but we can at least look through the porthole in the door at the end of the alleyway,' countered Jimmy, unwilling to forego even the remotest opportunity of discovering Peter's whereabouts. 'It's better than doing nothing.'

Trying to see through the porthole in the door at the end of the working alleyway with rain and spray bombarding the glass was hopeless, not to mention the reflections thrown by the alleyway lights which even in the best of conditions would have made night-time observation impossible. 'Can't see a bloody thing,' declared Steve, turning frustratedly away and raising his arms in despair. 'The only way we're going to spot anything is if we physically open the door.'

'Then let's open it,' proposed Jimmy, forcefully, pushing past Steve, grabbing and turning the door handle. 'If he's out there at all we'll be able to see him, without stepping over the coaming,'

Steve leant his own weight to the door which gradually inched open against the force of the demented southeaster - and the hydraulic closer that prevented it slamming shut, even in the fairest of weather. The pandemonium that greeted them was as terrifying as a wailing banshee. The wind screamed through the aerials and rigging, and shrieked through the gap between the deck cargo of wool and the midships accommodation from where the pals gazed into the darkness, desperate for a sight of their friend. But Peter wasn't there, the only movement being the cascades of water that broke incessantly over the starboard rails and swished around the after well-deck before gurgling away through the scuppers. The door closed slowly behind them, nullifying the din which made any sort of rational thought process impracticable.

'We'd better report him missing,' said Steve at length, all but convinced that Peter had unwisely gone outside and been swept away, and that any further searching would be both futile and time wasting.

'S'pose so,' agreed Jimmy, who just couldn't believe that Peter had simply vanished into thin air, let alone been washed over the side. 'But I bet he's around here somewhere, if only we knew where to look.'

'There's just one other thing,' speculated Steve, as a last resort before disturbing the Second Steward to announce Peter's disappearance. 'We've only looked outside on the weather side of the ship. If he's out there at all he's not going to be standing there getting soaked to the skin, is he? My guess is that he'll be on the lee side, under some kind of shelter.'

'Well he certainly wasn't on the passengers' promenade deck,' declared Jimmy, striving to think of some other sheltered location where their pal could be skulking. 'It was one of the first places I looked - and he wouldn't be in any of the lifeboats. Tell you what, we'll have one last look on the lee side of the after well deck. We'll be able to see out of the door at the end of the engineers' alleyway, and if he isn't there we'll have to report him adrift.'

Crossing to the lee side of the ship via an athwartships alleyway they confronted the door at the after end of the engineers' alleyway. Being partially sheltered by the deck cargo of wool it wasn't as difficult to open. Nevertheless, the row was still nerve shattering and it was equally as impossible to see anything as it had been on the weather side, owing to the rain and the spray. There was less water swilling about but it was still pitch-black, the only things visible being the lifeline snaking across to the sailors' and firemen's accommodation, and the shimmering reflection of a bulkhead lamp that was mounted directly above them. 'Couldn't see anyone,' said Jimmy, letting the door close behind him. 'There's only wind and water out there.'

They were about to turn and report to the Second Steward when Steve had the briefest inkling that he'd glimpsed something through the diminishing gap in the closing doorway - a faint glimmer, maybe, that couldn't be previously seen. No, couldn't have been, must have imagined it, he thought, holding the door ajar and staring again into the darkness. But wait, there it was again, just for a mini-second, in the lee of the deck cargo of wool, as if someone was standing there smoking.

'Jimmy - I think he's out here,' he called, excitedly, beckoning to Jimmy who was already half way along the engineers' alleyway, to report their fear that Peter might have committed involuntary suicide.

Jimmy did an abrupt about turn and was soon following Steve's pointed finger. 'You're right,' he concurred, as the glowing end of a cigarette penetrated the torrential rain which slanted almost horizontally down stinging the flesh like slivers of glass. 'And if I'm not mistaken,' he added, as a second cigarette end flared in the darkness, 'there are two of them out there, not one.'

'What the hell do you think you're playing at?' challenged Steve, when he and Jimmy eventually arrived in the lee of the deck cargo of wool, having safely negotiated the after well deck by hanging on to the lifelines. 'We've been worried to death about you, you silly bugger. Why didn't you tell us where you were going?'

'I needed a breath of fresh air,' replied Peter, drawing heavily on his cigarette, the ash from its tip being torn away by the tempest. 'I didn't want to get caught loafing about in the passengers' accommodation so I came out here. It isn't too bad all considered.'

'That's right,' volunteered Peter's companion, who was all but invisible in the darkness. 'I saw him standing out here on his own and came to investigate.' The voice belonged to Dingwall Patterson, who Steve concluded was another one who ought to have his head tested.

'You must be bloody mad, the pair of you,' lectured Jimmy, hunching his shoulders as the refrigerated air blowing up from the Antarctic penetrated his flimsy T-shirt, 'standing out here in the cold when it's warm and cosy inside.'

'Not a bit of it,' answered Dingwall, motioning upwards and backwards at the looming deck cargo of wool. 'It's comfortable enough standing here. The wool makes an ideal wind-break, and the rain's blowing over our heads. Here, feel my pullover - it's as dry as the day it was knitted.' Steve felt the jersey and had to admit - there was hardly a trace of dampness. But dry or otherwise it was no excuse for taking unnecessary risks, just for a breath of fresh air.

'And there's another thing,' continued Dingwall, gesturing at the tortured ocean before either of the Samaritans could protest. 'Just take a look at that. Have you ever seen anything so magnificent?'

Steve and Jimmy had been so preoccupied with tearing a strip off Peter that they hadn't even noticed the raging extravaganza on the seaward side of the bulwark. They turned and were flabbergasted as the mighty and supposedly serene Pacific was flayed into a luminous but savage fury, into ribbons of spume that vanished like wraiths in

270

the storm. The decks were as stygian as the crypt but the ocean was as white as driven snow. It was another of the world's natural wonders, the more striking for its dazzling brilliance.

'It's phosphorescence,' shouted Dingwall, clinging on to the lifeline as the *Alice Springs* leant even further over to port and seawater gushed up her scuppers before draining away, gurgling and swirling. 'It's only seen at night, when the water displaced by a ship's headway, or by wave movement, appears as a sheet of white light. It's caused by billions of plankton - or more precisely, the heat generated by their disturbance.'

Dingwall was right, the spectacle was breathtaking; but from Steve's point of view it was still utter madness to be standing on deck when the advice had been not to. 'All very interesting,' he replied, although his words were aimed specifically at Peter as he and Jimmy took a tighter hold of the lifeline and edged cautiously back towards the superstructure. 'But we're going back to our cabins and I suggest you two do likewise. Anyway, Peter,' he added, as a torrent of water filled the well-deck, saturating his shoes and soaking the bottoms of his trousers. 'Your bed's sopping wet so you'll be needing a full change of linen.'

Steve felt mightily relieved as he and Jimmy regained the sanctuary of the accommodation. Over the past couple of hours his moods had switched from annoyance at discovering his cabin a shambles to concern over Peter's disappearance. He'd been livid at his cabin mate's irresponsibility, for failing to inform anyone of his whereabouts; but now that the anger had subsided he felt a surge of joy knowing Peter was safe and that his fears had proved ultimately baseless. In fact, he'd suffered a whole string of emotions, and on reaching his cabin he felt suddenly exhausted and desperately in need of his bed.

'G'night, Jimmy,' he sighed, turning to face the galley boy who was about to enter his own quarters. 'And thanks for helping me out. What with Peter playing silly buggers and all, I'd have been in a right old pickle.'

Steve was soon dead to the world, and didn't hear Peter creep into the cabin to strip his bunk of the soaking-wet linen. Luckily, the mattress didn't need changing but even so, Sec hadn't been pleased at the untimely interruption as he was about to climb into his bed.

'Peter, you're bloody useless,' he'd censured, when the pantry boy appeared at his door with an armful of dripping bedclothes. 'How did they get in that state?'

'Steve left the porthole open,' Peter had answered, guiltily, being as economical with the truth as possible without actually telling a lie. 'I'll have to tell him off in the morning.'

Sec had grudgingly issued a fresh set of bedding but had viewed the excuse with scepticism, suspecting that whatever story Peter had concocted, he was no less the villain than Steve.

As it happened, Steve was able to repay his debt to Jimmy far more quickly than he'd imagined, with Peter adding his own contribution, although initially as a reluctant volunteer. It must have been sometime around two in the morning when he was brought instantly awake by an unremitting clamour that seemed to be emanating from the galley. He lay there a moment, straining to identify the racket which he'd have normally associated with a scrapyard. His wait for an answer was brief, for as a louder and even deeper-toned resonance reverberated along the alleyway there came a knock at the door and Jimmy's face appeared in the opening.

'What's causing all the commotion, Jimmy?' asked Steve, rubbing sleep from his eyes while squinting in the glare from the light bulb. 'Sounds like a bloody great car smash.'

'All the utensils have broken free in the galley,' answered Jimmy, giving Peter a shake in the mistaken hope of a response. 'And that louder crash, just as I knocked on your door - I reckon that was the stockpot taking a nosedive and if it was, there'll be a hell of a mess to clear up. I was hoping you'd give me a hand?'

Steve climbed from his bunk without protest, only too pleased to assist; but Peter showed no sign of life, only apparently waking after Jimmy had yanked off his bedclothes.

'Fuckin' hell, Jimmy,' complained Peter, huffily, pulling his blankets back over his head and snuggling down into his bunk. 'I heard you. Bugger me, it's only a few pots and pans. Surely you can stow them away on your own without bothering everyone else.'

Steve was furious. 'You lazy bastard,' he stormed, tearing off Peter's bedclothes and throwing them on the settee. 'After the trouble

272

you've caused the least you can do is help us clear up in the galley. We owe Jimmy that much - both of us.'

Peter leapt up from his bunk, eyes blazing, intent on launching an assault; but Steve was prepared and drew back his fist, determined to retaliate first. Peter hesitated. The fist looked as hard as a rock, and the resolve on the face of its owner was as menacing as the knuckles themselves. It prompted an abrupt change of heart. Peter shook his head and the fire subsided, the atmosphere cooling with his eyes.

'Yeah........all right, I'm coming,' he mumbled, lacing his shoes and slipping his pee jacket over his shoulders. 'I'll be along in a minute.'

As they entered the galley the devastation was immediately apparent. Pots and pans were rolling and sliding, clattering into each other and any immovable object, while the stockpot lay tipped on its side, only prevented from following suit by the opposing handles and tap. Underneath it all was a brown gooey mess that represented gallons of accumulated stock.

'What a shithouse,' declared Jimmy, dejectedly, surveying the chaos that he admitted could have been thwarted with foresight. 'We should have taken it off the stove. We didn't think it'd move with all that stock in it - not with the fiddles up and all. Now, where do we start?'

The answer came from an unexpected quarter. 'Well, let's get as many of the pots and pans into the sink as we can,' suggested Peter, showing a willingness that had been absent only a few minutes earlier. 'They won't roll around in there - and most of them'll need strapping up anyway so it'll be killing two birds with one throw.'

'Then let's go to it,' echoed Steve, hoisting a huge aluminium pot into the stainless-steel sink which was almost as large as a bath. 'Most of them'll fit in here for the time being - and we can strap 'em up afterwards.'

The slippery deck, along with the corkscrewing motion, made it difficult to stay upright; but all three went to work with a purpose, Steve and Jimmy to restore the galley to its usual pristine condition, while Peter was eager to rebuild bridges. In this latter respect both Steve and his cabin mate felt awkward with neither wanting to alienate the other. Despite Steve's hesitance earlier in the trip along with Peter's cavalier attitude they'd become extremely close, engaging in the occasional quarrel but speedily settling their differences.

'Sorry about that bit of argy-bargy,' apologised Peter, as he swept a pile of sludge towards the roasting tray that Steve had commandeered as a scoop. 'But I was still feeling under the weather. I didn't mean to have a go at you, honest?'

The apology was graciously accepted. 'Yeah, I know,' answered Steve, warmly, throwing an arm around a relieved shoulder, before adding. 'But if you'd taken a swing at me I'd have still given you a bop on the nose.'

'Thanks for that, you blokes,' voiced Jimmy, as with the clean-up operation over and the utensils stowed away he locked up the galley and slipped the key into his pee-jacket pocket. 'I'd have been there till breakfast if it hadn't been for you two. The only thing bothering me now is what Ted's gonna say when he finds out the stockpot's empty.'

'That's his problem,' answered Steve, knowing that regardless of who was at fault it was Jimmy who'd shoulder the blame. 'He's the Chief Cook and you're only the galley boy - and as far as the stockpot was concerned he could easily have shifted it himself.' The statement was of minimal solace; but the fact that the basic ingredient of soups and sauces was now at the bottom of the galley rosie was Ted's worry, and Steve felt sure he'd get over it somehow.

Morning found the *Alice Springs* bowling along under a windswept sky, the undulating seas being tangible evidence of the storm's ferocity and the havoc it had precipitated. In retrospect it probably hadn't been a particularly large weather system, or maybe they'd only clipped the edge of it; but whatever, its malevolence had been real and between-times a cause of concern.

Further evidence of the turbulence came in the form of huge clumps of seaweed that littered the ocean like floating molehills or had been washed aboard during the night. This was often an indication of land in the vicinity, or that the water was unusually shallow, although neither of these appeared obvious. The Alice Spring's position at the time was somewhere between Pitcairn and Ducie Islands, both only specks on a chart and separated by four-hundred miles; but it was also possible there were tiny atolls in the area that with the exception of the officers the crew would be totally unaware of.

Vessels of the Australasian and Pacific Steam Navigation Company called sporadically at Pitcairn and other of the more minuscule Pacific islands to collect and deliver mail, lift various small parcels of cargo or to drop off supplies, staying only a few hours before resuming their passages to wherever. However, the *Alice Springs* wasn't one of these, instead operating what the company called its 'Express Service,' calling at principal ports only, shifting the bulkier and more regular items in the speediest possible time-scale.

As Steve proceeded aft to empty the rosie he had to negotiate the brooms and hoses that the deck crew were using to clear away the accumulated seaweed. One of those so employed was Dingwall Patterson who'd gathered a sizeable stack of it adjacent to the starboard rail.

'See this,' called Dingwall, holding up a string of seaweed as Steve struggled past with the rosie. 'It's probably loaded with all those pieces of plankton I was telling you about. Take's some believing, doesn't it? But it's highly likely, even though it's completely invisible.'

It certainly did take some believing and Steve wasn't totally convinced. He picked up some weed and examined it, but apart from the moisture and some drying salt it appeared free of anything remotely capable of irradiating an ocean. If the story had been told by anyone else he'd have suspected a leg-pull, but he was learning that Dingwall was something of an academic, and that the man from the western isles was every bit as knowledgeable as that other exponent of sea lore, the Bosun.

An amusing consequence of the storm's aftermath, and an example of everyday negligence and Peter's flippancy, occurred shortly before breakfast. He was removing items from the elevator without using the requisite pantry cloth when he came a cropper. The second of two trays of bacon was hotter than he expected, and he laid it hurriedly across the fiddles to prevent it searing his fingers. Steve had witnessed the incident, and was about to place the tray in the press when the ship took a dive, sending the tray flying while at the same time scattering its contents.

'Sod it,' snarled Peter, as he recovered the tray and commenced scurrying around on all fours to retrieve arguably the tastiest ingredient of a full English breakfast. 'That's the last thing I needed. Gimme a hand before Sec and Archie turn up. They'll go fuckin' spare if they find out what's happened.'

Steve, who'd been busting a gut laughing, could hardly believe it. 'What! You don't think we're going to eat this, do you?' he queried, taking the tray and rearranging the rashers as neatly as when they'd arrived from the galley, 'not after it's been on the floor.'

'No, we're not,' answered Peter, tossing the last of the streaky on the tray, 'but it's too good to waste, and plenty good enough for the officers and engineers - and passengers too come to that. We'll just make sure that when it comes to getting our own breakfasts we'll take our own bacon from the other tray.'

Steve went along with the exercise because he couldn't think of an alternative - but he wasn't happy. 'What if someone finds a bit of grit in their breakfast?' he protested, as Peter positioned the tray at the front of the press so that the errant rashers would take precedence. 'The deck hasn't been scrubbed since yesterday evening, so it's bound to have accumulated dirt.'

'Don't worry about it,' replied Peter, his face creasing into a wicked grin as he lounged nonchalantly against the worktop. 'They'll just think the bacon's a little crispier than usual.'

As the day progressed the storm blew itself out, so that by teatime the Pacific Ocean was behaving more like a playful kitten than the tiger of the overnight period.

'Doesn't seem possible, does it?' said Dingwall Patterson, who'd sidled up to Steve as the latter leant on the rail in the forward well-deck, mug of tea in hand, contemplating what was after all a greatly-changed seascape from the one that Dingwall had expounded upon earlier.

'No, it doesn't,' agreed Steve, who found it hard to believe that such a dramatic improvement had taken place so rapidly. 'But our bedroom steward told me as much yesterday,' he added, repeating what Archie had told him at the storm's onset, 'that weather conditions at sea change far more quickly than ashore.'

'That's basically true,' said Dingwall, taking a Rizla from his tin of Old Holborn and stringing a measly strand of tobacco along its entire length, before rolling a cigarette the thickness of a matchstick, 'but it's a bit more complicated than that, what with all the other factors involved.'

'Such as?' probed Steve, who'd held a keen interest in weather-related topics since being a pupil at primary school, where along with the other kids he'd helped take the readings from the school's own weather station.

'Such as........when you're sitting comfortably in your own living room after they've forecast rain,' elaborated Dingwall, igniting his roll-up which flared so fiercely it resembled a touch-paper rather than a cigarette. 'You can see the cloud gradually thicken - often over a prolonged period, with the wind slowly increasing until eventually the rain begins falling. Out at sea, especially if you're heading into the weather, the change obviously happens more quickly, owing of course, to the combined speeds of both ship and depression. You also have to take into account that out here at sea there are no mountains and so forth to either deflect or delay the weather front.'

'I see,' said Steve, absorbing everything Dingwall had recounted, despite being already conversant with the 'mountains' element of the equation. 'And I suppose if a ship and the weather are travelling in the same direction then the opposite applies?'

'Naturally,' replied Dingwall, pinching out the end of his roll-up and tossing the dog-end overboard. 'But that's not the end of the story. Sometimes a ship can outrun the weather and escape it altogether, depending on the direction either one or the other is heading. Of course, the skipper has no control whatsoever over the track of a storm system, but he can take evasive measures if he's a mind to. Like last night for instance, although in that case we were tracking across the weather rather than away from it. If you happened to be watching the wake yesterday afternoon you'd have noticed us take a turn to the south-east. That's why we only caught the tail-end of that little beastie. If the Old Man had decided to continue on his original course the cargo of wool would probably have been blown all the way to Hawaii and we'd have been looking for a dry dock to repair the damage. As it was we came through virtually unscathed.'

'And I guess that was the reason it turned colder last night,' volunteered Steve, who'd become fully engrossed and was in danger of forgetting the time.

'Exactly,' answered Dingwall, who was clearly the master of his subject without being unduly patronising. 'Because as you probably already know, the air-stream behind a weather system is always cooler than before it. It's all basic weather lore, really.'

'Fascinating,' said Steve, finally glancing at his watch and realizing he ought to be strapping up the afternoon teacups. 'We'll have to have another chat some time.'

'Certainly,' replied Dingwall nodding appreciatively. 'I'm always willing to help further a youngster's education.'

'There's just one other thing,' said Steve, suddenly remembering something he'd been dying to ask, ever since the DBS's arrival. 'That's if you've no objection to me being personal.'

'What's that?' enquired Dingwall, head cocked inquisitively, wondering what was about to land on his doorstep.

'Well........ventured Steve, hesitantly, not entirely sure he should be asking. 'How come you have the name Dingwall? I thought Dingwall was somewhere in Scotland. Is it your real name? Or is it just a nickname?'

'No, it's my real name, right enough,' answered the islander, relieved at the question's innocence. 'It was my mother's idea. You see, my maternal grandmother hailed from Dingwall, and for whatever reason my mother thought it would be a suitable name for her second-born. In truth, I'm only glad they didn't name me after my grandfather's birthplace. He came from Lochboisdale, on South Uist. That would've been a terrible mouthful.'

They chuckled as Steve took his leave, a contented glow warming his innards as he pondered this latest encounter with Dingwall. He'd known the fellow for less than a fortnight, and they'd only conversed with any real purpose since the previous evening; but in that relatively short time he'd acquired a considerable liking for the man, and regarded him as something more than just a seagoing encyclopaedia.

In the days to come Steve also discovered that in addition to being a kindly guru Dingwall was a political animal, a sea lawyer for want of a more suitable appellation, who carried a weighty grudge against the British Establishment and British shipowners; mostly for the injustices perpetrated against British seafarers for which he considered the owners, with the Establishment's tacit collusion, responsible. Much of his bitterness was reserved for the manner in which his own family had been treated during wartime, although the same had applied to any family where a merchant seafarer had been the principal provider.

Like most British citizens, especially those with no maritime connections, Steve had been completely ignorant of the discrimination practised against seafarers by a tight-fisted British shipping industry, with total disregard for the effect on the men and their dependants. But through listening to people like Dingwall, and others who'd been in a similar position, Steve became better enlightened; although if the truth be told, what with him believing Britain was a paragon of fairness, he at first found it difficult to stomach. However, he was learning, little by little and no matter how disagreeably, that his history lessons at school had been hugely embellished, highlighting the so-called glories of Empire and so on, but neglecting the inherent brutality and misery; all part of what the Establishment decreed should be believed, rather than the shocking reality.

'No! You're bullshitting,' Steve had protested, when Dingwall first told how in World War Two, British seamen had had their pay terminated from the instant their ship was torpedoed, leaving the families to fend for themselves, either until the men were rescued and able to find further employment; or in the case of those who died, until some other family member assumed the role of breadwinner. 'This is Britain we're talking about - the greatest country in the world.'

'Oh! It's true right enough, great country or not,' replied Dingwall, in no uncertain fashion, determined that Steve should understand, and that the blinkers be permanently removed. 'Back where I come from you're either a crofter or a seafarer, with seafaring being the main occupation simply because there's so little alternative employment. My father was a prime example.'

'What was so special about him?' enquired Steve, not sure he

279

should be asking for fear of hearing something unpalatable. 'If what you say is true, wasn't everyone in the same boat?'

'Exactly, that's the point,' answered Dingwall, trying his best to overcome Steve's mulishness without sounding unduly offensive. 'It would have been precisely the same if your father had been a seafarer - it didn't matter a toss where they came from or who they were. Now, as I was saying. My dad - he was a greaser, by the way - was torpedoed on three separate occasions, and in each instance his pay was suspended from the moment his vessel was sunk. The last time it happened he didn't survive so my mother had to cope on her own - well, at least for the next three months, until my elder brother got a berth on a puffer, trading along the Clyde. He was only thirteen at the time so you know they weren't paying him much - not that he'd have been earning a great deal more if he'd been thirty, mind you. Anyway, as soon as he turned fifteen he went off to sea school and then away to sea on a tanker. His ship was torpedoed on his very first voyage and exploded with the loss of all hands. That's why I'm here lecturing you, so I know exactly what I'm talking about - and don't you dare to suggest otherwise.'

Steve had felt suitable humbled, the more so after the Bosun had corroborated the story; not specifically regarding Dingwall's personal circumstances, but the whole rotten business in general. 'Dingwall's got it spot on,' the Bosun had advised, only too happy to confirm the account, and to supplement it with his own summary of what had after all been a deplorable state of affairs. He went on to sermonize that when he first went to sea as a deck boy in the early years of the century, when the gulf between rich and poor was as expansive as ever and causing ever-more heated disagreements in parliament, he'd walked up the gangway of a rusty old tramp in Cardiff docks, carrying his very own bedding because the company refused to provide it. That kind of stinginess, along with a host of other grievances, had prevailed throughout the 'twenties' and 'thirties', extending into the nineteen-fifties.

'Even after the Second World War men were still paying for their own grub on some ships,' the Bosun had continued, eager to drive home his message, 'mostly coasters, mind you - but even on some of the tramping companies the food was barely adequate, hardly meeting Board-of-Trade entitlements. I know things were tough ashore during the war and immediately afterwards, what with rationing and all, but folk would have rioted in the streets if they'd had to exist on what some merchant seamen were expected to live on.' Steve was totally disillusioned. Here, aboard the *Alice Springs*, he was eating far, far better than he'd ever done - notwithstanding that he'd always been pretty well fed - because the food was easily the equivalent of that in a five-star hotel; and this was only a freighter, without the cuisine of a liner.'

And I'll tell you another thing,' added the Bosun, just when Steve was beginning to think he'd heard the worst of it. 'When we were home on leave during the war we were often treated as cowards, conscription-dodgers if you like, just because we didn't wear uniform. Can you imagine how the blokes must have felt - after what they'd been through, simply because an ignorant public weren't kept properly informed?

Steve felt thoroughly sickened, especially after learning that the Merchant Navy had lost a greater percentage of its manpower in the conflict than any of the armed services, including a scandalous number of boy ratings who were barely into their teens. Yet this factor routinely passed without comment, as if by simply being civilian seafarers their sacrifice wasn't worth mentioning. It had been a difficult lesson to digest but he did digest it, vowing that when he returned home he'd ensure that as wide an audience as possible learnt the true extent of just how shabbily the men had been treated.

He could only reflect upon what the Bosun had been telling him for ages, that in the years since the war the seafaring life had changed beyond all recognition, and that if a seaman from the 'twenties' or 'thirties' was suddenly to find himself aboard the *Alice Springs*, or any other British vessel, come to that, in the early 1960s, he'd have thought he was witnessing a miracle. As a parting shot the Bosun had added, 'Just you remember, Son. These are the best times to be a seafarer and if I were you I'd make the most of them, because they ain't gonna last forever.'

As if to deny the impression that in the most recent two decades the shipowners had gradually become spendthrift, an example of their cheese-paring - or to be more precise, that of their on-board representatives - presented itself when the *Alice Springs* was only a few days from Panama, when the Second Steward appeared flourishing a sheet of paper.

'All of your cabins are going to be redecorated,' announced Sec, scanning the document to see whose names were first on the list. 'Steve, Peter........your cabin's going to be painted first so until it's completed you'll have to sleep in the hospital.'

'So, who gets to do the painting?' asked Peter, suspiciously, indicating he already knew the answer. 'Do we get to do it on overtime?'

'No, you don't,' replied Sec, who appeared decidedly uncomfortable, as if Peter's suggestion would have been the proper course of action to adopt. 'The Chief Steward's been talking it over with the Mate and they've decided that a couple of deckies'll do it on daywork,'

'Fuckin' old skinflint,' complained Peter, bitterly, slamming the door of the hot-press in disgust, so that the dixies and carousel rattled in protest. 'We could have done it in the evening after work, and earnt an extra few bob into the bargain.'

'Don't blame me,' answered Sec, turning to Archie and Ruby whose cabin was next on the rota. 'I'm only the messenger - but if it's any consolation I agree with you. I'm just wondering what's going to happen if someone falls ill or gets hurt while the hospital's occupied.'

'I bet the old bastard hasn't even thought of that,' grumbled Peter, contemptuously, grabbing a stack of saucers and loading them noisily into their rack. 'Or if he has he doesn't give a monkey's.'

'Well, that's it in a nutshell, isn't it,' ventured Archie, who wasn't too bothered about the extra overtime but was a little miffed at being ousted from the comfort of his own cabin for the sterile surroundings of the hospital. 'It's a stitch-up - you can read the Boss like a book. He works out a way of getting the decorating done without damaging the catering budget, has a sly word with the Mate and the deckies get to do it on daywork, with no extra cost to either department. A bottle of scotch for the Mate and the deal's wrapped up.'

'That's as maybe,' agreed Sec, folding the sheet of paper and slipping it into his beast pocket before breaking the news in the galley, where he knew he'd get a further ear-bashing. 'But at least you'll be getting some additional overtime after Panama, what with 'Channel Night' and so on.'

'Big deal,' sulked Peter, as Sec left the pantry and descended the companionway to the galley. 'But we'd have gotten that anyway - and the extra few bob from the painting job would've been useful.'

Steve too would have been grateful for a little extra overtime, for while he was far better paid than he would have been ashore his wages were still less than half those of a fully-fledged steward. Steve's monthly wage as a first-tripper was £14/12/6d all found, plus the customary daily overtime and accumulated leave pay, the latter of which would be added at the voyage's completion. This compared very favourably with the £2/10/6d he'd been earning for a six-day week in the signal box, but was infinitely less than the £36 being paid to stewards like Keith while Archie earnt several pounds more. But what had really intrigued Steve was Sec's parting remark, and the overtime it ostensibly promised. 'What's all this about Channel Night?' he asked, when Peter had finally stopped whinging and he managed to get a word in edgeways. 'And why does it mean we should get some extra overtime?'

'Oh! It happens towards the end of every trip,' answered Peter, surprised that Steve should be asking. 'Actually, it usually lasts for several nights in succession. That's because there's so much to do that we'd never get it done if it didn't.'

'And what does it entail?' pressed Steve, who liked to hear the nuts and bolts of a story and not just a vague passing reference. 'I guess we have to work - but doing what, exactly?'

'Well - cleaning, of course,' replied Peter, showing just a little irritation at what to him was an idiotic question, 'what do you think we do - stand on our heads and watch television? No, we give the pantry and saloon, smoke rooms and lounges - alleyways too come to that, an extra special clean up, and touch up any chipped paintwork. It's so that when we arrive back in London everything's shipshape and Bristol fashion. That's why they're tarting up the cabins.'

'Fair enough,' thanked Steve, a tad embarrassed as Peter glanced sideways, perhaps wondering at his cabin-mate's intellect. 'It's just that I'd heard of 'The Channels', but not about Channel Night and so on.'

The *Alice Springs'* hospital was a starkly barren affair located at the forward end of the working alleyway, directly opposite the galley. Over the previous four months it had hosted Steve only twice, firstly when he'd consulted the doctor with regard to his damaged front tooth, and on visiting Danny when the Tiger was suffering from bladder stones. The unfortunate steward had occupied one of a pair of cots that were suspended from the deckhead in much the same way as a hammock, an arrangement that allowed the cots to remain static, even if there was a hurricane blowing. With the exception of the daily surgery Danny had been the only inhabitant, at least until now, and the lack of occupancy showed. The cots were bereft of bedding, there were no personal effects and the pair of empty lockers with their doors agape reminded Steve of 'Old Mother Hubbard'. The furnishings were completed by a pair of canvas-seated chairs and a solitary medicine cabinet that was bolted to the starboard bulkhead. 'Sod all in there, I shouldn't wonder,' groused Peter, dumping his linen on one of the chairs before exploring his temporary abode. 'A few bandages and plasters maybe, some codeine and iodine and a few other odds and sods and that'll be just about it,' he mumbled, tugging vainly at the cabinet's locked door before plonking himself down on a cot.

Peter's perpetual moaning about the sequestered overtime, along with having to sleep in the hospital, was becoming a mite tedious and it was Steve who was feeling the brunt. 'For Christ's sake, Peter,' he pleaded, hoping for a change of record, 'put a sock in it. Whether we like it or not the Chief's made his decision, and as for sleeping in the hospital - we're only in here for forty-eight hours so surely you can put up with that?'

'That's not the point,' snapped Peter, seemingly aggrieved that Steve should have apparently chosen to take the side of authority when in his view the entire catering department should have revolted. 'We should have all gone along to the Boss's office and told him we weren't going anywhere unless we got to do the painting ourselves,' he argued, lighting a cigarette and tossing the still-flaring match carelessly into an adjacent but fortunately empty waste-paper basket. That would have taught him and who knows, we might even have ended up with the overtime. Instead of that we just gripe among ourselves and let the old bastard get away with it.'

It was a valid enough basis for argument, and despite Peter's bellyaching Steve found himself broadly in agreement. Most working people, especially unorganized labour and more specifically seamen who were scattered to the corners of the earth, were all too ready to concede and be trampled on rather than stand up for their rights. He thought back to what Dingwall and the Bosun had told him, about how seafarers had been routinely mistreated and yet the owners had almost always overmastered. He reasoned that to have made a great fuss in wartime would have been self-destructive, attracting little public sympathy; while the owners and the government would have had a field day, portraying the men as unpatriotic by placing personal interest ahead of the national need. But this was nearly twenty years later, and remembering what Dingwall had told him he acknowledged that seafarers sometimes ought to be more vociferous in order to achieve their objectives. He didn't hold with striking - never had; that was also self-defeating and it would take months, perhaps years, to make good the lost pay for what little might be gained in return. Anyway, striking at sea would almost certainly be regarded as mutiny and lead to the crew's eventual arrest and possible imprisonment. But simply refusing to vacate your own cabin could hardly be regarded as mutiny, not so long as you honoured your contract. And who knows, an unwillingness to cooperate might even have resulted in the Boss backing down and reconsidering his position. But that was all largely hypothesis; the deal was done and they had to accept it.

Steve left Peter to grumble away to himself and wandered aft, to where one of the Junior Cadets was lowering and folding the ensign. It was a simple ceremony that took place every evening at sun-down and as the Bosun had once explained, was intended to show that the sun would never be allowed to set on the British Empire. The 'Red Duster', as it was affectionately known among seafarers, would be stowed away until sun-up when it would be re-hoisted, a scarlet banner symbolizing not only the ascendancy of the British Merchant Navy but by association, the aforementioned Empire.

Given what he'd recently learnt Steve couldn't help thinking how false it all seemed, proclaiming the illustriousness of British

Imperialism while the very people who'd created the Empire, namely ordinary men and women from Britain and her colonies, had been treated like the scum of the earth. He regarded it all as counterfeit - but was abruptly brought up with a jerk. He was suddenly aware of his politicisation since first becoming associated with Dingwall. Until a few days ago he'd always accepted what his government and the media had told him, whereas now he was taking a totally different slant on the world, with his very own homeland coming under ever-increasing scrutiny. Upon reflection he really ought to have known better because after all, he'd only just been to Australia. Okay, he'd already known of how little more than a century earlier some British children, often barely out of their cradles, had been sentenced to transportation for stealing perhaps a slice of bread, simply because they were hungry. But he'd more recently learnt how Australia and some of its off-lying islands, notably Norfolk Island and Tasmania, had been hell on earth for transported British convicts - many of whom had been convicted for what those of Steve's generation would have considered trivial - with merciless floggings and forced hard labour being the mandate of an imperious Establishment.

And that wasn't the extent of the cruelty by any means. The Royal Navy in particular had been notorious for the brutal ill-treatment of its ratings, while the inhumanity of slavery, of which the British had been amongst the most barbaric practitioners, had only relatively recently been abolished. This new-found knowledge made Steve feel ashamed because according to conventional wisdom, wasn't it the Spanish and Portuguese, along with other unenlightened nations, who'd behaved like savages whereas the British had been flowers of virtue? It had come as a nasty shock to find that Britain had been equally as vicious and sometimes worse when it came to stamping its mark on those it had colonised and governed. The fact that during the last century and a half, although more specifically in the last twenty years, the nation had supposedly become more civilised was of small consolation, the more so as Steve vividly recalled hearing on a BBC news bulletin how a tribesman in the East African colony of Kenya had received twenty-one lashes for actively opposing his rulers, and this was in the mid nineteen-fifties.

In retrospect, he'd been foolish and naïve to doubt Dingwall when he'd tried to instil how poorly the seamen had been treated. The lesson had been painful, but the recent instruction had opened his eyes far wider than his schoolroom history classes, not to mention the blinding propaganda peddled by a mealy-mouthed media on behalf of an unprincipled State.

Still, that was now all in the past. The wrongs couldn't be righted; but there ought to be greater transparency, Steve thought, so that the population at large knew how poorly their country had conducted itself - and in some instances continued to conduct itself - both at home and in its overseas territories. Whether or not they'd be interested was a different matter. He had a sneaking suspicion that most would just bury their heads and pretend it had never happened, or simply dismiss it as, 'that's how things were', and regard it as no longer relevant; but better to know the truth, he concluded, than be treated like a cultivated mushroom.

Steve found his brooding as cheerless as Peter's moaning; but his mood was lightened on the morning of their arrival at Panama thanks to an hilarious incident that perhaps only one of the catering staff had anticipated. He suspected something amiss when he heard a metallic 'clunk' and a yelp as he was cleaning the engineers' wash-room. He poked his head around the door to find a traumatised Ruby, a blood-soaked handkerchief pressed to his nose, being led towards the hospital by Donald who was doing a pretty good job of playing the caring nursemaid without actually bursting out laughing.

'Now, now, then' consoled Donald, as he winked at Steve as the latter gazed on in amazement. 'It's only a bloody nose. I've sent for the doctor and he'll have you fixed up in no time.'

'What's happened?' enquired Steve, as eager as anyone to learn the cause of the bloodshed. 'Ruby walk into a door?'

Donald shook his head, and whispered, 'No, nothing like that. You wouldn't believe me if I told you.'

Steve didn't have to wait for Donald's account, for as soon as he arrived back at the pantry he found Keith and Peter doubled up at how Archie had caused Ruby's injury. 'Smacked him in the face with a tea tray,' said Keith, when Steve pressed them both for an answer.

'Why would he do that?' asked Steve, hardly able to credit that

Archie could be in any way violent. 'I thought him and Ruby were lovers.'

'They aren't now - well, not for the time being at any rate,' answered Keith, wiping a tear from his cheek with his handkerchief. 'And the way Archie's carrying on they won't be for the foreseeable future.'

'What did they fall out over?' pressed Steve, impatient to be given the broader picture. 'They seemed to be getting along so well together.'

'They were until Archie caught Ruby sidling up to Sean Cassidy,' answered Keith, incredulously. 'Can you believe it, Archie getting jealous, just because Ruby was chatting up one of the firemen? And Sean of all people - as if he'd be the slightest bit interested in Ruby. I told you we'd be seeing the real Archie, didn't I? But I didn't expect the little green-eyed monster to get the better of him over someone as unlikely as Sean.'

'I don't care what it was all about,' intruded the Second Steward, clearly concerned that the issue should be speedily resolved without a great deal of boat-rocking. 'But we've got to get Archie out of this mess somehow, before either the Boss or the Skipper get wind of it. Archie's been a bloody good mate, no matter what his sexuality, and regardless of the fact that he belted Ruby with tray he doesn't deserve a logging. Now what I propose is this. You lot keep your mouths shut and I'll smooth things over with Ruby. A bottle of gin ought to do it. I'll mark it down as a breakage and hopefully that'll put an end to it.'

'What about the doctor?' queried Peter, spotting a possible flaw in the Second Steward's strategy. 'He'll have to enter something in the incident book. Won't that give the game away?'

'I've already thought about that,' replied Sec, to Peter's obvious irritation. 'The doc's a decent bloke too, and he'll think it just as preposterous. I'll just ask him to enter it as a nosebleed, bung him a packet of Players and no-one'll be any the wiser.

And that is exactly what happened. Sec played the part of pacifier, and with the promise of a bottle of Gordon's persuaded Ruby that Archie's jealousy had been fuelled purely by his feelings for his cabin-mate. For his part, the doctor played along and the matter was swept under the carpet. Archie and Ruby hardly spoke to each other for a fortnight, in the company of others at any rate; although it was widely suspected they'd kissed and made up and that the exhibited estrangement was largely for the benefit of others.

Later that morning, as the *Alice Springs* was making her approach to Balboa on the Bay of Panama, Steve went aft to empty the rosie before they entered the series of locks, lakes and channels forming the route of the Panama Canal. The bin wasn't full, but if it wasn't emptied it would be overflowing long before they reached the system's Caribbean extremity. It also gave Steve the ideal opportunity to survey the scene on the Pacific side of the isthmus, an area much altered since the Spanish explorer Rodrigo de Bastidas first discovered it some four-hundred-and-sixty years earlier.

'You'd better save some of that for the mules that'll be towing us through the locks,' called a voice from the boat deck, as Steve stepped out on the after well-deck on his way to the rubbish chute. 'We don't want them going hungry, do we?'

Steve turned around and looked up and there stood Donald and Keith, faces beaming as they peered down on the pantry boy whom they'd assumed would be ripe for some fun. Indeed, many first-timers through the Panama Canal had been caught by that very same chestnut; but Steve was a railway aficionado, and knew very well that the mules being referred to were electric locomotives, and that their diet was generated by a power-station. And thereby he turned the tables, presenting his colleagues with a two-fingered salute before continuing his way aft with the rosie.

18

It had been hoped that shore leave would be granted, in either Balboa, Colón or perhaps both, but the wish had been stymied. The *Alice Springs*, the crew were informed, wouldn't be calling at either but would be making a direct transit of the canal, their next port of call being Curaçao in the Netherlands Antilles. However, there was a welcome delivery of mail, and among a bundle of correspondence for Steve were a number of letters from Maxine.

Steve tore open the envelopes from Maxine and commenced reading, stuffing those from home into his pee-jacket pocket until later. For his part, he'd written several letters to Maxine and one each to his parents and grandmother during the lengthy crossing of the Pacific; and he'd popped these in the box in the working alleyway shortly before their arrival at Balboa. There was nothing from Glenda - but that was only to be expected; and when all was said and done, he hadn't sent her anything either.

Maxine's effusions were a mosaic of romantic exuberance and longing. She was clearly deeply in love, and he fervently hoped that his scribblings to her had painted a true reflection of his own feelings. She'd hardly been out of his mind since he'd left New Zealand, and the arrival of her letters fanned the flames of his migratory ambition. He was dancing on air, and already counting the days until he could begin the process of arranging a permanent reunion with his sweetheart.

He'd become so engrossed with Maxine's outpourings that he completely forgot about the pantry; until a whispered word in his ear from the Second Steward reminded him that this wasn't Daddy's Yacht, and that he could drool over his girlfriend's jottings for as long as he liked in his own time. Meanwhile, he should replace them in their envelopes and assist Peter in cleaning out the refrigerator, before turning his attention to some teacups and a packet of plate powder.

Steve had learnt from his atlas that the Panama Canal actually runs in a north-westerly direction between the Pacific and Atlantic Oceans and not from west to east as is generally surmised. He'd also gleaned that the canal is in reality a series of lakes connected to each other - and to the sea at either end - by the only true stretches of canal. However, that didn't detract in any way from what was after all a civil-engineering masterpiece that due mainly to yellow fever and malaria, had cost a great many lives to construct. Finally opened in 1914, the Americans controlled the waterway and were responsible for its operation throughout, having completed the project after an earlier French attempt had been aborted. The land for several miles on either side of this vital maritime link was known as the Panama Canal Zone and also came under United States jurisdiction. However, American governance didn't extend to the ports of Colón in the north and Panama City in the south which both retained Panamanian sovereignty.

After entering the canal beneath the newly-completed Bridge of the Americas which linked the North and South American continents, the *Alice Springs* negotiated the Miraflores Locks and traversed a small but picturesque lake before entering the Pedro Miguel Locks which lifted her up to the Gaillard Cut, a steep-sided, jungle-clad excavation that after several miles led into the Gatun Lakes. The lakes had been formed by the flooding of an elevated valley, the water being drawn from the adjoining Chagres River. The inflow from the river was regulated so that as the locks at either end of the canal filled and emptied, the depth of water in the central section remained constant.

A peculiarity associated with the Panama Canal which Steve didn't fully comprehend was that for some reason the sea level at the Pacific end varied by several meters from that in the Caribbean. According to the Bosun it had something to do with the tides which in the Bay of Panama were apparently wide ranging, whereas in Limón Bay on the Caribbean side they were only marginal.

By this stage of his seagoing career Steve had become semi-conditioned to the blistering heat of the Red Sea and Indian Ocean, but he was totally unprepared for the steamy, debilitating sauna of Panama. Daytime temperatures didn't reach the dizzying heights of those attained in the Arabian Peninsular and north-eastern Africa but were typically around the ninety degrees Fahrenheit mark; and allied with a saturated atmosphere conditions were truly enervating. He'd never taken so many cold showers as he did over the following twelve hours, not only to wash away the sweat, but also to seek relief from the suffocating, strength-sapping humidity.

'Bloody hell,' he complained, as he loaded the steaming hot components of lunch into the hot-press, wiping perspiration from his brow with the back of his hand to prevent it dripping into a tray of lamb cutlets. 'I knew it'd be hot but I didn't expect it to be this oppressive. It's a good job I've plenty of T-shirts.'

'Now you can understand why it was an ideal breeding ground for disease,' pronounced Archie, who outwardly at least seemed to have brushed off his differences with Ruby. 'It must have been a death-trap before the advent of modern insecticides and medicines - penicillin and the like. They must have been dying like flies.'

It wasn't until the afternoon, when the *Alice Springs* was well into her transit, that Steve and Peter were able to go on deck in the forlorn hope of a breath of fresh air, and to view the jungle-wrapped islands and mountains that were a dominant feature of the landscape. Unlike at Suez there was no obvious evidence of convicts toiling away in this broiling strip of Central America. Instead, the air was alive with all manner of colourful and strange-sounding birds, while the greenery itself resounded to the squeals, yelps and chatter of countless yet largely invisible animals.

'I bet there's a load of monkeys in there,' ventured Peter, nodding at the undergrowth and breaking the silence that hitherto had been punctuated only by the voices from the jungle and the birds soaring overhead, 'and crocodiles too, I shouldn't wonder.'

'Do they have crocodiles in this part of the world?' queried Steve, who was by no means an expert in zoological demography, but understood crocodiles were mostly to be found in Africa, Australia and parts of Asia. 'I thought it was mostly alligators and cayman in this neck of the woods.'

'Call them what you like,' responded Peter, indifferently, 'they all look the same to me.' Steve chuckled. He couldn't argue with that, any more than he could argue that there were alligators rather than crocodiles in the Panamanian jungle. For all he knew there might be neither or both.

Unlike the Suez Canal, which owing to its restricted width was effectively a one-way street, two-way traffic was the rule of the road at Panama. And so it was that during the course of her transit the *Alice Springs* passed a number of other vessels proceeding in the opposite direction, including Blue Star's *Tacoma Star* on her way from Liverpool to Vancouver, and the Pacific Steam Navigation Company's *Santander*, outward bound from Glasgow to Valparaiso.

By nightfall the *Alice Springs* had completed her transit, having navigated the Gatun Locks before passing the conjoined cities of Cristóbal and Colón and entering the Caribbean Sea. At each flight of locks the mules had performed admirably, enabling the *Alice Springs* to cross an entire continent in a distance of only forty-eight miles, so avoiding a lengthy and potentially hazardous detour through the tortuous Straits of Magellan or around the infamous Cape Horn.

19

By the simple procedure of slipping into the Caribbean it was as if a pall had been lifted, and in the space of only a few miles the air was as fresh - or as fresh as it was ever likely to be in these latitudes - as it had been earlier that morning. 'Thank Christ for that,' rejoiced Steve, as he and Jimmy observed the fading lights of the Panama Canal Zone receding gradually into the distance. 'That has to be the most uncomfortable place on the planet.'

'Yeah? Well - just think how unpleasant it was for us in the galley, or the lads in the engine room,' responded Jimmy, with little sympathy. 'Talk about sweating over a hot stove - and I can only imagine what it was like for the black gang.' It was a pertinent point. Other people seemed to have coped despite the discomfort, so it was probably a case of Steve being less acclimatized than they.

Since well before their arrival at Panama, the Chief Steward had been making sarcastic comments about the length of Steve's hair, which hadn't been cut since they were in Sydney. The latest swipe came on the morning following the canal transit, when he spotted Steve sweeping hair from his eyes while scrubbing out the engineers' alleyway. 'Chapman!' he snapped, causing Steve to jump out of his skin. 'Your hair's a bloody disgrace. If it gets any longer you'll be able to sit on it.' Steve had to agree that the length of his hair was becoming both troublesome and unsightly, and may have contributed to his discomfort back at Panama. In retrospect he should have had it cut in New Zealand because as far as he was aware there was little he could do about it here. He could see where the Chief was coming from given that over-long hair wasn't really desirable in the vicinity of food and so on - but he'd had just about enough of the sniping.

'Well, I can't get it cut miles from anywhere, can I?' he rasped, gesturing at the ocean which was all but invisible from the alleyway. 'It'll have to wait until we get home.'

'Oh, no it won't,' answered the Chief, bluntly, poking the tip of his ballpoint into Steve's forelock and twisting it away from his eyebrows. 'We'll be in Curaçao in a couple of days' time. You can get it cut there instead of going out on the piss.' And with that he left Steve to contemplate the prospect of getting his haircut on an island he was completely unfamiliar with, and where the whereabouts of the nearest barbershop could only to be guessed at.

'Arsehole,' growled Steve, beneath his breath, as soon as the Chief was out of earshot, but clearly enough to de-cypher by anyone who could lip-read. 'If he thinks I'm going to waste time getting a haircut in Curaçao he's got another think coming. There must be someone on board who's handy with a pair of scissors.'

'Have a word with either Archie or Ruby,' suggested Peter, when Steve enquired about the possibility of obtaining an on-board haircut. 'Most women are dab hands at sewing and knitting - home perms and the suchlike, so maybe either of those two are useful at hairdressing.'

'I should say so, Duckie,' clucked Ruby, when Steve posed the question of whether or not he was an occasional hairdresser. 'They don't call me the Mister Teazy Weazy of the working alleyways for nothing, you know. Tell you what, we'll cut it this afternoon - and don't you worry. We'll soon have you looking like Cary Grant.'

Steve had never aspired to having film star looks, and it wasn't a priority now. Rather, his main concern was that his hair should be made more presentable. It was with this in mind that straight after lunch he took the chair from his cabin and positioned it in the forward well-deck, as close as possible to the superstructure, where they couldn't be seen from the wheelhouse. Ruby put in appearance soon afterwards, a shower curtain draped over his right forearm while in a small canvas bag he carried a safety razor, a semi-toothless comb and some nail scissors. Steve viewed the approaching tableau with foreboding. He'd been expecting Ruby to be equipped with all the paraphernalia of a professional hairdresser; although as he readily accepted, it would have been impracticable given that the steward had arrived on board carrying only his personal belongings. It was with this less worrying thought that he sat back in his chair while

Ruby made ready his tackle.

'Now then, Duckie,' chortled Ruby, tucking the edge of the shower curtain beneath Steve's collar and draping it over his torso. 'I haven't got any clippers so I'll cut the bulk of it with the scissors and tidy your neck with the razor. If nothing else, it should put a stop to the nagging.'

And so, Ruby began snipping away with the nail scissors, which weren't as sharp as they might have been owing to their more usual vocation being the clipping of his - and more recently - Archie's toenails. Every now and again Steve winced, the scissors having yanked out some hair rather than cut it. Ruby apologised, promising to be more careful in future, although from Steve's perspective any extra diligence was negligible. Not only that, but to his gathering consternation the hair accumulating around his ankles was gradually assuming cushion-stuffing proportions; and he also noticed that his tonsorial makeover was attracting an audience, some of whom were grinning like Cheshire cats, even though in certain instances they could have done with a haircut themselves.

'I hope you're not taking too much off, Ruby,' cautioned Steve, as a two-inch clump of his mane, snipped from somewhere in the region of his left ear, landed in front of him. 'I don't want to look like a monk.'

The onlookers tittered, although Steve wasn't sure if it was in response to his quip or more disturbingly, in appreciation of Ruby's expertise.

'I told you not to worry, didn't I, Duckie?' answered Ruby, flourishing the nail scissors in the fashion of a fully-qualified coiffeur. 'I know what I'm doing - and don't you take any notice of these silly buggers,' he continued, indicating the encircling assemblage, some of whom were now in uncontrollable fits of laughter.' They can spend the rest of the trip looking like orang-utans if they want to, whereas you'll be as smart as a pageboy.' Steve relaxed - slightly, although if the truth were known he'd be happier when Ruby had finished.

He didn't have too long to wait. In due course, Ruby took a few paces back to admire his handiwork before shaving Steve's neck with the razor. He then withdrew a six-inch paintbrush - borrowed from the Bosun - from his waistband, and began sweeping away the locks, some of which had slipped beneath the shower curtain and were prickling the skin on Steve's shoulders. Finally, he produced a compact-mirror from his breast pocket and brandished it for Steve's appreciation. 'There!' He announced, triumphantly, beaming broadly as the gathering applauded and nodded. 'What do you think of that? I told you I could cut hair, didn't I?'

Steve opened his eyes - and nearly fell out of his chair. The image in Ruby's mirror was far removed from the one he'd been recently used to. Gone were the long flowing tresses. In their place was something resembling a scrubbing brush - and a badly-worn scrubbing brush at that. None of his remaining hair was more than an inch in length with most of it considerably shorter. It was littered with notches, while the section immediately above and behind his left ear was as bare as a freshly plucked chicken. Steve was mortified, and straight-away knew that he'd become the victim of a practical joke. It was patently obvious that Ruby was no Teazy Weazy. In fact, his efforts showed more of an affinity with Fleet Street than any high-class salon in Mayfair.

Steve's unease turned to anger. 'What the fuck have you done?' he roared, rubbing a hand through what was left of his hair while using language that was quite unbecoming. 'I look like a fucking hedgehog. I thought you said I'd look like Cary Grant. Cary Grant's hair doesn't look like this.'

'It would do if I'd cut it,' answered Ruby, huffily, feigning offence; although a crafty wink at the still enthralled audience revealed that as far as he was concerned the farce still had some way to run. 'And anyway,' he persisted, shaking the hair from the shower curtain before folding it and tucking it under his arm. 'At least there's nothing left for the Chief Steward to whittle about.'

Steve wasn't sure about that. The Boss wasn't renowned for his sense of humour, and he was convinced that with his hair looking as if it had been cut with a cheese-wire he was due for some further invective. Still, as he quickly accepted, and as was often the case, it was no use complaining, especially given that on this occasion he'd been the instigator of his own embarrassment. His hair had been cut to the bone and would take weeks if not months to regrow. In this instance, the old saying that there were only a few days between a bad haircut and a good one just didn't hold water, and wouldn't do for the foreseeable future.

As Ruby stalked off and the gallery dispersed, Steve slumped despondently in his chair. Then, unexpectedly, he too suffered a fit of the giggles, as like a bolt from the blue he also appreciated the funnier element of the side how. For that was what it had been, a diversion from the humdrum routine of a cargo ship. Aboard the passenger liners there were cinemas, theatres and all manner of distractions, with some of them available to the crew, if only in their off-duty hours. There was the 'Pig and Whistle' -the crew bar - where they could gather at the end of the day; or maybe someone would organize a 'Sod's Opera', with any number of individuals playing the part of maybe Charlie Chaplin, Max Miller, perhaps the Tiller Girls or even the Beverly Sisters. But ships like the *Alice Springs* didn't provide entertainment of that sort so Steve's haircut had been a proxy, an alternative form of amusement. Nevertheless, that didn't mean he was any more thrilled with his haircut, or that Ruby would escape retribution.

'I suppose you could say it was in lieu of a crossing-the-line ceremony,' Said Dingwall Patterson, as Steve and the man from South Uist sat out on deck, breathing in the late-evening air. 'You got away with a lousy haircut, whereas when I first crossed the equator they painted me from head to toe with lubricating oil that had been mingled with soot from the funnel. It took a fortnight to get myself clean.'

Steve had to admit that compared with Dingwall he'd gotten off lightly. He had indeed escaped the dreaded crossing-the-line ceremony - twice, to be precise, as the *Alice Springs* had recrossed the equator somewhere north of the Galapagos Islands. Fair enough, he wouldn't be allowed to forget his makeshift haircut in a hurry - and nor could he given that on every occasion he looked in the mirror it was glowering back at him; but it was eminently preferable to the tar and feathers treatment that he might have been subjected to on another vessel. And as for the Chief Steward: far from administering the expected bollocking the Boss had laughed like a hyena. In fact, for the following few days the atmosphere in the catering department was as genial as anyone could recall - not that it was ever overly subdued - as no one could remember the Chief being anything but a misery, let alone being reduced to fits of laughter.

For a good five minutes Steve and Dingwall sat without speaking, staring into the darkness and relaxing in the warmth of the evening; before Dingwall nodded vaguely away to starboard, and said, 'Columbia and Venezuela are somewhere over there. Take a deep breath and you can smell them.'

Steve glanced at Dingwall before doing as the man had invited; but following a prolonged analysis wasn't convinced he could smell anything extraordinary. 'Maybe,' he replied, sceptically, taking another sniff of the air, just on the off-chance that he might have previously missed something. 'But even if I can, and I'm not saying I can - how on earth can I smell somewhere that's miles away over the horizon?'

'Because they're not very far away at all,' answered Dingwall, again nodding absently in a southerly direction, indicating roughly where he imagined either Columbia or Venezuela existed. 'In fact, they're really quite close, and the border between the two is somewhere over there.' He emphasised his remark by extending an arm and drawing an invisible arc from forward to aft and back again, as though the frontier might be anywhere within the delineated radius. 'And as for the smells,' he continued, rolling and finally igniting one of his spindly cigarettes, 'in this part of the world the seasons are very much the same. It's always warm in these latitudes, the more so over a land mass. That's why when the heat increases during the daytime it draws in the air from the sea, helping to keep the coastal areas cool. Then, when the temperatures lower again in the evening, an off-shore breeze is created and the fragrances are carried on the breeze. Mostly it's from flowers and trees - but not always. That's why in some parts of the world you can sit offshore after dark and the air seems to be laden with honeysuckle, while in others, the Middle East and southern Asia, for instance, it can stink like a field of rotten sprouts.'

Steve drew another deep breath, and was eventually persuaded there was some kind of scent in the offing, although if he hadn't been told he was certain it would have passed undetected. But it was yet

299

another addition to his rapidly expanding intellectual stockpile; and as Archie had advised back in Newcastle, that's how wisdom was gained, through experience and by listening to others. By paying attention to people like Archie, Dingwall and the Bosun, Steve was absorbing an incredible amount of knowledge, and he couldn't help thinking that the boy who'd left home as an innocent and credulous teenager was returning as a wiser young man. That said, he wasn't so conceited as to become a know-all, for as the sages had taught him, he'd never grow so old that he couldn't learn anything new.

As a parting gesture, Dingwall threw back his head and inhaled deeply before slowly releasing the intake, as if savouring the delights of a garden. 'That smells very much like an Araguaney Tree if I'm not very much mistaken,' he declared, as Steve looked on in amazement. 'It's the national tree of Venezuela. Its flowers are trumpet-shaped and golden, and it smells like a posy of freesias.'

'How can you be so sure?' called Steve, sniffing the air as Dingwall strode purposefully back to his cabin. But the islander, who could be as deaf as a post when he wanted, was gone, and Steve was left wondering if even Dingwall wasn't shy of a leg pull.

Early in the morning of the second day out of Panama, the *Alice Springs* negotiated the narrow channel linking the southern Caribbean with the charming, almost landlocked harbour at Curaçao. Steve was up with the hummingbirds, and it still wasn't light when he arrived on deck to observe the berthing proceedings, and - hopefully - to gain a glimpse of the capital. Initially there was little to see save the oil tanks and refineries that serviced the bunkering industry, bathed as they were in the glare from a proliferation of arc-lights that in addition to illuminating the immediate locality made a pretty good fist of dazzling the onlooker. However, daylight arrives quickly in the tropics, and as the *Alice Springs* exited the channel and approached the capital, Willemstad, reputedly the jewel of the Dutch West Indies, the outline of the colonial-style buildings could clearly be seen against the skyline, and within minutes the first burst of sunlight was blossoming over the rooftops.

'We're here until nightfall,' said a voice that Steve immediately recognised as the Bosun's, 'so you'll have time for a decent run ashore. But then, the petty officer, who was proceeding aft to help oversee the berthing operations, added a caveat. 'But if I were you I'd give Happy Valley a miss.'

That was intriguing, thought Steve, as the Bosun made his way across the after well-deck and began scaling the ladder to the poop. I wonder what that was all about. Still, that was of no immediate concern, not with a scrub-out awaiting along with his other cleaning commitments. Nevertheless, he'd have to enquire what the comment had signified, and the man with the answer would be Keith.

'Because it's a whorehouse,' answered Keith, as the steward delivered more soiled crockery to the pantry as the post-breakfast strap-up intensified.

'Quite a number of whorehouses, actually,' added Donald, who'd overheard the conversation and had no intention of remaining a reticent bystander, not when such a salacious topic as Happy Valley was under discussion.

'That's right,' added Keith, casting a disapproving glance at Donald for having stolen his thunder. 'In fact, it's a collection of wooden huts in the countryside, and if you want a good time in Curaçao then there's no better place than Happy Valley. Mind you, you'll probably end up paying for more than a ten-minute romp on a filthy mattress - if you get my meaning.'

'And not only that,' added Donald, this time without apparently annoying anyone. 'The taxi drivers are bunch of fuckin' robbers. They'll charge a Dollar to drive you out to Happy Valley but twenty to bring you back.'

'That's a bit of an exaggeration,' rejoined Keith, who despite the impression of a few seconds earlier was still seemingly piqued by the intrusions. 'But five - maybe ten, top whack. And if you choose not to pay it's a bloody long walk to the port.'

Having learnt that Happy Valley was nothing more than a knocking shop Steve was no longer interested. He'd no intention of going there, although he was certain there were others who would.

The notice at the head of the accommodation ladder stated that the *Alice Springs* would be sailing from Curaçao at six, with shore leave expiring at five. During the intervening hours she would replenish her tanks with both fuel and fresh water, more than sufficient to see her safely across the Atlantic and back to her home port of London. As was customary in places like Curaçao the bumboats were soon in attendance, peddling a variety of souvenirs, consumer goods and other items of interest, both locally-produced and imported. However, with his pockets only containing a small amount of Australian and New Zealand coinage Steve gave the traders a miss, as in the absence of a sub he could barely afford himself a beer.

Most of the crew who were able to get ashore did so, Steve joining Jimmy and Keith after Norman and John said they weren't interested, while Peter and Donald were working. Archie and Ruby drifted off for a snorter with Sec while Sean Cassidy and his cronies were seen leaving town in a taxi, making in all probability for a collection of huts in the countryside.

Willemstad transpired as a pretty and compact city of predominantly Flemish-style architecture, the multi-shaded colour-washed buildings exuding a freshness that helped temper the stifling humidity. Bars and other small businesses abounded while a handful of markets, including a floating market, did business selling locally-grown produce, artefacts and other eye-catching merchandise. However, time like money was of the essence, and after wandering aimlessly around the various retailers Steve and his companions sought an establishment where their remaining liquidity might be more rewardingly converted.

Owing to the abysmal exchange rate the remnants of Steve's Australian and New Zealand, 'Pounds, Shillings and Pence', didn't buy very much in Willemstad, where American Dollars were greedily accepted although Guilders was the recognised currency. In fact, Steve and Jimmy could only muster sufficient for a beer each between them. 'Here, I'll treat you to a glass of blue Curaçao, offered Keith, a proposition readily accepted by Jimmy but declined by Steve who found the colour decidedly off-putting.

'You don't have to have a blue one if you don't want it,' coaxed Keith, keen that both boys should sample this delightful native liqueur. 'It's naturally colourless but it's tinted to add a touch of mysticism, otherwise you'd probably think it was an everyday bottle of rotgut. You can have an orange one if you'd prefer. The taste is identical.'

Steve was eventually persuaded and accepted a Curaçao with the alternative colouring, the orange-flavoured tanginess tickling his tastebuds like they'd never previously been tickled. 'Mmmm........that's scrumptious,' he enthused, licking his lips and sipping again from a glass that while containing significantly more than a British measure, wasn't quite as full as he'd have liked. 'I wish I could afford another.'

'Yeah........well, one's enough to be going on with,' answered Keith, drinking up and glancing at his watch. 'You'll be able to treat yourself to as many as you like back in London, but it's time we were moving. It's already past four o'clock.'

Most of those who'd ventured ashore were aboard by the five o'clock deadline, the only laggards being Sean Cassidy and his pals who came jogging along the quayside some thirty minutes after the expiry hour. This was a risky exercise given that if bunkering and other ship's business was completed prematurely, it wasn't unheard of for vessels to depart before the advertised sailing time.

As expected, Sean and his entourage had squandered their cash on the dubious delights of Happy Valley and hadn't a ha'penny between them. Nevertheless, they'd still intended hiring a taxi for the return journey, planning to cut and run on the outskirts of town leaving the driver screaming for his money. However, like most of his associates the driver they'd approached was wise to the wiles of the bullyboys. He'd insisted on being paid first, demanding ten American dollars or the local equivalent before he'd even consider carrying them. Sean had turned nasty, calling the driver all the thieving bastards in the Caribbean and threatening to kick a hole in the taxi's radiator. But the driver had refused to be intimidated, a lengthy blast on his horn summoning a throng of his brethren who appeared as from nowhere clutching wrenches and hammers and clearly prepared for a skirmish. Sean would have doubtless obliged; but his mates were more timid, preferring instead a three-mile walk to a spell in a Curaçao gaol, where the hosts might be considerably less amiable than their Antipodean counterparts whose own credentials in the humanitarian field would have horrified Amnesty International.

That evening, as the *Alice Springs* edged out into the broader

Caribbean, towards the islands of Hispaniola and Puerto Rico, Steve and Peter took a blanket each from their bunks with the intention of sleeping alfresco. Owing to the presence of the deck cargo they couldn't sleep on the hatch cover as they had done previously so they decided to sleep in the wool. They were back in their cabin within minutes, covered in dust and itching like flea-bitten hounds. Neither had considered that sheep weren't the cleanest of creatures, or that that the fleece might be lousy with ticks.

The following morning, as Steve was emptying the ash trays in the engineers' smoke room, the Second Electrician, who'd been absorbed in an out-of-date and tatty edition of a periodical called, 'The Marine Engineer', laid his magazine on the coffee table, and announced, 'I see that the Union Steamship Company has ordered an inter-island ferry. She's to be built on the Clyde, and is due to be delivered next year. Just thought I'd mention it as I'd heard you were thinking of emigrating.'

Steve felt a fluttering inside, but he didn't exactly know why. 'Honest - no kidding?' he gushed, making a dive for the journal but suddenly becoming more cautious. 'But won't she be crewed by the Kiwis?'

'Not for the delivery voyage,' answered the Second Electrician, rising from his armchair and stubbing out his Senior Service in one of the ashtrays that Steve had only recently emptied. 'The skipper and officers maybe, but the remainder of the crew will mostly be drawn from the pool. Saves the expense of flying a planeload of their guys half way around the world while the British lads will be working their passages. And the important thing to remember is that once they arrive in New Zealand the crew can remain in the country and apply for New Zealand citizenship without danger of being deported.'

Steve was jubilant. 'Thanks, Second,' he acknowledged, as the electrician exited the smoke room and headed for his engine room workshop. 'I'll borrow this 'maggy' if I may.'

However, Steve's elation was only temporal. The Union Steamship Company may have ordered a ferry from a Clydeside shipyard, and may have been looking for a crew; but what use was that to him? he thought, with him in the middle of the Caribbean. It was all very frustrating. His best prospect, he reasoned, tucking the magazine inside his pee jacket where hopefully it wouldn't be seen, was to visit the Union Steamship Company's office on Tower Hill as soon as he arrived back in London, to apply for a post before all the vacancies were taken. It was a bitter-sweet pill, promising a possible return to Maxine on the one hand, without the expense and paraphernalia of the official emigration process, but also leaving him in limbo, in no immediate position to further this newly-found option. In the event he replaced the magazine on the coffee table. The article concerning the ferry comprised mostly technical stuff that was of little personal interest. It didn't even mention a name for the vessel, assuming a name had been chosen. He decided he'd just have to play it by ear, crossing his fingers that all the positions for junior catering staff hadn't been filled before he could make his application. And if nothing else, it - or something similar - did at least offer a possible alternative if he encountered difficulties at New Zealand House.

For the next couple of days they made steady progress in a north-easterly direction, as if the *Alice Springs* herself could smell the tangy salt air of the English Channel and was increasingly eager to be home. But there was plenty of steaming to do between here and the Thames estuary, and on the morning of their approach to the Mona Passage, the channel that would take them free of the islands and into the wider Atlantic, the sea resembled aquamarine while the sky was a crystal-clear blue. However, there was a blot on the horizon, because far away to the south-east rose a towering cloud-bank, mushrooming upwards like the aftermath of a nuclear bomb-burst.

'Looks like a right vicious bastard,' said the Bosun, nodding towards the cumulonimbus as Steve played the hose around the rosie's innards. 'Still, it shouldn't bother us. We'll be well clear of here by nightfall - but I wouldn't want to be on either Jamaica or the western tip of Cuba if it carries on its present trajectory. I wouldn't mind betting that it's already blown some roofs off in the Windward Islands.'

Does that mean it's a hurricane?' asked Steve, straightening and gazing away to the south-east where the cloud seemed to have grown even larger and more threatening in the space of only a few seconds.

'Not necessarily,' replied the Bosun, tapping out his pipe on the rail and reaching for his pouch of tobacco. 'But we can't rule it out. It's still a bit early in the year for hurricanes, but it could be a tropical storm and they can be nearly as spiteful. In fact, if the conditions are right they often develop into hurricanes.'

'But don't they occasionally change course?' asked Steve, reeling in the hose after ensuring that the rosie was clean. 'I don't fancy getting mixed up with one of those.'

'Well, it shouldn't be anything for us to worry about even if it does,' answered the Bosun, firing up his pipe and emitting a plume of smoke that would have done credit to the *Alice Springs'* funnel. 'Ships like ours are built to withstand hurricanes - in fact, anything the elements can throw at them. If that little beauty does catch us up - and I don't think it will - we might get a shaking; but the worse that's likely to happen is that you'll lose a few cups and saucers while we keep an eye on the deck cargo.'

'Thanks, Bose,' said Steve, picking up the rosie and heading in the direction of the pantry. 'You've cheered me up no end. I thought we'd seen the last of the weather systems.'

'Not on your life,' called the Bosun, as Steve descended the ladder to the after well-deck. 'We may have had a couple of squalls, but you haven't seen anything yet.'

It was true, Steve reflected, as he positioned the rosie in its customary corner of the pantry. They'd come through that gale in the Channel, and they'd caught the edge of a storm in the Pacific; but those apart, meteorologically speaking, the trip had been pretty much benign.

As if to confirm the inevitable, shortly before lunch order was issued to batten down, as weather reports indicated that a tropical storm that had formed in mid-Atlantic was rapidly developing into the first hurricane of the season, and had been given the code name, 'Avril'. It was expected to track in a roughly north-westerly direction, passing right across Jamaica and clipping the extremities of western Cuba and the Yucatan Peninsula before causing havoc in northern Mexico and Texas. According to news bulletins picked up by the Junior Sparky it had already destroyed crops and flattened buildings on St Vincent and The Grenadines, and at that stage it was far from achieving its potential. It was more or less as the Bosun had predicted, and although the *Alice Springs* was expected to be well clear of the storm's projected curvature, the order to batten down had been issued primarily as a precaution.

'I guess you must have been in plenty of hurricanes in your time, eh, Archie?' queried Steve, as he loaded trays and dixies into the hot-press as they prepared for luncheon.

'Not just hurricanes but typhoons and cyclones too,' answered the bedroom steward, as he placed serving spoons and slices into the various food-bearing receptacles. 'Mind you, it's only a matter of terminology. In the Pacific they're known as typhoons while in the Indian Ocean they're cyclones. Out here in the Atlantic they're hurricanes - but whatever you call them they'll all blow the hair off a dog.'

'I bet this hurricane won't be as bad as the one in Archie's cabin last night,' intervened Peter, cheekily, while taking pre-emptive evasive action so as to avoid the expected back-hander. 'If the racket that I heard is anything to go by they must have been going at it like the clappers.'

'Hmfff! Your only jealous,' responded Archie, loftily, refusing to bite, thus making Peter's ducking and weaving manoeuvres pointless. 'If you'd got a woman on board you wouldn't be worrying about what other people were doing - you'd be concentrating on the job in hand; and anyway, you shouldn't have been listening. What Ruby and me get up to is our business - it's got nothing to do with you.'

If Peter thought he'd got away with his taunt he'd another think coming. He was busying himself at the sink, thinking what a clever boy he had been, when Archie aimed a well-directed flick with his pantry cloth, catching Peter squarely on the ear, causing him to yelp in agony. Peter went ballistic, and was about to retaliate with a cupful of soapy water when in walked the Second Steward. Peter's self-restraint was commendable, but wasn't swift enough to prevent the Second Steward suspecting some sort of nonsense. Sec - who hadn't forgotten his dousing when Steve had lobbed a dishcloth at Archie - glanced first at Archie and then at Peter, before venting his wrath on the latter.

'I hope you weren't going to do what I think you were going to do,' he chastened, glaring at Peter as the pantry boy sheepishly returned the cup to the sink and carried on with the strapping up, 'because if I thought you were you'd be working your arse off till Christmas. Now stop buggering about, because straight after lunch we've got to think about battening things down.'

Sec's intervention was a timely reminder that skylarking was acceptable so long as the job - and he in particular - weren't affected. It prompted Steve to remember the outstanding matter of his haircut, for which Ruby still hadn't been paid.

The battening-down exercise was necessary but ultimately needless. In the event, hurricane Avril passed well to the south and the *Alice Springs* was comfortably clear of the islands as Steve and his mates began the tiresome process of returning everything to its rightful abode. 'Fuckin' waste of time that was,' groused Peter, removing a bevy of milk jugs from their refuge in a cardboard box that had been wedged between the fridge and the plate racks. 'All the time it took us to stow this lot away, now we've got to break it all out again - and for what? Hurricane? What hurricane? I get more wind after a couple of pints of Carlsberg.'

That evening, the setting sun resembled a fireball about to explode; a fitting end to the day, Steve thought, given the volatile nature of the atmosphere. As he had done on numerous evenings in the tropics he kept watch for the legendary 'green flash' that supposedly illuminated the heavens at the instant the sun disappeared, but as always the flash was absent. From Steve's point of view it was an occurrence that was frequently talked about but seldom if ever observed, and he was beginning to wonder if the spectacle even existed, or if it was a product of a yarn-spinner's dream.

The opportunity to settle his account with Ruby arose the very next morning, when Steve arrived first at the pantry and set about making the tea. It was an unwritten rule that the earliest arrival would prepare tea and make toast for the others. And so it transpired that whilst the tea was brewing, Steve shoved several slices of bread under the salamander before lining up the mugs on the work surface. Now then, every steward had his own allotted mug to which Steve added sugar and milk - to every mug, except Ruby's. Ruby shunned both sweetener and dairy products, believing them fattening and toxic and to be totally avoided if you wanted to remain healthy and trim. Therefore, when he came to Ruby's mug he added a whopping great spoonful of salt, before hurriedly buttering some toast and retreating to the sanctuary of the saloon.

Ruby, who was unusually the last to tick on, was oblivious to everything as he waltzed into the pantry with a cheery, 'Good morning, boys,' whilst making for his early-morning cuppa. Now, the previous evening, he and Archie had assisted the Second Steward in polishing-off a bottle of Drambuie, so that this morning he had a mouth like a tray of cat litter. For that very reason he took an extra-long swig from his mug, not only to nullify his thirst but to sluice away a mouthful of slough.

The reaction was both instantaneous and volcanic. Any ladylike pretensions vaporized as a fountain of tea redecorated the pantry bulkheads. At that very same instant Ruby spotted Steve through the servery. Without pausing to consider whether or not he'd correctly identified the culprit he grabbed a sopping-wet dish cloth and hurled it through the servery hatchway. The deed was both reckless and dire. Expecting just such a backlash, Steve dived through the door to the passengers' promenade deck at the very same instant the Chief Steward entered the saloon from his office. Steve's split-second timing was immaculate; not so the Chief's as the senior catering officer strode headlong into the projectile's flight-path.

The missile hit the Chief in the face, sending his spectacles flying and saturating the front of his shirt. The laughter that had been emanating from the pantry evaporated as the stewards, not wanting to be associated in any way with the unfolding drama in the saloon, slunk away on their respective scrub-outs. Meanwhile, Ruby stood rooted to the spot, gaping in horror as the Chief Steward, once the shock had subsided, flew into an apoplectic rage.

'You useless fuckin' fairy,' he blustered, while recovering his thankfully unbroken spectacles from the table on which they'd landed, completely forgetting that the door leading to the passenger accommodation was still ajar. 'I always did think your sort were a bunch of fuckin' space wasters. Now get in here and clear up this mess - and you can dhobi my shirt when you've finished.'

And therein lay the Chief's dilemma. Normally, anyone guilty of assaulting a superior, intentionally or otherwise, would have been dealt with most severely by the Captain: a whacking great fine at the very least not to mention the inevitable logging. But what with Ruby being a DBS, with no money in the ship and a discharge book in the custody of the Shipping Federation, the only recourse was to bawl Ruby out and generally make his life wretched.

As for Ruby, once he'd recovered from the initial bollocking and realized there was little else in the Chief's armoury, his self-confidence returned and he became the embodiment of bogus repentance. He scampered into the saloon with a handful of cloths with the intention of making amends. 'There, there, Chiefy, he fussed, dabbing at the Chief Steward's shirt as if soaking up ink with a blotter, 'we'll soon have you clean and dry. Don't know what came over me. I just had this instinctive urge to sling a dishcloth at someone. Must be to do with my age.'

Ruby's efforts at appeasement were futile. In fact, the Boss's temper was spiralling so rapidly out of control that he seemed on the cusp of a brainstorm. 'Get out of my sight, you fuckin' woofter,' he snarled, as Ruby, suddenly unsure of his ground, backed hesitantly away before turning and fleeing for the exit. 'And if I so much as clap eyes on you at any time in the next fortnight I'll stick my boot so far up your arse you'll think it's your fuckin' birthday.'

Unbeknown to the Chief Steward, the two well-upholstered lady passengers, having been wakened by the commotion, had been eavesdropping at the slightly-open door. As the Chief hustled past and up the companionway leading to his own and the passengers' accommodation, stripping off his shirt and still muttering something about useless 'brown-hatters' and 'gingers', they suffered a fit of the giggles, causing a further cascade of resentment. He turned, and was about to shout something about two overweight gluttons having nothing better to do, when he remembered who was paying his wages.

'Sorry about that, ladies,' he apologised, crossing his arms to cover his chest and upper abdomen, trying his best to display a modicum of decency while fuming like an overloaded circuit-board, 'just a little bother in the saloon. Nothing to worry about.' And without further ceremony he vanished into his cabin, by now incandescent with anger.

Meanwhile, Ruby was out on the prowl, searching for Steve, and found him on his hands and knees, scrubbing out the engineers' alleyway. The pantry boy had been anticipating the showdown and rose warily to his feet as Ruby, wagging a forefinger as if scolding a delinquent schoolboy, minced menacingly over the oilcloth. It was Ruby's uncharacteristically aggressive attitude that persuaded Steve that he wasn't about to be offered an olive branch, more likely a slap on the cheek; so it was with this in mind that he reciprocated first, surprising Ruby with a flick on the nose.

Now as everyone knew, Steve and violence were totally at odds with one another, so the powderpuff nature of the 'punch' had been intended more to intimidate than harm. However, the effect on Ruby was pure tinsel-town, as if he'd been flattened by a John Wayne haymaker. 'Ow!' he squealed, reverting to type and landing on the seat of his pants in a puddle of warm soapy water. 'What did you do that for? I wasn't going to hit you, just give you a good ticking-off.'

'Well, I didn't know that, did I?' answered Steve, hauling the now blubbing steward to his feet. 'The way you were stomping down the alleyway I thought you were looking for a punch-up. Anyway, you do make a mountain out of a molehill. It was only a tap on the beak.'

'It was hard enough to make my nose run,' protested Ruby, tearfully, dabbing his eyes with a handkerchief whilst pretending he wasn't really crying. 'And anyway, you deserve a telling off after what you did.'

'I deserve a telling off?' remonstrated Steve, incredulously, having difficulty believing his ears. 'After the mess you made of my hair did you honestly expect to get away with it? You can thank your lucky stars you didn't get clobbered there and then. Now! It looks like you've pissed yourself, so if I were you I'd go back to my cabin and change my trousers. And then, I think the best thing we can do is to forget any of this ever happened. Deal?'

'Deal,' answered Ruby, eventually and still somewhat resentfully, but accepting Steve's hand as a token of a mutually declared truce.' But I still think you were a bit heavy handed.'

As Ruby trudged dispiritedly away, water still dripping from his backside and doubtless feeling that the entire world was his enemy, Steve felt a jab of remorse. He was about to call out and offer an apology when the Senior Cadet slid down an adjacent companionway and made for the door leading to the after well-deck. As he brushed past Steve, stepping over the pool of soapy water and around Steve's bucket, he announced. 'There's something out here that might interest you.'

Steve gazed after the despondent Ruby, unsure if he should follow or pursue what was animating the cadet. Finally, persuaded by the sight of several off-duty engineers vacating their cabins and making for the after well-deck Steve followed suit, stepping over the coaming into the dazzling sunlight. There he discovered seemingly half of the *Alice Springs'* crew, apparently galvanized, crowding the port side rail and staring at a pall of smoke in the distance.

Steve, his curiosity now fully aroused, muscled in between Dingwall Patterson and the Bosun, and asked, 'What's all the fuss about? I can't see anything for smoke.'

'You will if you're patient,' answered Dingwall, pointing in the general direction of the clag that had partially cleared to reveal a rusty and weather-worn freighter that in an ideal world would already have been sent to the breakers'. 'She's a 'Rusky', and in plenty of trouble by the look of it.'

'You can say that again,' agreed the Bosun, who's pipe was emitting almost as much filth as was pouring from the rust-bucket's funnel and engine room skylight. 'There are two black balls at her masthead so she's obviously not under command - but why is she laying the smoke screen?'

'Maybe a boiler room fire,' suggested Dingwall, rolling a spindly-thin cigarette from his tin of tobacco and papers. 'One thing's for sure, she's an old coal burner - no doubt about that. You can smell 'em from miles away.'

'I suppose we'll be picking up survivors,' volunteered Steve, who'd quickly become fascinated by the unfolding panorama that was brimming with intrigue and which in his heightened imagination might easily have been created by Joseph Conrad. 'Looks to me like she's had it.'

'No, they'll sort it out one way or another,' replied Dingwall, lighting his roll-up which flared like a freshly-lit gas mantel. 'It's probably only a funnel fire.'

'Perhaps,' countered the Bosun, sounding decidedly sceptical, fearing the Russian's situation was more serious. 'But I doubt it. More likely a bunker fire, I'd say, judging by the fact that whatever it is it's been burning since well before dawn. She was spotted on the radar while it was still dark, then when it got light one of the lookouts noticed this blanket of smoke on the horizon. The Senior Sparky tried raising her on the radio but she didn't answer. That's why the Old Man altered course to investigate. Whatever, she'd have to be on the verge of abandonment before seeking help from the likes of us.'

'Why's that? pressed Steve, wondering why on earth a vessel in distress had to be literally sinking before accepting the assistance of others.

'Because,' answered the Bosun, pointing out the hammer-and-sickle device on the other ship's ensign, 'the Ruskies wouldn't want westerners getting any closer than necessary - and for a very good reason. See what she's carrying on deck?'

Steve had been so preoccupied with the old steamer's plight that he hadn't even noticed what appeared to be segments of aluminium pipeline forming her deck cargo. 'So what, he answered, at length, looking vaguely perplexed as to why such an apparently innocuous cargo should be shrouded in mystery. 'What's so unusual about a shipload of pipework?'

The Bosun shook his head, having spotted what others may have missed. 'They're not pipelines, Son,' he answered, pointing at what now materialized as a prominent red star on the side of each cylinder. 'If I'm not very much mistaken, those are guided fuckin' missiles.'

20

It was a prelude to what would later become known as, 'The Cuban Missile Crisis', a stand-off between the United States of America and the U.S.S.R. which probably resulted in the most critical phase of the 'Cold War', almost triggering a full-scale nuclear conflict.

Following the overthrow of the corrupt, American-backed Batista dictatorship by the forces of Fidel Castro in 1959, the American C.I.A. trained and equipped an army of pro-Batista exiles with the aim of regime change in Cuba without apparent U.S. involvement. A landing was subsequently made in southern Cuba in April 1961 which was popularly referred to as the Bay of Pigs Invasion. The incursion rapidly became a fiasco when the exiles, with covert American support, were routed by the Cuban defenders. The Bay of Pigs episode, although not at the time directly related, almost certainly accelerated the creation of a Russian nuclear arsenal in Cuba in response to the installation of American missiles, firstly in the United Kingdom in the late nineteen-fifties, but more recently in Italy and Turkey. What it unarguably amounted to was that the Cuban Missile Crisis had its beginnings considerably earlier than the August 1962 date that is commonly quoted.

'Does that mean there's going to be a war?' asked Steve, cautiously, having listened carefully to what the Bosun had to say about the Bay of Pigs and Cuba's now inflammatory relationship with America, especially given that Cuba wasn't so many miles distant.

'I sincerely hope not,' rejoined Dingwall, who clearly had no definitive opinion and was only prepared to state the obvious. 'But the Yanks are a trigger-happy bunch and I wouldn't put anything past them. Given that they've already taken a drubbing, albeit by proxy, they're likely to shoot first and ask questions later.'

'What do you reckon, Archie?' asked Steve, picking over his poached eggs on toast as the topside catering staff settled down to their breakfasts, with the Rusky now some miles astern. 'The Bosun seems to think that if there's any more trouble between America and Cuba then the Russians'll take the side of the Cubans.'

'Oh, I wouldn't think so,' replied Archie, as if the sight of a solitary freighter carrying what appeared to be missiles wasn't in itself indicative. 'We can't even be sure that they were guided missiles - and we don't really know where she's going. And anyway, the Yanks and the Russians have been sniping at each other ever since the overthrow of Hitler and it hasn't come to anything yet.'

'Doesn't mean it won't this time,' interjected the Second Steward, adding his own two-pennyworth, and keeping the pot on the boil. 'Look what happened in the run-up to the First World War. A lunatic gunman shoots an Austrian duke and before you can say 'Jack Robinson' it's steamrollered out of control.'

'Yanks'd wipe the floor with the Ruskies anyway,' barged in Peter, with his customary lack of intelligence, the fact that there'd be no winners in an all-out nuclear blitzkrieg having totally escaped him. 'So there'll be nothing for us to worry about, anyway.'

'You silly little twerp,' snapped Archie, rounding on Peter and slamming his mug so violently down on the table that its contents slopped over the edge. 'Hasn't it occurred to you that if there was a nuclear war then we'd all be wiped out, and there'd be nothing that any of us could do about it? You need to get some savvy into that coconut shell of a skull of yours - dopey little eejit.' And without further fuss and palaver, Archie rose from his seat and stalked off in the direction of the passenger accommodation, leaving most of the gathering, and Peter in particular, not only a little startled but also a little bit wiser.

'Archie's right, you know,' said Donald, at length, picking up the conversation, as if Archie's unlikely outburst had added another dimension to the topic, and that there was no escaping the conclusion. 'I've been reading this book I picked up in Adelaide. It's by Neville Shute and it's called, 'On the Beach'. It's set in south-eastern Australia in the aftermath of a nuclear showdown. The northern hemisphere has been virtually obliterated and the fallout is drifting in a southerly direction, with Australia being the only safe-haven on earth - at least in the short term. I haven't finished it yet, but what with the cloud getting closer and closer and some of the characters talking about taking suicide pills, I can't see a happy ending. I know it's only a novel - but it certainly exercises the grey matter.'

'And that's why Archie's given Peter a bollocking and gone off in a tizz,' added Keith, mopping a dollop of marmalade from his plate with the corner of a slice of toast. 'He's no idiot, and for all his debonair outlook on life he's got a sensible head on his shoulders. I must admit, I'd heard about the Bay of Pigs ages ago, but I honestly didn't think it'd come to anything.'

For a few gloomy seconds the men sat in silence, contemplating the near-certain Armageddon should nuclear war become a reality rather than the chimera that the sight of a woebegone freighter had generated. A couple of hours earlier everyone had been carefree and happy, laughing their heads off at how Ruby had water-bombed the Boss; now here they all were, fretting needlessly over something that most likely wouldn't happen.

It was the Second Steward who dragged them out of the doldrums, by unexpectedly announcing that from the following Monday the entire catering department would be on an additional two hours overtime, cleaning and painting those areas of the midships accommodation and catering areas that hadn't already been seen to. 'That's a good seven days extra overtime,' he concluded, rising to his feet and sliding his plate through the servery with one hand while brushing crumbs from his shirt with the other. 'And, oh, yes,' he added, cheerily, acknowledging that women and booze excepted a seaman's pay packet was his principal preoccupation. 'I've also heard that after calling at Dunkirk we'll be docking in Liverpool, not London, so that'll mean another day's pay to look forward to. By the time we pay off you'll be loaded.'

Sec's good humour worked wonders and by lunchtime, if all the earlier pessimism hadn't exactly been eradicated, an air of normality prevailed. Steve certainly felt happier; not substantially owing to the

316

prospect of a larger than expected pay packet, but because having had time to reflect, he was coming round to the view that whatever their differences, neither the Americans nor the Russians would be stupid enough to engage in a nuclear knockabout.

'That's typical of the bloody Yanks,' complained Dingwall Patterson, as he and Steve, along with Jimmy Craddock, discussed the days extraordinary events over a smoke and a supper-time cocoa. 'They reckon there should be one law for them and another for everyone else.' His disdain for the western hemisphere's self-acclaimed figurehead was palpable as he spat contemptuously over the rail, wiping his mouth on the back of his hand before continuing to denigrate the Americans. 'Talk about corrupt - they're one of the most unscrupulous nations on earth.'

'What! Even worse than the British?' cheeked Steve, with just a hint of sarcasm, remembering his earlier exchanges with Dingwall in which the entire ills of the British Establishment and Empire had been paraded over the bonfire. 'I didn't think any nation could behave that despicably.'

Steve sensed a critical eye, as though Dingwall was wondering if his newly-converted disciple had forgotten the earlier lessons or was beginning to have reservations. But Steve was no 'Doubting Thomas'; he'd heard sufficient from others to convince him that Dingwall's preachings were historically accurate. It was just that he couldn't help thinking that the fellow's malediction of virtually everything British might be clouding his judgement because when all was said and done, wasn't America Britain's closest ally?

'They're both as bad as one another,' answered Dingwall, apparently satisfied that Steve was simply being facetious and wasn't in any way wavering. 'Either of 'em'd shit on their own grannys' doorsteps if they thought it'd suit their agendas.'

Steve and Jimmy exchanged glances, as if each was unsure where this latest round of tutelage was leading. They didn't have too long to wait, for as soon as Dingwall had fashioned yet another skinny roll-up he launched into a scathing denunciation of American foreign policy.

'Just lately the Yanks have been getting far too big for their boots,' he declared, solemnly, exhaling a stream of smoke while brushing a flake of still-burning ash from his shirt front. 'And they'll get a bloody sight worse unless someone does something to stop them.'

'What makes you say that?' asked Jimmy, who until earlier this morning - and like most other youngsters - hadn't paid very much attention to world politics, or domestic politics either, come to that. 'I suppose they're only looking after their own interests, same as everyone else.'

'That's exactly the point,' protested Dingwall, showing just a hint of frustration that his message was failing to hit home. 'But they're not like everyone else. They are looking after their own interests, but in so doing they're meddling in the internal affairs of other countries, Cuba for instance, actively organizing and arming right-wing terror squads to oppose left-wing dictatorships; and in some instances democratically-elected left-wing governments. At present it's mostly in Latin-America, on their own doorstep - but I can see it happening elsewhere, and before long the Yanks themselves'll become involved in the actual fighting, especially if their puppets are getting a walloping.'

Most of this was way above Jimmy who was shaking his head; not necessarily in disbelief, but as if whatever took place in Cuba or wherever was of no immediate concern. 'I can't see what all the fuss is about,' he declared, clearly wearying of the topic and wanting to shift the conversation onto something – anything - more stimulating. 'This is all happening on someone else's patch, so what have we got to worry about.'

It was like a rerun of Archie's disagreement with Peter, and Dingwall was becoming disillusioned. An erudite cvangelist he may have been, but where perceived Philistines like Jimmy were concerned he lacked the necessary patience. Nevertheless, he drew a deep breath; and seeing that Jimmy hadn't wandered off and was seemingly prepared to listen he continued, moderately hopeful that his sermon wouldn't be wasted.

'Don't you know that much of eastern England is littered with American airfields, each of them home to squadrons of bombers that are fully geared-up to strike at the Soviet Union? And these aren't conventional weapons, you know, but nuclear-equipped B47s and B52s, all of them capable of destroying the world single handed, let alone a city like Moscow. So you see where it matters to us? If you don't, you're a bigger ignoramus than I thought.'

Jimmy resented the suggestion that he might be an ignoramus, even if being a native of faraway Scotland he hadn't realized that a considerable chunk of East Anglia, not to mention locations further afield such as in Berkshire, Lincolnshire and Oxfordshire, were considered by many to be nothing but American aircraft carriers, first in the line of fire should the Russians respond to any first strike by the Pentagon. Instead of protesting he absorbed the information and appreciated the likely implications, not only for those in the immediate vicinities, but also for humanity at large.

Steve, on the other hand, had known of bases like Lakenheath and Mildenhall, having passed them on numerous occasions during trips to the East Coast resorts. But knowing of their existence didn't necessarily mean he'd been aware of their significance, or of the destructive hardware contained behind their fences and barriers. It was certainly all very thought-provoking, even if he was gradually adapting to the idea that although these armaments existed, they were meant as a deterrent rather than a battle-cry.

'So you see,' continued Dingwall, at long last satisfied that both Steve and Jimmy were in total possession of the facts. 'That's why issues like this are so important, because you know very well that whatever course the Yanks embark on the Britts'll trot along in their wake.'

'So, what about Cuba?' asked Steve, realizing that owing to Jimmy's misplaced derision Cuba had been somehow sidetracked. 'What can you tell us about that?'

'Ah........Cuba,' replied Dingwall, as if he'd suddenly remembered his predetermined subject without having to be reminded. 'That's a political flashpoint if ever there was one.'

'Why's that?' asked Steve, wondering why a tropical island, albeit a rather large tropical island, should represent any more of a tinderbox than the other specks of land in the Caribbean. 'What's so different about Cuba.'

'Simply this,' replied Dingwall, raising an index finger as if to emphasise the fact that Cuba was far-and-away removed from places like Barbados and Aruba. 'The Yanks are bloody petrified of even the word, communism, let alone the doctrine itself, even though the vast majority of them don't even know what it means. Unbelievable, isn't it? Especially as some of the poorer Americans are among the most impoverished people on earth. To fully understand all this you have to go back to the Cuban revolution of a couple of years or so ago. Prior to that the island had been governed by an American puppet dictator called Fulgencio Batista. In those days it was a playground for corrupt and wealthy American politicians, while the Mafia owned and operated the casinos, brothels and nightclubs in cities like the capital, Havana. Anyway, while this bunch of wasters and the Cuban elite were leading the life of Riley the poor bloody peasants were living in squalor and hunger, with the children especially suffering from malnutrition and disease, not to mention a lack of education. All this was anathema to a lawyer called Fidel Castro, so along with a guy called Che Guevara he assembled a guerrilla army and - well, the rest is as the Bosun said earlier.'

'Anyway, I'm off to bed,' announced Dingwall, tipping the dregs of his cocoa into a scupper, apparently happy that whenever further tensions arose involving the Americans - as surely they would - the possible repercussions and spin-offs wouldn't be so flippantly dismissed. 'Trying to educate you two has just about buggered me up.'

'Cor!' He hasn't much time for the Yanks, has he?' whispered Jimmy, as Dingwall sloped off and disappeared into the after accommodation, acknowledging the presence of an off-duty EDH who sat by the doorway, studiously clipping his toenails.

'Dingwall hasn't much time for any kind of governmental organization, whatever the nationality,' answered Steve, offering Jimmy a Rothman's before fishing around in a trouser pocket for his lighter but finding a box of Swan Vestas. 'I don't think it's quite so much the authority he objects to but the unfairness that goes hand in hand. And in Dingwall's eyes the Yanks - not to mention the British - are among the world's worst perpetrators of injustice. Nevertheless, I'm sure he knows what he's talking about because the Bosun says very much the same.'

'Do you think he's a communist?' asked Jimmy, accepting a light and inhaling a deep draught of nicotine. 'Or is he just bitter and twisted?'

'What? Dingwall? No, I don't think he's a communist, and I don't think he's bitter and twisted,' replied Steve, tossing the extinguished matchstick over the side and filling his own lungs with smoke. 'But I certainly think he's a socialist - which as I see it is a long way from being a communist. That's why he has such stringent views on corruption, inequality, and so forth. And one of the reasons I believe him is that he and his family are some of those who happen to have been on the receiving end.'

21

Peter was the absolute limit - well, Steve thought so when he arrived early at the pantry the following morning and discovered that his cabin mate, who should have emptied the rosie the previous evening, hadn't done so leaving it full to the brim and humming like a municipal dustcart. Still, rather than create a to-do he decided to empty it himself, the ideal opportunity, he thought, to clear his head of its overnight gunk.

As he upended the rosie, watching the rubbish plop noiselessly into the Atlantic, he ruminated that somewhere to the west lay Bermuda; and that they hadn't yet passed the Azores, north of where the weather could be expected to deteriorate into something the British were more used to. That allowed the promise of at least another day or so's bronzying, to top up his tan before submitting to the greyer skies of the more northerly latitudes. Having emptied and hosed out the rosie he stood studying the wake which in the clear morning air extended all the way back to the horizon, an arrow-straight line that exemplified the art of the helmsman. He glanced at his watch. It was almost 6.00am, time to turn to, and to bollock Peter for being so forgetful about the rosie. He stooped down to pick up the bin - and almost suffered a cardiac arrest. 'Christ, Eddie!' he exclaimed, leaping back in surprise, letting drop the rosie that clanged tinnily against the taffrail, 'I didn't see you sitting there. You almost frightened me to death.'

Eddie Clooney was a wiry, Dublin-born fridge greaser, who stood only five feet four in his stockinged feet and was built like a featherweight boxer. He was a pal of Sean Cassidy, and like the oversized fireman, and not withstanding the disparity in stature, could soak away booze in a fashion that men of twice his body-mass would be proud of. This, along with an ability to smoke his way through forty Gold Flake a day, exacerbated an issue with his health. A diagnosed diabetic, it was the probable reason why Eddie, who was slumped against the after bulkhead of the petty officers' quarters, reacted glassily to Steve's astonishment. That in itself was sufficient to arouse Steve's suspicions, for although he and Eddie kept totally different company and were far and away from being buddies, they usually acknowledged each other in passing.

'Are you all right, Eddie?' asked Steve, having recovered from the initial shock of discovering that he hadn't been alone, and it began to sink in that perhaps Eddie wasn't as well as he should have been. 'You look a bit peaky to me.'

It was to prove a profound understatement. Steve took a faltering step forward, squatting down on his haunches and peering into the other man's eyes which remained focussed on some faraway, invisible object, as if Steve himself was as transparent as a freshly-cleaned window. It was as if Eddie had spent the night on the bottle and hadn't yet come to his senses. But there was something else, something that was beginning to make the hairs on Steve's neck twitch and bristle. His uppermost fears were confirmed when he laid a hand on the greaser's shoulder, only to watch him topple over on to his side, his head coming to rest against the hose-reel. Steve sprung back in alarm, because it was only then that he finally grasped that Eddie wasn't just dead to the world but was, quite literally - dead.

Steve had never previously encountered a corpse, and the sight of Eddie Clooney laying motionless against the fire-hose left a numbness he found hard to handle. He stood glued to the deck, staring at Eddie, wondering what to do next but unable to co-ordinate any kind of meaningful action. Instead, he had this weird recollection of accompanying his family in visiting an aged aunt in the days following the death of his uncle. It had been several years ago but the scene was as vivid as if it had been only yesterday. His aunt had invited them into her front parlour to view the cadaver which had yet to be sealed in its coffin. His parents had ventured over the threshold but Steve had declined, electing to stay outside with his younger brother, using the pretext that he would rather remember his uncle as he was; notwithstanding that he'd only met the gentleman on one

323

previous occasion, when he was only about five years old, and he hadn't a clue what the fellow looked like.

After what seemed like an eternity, but what in reality must have only been a few seconds, Steve was jerked from his macabre reverie by the sound of a door opening on the starboard side of the deck house, and out popped the bald-headed pate of the Carpenter. The senior petty officer was taking the air, clearing his sinuses of the accumulated clag of an evening spent playing cribbage with the Bosun, during which they'd consumed a bottle of Daiquiri and emptied a pouch of tobacco.

'Hey! Chips,' called Steve, in a sort of shouted whisper that was meant to be heard by one person only, as if he was afraid of alerting the ship at large to the catastrophe that had overtaken a comrade. 'Have you got a minute - I think we've got a problem with Eddie.'

The Carpenter sauntered over until he and Steve stood contemplating the lifeless figure of what until relatively recently had been a living, breathing human being. 'He's dead, no doubt about it,' declared the Chippy at length, as he stepped forward and with an extended forefinger and thumb, closed the unfortunately fridge-greaser's eyelids. 'Tell you what, you nip for'ard and inform one of the officers while I cover him up. At least that'll get the ball rolling, as well as showing some respect for Eddie. We don't want him becoming a peep show, do we?'

Anxious to be doing anything rather than nothing Steve, completely forgetting the rosie, made straight for the nearest bridge wing, from where he could enter the wheelhouse and report to the officer of the watch. The Mate had the four till eight, and he lost no time at all in phoning the Captain while detailing a deck hand to rouse the doctor who if nothing else, would be required to confirm the fatality. In the meantime, Steve was advised to return to his duties and to keep his mouth shut, at least until the earthly remains of Eddie Clooney were safely concealed, somewhere in the ship, while a suitable means of disposal was agreed upon.

Steve didn't hurry, knowing he'd a watertight excuse for not turning to when he should have. It wasn't surprising, therefore, that when he belatedly arrived at the pantry, to fill his bucket and begin his scrub-out, the grapevine had flourished and the news had already leaked out. 'Hey! guess what, exclaimed Peter, eager to impart what he thought was a scoop but what in reality was now common knowledge. 'They've found Eddie Clooney, dead as a Dodo behind the after deck house - suffered a stroke, according to the peggy.'

'I know, and he didn't - not as far as I know, anyway,' rasped Steve, a little annoyed that the rumours were already circulating before the facts of the matter were known. 'As far as I'm aware he just sat down and died - and I should know because I was the one that found him.'

'What? You?' queried Peter, in a disbelieving fashion that suggested Steve was simply creating the story to deflect attention from his tardy appearance. 'What were you doing up on the poop at that time of the morning?'

'Doing what you should have done last night,' answered Steve, grateful for the opportunity of chastening Peter without having to broach the issue directly. 'If you'd emptied the rosie when you should have done I needn't have gone up there at all. As it was the bin was overflowing so I decided to empty it myself. That's when I came across Eddie.'

Peter shut up like a clam before eventually mumbling an apology. 'Sorry about that. I might have guessed something had happened after you left the cabin early but didn't turn to with the rest of us.' And then, as if lost for something more constructive to say, he asked, 'Wanna slice of toast?' And there's some tea in the pot if you want it.'

Peter was spared further embarrassment when Keith entered the pantry with news that there was an almighty row taking place in the Chief Steward's office. 'Something to do with stowing Eddies body in the handling room by the sound of it,' declared Keith, slipping a tray-load of crockery into the sink, having retrieved it from the engineers' duty mess where it'd been used by the overnight watches. There were also a few uneaten sandwiches that would normally have been dumped in the rosie - except that the rosie was still on the poop. 'I couldn't catch it all, not with the door closed, but the Boss wasn't happy and was making his views known in no uncertain terms. I think the other person involved was the Senior Cadet.'

'I'm not surprised he wasn't happy,' answered Steve, amazed that such a course of action was even being contemplated, especially were the storage of food was concerned. 'There'd be hell to pay if the passengers found out, not to mention what might happen when the crew got wind of it.'

It later emerged that the Chief Steward wasn't the only dissident. After the Chief had flatly rejected the idea on the grounds of health and propriety, the Bosun had objected to Eddie's remains being stored in the paint locker, even though in each instance it would only be until a more fitting location was identified. 'You've got to remember that we're only just out of the tropics,' argued the Bosun, to the frustration of the hapless Senior Cadet who'd been lumbered with the task of finding a suitable temporary resting place for Eddie. 'It'll be as hot as hell in there by lunchtime, and he'll stink to high heaven by teatime. No, I'm not having it - you'll have to find somewhere else.'

As Steve crossed the after well-deck while venturing aft to retrieve the rosie - Peter having adamantly refused to go anywhere near the poop until Eddie had been removed to wherever - he encountered the Senior Cadet who was scratching his head and clearly in a state despair. 'No one wants the poor bugger,' complained the trainee officer, pushing his fingers through his hair, as if massaging his scalp would spark at least a glimmer of inspiration. 'It'll only be a stop-gap measure, while they check with his next-of-kin regarding funeral arrangements. If they agree to a burial at sea then all well and good; we can get rid of him either today or tomorrow. Otherwise he'll go into one of the insulated spaces in the lower tween-deck until we get home and his family can organize a shore-side interment. It's just that the Mate didn't want the hassle of stowing him away below decks, only to have to drag him out again if it's decided to bury him at sea.'

To Steve's way of thinking any of the refrigerated cargo spaces would have made an ideal makeshift mortuary, even if it was for only twenty-four hours; so long as Eddie didn't get lost among the thousands of frozen lamb carcasses and end up in a hotel restaurant. He said as much, causing the apprentice to laugh, momentarily loosening the shackles.

Leaving the Senior Cadet to pursue what to anyone's way of thinking was an impossible assignment, Steve climbed the

326

companionway to the poop and slipped beneath the cordon that the Carpenter had strung around Eddie. He collected the rosie and hurriedly returned whence he'd come; not owing to an irrational fear of the departed, but because he didn't want to be seen loitering about as if displaying any sort of ghoulish curiosity. In fact, it appeared that apart from the doctor, who in the company of the Mate had pronounced Eddie dead and ready for burial whatever the arrangement, no one had visited the poop since Steve had left Eddie with the Chippy; not even one of the Junior Cadets whose responsibility it was to hoist the Red Ensign, an ensign that this morning was conspicuously absent.

As it evolved all the bickering proved needless, as it was quickly established via radio that Eddie Clooney had no next-of-kin, and that in the event of his death the disposal of his mortal remains should rest with the company; which in simple terms meant the captain of any vessel in which he was currently engaged. It therefore fell to the Carpenter to oversee the body's removal to his shop in the fo'c'sle where he'd prepare it for burial at sea. He would sew it into a canvas shroud that had been purposely weighted, passing the final stitch through Eddie's nose and in so doing fulfil two important objectives. Firstly, it would ascertain that Eddie was in fact dead, despite him having been certified so by the doctor; and secondly, it would ensure that when Eddie went over the side he wouldn't slither down the shroud in a heap but would sink with dignity, laid out as if in a funeral parlour with his hands clasped over his midriff. In order to waste no further time than was necessary the committal proceedings were scheduled for four o'clock that very afternoon.

Eddie's blanketed body was subsequently spotted being transported for'ard on a hatch-board, one end supported by Sean Cassidy who it was said was sobbing his heart out, the other by the Donkeyman who apparently appeared stonily emotionless and to whom it was just another obligation. 'Saw it with my own eyes,' sang Ruby, bustling into the saloon, arms full of crisply-laundered tablecloths, and whose differences with Steve seemed forgotten. 'Who'd have thought that a ruffian like Sean Cassidy would have had feelings of any sort, crying his eyes out like a newly-born babe. He must have a soft spot somewhere.'

Steve, who'd been cleaning the Junior Sparky's porthole surround with a compound of brick-dust and oil, thought it perfectly natural that any individual should demonstrate their grief at the loss of a colleague; and the fact that the person being referred to was a brawling, gargantuan beer-swiller was largely irrelevant. Everyone had their emotions, and while in most instances Sean Cassidy showed no sentiment whatsoever, the fact that he openly cried for Eddie Clooney indicated that somewhere beneath the surface lurked a grain of common humanity.

'You may depend he has,' agreed Steve, vacuously, his thoughts drifting laterally towards something he considered almost, though obviously not entirely, as cheerless as Eddie's demise. 'But you know what? I think it tragic there are no next-of-kin, probably no family whatsoever that he knew of, and no one to mourn him - except people like Sean and the black gang. I wonder if he even had a home?'

'Doesn't seem like it,' answered Ruby, wafting a tablecloth free of its folds before laying it squarely on a table. 'According to the Lamp Trimmer, wherever he paid off he made straight for London and the docks. Apparently, he'd lodge at the Custom House Flying Angel until his money ran out then he'd sign on another ship.'

'Not much of a life, was it?' offered Steve, dolefully, stowing his cleaning materials away in their designated locker. 'Months at sea followed by a week in the dockside pubs then back again to sea. Still, I suppose when you've no home or family any company's better than none.'

By 3.45pm a sizeable crowd had assembled in the after well-deck, to pay their final respects to Eddie Clooney who'd already arrived, enshrouded in canvas and on a hatch-board supported by trestles. Rather than the blanket that had enveloped him earlier, his supine remains were respectfully draped in a Red Ensign. The entire ensemble had been positioned in close proximity to the port side rail, the hatch-board actually a few inches higher than the rail so that at the appropriate moment the inboard end could be lifted allowing the body to slip effortlessly overboard. Most of the off-duty crew were in attendance; and even the passengers were represented, by the doctor and the two overweight ladies who were somehow manoeuvred down the almost perpendicular companionways by the luckless Junior Cadets. While certain of the crew considered it fitting that the passengers had made the effort, others thought the presence of the two fleshy females owed more to morbid voyeurism than any genuine deference to Eddie with whom they obviously hadn't been acquainted. Still, that was by the by and for the most part all seemed satisfied with the turn out.

At 4.00pm precisely the Captain appeared, accompanied by the Second and Third Mates and followed by the Senior Cadet who seemed a thousand times happier than he had been. The congregation parted to allow the officers through, the Captain taking up station abaft Eddie's head while the Mates and Cadets flanked the bier. At a given signal from The Senior Cadet the Mate, who was observing proceedings from the port side bridge wing, rang, 'Stop Engines', on the engine room telegraph; and as the *Alice Springs* drifted lazily to a standstill the assemblage gathered around as The Captain withdrew Bible and prayer-book from a pouch.

The service was brief but respectful. Following a reading from Chapter Fourteen of St John's Gospel The Captain said a few words of his own, referring to Eddie as a valued member of the *Alice Springs'* crew who would be greatly missed by his shipmates; although in reality he'd only met the man twice, when logging him for dereliction of duty while being drunk and incapable, and for being abusive to the Second Engineer. There ensued a short prayer of committal followed by the Lord's Prayer and blessing, at the conclusion of which the Second Mate nodded; a signal for a tearful Sean Cassidy and sombre Donkeyman to gently raise the hatch-board allowing Eddie to slide effortlessly overboard. At that precise moment there came a mournful blast on the siren as the *Alice Springs* paid her own final tribute to a crew member who'd prematurely, 'signed off'. There were a few mumbled 'Amens', and the handful of Catholics crossed themselves as the gathering dispersed, most in agreement that although Eddie undoubtedly had his faults, by and large he'd been a decent enough fellow. And so it was that as Eddie Clooney made stately progress to the bottom of the North Atlantic, the Mate rang, 'Full ahead', on the engine room telegraph, the voyage having been only cursorily interrupted.

That evening Eddie Clooney's belongings were divvied up between his former engine room messmates, although in truth most of his clothing proved virtually useless owing to his diminutive proportions. It was therefore offered to an equally pint-sized deckhand called Thomas Llewellyn, a cadaverous-looking native of Aberystwyth, who snapped it up, along with Eddie's battered suitcase, without apparent thought for the previous owner. There were no such problems in disposing of the remnants of Eddie's final pack of 200 Gold Flake. They disappeared like snowballs in a heatwave, as did a half empty bottle of Gordon's. It was decided that what little cash he had left wasn't worth sharing but should be played for over a game of rummy - fittingly won by Sean Cassidy who would doubtless squander it in some Merseyside alehouse. And that, for the *Alice Springs,* his former shipmates and the British Merchant Navy, was the end of Eddie Clooney, a humble Dublin-born fridge greaser who would indeed be missed - if only until his money was spent.

The final week of the voyage was notable, as far as the catering department was concerned, for the additional overtime previously promised by the Second Steward. As Steve had discovered, Channel Night proper was generally accepted as being the final few nights of a voyage, when all the last-minute cleaning and maintenance chores were attended to; although on this occasion it would last for several nights longer owing to the owners' decision to make a pre-arranged ship inspection at Liverpool. No one really objected, thanks to that exceptional phenomenon known to all merchant seamen as, 'The Channels', a feeling of exhilaration associated with homecoming and a reunion with loved-ones. And so it was with Steve, who despite his longing for Maxine and an expeditious return to New Zealand, was eagerly anticipating the re-engagement with and fellowship of his family; a pint with his dad, a hug from his mum and the oft-missed banter with his brother. In short, despite the additional overtime, extending the working day to a good sixteen hours - with half-hour morning and two-hour afternoon breaks - all were in a happy frame of mind and went about their jobs with a zeal.

At the onset of the extended overtime Steve was allocated the troublesome grind of removing scorch marks from the hot-press and salamander, an unenviable labour that Peter had evaded by volunteering to sugi the overheads (asbestos-coated pipework, cables, etc.) in the working alleyway, a less arduous task than that with which Steve had been saddled. He decided to tackle the salamander first as it was clearly the more tarnished piece of equipment. Theoretically it shouldn't have been difficult, the heat-generated discolouration only extending for the half an inch closest to the elements. Initially, he toiled away with wire-wool and sugi; to no effect as it transpired as the blemishes stubbornly refused to be shifted.

'Nip down to the galley and ask if you can borrow a tin of SOS paint,' suggested Archie, who could see that Steve was in trouble and in need of some counsel. 'It'll cover those marks up in no time and no-one'll be any the wiser. It's what they use on the ovens, and they look virtually new when they've finished.'

Steve suspected a prank; something along the lines of, 'jugs for jugged hare', or, 'green oil for the starboard navigation lamp', but he slipped down to the galley, at least prepared for some monkey-business. But no, for there, seated on the deck adjacent to the stove sat Jimmy Craddock, dipping his paintbrush into a tin bearing the legend, 'Silverene', which the galley boy was using to obliterate the scorch marks from the ovens. 'I was beginning to think it was another leg-pull,' confided Steve, as Jimmy put the finishing touches to his masterpiece, 'but now I can see what Archie was getting at - but why do they call it SOS paint?'

'Shite over shite, Son,' called a voice from the other side of the galley where Norman was de-scaling the steamer. It's a load of old tat but it does the trick, even if it is only temporary.'

The tin of Silverene made short work of improving the appearance of both hot-press and salamander, and Steve couldn't help wondering why he hadn't been told about it earlier as it would have made life a great deal easier. Peter for one must have known about it, so Steve concluded that silence had prevailed for the sole purpose of making his existence more awkward.

Steve became quickly amazed at the difference facilitated by the additional overtime. For instance, the timber panelling in the saloon and passenger areas was totally revitalised using lukewarm water and vinegar, an age-old remedy that still produced sparkling results despite the availability of more up-to-date cleansers. Paintwork was sugied for the umpteenth time in a month, while mirrors were wiped with a damp chamois before being burnished with a soft linen cloth. The timber panelling had also been given a final polish with linen for as Ruby advised, 'Cotton leaves an awful lot of 'fuzz'.'

All the silverware was given an additional dip and polish, while most of the glassware ended up in the sink where the pantry boys were kept particularly busy as water jugs, tumblers, wine glasses, flower vases and ashtrays were sluiced in warm soapy water before being dried and returned to the tables. Archie remarked that, 'In days gone by on some of the passenger liners, if a water jug had a 'tide-mark' around the interior then it had to be cleaned with potato peelings - and jolly hard work it was too.'

Tea and coffee pots, along with the coffee percolator, were all subject to special attention owing to their propensity to stain. On this occasion it was Peter who drew the short straw, being detailed to clean out the coffee percolator which was an archaic contraption, similar in appearance to the geysers found in inter-war sculleries to heat water for washing-up and bathing. On this occasion, as Peter was carefully removing the filter, it split across the middle spilling its contents into the reservoir. By the time he'd finished, draining off the coffee and removing the now useless coffee-grounds, he could easily have passed for a Negro. 'Fuckin' thing,' he cursed, throwing what remained of the filter into the rosie. It's about time they dumped this fuckin' geriatric and invested in something more modern.'

Meanwhile, Steve had had his own problems, scrubbing out the interior of the hot-press which never completely cooled down and possessed all the qualities of a sweat-box. He too was swearing about 'galley-slaves' and 'saunas', although he acknowledged that the job needed doing.

By the end of the additional week's overtime there wasn't an inch of the catering and circulating areas, not to mention their associated alleyways, that hadn't received attention of some sort; either a lick of fresh paint, the caress of soapy water or the taste of scouring cloth and vinegar. The same applied to every stick of furniture before it was industriously buffed up with linen. In fact, and when the cabin repaint was taken into account, the entire midships accommodation area looked as spick and span as if the ship had been newly refitted.

Eventually, shortly before midnight, immediately prior to the *Alice Springs'* scheduled arrival at Dunkirk, Sec called a halt, satisfied that all that could be done had been done and that a blind man would be ecstatic at spotting anything neglected. 'Right, lads,' he announced, striding into the saloon carrying a battered case of Tennant's that if he was to be believed, had slid from its stack as the ship took a roll and was in no fit state to be retailed. 'I think you've earnt this. If the owners find anything amiss then it won't be through any fault of yours.' And to the two boy ratings, he added, handing them each a can of lager, 'Make yourselves scarce and stay out of sight, because if the Boss finds you drinking it won't just be you for the high jump - I'll get a bollocking as well.'

Steve snatched a can-opener from a startled Keith, and with a hurried, 'Cheers, Sec,' chased Peter down to and along the working alleyway, across the after well-deck and up to the poop where Jimmy Craddock was already in residence, sprawled in almost the exact location that Steve had discovered Eddie Clooney; the only difference being that on this occasion the incumbent was alive and supping from his own can of lager.

The night was chilly but clear, and far away to the north-east, on the island of Ushant, loomed the most powerful lighthouse in Europe, its beam an indication that they weren't so very far from home. A scattering of white horses were being driven on by a freshening breeze, meaning in all probability that tomorrow, holidaymakers from Blackpool to Brixham would be seeking refuge from the notorious British summer in an assortment of sea-front shelters and amusement arcades.

Steve took a seat beside Jimmy, protected from the breeze by the bulk of the after deck-house; but Peter remained standing, for although he'd visited the poop on numerous occasions since the passing of Eddie, he still felt an unexplained 'presence'.

'Sit down, you silly bugger,' urged Jimmy, draining the remnants from his can before tossing it carelessly overboard. 'He can't hurt you now, not where he is. He's probably having a drink with the crew of the Titanic for all we know.'

333

Steve thought the joke pretty tasteless, especially considering that something not dissimilar to the fate of the White Star liner could befall any of them at any given moment. It didn't have to be an iceberg. There were plenty of ships out there even now, in the middle of the twentieth century, that weren't equipped with the latest navigational aids; some of them, most particularly the older flag-of-convenience vessels, didn't even have the luxury of radar. That was enough to scramble the wits of even the most seasoned shell-back, especially in the congested waters that the *Alice Springs* was now entering. Hair-raising encounters between merchant vessels were commonplace, and although separation zones had provided a basis for discussion among various European governments - including the British - since a recent spate of near-misses and collisions, nothing had so far been formalized, and the restricted sea lanes of the English Channel remained a potential holocaust.

22

The weather was true to its reputation, and an annoying drizzle was falling over the low-lying city of Dunkirk as a brace of tugs, one of apparently Edwardian vintage, shepherded the *Alice Springs* past the curving breakwater and into the docks where the quaysides were crowded with shipping. Steve, who was wearing his wind-cheater as protection from the breeze and sporadic outbreaks of rain, lounged against the starboard rail in the forward well-deck, periodically wiping moisture from his spectacles as he strove to identify landmarks both within and on the fringes of the harbour, the proximity of which was heavily industrialised with both chemical and steel-forging complexes. It was only eight o'clock on a July evening, but with the heavy overcast and smoke billowing from the factory chimneys, it could easily have been two hours later.

While the ship had glided ever closer inshore he'd scrutinized the beaches and sand dunes that only twenty years earlier had born witness to the most calamitous defeat ever inflicted on the British military. It had happened before he was born; but he remembered his parents talking about those who'd battled, survived or were slain, and of the fishermen, pleasure-craft owners and other part-time seafarers who'd endangered their own lives on rescue missions, making countless crossings between harbours and creeks in the south-east corner of England and the blood-drenched beaches that once rang to the cacophony of combat, but that this evening lay empty and quiet. Every so often he'd suspected the ghostly revelation of some twisted finger of metal, perhaps a remnant of some ill-fated rescue craft or item of military equipment; but it may just as easily have been a marker pole indicating the seaward end of a semi-submerged groyne or breakwater.

But there was no mistaking the sinister-looking caverns that punctuated the harbour's perimeter; the remains of a super-efficient, maritime-warfare support-system, but which were now seaweed-clogged depositories for all manner of nautical detritus. 'U-boat pens,' stated Dingwall Patterson, who'd also braved the weather and was likewise scanning the warren of tunnels that penetrated into the darkness and possibly extended beneath the bustling streets of Dunkirk. 'It was generally accepted that the U-boat bases were mainly in the Biscay ports,' continued Dingwall, pulling his oilskin more tightly around his shoulders as a heavier burst of drizzle threatened to drive them into the drier and more hospitable bounds of the superstructure, 'places like Lorient and La Rochelle, but they could be found almost anywhere from the northern tip of Norway southwards, all the way down to the Spanish border.'

'They must have been pretty wide ranging?' said Steve, glancing sideways at Dingwall. It wasn't so much a statement as a question as he wondered how the evil-looking, shark-like submersibles could have caused such appalling havoc among the allied convoys way out in the Atlantic if they'd had to travel such enormous distances; for when all was said and done, they were relatively tiny compared with conventional warships.

'They travelled thousands of miles,' answered Dingwall, wiping a bead of drizzle from the tip of his nose before it could trigger a sneeze. 'They'd run submerged on their electric motors for as long as possible; then, so long as it was safe to do so they'd blow their tanks and navigate on the surface under diesel power, recharging their batteries in the process. I suppose their endurance was only restricted by fuel capacity and supplies of food and ammunition.'

'Must have been pretty awful living conditions,' offered Steve, trying to imagine the cramped and stuffy accommodation areas and action stations for forty-odd men aboard what was indisputably a wickedly murderous fighting machine, but also a terrifyingly potential steel coffin.

'Bloody atrocious, I'd say,' replied Dingwall, absently smoothing his hair with the palm of his hand, sending a trickle of water down the neck of his oilskin, causing an involuntary shiver. He tightened the garment even closer around his shoulders, as if doing so would

336

atone for the error. 'I was once told by a German submariner who'd served aboard U-boats as a teenager that he'd been petrified for the entire duration of the commission - and I for one can believe it.'

Steve could believe it too, and no way could he ever imagine himself volunteering for the submarine service. For one thing it would be too claustrophobic, not to mention the never-ending fear of being depth-charged or rammed to oblivion by an enemy destroyer or frigate. But, he wondered, picturing seawater gushing through the ruptured hull of a condemned U-boat, and the entombed submariners scrambling frantically to escape but with no realistic chance of survival; were the incarcerated crew members ever given the option? He posed the question to Dingwall but for once the oracle seemed stumped. 'I suppose they might have - in the beginning,' he eventually mused, as he wiped a calloused hand over a bristly chin while striving for a credible answer. 'Although my guess is that as losses mounted among the more experienced men and volunteers became scarce, they most likely resorted to conscription.'

Later that evening, although it was past ten o'clock and no sub had been granted, Steve joined Donald and Keith for a run ashore, for a couple of beers and some late-night sightseeing. Being completely penniless he'd borrowed from Keith with the promise that it wouldn't be forgotten. The ten-shilling note was readily accepted in a waterfront bar, and the price of three beers was rewarded with four Francs change, the local currency having only recently been revalued at fourteen Francs to the Pound.

The establishment was a typical seaport watering hole, catering primarily for seamen and port workers. Only a handful of drinkers were present, most of them seated at bar-stools while none of the tables were occupied. A ribbon of smoke filtered the already dim light from the chandeliers and the atmosphere was heavy with Gauloise. Universally loathed by their critics, Steve found the scent of the fabled French cigarettes exhilarating, and he would certainly have invested in twenty if funds had been more plentiful and if he hadn't already been in debt. Furnishings were plentiful if time worn, and the tobacco-stained walls carried souvenirs that were the proceeds of decades of globe-trotting; perhaps a legitimate purchase like the kaleidoscopic butterfly tray from the jungles of darkest

Brazil, but just as likely a purloined or salvaged artefact from a world-famous icon, such as a lifebelt from the French liner, *Normandie,* which hung above the entrance to the toilet.

The *Normandie,* a one-time Blue-Riband holder and arguably the most luxurious liner ever, was laid up in New York at the outbreak of the Second World War. A couple of years later she was seized by the U.S. Authorities with a view to rebuilding her as an aircraft carrier. The idea was never carried through and it was agreed that she would be adapted as a troopship. It was while undergoing conversion that she caught fire and capsized, being later broken up as a constructive total loss at her moorings.

Once served, and until their departure, the pals were largely ignored by both the barman and his Gallic clientèle - a nod and a mumbled *au revoir* being acknowledged by smiles and what the latter-day English call, 'Franglais'.

From closer quarters the area surrounding the port appeared utterly devastated, clearly still suffering from the ravages of Nazi occupation. Lighting wasn't as bright as it might have been and the thoroughfares were potholed and broken. In fact, many of the back streets and alleyways were cobbled; although huge swathes of cobble-stones were missing making the likelihood of an accident an everyday hazard for pedestrians and cyclists alike. Of the surviving dwellings few were entirely intact, with crumbling brickwork and windows that were either boarded-up or shuttered. The latter may simply have been a householder's mode of protecting his privacy, for as Donald pointed out, waving a hand at what remained of the surrounding residential district where only an occasional light suggested that some of the properties were occupied. 'It's a way of life on the Continent. They close the shutters at night in the same way that we draw our curtains. Then, down in the south, along the Mediterranean and in countries like Portugal and Spain, closing the shutters is a way of excluding the heat, as well as being a night-time blackout. They're also a pretty useful security measure.' It was an easily appreciated logic; but in Steve's blinkered view it didn't account for the town at large appearing semi-derelict, an opinion he voiced without thinking although with hindsight the reason was obvious.

It was a classic example of yet another abject failure of the British educational system, as Keith so eloquently explained. 'You have to remember that places like Dunkirk and Rotterdam were all but destroyed in the war, and have had to be completely rebuilt. Don't forget, these streets saw weeks of hand-to-hand fighting. Then there was the pounding from tanks, heavy artillery and the Luftwaffe as the Jerries sought to dislodge the forces covering the evacuation. When you think about it, it's a miracle anything was left standing.'

'That's right,' added Donald, whose own family had been bombed out of their terraced house in the Ardoyne, but had survived thanks to an Anderson Shelter. 'It was bad enough in Belfast, not to mention places like Plymouth and Coventry, but it was nothing compared with what these poor bastards had to cope with. Some of them hid in cellars and suchlike but most just fled and quite literally became refugees in their own country, sheltering in roadside ditches and along riverbanks - anywhere away from the fighting.'

Like the U-boat pens it was a stark reminder that the scars of modern warfare took a great many years to erase. Indeed, as he'd made his way to the docks on a Metropolitan Line underground train some five months earlier Steve had been shocked by glimpses of bombed-sites and wasteland in the City and East End of London, years after the end of hostilities. In one fleeting instant, as the train had emerged from a tunnel close to Farringdon station, he'd spotted the bombed-out remains of a factory with a tree growing out of a chimney, a bizarre side-effect of twentieth century war-mongering. 'They didn't teach us any of that at school,' he complained, forever seeming on the receiving end of some sort of lecture. 'We only had two half-hour periods of history a week and, well - I don't suppose they considered the Second World War to be history, not with it only ending in the mid nineteen-forties. They taught us about The Blitz and the Battle of Britain, about Alemein and D-Day, but they only glossed over what happened here. If anything, they made Dunkirk sound more like a glorious victory, but now I know it was nothing of the sort.'

'It most certainly wasn't,' answered Keith, whose uncle had been one of those fortunate enough to be rescued, enabling him to give a full account of the carnage. 'It was a fuckin' rout, no matter how you try to glamorize it. Mind you,' he continued, leading the way out of a dingy alleyway into a more brightly lit square where it seemed as if a party was gaining momentum. 'It wasn't really the troops' fault. They were trying to hold off a modern, well-equipped army and air force with small-arms and light artillery, having abandoned their own obsolete heavy weapons. They didn't stand a chance, not without proper air cover and suitable hardware.' And then, after a few seconds thought, he added. 'The only good thing about it was that so many were eventually evacuated.'

'Still, the ones who were saved did at least get a well-deserved break,' rejoined Donald, pointing the way to a gaily adorned café with red, white and blue bunting draped across the frontage, and crowds spilling out in the street. 'A couple of weeks leave must have done 'em the power of good.'

'I suppose so,' replied Keith, taking a seat at the only vacant pavement table and waving for the waiter's attention. 'But I remember my Uncle Alf telling me that they all felt ashamed - as though the Army had let everyone down.' Then, after ordering three beers from the moustachioed, black-aproned waiter, he continued. 'And another thing Uncle Alf told me was that there was no rest and recuperation for the poor bloody French and Belgian squaddies. Those who were evacuated were shipped straight back across The Channel, and before they had chance to say, "Sod this for a game of soldiers", were back in the thick of the action.'

Thankfully the drizzle had stopped, and the chairs on the pavement had been thoughtfully dried so that the patrons could sit down in comfort. From his seat overlooking the square Steve could see that the buildings in this part of Dunkirk were largely new, with a handful of older yet beautifully restored properties occupying the intervening gaps. It was exactly as Keith had described it. In contrast with the dimly-lit lanes that encircled the port, the streets in the centre of town were highly illuminated as the beams from recently-installed sodium lamps reached into even the gloomiest corners, complementing the softer yet warmer glow emanating from bars and cafés. Even now, at thirty minutes to midnight, the town was alive with people celebrating and the festivities showed little sign of abating. 'I wonder what the shindig's in aid of?' queried Steve, lifting

340

his glass of 'Flanders' ale and raising it in deference to a pretty young blonde who was smiling at him from a neighbouring table.

'It's the fourteenth of July - Bastille Day,' enlightened Donald, taking a quaff of his own beer while helping himself from the bowl of savouries that the waiter had set on the table. 'It's a National holiday - the most important and popular in the French calendar, and everyone's out to enjoy it.'

As if to emphasise the point, and before Steve had chance to protest, he'd been jerked to his feet by his blonde admirer and hauled into a swirling ring of humanity, who were dancing to the lively music of a piano-accordionist who was swaying to the rhythms of his own energetic performance. For once he felt no inhibitions as he mimicked the girl and other revellers in linking arms and galloping first in one direction and then the other in a gigantic and growing orbit, stopping every few seconds to twirl on the spot with his partner before reeling away on the next lap of the circuit. An ability to dance wasn't a prerequisite and many a toe was trampled before the accordionist called time and slowed the tempo into something approaching a romantic nocturne, at which stage the circle broke up.

'You didn't fancy joining in, then?' asked Steve, mischievously, slumping breathlessly into his chair as the girl returned to her table, her joyful expression turning to an obvious scowl at a comment from one of her party.

'Too much like hard work for me,' answered Donald, who along with Keith had been clapping in time with the music but had shown no inclination to participate.

'You seem to have a devotee there,' said Keith nodding at the adjacent table where the blonde and a squat, swarthy, dark-haired individual of pugilistic stature seemed engaged in a heated argument. 'Are you going to follow it up?'

'No bloody fear,' announced Steve, burying his head in his collar and doing his best to evaporate. 'I reckon that's her boyfriend she's rowing with, and he looks like a bit of a handful.'

'They certainly know how to enjoy themselves, that's for sure,' declared Donald, ignoring the squabble at the adjoining table and motioning at the on-going revelry. 'We don't seem to do anything like this on public holidays in the United Kingdom, especially the Welsh,

Scots and English.' Donald paused as a brief but colourful firework display exploded over the municipal buildings, temporarily drowning any attempt at conversation. 'All right, the Irish make the most of St Patrick's Day,' he eventually continued, as the last of the pyrotechnics fizzled out, 'but that's only to be expected what with all that Guinness floating about. Then there's the Orangemen in Ulster. They were probably making pratts of themselves a couple of days ago, strutting up and down the High Streets behind their banners and fife-and-drum bands, but their main purpose is to cause trouble and resentment rather than to have a good time. No, when you think of it there's a lot we can learn from the Continentals.'

Steve was aware that Donald was a Catholic, and knew that he was referring to the Twelfth of July Orange Day marches in Belfast and Londonderry. He longed to learn more about the years of conflict between the province's Loyalists and Nationalists, but suspected that whoever he asked, especially if they were Irish, he'd get a one-sided view of the argument. Anyway, he'd had sufficient in the way of cerebral exercise for one day and decided to place the topic on the back burner, intending to revive it in the morning.

But that was as far as it got, for it was announced over breakfast that after the briefest of visits the *Alice Springs* would be sailing for Liverpool at six. For whatever reason, the historic issues surrounding Protestant and Catholic were forgotten, and the subject was never resurrected.

Throughout the morning the *Alice Springs* was gradually relieved of her deck cargo, along with several parcels of refrigerated and general merchandise. On the opposite side of the basin the Panamanian freighter *Peter*, another superannuated relic, discharged her deck cargo of timber from the Baltic, while ahead of the *Alice Springs* a Greek-owned liberty ship - whose name Steve couldn't pronounce - was loading a shipment of steel from the smelters, a trainload of forgings having drawn alongside with another one waiting in the sidings. The Industriousness of the port, France's third largest, was evidence that although the city hadn't yet fully recovered from its trauma then it wouldn't be long in the doing.

23

'It's dinner at seven o'clock this evening - not six-thirty,' informed Sec, pushing into the pantry and laying a wad of menu cards on the work surface as Steve and Peter, along with the stewards, prepared coffee for the officers and passengers. 'What with sailing at six it would have been a bit of a scramble so the Mate asked the Boss if we could postpone it for the extra half hour.'

'Any idea when we'll be arriving in Liverpool?' asked Steve, taking a luncheon menu from the pile and pinning it to the pantry noticeboard, alongside the buff-coloured Board of Trade document detailing the minimum rations entitlement for the crew.

'Dunno for sure,' answered Sec, squeezing between Peter and Archie, both of whom were piling up trays with the entire accoutrements for coffee before setting off for the lounges and smoke-rooms, 'but I should imagine it'll be another two days.'

'That's okay then,' announced Peter, who was rubbing his hands together in anticipation. 'That means we should be there in ample time for a pint. It sounds as if we'll be too late to pay off so do you reckon we'll get any 'Channel Money' - you know, for a beer and so on?'

As they awaited an answer Steve began inserting the remaining menu cards into their folders. As in the pantry, another copy would have been posted on the board in the galley, the various courses having been agreed upon by Ted and the Chief Steward in consultation, bearing in mind the remaining stores and provisions.

'It's being sorting now,' replied Sec, edging away from the mêlée, before he was bombarded with any more questions, 'but you won't be getting it until after we've docked and all the formalities have been completed.'

As he placed the menu folders on their respective tables Steve couldn't help wondering if the run up to Liverpool would be worth the added expense in wages and fuel costs given the paltry amount of cargo discharged at Dunkirk. In his opinion it would have been more economical to have paid off in London and then transshipped the French portion on a smaller vessel; one of the coasters that the company frequently chartered for just such a purpose.

'Normally that's what would have happened,' advised the Bosun, when Steve later bumped into the petty officer who was supervising the battening down of the hatches from which the Dunkirk cargo had been landed. 'But rumour has it that as soon as we've discharged in Liverpool the ship's going into dry dock at Birkenhead, see if they can't sort this boiler problem out once and for all. Apparently, that's why we're making for Liverpool rather than London.'

'I thought they'd fixed the engines,' said Steve, who like almost everyone else on board hadn't been aware of any ongoing difficulties with seawater ingress following the breakdown in the Indian Ocean.

'Well, there's only so much they can do on the high seas,' answered the Bosun, bravely positioning a wedge in one of the brackets between the hatch coming and the tarpaulin while a deckhand took aim with a mallet. 'At least if they get her in Cammell-Laird's they'll be able to strip everything down and get to the bottom of it.'

From Steve's uncompromising angle it still made absolutely no sense at all to send the *Alice Springs* on a seven-hundred mile jaunt up to Liverpool at goodness knows how many gallons per mile when distinguished companies like Harland & Wolff Ltd and R.H. Green & Silley Weir had perfectly good ship repair facilities on the Thames. 'Surely they could have done that in London?' he pressed, pointing out that there were a couple of dry docks in the Royal group along with machine shops and a fully-equipped fitting out basin. 'It would have saved time as well as money - and we'd have gotten home sooner.'

'They probably could have,' replied the Bosun, picking up another wedge and moving along to the next bracket, followed by the deckie with his mallet. 'But I suppose they considered that seeing as how Cammell-Laird's built the old girl, they were the best ones to fix her.'

It was shortly after six when the mooring lines were eventually released and the *Alice Springs* inched slowly away from the quayside, swirls of muddy water bubbling to the surface as the tugs performed their manoeuvres. Amid a cacophony of tooting from her Edwardian consort, and the booming of the her own siren, she was swung a full 180° before slipping silently past the derelict U-boat pens and out of Dunkirk on the final stage of what from Steve's point of view had been a truly epic adventure. She would initially sail in a south-westerly direction, hugging the coast in the wake of the *St Germaine*, an SNCF train ferry that had sailed from Dunkirk just a few minutes earlier. The French vessel was making for Dover's Western Docks, but once the Channel was crossed the *Alice Springs* would adopt a more westerly course, heading for Cornwall and The Lizard.

Steve saw little of the departure, having been despatched with disinfectant and cleansing materials to the passengers' lounge where one of the corpulent ladies - the younger of the two - had thrown up on the freshly-cleaned carpet. She insisted it was a bilious attack caused by eating contaminated shellfish while ashore in the city, whereas the doctor maintained that she'd made an absolute pig of herself over lunch, and considering the amount of curry she'd consumed it was a wonder she hadn't shit herself as well. Whatever, it didn't prevent her enjoying pre-prandial drinks with her travelling companions, or from stuffing herself silly over dinner.

'The greedy bitch has only ordered a second portion of Yorkshire Pudding,' whispered Ruby, incredulously, finding it difficult to believe that someone who'd evacuated their stomach only an hour or so earlier was eating with the appetite of a horse. Sliding a stack of soiled crockery through the servery and collecting a trayful of crème caramels, he added, 'I wouldn't be surprised if she has several of these as well - so if I were you, Steve, I'd be ready with my mop and bucket.'

A late dinner inevitably meant a late finish, and it was almost dark by the time the catering staff in general - Peter carrying his portable wireless which was once again tuned into radio Luxembourg - sat on the hatch cover in the after well-deck, enjoying the fading twilight as the final tinges of a fine summer's day slipped silently beneath the horizon. The day had been pleasantly warm with appreciable amounts of sunshine, the previous evening's depression having drifted away over the low countries, taking its irritating drizzle with it. The claustrophobic effect that had lain heavily over the *Alice Springs* for the month or so's passage from Napier had been lifted with the discharge of the deck cargo. Forward-facing cabins were again blessed with daylight, while the favourite pastime of idling away time on a hatch cover could once more be indulged in.

Despite the gathering nightfall a scattering of gulls still performed last-minute aerobatics, crying and mewing before wheeling away to roost among the chimneys on Dover's grey-slated rooftops. Meanwhile, the *St Germaine* had sped between the piers at the western end of the harbour and was hidden from view, her voyage almost over in the time it takes to play a twenty-overs-a-side cricket match. She'd re-emerge sometime after midnight, only instead of carrying railway wagons laden with merchandise her cargo would consist of Wagons-Lits sleeping cars full of slumbering passengers, some of whom would have dropped off to sleep at London's Victoria Station, and wouldn't awake until the train arrived at Paris' Gare du Nord.

'Can't be a bad life, working on one of those things,' said Peter, nodding towards the distant but brightly-lit harbour and the now vanished *St Germaine,* that was probably already tying up in the specially-designed train ferry dock. 'Home every night - or every day. Must be bloody marvellous for anyone who's married with kids.'

'Don't you believe it,' answered Donald, who himself had been married for over ten years and had half-a-dozen children of his own. 'You can't beat getting away from the wife and nippers. 'Oh! It's fine for the first several days when you arrive home on leave, snuggling up to the missus at nights, and having a bit here and there when you want it. But then she starts cackling on about how the lawn needs mowing, or the toilet cistern needs a new washer - all those things that you don't have to bother about at sea. Then the bloody kids get the wants - can I have this, will you buy me that, that's despite the fact that I always arrive home with a load of presents. No, you can't beat a long deep-sea voyage. It's nice to see them now and again, but after a couple of weeks using a screwdriver I'm ready to re-sign those articles.'

Even though he was single and unattached Keith agreed that sailing deep sea was preferable to home trade or 'Channel hopping' - although for different reasons. 'And another thing is you don't get to save much money when you're ashore every night,' he advised, wiping a small pool of spilt coffee from the hatch cover and sitting down where Norman had stood his mug. 'If you're not at home, shelling it out on the housekeeping, you're pissing it all up the wall.'

'I reckon you're far better off not being married - full stop, deep-sea or otherwise,' said Norman, who'd been listening intently to the exchanges, comparing other people's views with his own. 'And you don't have to go out on the piss every night. You can go to the pictures, to the mission, go for a walk, do a spot of sight-seeing or simply stay on board. You don't have to blow all your money. And another thing is, you don't have to send an allotment home to the missus - you can pay it directly into your own bank account instead.'

'Well said, my man,' concurred Archie, who was obviously single, liked a drink - lots of drinks if the truth be told - and was considered by most to be, 'not without a few bob'. 'My sentiments entirely. I'm no millionaire but I enjoy the comforts of life. A few cushions scattered around the cabin and curtains at the porthole - and my little cottage in Sandbach is as snug as you're likely to find. No, I don't mind spending money - but I wouldn't squander it.'

The mention of Archie's cottage in Cheshire prompted a change of tack - but one that was a little unchristian. Everyone knew that Archie was as queer as a three pound note, and that he shared his home with another homosexual called Alan who wasn't a seafarer but worked for the local council, doubling as housekeeper for the months that Archie was away. But with Ruby's appearance on the scene John was wondering which of the relationships would prevail, so he decided to bugger the consequences and tackle the question head on. 'I suppose you'll be glad to see that mate of yours, Archie?' queried the butcher, mischievously, while watching for Ruby's reaction.

Archie shifted awkwardly on the hatch cover, having been caught on the pot, so to speak. Eventually, after an extended pause during which Ruby never batted an eyelid, he answered, 'Of course I will. He's my best friend and has been for years. It'll be like going home to

347

my brother.'

'It's all right,' broke in Ruby, imperiously, linking arms with Archie and eyeing the gathering defiantly. 'I know all about Alan. Archie told me about him at the very beginning - and it's the same with me. I'll be going home to the house I share with my friends at Kingston-upon-Thames. I've known them for yonks and we get along like nobody's business, but it doesn't mean we can't have relationships with others.'

It was time to take the heat out of the situation, thought Steve, so he gamely took the bull by the horns. 'I'm like Archie and Ruby,' he announced, not immediately realizing the silliness of the statement until Ruby tossed his head with an aloofness that suggested Steve was taking the piss, and the rest of the crowd began sniggering. He belatedly cottoned on and grinned, but proceeded as if his slip of the tongue had been an intended part of his address. 'I'm looking forward to seeing my family again. After we've paid off I'll be catching the first train to Euston. What about you, Donald?'

'Me?........Oh!........'I'll probably hang about Liverpool for a few hours, have a few pints and then catch the overnight ferry to Belfast. I should be home before breakfast.'

'I'll be catching the afternoon train to Glasgow, said Jimmy, who'd joined the congregation after everyone else owing to the later than expected clean down. 'I'll be seeing my mum, and if it's not too late I might nip down to the Locarno.'

Keith and John were of the same mind as Steve. They'd be going straight home - as was Peter to an extent. 'I'll probably poke my head around the door, say "hello" - that's if anyone's in,' he articulated, in a tone that was utterly devoid of optimism, 'then I'll be seeing my mates. They've all said that anytime I need a roof over my head................' Peter's voice tailed off, as if he'd said all he really wanted.

What a sorry state of affairs, thought Steve, guessing that Norman's situation was similar to Peter's but with marital complications. It was as if Norman had been reading Steve's mind, and the cook needed no invitation. 'I'll be staying with one of my cousins,' he announced, draining his coffee before delving around in his pocket for the makings of a roll-up. 'I wrote to him from Nelson and got a reply in Panama. He said I could stay as long as I liked, get this mess with my missus sorted out then see where we go from there. But it doesn't look like I'll be coming back anytime soon, not with me getting involved with solicitors and so on. Pity really. I've been on the *Alice Springs* for over a year now - she's one of the best ships I've ever sailed in.'

The glow of Dover was rapidly receding astern, and a lightening of the western sky indicated they would soon be abeam of Folkestone. Beyond Folkestone lay Hastings, Eastbourne and Brighton, but Steve had no intention of spending the night on deck just to witness the passing of an assortment of seaside resorts. 'Well, I don't know about you lot,' he mumbled, his words distorted as he stretched and stifled a yawn, 'but I'm turning in. See you all in the morning.'

But curiosity got the better of him, and he wandered round to the opposite side of the well-deck from where the coast of France was still discernible thanks to a sprinkling of lights. Far away to the south-east the underside of a low-lying ribbon of cloud reflected the street-lamps of Calais, while further west the Cap Gris-Nez lighthouse, its beam pulsing every five seconds, was said to be visible for almost thirty miles in any seaward direction. But it wasn't the coastal lighting that he found most magical. The Channel itself was aglitter with otherwise invisible craft, ranging from cross-channel ferries to tramp steamers, oil tankers, cargo liners and coasters; not to mention one vividly illuminated passenger liner that was rapidly overhauling the *Alice Springs* as if his own ship was merely a tortoise. All these, along with a multitude of blinking navigational beacons, made the otherwise blackened seascape seem a reflection of the starlit heavens.

It was generally accepted that the English Channel, especially where it funnelled through the Straits of Dover, was one of the most congested sea areas in the world, ranking alongside the Straits of Malacca in terms of everyday shipping movements; the latter being the more highly overcrowded owing to a width of less than three thousand yards at its southern end, where it squeezed between Singapore and Sumatra. But the statistics were largely irrelevant as Steve studied the darkened panorama. What a nightmare, he thought, for the navigating officers and watch-keepers who had to be fully alert for any rogue vessels that considered the rules of the road, insomuch as they existed, applied to others rather than themselves. It was all very fine that well-equipped ships like the *Alice Springs* were kitted out with radar and a host of other navigational wizardry; but what on earth must it be like in foggy, overcast conditions, knowing that your nearest neighbour was possibly an ancient, under-manned, poorly maintained and ill-provisioned cowboy who was ploughing along without a clue as to his whereabouts let alone the proximity of others. In the absence of any universally recognized separation zones there were vessels plying here, there and everywhere, all of them potential collisions if an adequate lookout was ignored. Indeed, it was a standing joke among British seafarers that some flag-of-convenience vessels that should have had a complement of sixty were crewed by fifteen men and a dog, and that if those fifteen men were more pressingly engaged, perhaps drinking or playing cards, it was a fair enough bet that the dog was the one keeping watch.

'Nothing to worry about whatsoever when the weather's clear, not so long as you keep your wits about you,' assured the Senior Cadet, when Steve broached the subject the following morning as the former was shaving in the engineers' washroom, the plumbing having failed in his own quarters. 'It's different when it's foggy mind you, or when it's blowing a blizzard,' added the apprentice, rinsing his razor beneath the hot water tap and dabbing a cut with his towel. 'Then you have to creep along with the siren bellowing, eyes peeled in every direction while hoping everyone else is doing likewise. I tell you, at times like that it can be hairy.'

Another snippet furnished by the Senior Cadet, before Steve left him to his ablutions and before he could cut himself further, was that the brightly-lit passenger vessel that had overtaken them during the night had been the Dutch liner *Oranje* of Royal Rotterdam-Lloyd, outward bound for Jakarta and the wider East Indies.

By seven o'clock the *Alice Springs* was to the west of the Isle of Wight, and the amount of noticeable shipping, although considerable, was more scattered than in the more restricted waters nearer Dover. Nevertheless, one vessel in particular warranted special scrutiny. 'Cor, just look at that,' called Peter, frantically beckoning Steve to the saloon windows and pointing obliquely at some as yet unidentified treasure that was causing him untold excitement. Steve hurried through from the pantry; and following Peter's outstretched arm was thrilled by the sight of Cunard's *Queen Mary,* inward bound at the end of her five-day dash from Manhattan, having called briefly at Cherbourg before completing her voyage at Southampton. The boys stood in awe as the great and legendary Cunarder swept past in a welter of spray. She was barely half a mile distant, and passengers were clearly visible on her promenade decks, perhaps taking a final constitutional prior to breakfast. 'I bet there's some money sloshing around on there,' scoffed Peter, as the last of the British Blue-Riband holders powered speedily in the direction of the Nab Tower where she would turn and make a more leisurely approach to the Ocean Terminal through Spithead, The Solent and Southampton Water. 'Film stars, pop singers, businessmen, politicians - anyone who's never had to work for a living. We must be fuckin' mugs, skivvyin' away on here while they live the life of Riley.'

The bitterness wasn't lost on Steve, notwithstanding that Peter seemed to have a perpetual chip on his shoulder and appeared to bear malice toward anyone of greater material standing, even if it had been achieved through talent and sheer hard graft. Probably to do with his upbringing, he thought, as he meandered back to the pantry while the *Queen Mary's* passengers put the final touches to their packing. Whatever, there was little that he could do about it. The only hope was that as Peter matured - and hopefully became wiser and less cynical - he would grow to accept what life threw at him and not be so envious of others because if he didn't, he was almost certainly heading for a miserable and lonely seniority.

By 4.00pm the *Alice Springs* was rounding The Lizard, the most southerly point on the British mainland and the only sliver of the United Kingdom to extend below fifty degrees north. This distinction didn't make the Lizard Peninsular especially tropical although the area, along with much of southern Cornwall, was noted for its ability to sustain a wide variety of sub-tropical plant life including a weather-hardened assortment of palm trees. As with the rest of the south-west peninsular, The Lizard was exposed to the worst of the westerly gales and the promontory itself was devoid of significant tree growth, and what scrubby specimens did exist had been bent by the strength of the wind.

And so it was on this afternoon that the morning's sunshine had evaporated in the face of an advancing weather system, with clouds massing to the west and the sea state sufficiently high to send the *Alice Springs* pitching and rolling in the conflicting currents as she rounded the famous old headland. On a positive note it wasn't yet raining and The Lizard lighthouse, along with its two massive foghorns and keepers' cottages, could clearly be seen on the cliff-edge. Along with the householders in the handful of properties scattered along the cliff-top, the lighthouse keepers at Lizard Point would be first to feel the lash of the storm.

A little earlier, as the *Alice Springs* had passed the quaint little fishing village of Coverack, the Bosun had handed Steve his binoculars and pointed to a slender spire on a hilltop. 'See that steeple?' he'd indicated, as Steve struggled to focus while the ship negotiated a patch of rough water. 'Well that's the parish church at St Keverne, and I live about three miles from there on the other side of the peninsular, in a tiny hamlet called Porthallow. Bloody lovely it is, down there. Looks out over Falmouth Bay, and it's sheltered from the westerly winds.' Gauged by the height of the landmass Steve could imagine Porthallow nestling at the foot of a steeply-wooded valley, with just a handful of cottages and maybe a pub encircling a beach. It sounded idyllic; and the Bosun added, jokingly. 'If they were to let me lower a boat I could be home within the hour, and it'd save me a three-hundred-and-fifty mile train journey.'

By sun-rise the following morning the South Stack lighthouse off the west coast of Anglesey was evidence that Liverpool was close. The sea had subsided during the night as the weather front had blown itself through, leaving an undulating swell beneath the vault of a windswept sky. The sun was full in their face as the pilot boarded at the Point Lynas pilot station, and by lunchtime the *Alice Springs* was abeam of the 'Bar' light-vessel, within sight of the Mersey estuary.

Steve was almost as excited as he had been as a child at Christmas, or when about to depart on his holidays. Archie, whose home wasn't so very far from the north Wales coast, had pointed out Great Orme's Head at Llandudno, and as the *Alice Springs* entered the Mersey he drew Steve's attention to the great sweep of beaches on the Wirral Peninsular between New Brighton and Hoylake. 'Along with Southport,' enlightened the bedroom steward, nodding over his shoulder in the direction of the Lancashire resort, 'those sands, and the beaches at Rhyl and Prestatyn, are the principal seaside attractions for this part of north-west England.' And almost as an postscript, he added, in reference to Britain's gradually growing affluent society. 'And now that more and more people have motor cars they're coming from further afield.'

Despite the loss of its tower the Tower Ballroom and funfair at New Brighton monopolized the Wirral skyline, and highlighted that this stretch of estuary and seafront was largely devoted to leisure. But over on the Liverpool shore the landscape was much more industrialised, almost exclusively in the form of the Mersey Docks and Harbour Board's dock system. Further upstream there were docks on either side of the river, those on the Liverpool waterfront extending beyond the 'Pierhead' to Garston, while those at Birkenhead, although important and substantial, didn't cover such an extensive acreage.

As the *Alice Springs* edged cautiously up the fairway, tugs standing by to guide her through the locks and channels leading in from the river, the forest of masts and funnels that protruded above the dockside warehouses represented a ship-spotters Mecca. Many of the funnels unmistakeably belonged to London-based companies, while several of those associated with Liverpool were less easily identified, at least from the distance that Steve was observing. It didn't help that any number of famous British shipping lines had adopted identical funnel colours. For instance, New Zealand Shipping Company, Royal Mail, Elder-Dempster and Pacific Steam Navigation Company were just a few that had opted for yellow, while those of Port Line were the same as the parent company, Cunard. And so it went on. Steve was able to distinguish a couple of Lamport & Holt Line funnels along with a Palm Line example; and at least two Brocklebank specimens were discernible amid the jumble of rigging.

A final cigarette issue had taken place prior to their arrival at Dunkirk, and the customs manifest had been completed during the run down Channel. And so it transpired, on this sunny afternoon with 'home' in the air, a launch drew alongside and transferred a pair of uniformed customs officers on to the already lowered accommodation ladder. 'Only two of them,' remarked Keith, gazing down from the forward end of the officers' and engineers' quarters as the pair of revenue men ascended the ladder and entered the superstructure, disappearing in the direction of the Chief Steward's office. 'Probably means it'll only be a formality. If they intended taking the ship apart they'd have sent the rummage crew, and they're like a swarm of fuckin' locusts.'

Steve had heard of the infamous rummage crew, the band of overalled customs officers stationed in almost every UK port, who would board inbound vessels at random at any hour of the day or night and all but dismantle a ship in their search for contraband and illegally imported cargo. They'd been known to remove bulkhead and deckhead panels, take apart furniture, empty lockers and drawers, rifle through suitcases and other items of luggage, drain off coffee percolators, shine torches into ovens, steamers and other cooking appliances, run mirrors along overheads and strip out cable trunking; and this was only in the accommodation areas, before they'd even thought about turning their attention to the vessel's much more capacious cargo-carrying compartments.

Steve wasn't unduly worried, other than from the point of view that an extended search might delay the clearance, leaving them confined to the ship until the officers were satisfied - or as satisfied as they could be - that everything was as stated in the manifest. For his part, he'd only had to declare the music box he'd bought for his mum, and the two-hundred Rothmans from the final cigarette issue. The cigarettes weren't a problem as they didn't exceed his allowance, his only concern being the music box that would almost certainly be liable for duty. At this stage he didn't know how much, and he wouldn't find out until he was handed the bill in the morning.

By two o'clock the *Alice Springs* was swinging in mid-stream between Birkenhead and Liverpool, the tugs lining her up with the Sandon lock entrance that would allow her access to the maze of channels and basins that made up the Liverpool dock complex. 'I've been told that we're tying up in the Huskison, Number Two Branch

354

Dock,' said the Second Steward, eager as always to keep his men informed as soon as the information became available. 'We should be alongside and finished with engines by teatime - that's according to the Chief Engineer.'

'How about Channel Money?' asked Donald, repeating the question that Peter had posed earlier. 'Any idea how much and when?'

'Should be about four o'clock,' answered Sec, helping himself to a cox's orange pippin from the basket that was replenished with fruit on a daily basis and located on a table in the saloon foyer. 'Two pounds for senior ratings, ten-bob for boys.'

'Two quid?' replied Donald, as if he couldn't believe his ears. 'What on earth's come over the Boss?' He had a win on Littlewood's?'

'Ours is not to reason why,' said Sec, smiling, while polishing the apple on the sleeve of his jacket before sinking his teeth into its flesh. 'Just think yourself lucky you've got it.'

Ten shillings, thought Steve - a reminder of what he owed Keith - as he gave the hot-press a final post-lunch wipeover. That's a small fortune. Should be able to have a decent night out on that. 'You going ashore tonight, Archie?' he asked, cheerfully, filling a bucket with hot soapy water before giving Peter a hand with the scrub-out.

'Too true,' answered the bedroom steward, removing the pantry cloth from around his waist and laying it on the hot-press to dry. 'I'm going to call in the Pierhead Hotel for a quick one and then, unless he's made alternative arrangements, I'll be meeting a friend up at Yates's.'

'How far's the Pierhead Hotel?' asked Steve, who was a complete stranger to Liverpool and knew nothing of the city and its attractions. 'I guess it's a fair old distance?'

'If what Sec says is true about us tying up in the Huskison Dock it's about a thirty-minute walk,' replied Archie, washing and drying his hands prior to making his way to the passengers' accommodation. 'And you can't miss it - it's slap bang in front of the Royal Liver Building.'

Steve had never even heard of the Royal Liver Building let alone the Pierhead Hotel, although he was prepared to follow the others - whoever the 'others' might be - and was eagerly anticipating his first night ashore in what was reputedly the liveliest seaport in Britain. 'The chances are we'll never even reach the Pierhead Hotel,' said Keith, assuming that most of the catering staff would be going ashore together and that they were in for a typical pub-crawl. 'There are so many boozers along Regent Road that we'll be literally spoilt for choice.'

With the scrub-out completed Steve found himself grabbing a smoke in the forward well-deck, admiring Canadian Pacific's outward-bound *Empress of England,* one of those elegant white liners that had so fired his original ambition, but which today evoked only a passing interest now that he'd come to appreciate the honest fundamentalism of a cargo ship. As the Canadian Pacific Liner slid gracefully past, bound for Quebec and Montreal, a tanker was being manoeuvred away from the Tranmere Oil Terminal at Birkenhead, while down towards the estuary the Lykes Bros Steamship Co's *Genevieve Lykes* was arriving in the river from New Orleans. As did the Thames at London, the River Mersey possessed a restless energy, which along with its backdrop of wharves and warehouses, towered over by the majestic silhouette of Liverpool's classic waterfront architecture, made Steve feel emotionally proud - not so much as a privileged onlooker, but as an integral part of the whole.

'Don't forget, there's no dinner tonight, lads,' said Sec, pinning a menu card to the pantry noticeboard, 'it's simply a basic high tea. No soup or other starters, only a main course and sweet.'

Hmm........thought Steve, welcoming the menu's uncomplicated but appetizing simplicity, rather than the five-course, multi-choice creation that constituted a typical dinner inventory. Sausages, creamed potatoes and peas, or liver and bacon, creamed potatoes and beans followed by either apple pie and custard or rhubarb and custard; or for those wishing for something lighter, the ever-present option of ice-cream. It'll be bangers and mash for me with apple pie and custard for afters. It'll make a jolly-good lining for my stomach.

In the event it was past four o'clock when Steve became aware of an unnatural silence; not the sinister stillness that had been so obvious in the immediate aftermath of the breakdown in the Indian Ocean, but the peaceful finality of the ship taking a well-earned repose. She wouldn't be paying off until the following morning but the voyage was now technically over, and the initial instalment of Steve's life at sea was rapidly drawing to a close.

With little requiring their immediate attention the boys were about to slope off when the Second Steward appeared and handed each of them a one-pound note. 'It's from the two lady guests you've been taking the piss out of for the past five weeks,' he advised, as Steve looked first at his pound then again at Sec, feeling suddenly guilty but also pleasantly surprised. 'They said they like to remember everyone, even the lads who wash up - so if I were you I'd nip topside smartish and thank them. They'll be leaving the ship in another few minutes so you'd better make haste.' Then, almost as an afterthought, he handed Peter an envelope, and added, 'And don't forget your Channel Money - Boss's office at four-thirty sharp.'

As if they - or anyone else for that matter - were likely to forget. A queue was already forming outside the Chief Steward's office as Steve and Peter pushed past, making for the aftermost of the starboard side staterooms to thank their benefactors who'd been the subjects of some spiteful if indirect abuse. Hopefully, the women had been totally unaware of the insults but nevertheless, Steve in particular felt suitably sheepish and would be glad when the errand was run.

In the end they were saved any embarrassment as Archie emerged from the stateroom carrying two bulging portmanteaus. 'Ah! Just in time,' proclaimed the bedroom steward, struggling past while nodding at a cabin trunk that lay between two single beds on which perched the overweight ladies. 'Grab that trunk between you and shift it down to the quayside. I'll be waiting there next to a taxi.'

Phew, that's a relief, thought Steve, as he and Peter hurriedly expressed their gratitude to the women before sizing up the task they'd been lumbered with. In the end it was a matter of which was the most awkward; thanking the ladies for their generosity or shifting the trunk from the room. Having determined that it would be best to carry it longways Steve led the way, inching along the alleyway with Peter behind and the two grossly-built females waddling along in their wake. After a ten-minute skirmish, trying their best to avoid damaging any of the recently-repaired paintwork, the lads claimed victory; and after the briefest of scares, when the trunk threatened to topple off the accommodation ladder and into the Huskison Dock, it stood innocently upright on the quayside. Archie and the taxi driver lifted it into the boot while the boys stood steaming in the sun. The ladies smiled sweetly and waved, squeezing into the taxi's rear seat as Steve and Peter waved back, believing that following their exertions they were worthy of their twenty-shilling tip.

'What's in the envelope?' enquired Steve, nosily, stuffing his Channel Money into his hip pocket along with his one-pound note. 'I didn't expect any mail this late in the trip.' Steve's last letter to his family - in which he'd stated that the *Alice Springs* would be docking in London within the fortnight - had been posted in Curaçao, and not withstanding that they'd been diverted to Liverpool he wasn't anticipating a reply.

'Search me - I'm just going to have a dekko,' answered Peter, a puzzled look on his face as he ripped open the envelope which had been redirected from the company's London office and bore a south London postmark. 'I wasn't expecting anything cos nobody knows where I am.' Within seconds of Peter unfolding the enclosed sheet of paper his face had lit up like the sun. 'It's from Maureen!' he exclaimed, jubilantly, while grinning like a Premium Bonds winner. 'Says she's sorry for dumping me in Sydney and that she's washed her hands of that other geezer. Reckons he was only interested in her because he thought all the drinks would be free. Says if I want to go and stay with her in the flat above the pub then I've only got to give her a ring.'

'That's marvellous,' answered Steve, feeling genuinely elated that Peter had something positive to look forward to rather than just mooching about with his mates; and that was despite having reservations that any sort of relationship would last. 'I'm really pleased for you, and I honestly hope it works out.'

With a few minutes to spare they leant on the rail at the after end of the passengers' promenade deck, admiring their fellow travellers. They were in exalted company, for also sharing the Huskison Number Two Branch Dock were the Blue Star Liner *Imperial Star,* the Moss-Hutchison freighter *Kantara,* Harrison's *Historian;* while lording it over the entire gathering like the goddess she was towered the Cunard Liner *Sylvania.* It was a fitting end to a memorable trip and the contentment showed; in Peter's eyes because at the end of a see-saw period he finally appeared to be wanted, and in Steve's because he'd become an established face in the crowd.

Keith was correct in his assumption that a sizeable number of the catering staff would be venturing ashore together, and barring the obvious exclusion of the Chief Steward there were only a handful of absentees: Archie who was meeting up with a mate; Ruby, who at the last minute had been invited to accompany Archie; Ted because he didn't feel like drinking; Norman because he did feel like drinking but owing to his excruciatingly painful little toe had decided to give it a miss; and The Second Steward who was obliged to stay on board and prepare for the owners' inspection.

And so it was that on the stroke of seven-fifteen the remaining seven scuttled down the accommodation ladder, Channel Money and tips in their pockets, to celebrate their homecoming with traditional seaman-like exuberance. As on the occasion of Archie's sixtieth birthday their money was pooled, the difference being that in this instance, owing to their imminent pay-off, the boys were required to pay a greater amount into the kitty. They willingly contributed five shillings each, all three of them aware they were being extremely generously treated.

It emerged that the stewards had benefited from handsome gratuities; even Ruby who as a DBS had no wages to collect, but who having worked his passage was entitled to a statutory shilling. Steve and Peter hadn't exactly hit the jackpot in terms of 'dropsy', as tips were colloquially referred to, although in light of their unexpected windfall they considered themselves lucky. And the same went for the lads in the galley, for the much-maligned ladies had also ensured that they weren't forgotten either. And so it was that the contingent from the *Alice Springs* made cheerful if increasingly unsteady progress from pub to pub along Regent Road, *en route* for the Pierhead Hotel.

The illuminated clock on the Royal Liver Building was showing ten thirty-one precisely when they finally tumbled into the full to bursting waterfront landmark. A barmaid rolled her eyes ceilingwards and was initially reluctant to serve them, pointing out that the 'bizzies' were outside just waiting for the chance to nick the premises for contravening the weekday licensing hours.

'They're not out there now,' slurred Donald, cocking his head over his shoulder in the direction of a side entrance, while grabbing hold of a chair-back to prevent himself toppling over. 'They've just shot off up the dock road like a greyhound with a rocket up its jacksie.'

The barmaid wrinkled her nose, reconsidering before finally relenting. 'Well........all right, then, but only one mind you,' she demurred, reaching for seven pint pots and lining them up on the bar top. 'You look like you've had enough already, and anyway, it's been like a madhouse in here and some of us do have homes to go to, you know.'

'No worries, m'dear,' assured Keith, collapsing into a chair at a recently vacated table, sweeping an empty light ale bottle on to the floor in the process. 'We'll be drunk up and out of here in no time.'

Steve declined a pint, settling instead for a half. The last thing he wanted was for the deckhead to begin spinning as soon as his head hit the pillow. Peter meanwhile was nursing a badly-split eyebrow, having tripped over a kerbstone in the vicinity of the Tate and Lyle sugar refinery. So, with John, Davy and Jimmy in close embrace, crooning an out-of-tune version of 'Auld Lang Syne', it seemed they'd all had an enjoyable time. In the event it was gone eleven when they were eventually persuaded to leave; in two separate taxis, three in an Austin Cambridge and four in a Standard Vanguard.

Most of the Liverpool taxi drivers knew the location of every ship in the port, from Gladstone Dock in the north to Garston in the south, including those on the Wirral side of the river. However, this didn't deter Steve, who was the only one of the four occupants of the Vanguard who was remotely coherent, from requesting, loudly and proudly, 'Huskison Dock, please driver. The *Alice Springs* - she's in Number Two Branch Dock.'

'I know where she is, La,' replied the driver, testily, tossing the words over his shoulder while keeping his eyes on the road. 'The only thing youse got to worry about is that if any of youse make a mess in the back there, yous'll be cleaning it up.'

Progress was rapid, only slowing as they negotiated a pile of debris outside a tavern called The Boathouse which only two hours earlier had been boisterous but peaceful, but now lay in ruins and resembled a casualty clearing station. Most of the ground-floor windows were shattered and splintered items of furniture littered the pavement and roadway. The police and ambulance service were in attendance and there was clearly a large count of injured, including a number of policemen. There'd obviously been an almighty punch-up; and although Steve couldn't swear to it, not in his pie-eyed condition, he felt certain that one of those being restrained was none other than Sean Cassidy while perched on the kerb, a blood-stained handkerchief pressed to his forehead, was who appeared to be Thomas Llewellyn. If Steve was correct, and he was convinced that he was, then Eddie Clooney's legacy had been invested in typical Cassidy-like fashion - with typical Cassidy-like consequences.

'Come on you two, stop playing with yourselves and show a leg,' called the night watchman, giving Steve a shake before focussing his attention on Peter. 'I know we'll be paying off in a few hours time, but that doesn't mean we can treat the ship as a holiday camp.'

'Piss off,' mumbled Peter, burying his head in his pillow, trying his best to suppress a pounding headache that was threatening to drive him bananas. 'We heard you the first time. Go and bother some-one else.'

Steve partly opened an eye and squinted at his watch. It read almost six o'clock but he showed little inclination to move. Still, as the watchman had said, today was pay-off day, sufficient incentive to motivate even the laziest lay-abed, even if it did require an effort. 'Come on Peter,' he urged, finally, shaking his mate who showed all the dynamism of a sloth. 'It's the last morning we need to get up early. After today you can sleep in as long as you like.'

They eventually managed to drag themselves into the pantry where Archie and Ruby were chatting away over tea and toast and only broke off to study the after-effects of the pub-crawl. Steve drew a cup of strong coffee. 'Christ,' he muttered, taking a swig of the liquid which lacked the customary milk but contained an additional spoonful of sugar. 'I hope this bastard works. I've got a head like a bloody pile-driver.'

'Get plenty of water down you, Duckie,' advised Ruby, who was buttering another slice of toast. 'You've probably piddled more than you've drunk and become dehydrated. That's why you feel like a prune - and another thing. Have a good breakfast, even if you don't feel like eating it. It's a dead-cert cure for a hangover.'

Steve couldn't have cared less about eating but he followed Ruby's advice, swallowing two pints of water before filling a bucket and setting off for the engineers' alleyway. But Ruby was wise, and as Steve settled down on his hands and knees he felt an upsurge of energy, so that by the time he'd finished his scrub-out and tidied-up the engineers' washroom he was desperately in need of some sustenance.

'Don't forget to strip your bunks,' reminded the Second Steward, filling a bowl with cornflakes and drowning them with half a pint of milk. 'Then just leave your dirty bedlinen outside the soiled linen locker and Archie'll stow it away. If everyone gets stuck in we'll be finished by eleven o'clock.'

'What's the idea of stripping our bunks?' enquired Peter, who although not yet fully recovered from the previous night's drinking looked a darn sight healthier than he had done. 'We usually just leave them as they are and the incoming crew change the linen.'

'I know what you usually do,' returned Sec, showing signs of irritation as the list of chores on his check-list grew longer by the minute. 'It's just that we don't have an owners' inspection at the end of every trip, and neither the Boss nor me want the accommodation areas looking like pigsties. So, just make sure that your cabins are clean and tidy then get on with your everyday chores.'

Archie had serviced his staterooms the previous evening, so while he helped out with the linen the boys cleared the remnants of breakfast and set about rearranging the saloon tables in a row athwartships, ready for the officials who'd be presiding over the discharge and pay-off proceedings.

Mornings like this were an encumbrance, to be worked through in a rush so as to be on your way as quickly as possible once you'd got your money in your pocket. By ten o'clock Steve was already finished and back in his cabin, dressed in his shore-going best, his recently dispensed-with working clothes forming the upper layer in a suitcase that had been progressively packed since the weekend. He was about to close the lid when there was a tap at the door and in peeped a red-headed youngster of minuscule build who announced, timidly, 'Hi! I'm Tommy. I'm from Greenock and I'm one of the relieving crew.'

Tommy was followed into the cabin by a giant of a lad who introduced himself as Gerry, proclaiming that he was from Kirby which explained the Merseyside accent. Gerry dumped his holdall on Peter's bunk and offered Steve a Senior Service, lighting one for himself before offering the match to Tommy who'd rolled a Vindiesque sparrow's leg from a tin of Old Holborn.

'You just up from the Vindi?' enquired Steve, remembering how he himself must have appeared only five months earlier, although it now seemed a jolly sight longer. To Steve's now experienced eye Tommy was the archetypal first-tripper, a suspicion confirmed as the Scots lad narrated his tale.

'Aye, I left there last Friday. By the time I got home the Federation office was closed so I went back again yesterday morning. There was nothing doing in Glasgow so they sent me to Liverpool instead. I've just spent the night at the mission.'

'You from the Vindi too?' asked Steve, directing the question at Gerry who was already donning a pee-jacket, his dungarees laying on top of his holdall which looked to hold little else than a sparsely-provisioned toilet bag along with a couple of changes of clean socks and underwear.

'No,' answered the Liverpudlian, pulling on his dungarees amid a cloud of smoke from his Senior. 'I went to Gravesend Sea School, but that was eight months ago now. I've just done a couple of trips on Lamport & Holt's *Raeburn*, down to BA. Had a fantastic time but I felt like a change. Everyone's talking about New Zealand so I'm fancying my chances on this tub.'

'You know she's going into dry dock?' advised Steve, just as Peter entered the room and contemplated the two new arrivals.

'Yeah, so they said,' replied Gerry, turning and smiling at Peter who proffered his hand in greeting. 'They reckon she'll only have a skeleton crew while she's over there - a Second Steward, a cook and a couple of boys as far as the catering department's concerned. I'm hoping they'll keep me on when she finally goes deep sea.'

'What do we do now?' asked Tommy, looking every bit as bewildered as Steve must have done as a novice.

'Finish your fag then we'll take you to see the Second Steward,' offered Peter, who himself had begun donning his shore-going clothes, stuffing his discarded dungarees and pee-jacket into his suitcase, hoping Maureen would launder them later. 'He's staying on board until his relief arrives tomorrow, after this so-called inspection that the owners have cooked up – although I reckon it'll be more like a beano. Tell you what, if what the galley's knocking up is anything to go by you'll have plenty of strapping up to do between you.'

As it happened Ted was another who'd fallen foul of the owners' inspection. Unluckily he too had been asked to remain on board and assist his replacement in preparing a feast for the owners who'd belatedly invited some local dignitaries; and like the Second Steward, he resented being taken for granted.

As the boys headed topside, Steve decided against mentioning that compared with the Vindi - which was usually likened to a concentration camp - the Gravesend Sea School was reputedly the equal of Butlin's. Gerry was too powerfully built to risk becoming embroiled in that kind of banter, not without knowing him better.

In the event the Second Steward was nowhere to be found, although a newly-arrived steward calling himself Wendy offered to take the new boys under his wing until their regular work routine could be organized. If Ruby was an example of the real McCoy then Wendy, blonde hair and all, was a thoroughgoing, out-and-out gender-bender. He pursed a kiss at a startled Tommy and ogled Gerry as if he were a male pin-up. But the real give-away lay in his appearance which was flamboyant, verging on the ludicrous, from the tip of his head to the toes of his brothel-creeper shoes. His snow-white jacket with purple epaulettes was a credit to the stewarding profession; but his trousers fitted so tightly that he resembled a girlish Max Wall, the lipstick, mascara and recently permed hair only adding to the impression that he was a leading character in a pantomime. Steve had heard about stewards like Wendy but this was his first physical contact. It was a parody that Peter whispered was usually to be found on the passenger liners rather than workaday freighters. Still, as Wendy piquantly made plain having overheard the remark. 'Any port in a storm Luvvy. I got the arsehole off the *Southern Cross* after an officer caught me giving a laundry boy a blow-job - and a girl's got to earn a living somehow.'

What about the laundry boy?' asked Steve, hesitantly, slowly recovering from the culture shock. 'What happened to him?

'Don't know for sure, Luvvy,' replied Wendy, fussily arranging coffee cups on a huge silver salver that only saw daylight on special occasions. 'Course, he got the heave-ho as well and the last I heard he'd applied to become a trainee hairdresser at a salon in Knightsbridge. If it's true he'll probably end up a fuckin' sight richer than all of us.'

Steve and Peter suppressed a fit of the giggles as they left Tommy and Gerry with Wendy, knowing Tommy was safe - so long as Gerry remained in attendance.

Instead of returning to their cabin the boys headed aft, Steve wanting to bid his farewells to the Bosun and to Dingwall Patterson. It was while ambling along the promenade deck that he happened to glance down and spot a row of limousines on the quayside. He initially suspected the cavalcade was that of the owners and their invited guests, but Peter knew otherwise.

'No, they're for us,' he explained, as they slid down the companionway to the after well-deck where the Bosun was engaged in discussion with a stevedore about how best to discharge a particular parcel of cargo. 'They're private-hire cars, and they're here to take us to the main line railway stations or wherever. Give it another half hour and the drivers'll be swarming all over the place, offering to drive us to Lime Street, Central or Exchange for a fiver a car load. Not a bad morning's work, is it? More than we earn in a week - for a ten-minute trip to the station.' Steve agreed. It did seem rather extortionate, but given the why and the wherefore he guessed it was a matter of choice. If he didn't fancy contributing towards the cost of a limo he could always opt for the bus.

'Don't know, son,' answered the Bosun, when Steve asked the whereabouts of Dingwall. 'One of the ABs reckons he saw him going ashore straight after breakfast and no-one's laid eyes on him since. I suppose he thought with a only a shilling to come he might as well bugger off. He can collect his discharge book from the Federation office whenever.'

'I wonder how he'll get home with no money or rail warrant?'

queried Steve, suddenly realizing that throughout all the hours they'd spent chatting with each other Dingwall had never once made a reference to home. OK, he'd made it plain that he was from the western isles, and had revealed where his grandparents had hailed from, but that wasn't quite the same as saying, 'home'.

'You don't have to worry about Dingwall,' reassured the Bosun, signalling to a winchman that one of the mooring lines needed tightening. 'He's a sea-gypsy, and more than capable of looking after himself. Sooner or later he'll sign on another ship and he'll be away again to goodness-knows where. And as for money - Dingwall was a dark horse, and for all we know he's probably sitting on a goldmine.'

'Yeah, I suppose so,' agreed Steve, resigning himself to the fact that he'd seen the last of Dingwall Patterson. 'But it's a funny old way of going on, not even bothering to say cheerio, especially considering we were mates. Still, thanks for everything, Bose. Might see you around sometime.'

'You never know,' answered the Bosun, as the boys each shook hands with the kindly petty officer who always had time for others, especially the younger generation who were in need of wisdom and counsel. 'And you take care - both of you.'

It was almost eleven, and Steve could picture a queue forming at the saloon entrance, a potential seventy-odd souls who'd soon have money to burn and in certain instances, discover the cost of their sins.

As they stepped carefully around some clutter and back towards the companionway they saw that the *Sylvania* had gone, having shifted up to the landing stage to embark her passengers for New York and Boston. In her place lay the opposite end of the spectrum, a rusting, forty-year-old tramp that was still eking a living humping whatever enticement was offered. In this case it was grain, and a huge floating silo had manoeuvred alongside to assist with the discharge. The once-white lettering on the steamer's bows had all but corroded away, but by shielding his eyes from the sunlight Steve was able to decipher her name: *Spartan Splendour,* a contradiction if ever there was one. Spartan she may have been but splendour she most definitely wasn't. Dangling forlornly at her stern and in need of replacement hung the ensign of Greece, supporting Peter's earlier contention that the *Lilac Hill* faced a future - such as it was - of neglect and ultimate decay. 'Come along,' said Steve, feeling suddenly depressed and eager to forget the rotting scrapheap. 'It's almost eleven o'clock - and time we collected our money.'

'They usually ask us if we're coming back next trip,' voiced Peter as they attached themselves to the rear of the queue that already numbered more than thirty, 'but I don't suppose that'll happen this time, not with the ship going in dry dock.'

'So, what d'ya reckon?' asked Steve, having no idea of the due process in situations where men were out of contract.

'Dunno,' answered Peter, nasally, wiping his nose on a sheet of toilet paper in the absence of a proper handkerchief. You'll probably get a telegram in a fortnight or so, telling you to report to some ship or the other - you might even get one tomorrow. Course, all that's assuming you haven't made other arrangements. Do you intend staying with the A&P?' as every seafarer referred to the Australasian and Pacific Steam Navigation Company. 'Or are you going to look somewhere else?'

'Well, for a start I'm going to have a word with the Union Steamship Company of New Zealand, see if I can't get a berth on that ferry. Failing that I'm going up to New Zealand House to find out my chances of emigrating. Whatever, nothing's going to happen overnight; and I don't want to be out of touch for any longer than necessary until something concrete's decided, so I might try my luck at coasting. That way I'll only be away for a couple of weeks at a time, so if anything does turn up with either the Union Steamship Company or the New Zealand High Commission I'll be more or less right on the doorstep.'

'You could always ask to work by,' volunteered Peter, eager to offer advice. 'You know, ask the Super if you can shift from one ship to another while the seagoing crews are on leave.'

'Mmmm........I hadn't even thought of that,' answered Steve, craning his neck to see to what extent the queue had shortened. 'Might be worth looking into. But anyway - what about you?'

'Me? Oh! I'll probably stay with this lot - maybe even the *Alice Springs* if they want me. It suits me down to the ground, especially now I've Maureen to consider.'

Meanwhile, the queue had moved on. The JOS and EDH immediately in front of them were discussing whether to have a couple of beers in the city before going to the station or wait until they got on the train. 'I know what I'm doing,' said Steve, as the deckhands shuffled forward to sign off articles and collect their discharge books, 'I'm going straight to the station.'

'Me too,' affirmed Peter, stuffing the tissue into a trouser pocket as they approached the first of the tables. 'But we should still have time for a couple of pints when we get there.'

Steve signed his name against number sixty-seven on the articles sheet and accepted the proffered discharge book, noticing as he did so in an adjacent column what appeared to be a huge sum of money. He could hardly believe it was his; but, important though the money undoubtedly was his immediate concern was his discharge. He flicked though the pages, completely ignoring the first half dozen which contained only his personal details and descriptions of certificates obtained. He eventually came to page number seven and the entries that mattered; his ship's name, its tonnage and official number followed by the dates of engagement and discharge. But it was to the opposite page, page number eight, that his eyes inevitably strayed. He read it once, twice, three times; the rubber-stamped verification, 'Very Good', on the counts of both ability and conduct. Those words alone were worth almost as much as the riches he'd glimpsed on the articles sheet. He couldn't shift his eyes from the book, repeatedly scanning the endorsements until a nudge between the shoulder blades suggested he ought to move on.

'Hey, we've got trains to catch too, you know. You need to get your arse into gear.'

'Sorry, I was miles away,' apologized Steve, hastily slipping his discharge book into his hip pocket and turning to find Jimmy grinning at him over Norman's shoulder. It was an excuse for some good-natured banter, with Norman chipping in for good measure as Steve moved along to the company's cashiers who were carefully counting out the cash.

No, it hadn't been a mirage, it hadn't been a trick of the light and he wasn't due an appointment at the optician's. Forty-six Pounds, fourteen Shillings and a Penny. He could hardly believe it as the money was laid on the table. It was an absolute fortune and far in excess of anything he'd previously calculated. Thanks to overtime and leave pay his total earnings were considerably more than he'd drawn but nevertheless, given the various stoppages............

'You coming back next trip?' asked a spotty-faced youth sitting next to the paymasters, Biro hovering above a list of names, several of which had already been untidily struck out. 'We can probably find you work until she comes out of dry dock.'

'Eh! What?' exclaimed Steve, engrossed in his payslip as he drifted away from the table while the youth exuded blank-faced indifference. Thinking on the spot he instantaneously made his decision. 'Uh!.......No!' I don't think so, he replied, turning to address his questioner. I've already got another berth waiting.'

And so the die was cast. In that one skimpy sentence he'd severed his links with the ship and inexplicably he felt suddenly vulnerable and isolated, even though he was sure that one way and another he'd find a route back to Maxine and a permanent future in New Zealand. Whatever, the brief stab of angst was soon forgotten as his attention reverted to his payslip.

'Any of youse need a lift?' queried a dwarf, who was strolling along the working alleyway in a black leather jacket, denims and Cuban-heeled shoes, the entire ensemble topped off by a cheese-cutter cap. 'I've got room for three more for Lime Street - a quid apiece if you're interested.'

The boys exchanged glances, wondering if it was worth twenty-shillings for the most cursory of rides to the station. Characteristically, it was Peter who made up their minds. 'What the hell, we're only here once - and a quid isn't going to break us, is it?'

'I'll meet you all at the top of the gangway in fifteen minutes, then,' said the driver, accepting three crisp one-pound notes and stuffing them into a wallet that was already bulging at the seams. 'I've just got to let the other two know and then we'll be away.'

'Now you know why he's all dolled up like a city slicker,' said Steve, not at all sure they were getting good value for money. That lot didn't come from British Home Stores or Marks and Spencer. That's all top-of-the-range-stuff, far too expensive for the likes of us.'

'He's already gone,' answered Donald, when Steve peeped into the

369

cabin shared by Keith and the Ulsterman, to repay the money he'd borrowed in Dunkirk. 'There was a bloke looking to make up a carload for Exchange station and he's been left here this past fifteen minutes. I wouldn't worry about it if I were you. He's obviously forgotten about it otherwise he'd have asked you beforehand.'

Events were now gathering pace, and in something of an undignified scramble it was time for the ultimate leave-taking. Firstly, Ted and Norman, Davy and John: the capable and generally affable bunch of galley rats who for over five months had sustained and nourished eighty-odd souls with only an occasional niggle between them. Then there was Archie and Sec, who in spite of his rawness had treated him as an equal and not as an irritating dog's-body. And finally, Ruby, who despite being a latecomer, the tantrums over that appalling haircut and the calculated backlash, had become just as well thought of as the rest. He would never forget them, any more than he could forget either Dingwall Patterson, Sean Cassidy or poor old Eddie Clooney. They'd all played their part in making his first trip to sea an unforgettable milestone.

There was a tear in Steve's eye as he vacated the cabin he'd first entered on a cool February morning, when frost had whitened the rooftops and he hadn't known what to expect. But, as he closed the door for the final time and joined Peter and Jimmy at the gangway there were no regrets, only the quiet satisfaction of a feat accomplished, perhaps an uncertain future but with a final port of call in in Manoao.

'Here, I'll carry those,' said the driver, indicating that the boys leave their luggage at the top of the accommodation ladder and make their way down to the car. 'The other two are already in there.'

The 'other two' happened to be the Lamp-trimmer and the Donkeyman, who were noisily celebrating their homecoming with a bottle of Bacardi which had already been two parts consumed. As Steve climbed into the rear of the Armstrong-Siddeley Sapphire, cheerfully declining the offered bottle, Peter and Jimmy sidled into the front, Peter clinging protectively to his precious wireless which he refused to let out of his sight.

The boot lid slammed shut and the driver slid into his seat, invisible to those in the rear. 'All ready lads?' he sang, firing the

Sapphire's ignition and slipping the engine into gear, the hum of the motor barely audible against the din being created by the celebrants. 'Then let's get going.'

As the limousine purred smoothly towards the gates of the Huskison Dock Steve glanced hurriedly over his shoulder. The old *Alice Springs* looked rather forlorn amid the dockside disarray. But she would survive and flourish - at least in the medium term - as he too would survive and flourish. The ship, along with all those wonderful - and sometimes not so wonderful - shipmates, had performed his seafaring baptism, steering him safely - although sometimes scarily - through the most momentous of teenage undertakings. She and they had nurtured and protected him, amused and occasionally enraged him but all thanks to them he'd prevailed. He settled more comfortably into his seat and against his better instincts accepted a swig of Bacardi; for when all was said and done, whatever other people thought he was now a fully-fledged seaman and no longer a lowly first-tripper.

Glossary of shipboard terms, some of which appear in this volume.

AB. *Able Seaman.*

Accommodation ladder. *Gangway from ship to shore.*

Aft end. *Rear section of ship (Tourist section on passenger liners).*

Articles. *Terms of agreement between ship-master and crew.*

AS. *Assistant Steward – usually referred to as, 'Steward'.*

Athwartships. *From Port to starboard and reverse.*

BA. *Buenos Aires.*

Bibby alleyway. *Cul-de-Sac.*

Bloods. *Passengers.*

Blues. *Navy Blue Uniform.*

BOT. *Board of Trade.*

Boss. *Chief Steward.*

BR. *Bedroom Steward.*

Bulkheads. *Walls.*

Commis. *Apprentice Waiter (Passenger Liners).*

Companionway. *Staircase.*

Cover. *A complete set of table cutlery.*

Deadlight. *Metal cover over porthole.*

Deck. *Floor.*

Deckhead. *Ceiling.*

Dhobi. *Washing clothes.*

Ducer. *Second Steward.*

Duty mess. *Set-aside dining area where duty engineers could eat out of uniform.*

EDH. *Efficient Deck Hand.*

Foar'ard. *Front section of ship.*

Fiddle. *Raised edge around table top to prevent items sliding off in rough weather.*

Fridge Greaser: *Crew member responsible for the day-to-day running of the refrigeration machinery.*

Heads. *Crew toilets.*

JOS. *Junior Ordinary Seaman.*

KG5. *King George V Dock.*

Leading hand. *Petty Officer.*

Lecce. *Electrician (Electrical engineer).*

Lockerman. *Steward in charge of lockers, e.g. Cruet locker, silver locker, fruit locker, etc. (Passenger liners).*

Maindeckman. *Steward in charge of Second Steward's gear (Passenger liners).*

MOT. *Ministry of Transport.*

Overheads. *Ledges, pipes, beams, etc. above the head.*

Peak (Also glory hole). *Stewards' accommodation (Passenger liners).*

Pig & Whistle. *Crew bar (Passenger liners).*

PLA. *Port of London Authority.*

Port side. *Left side of ship facing forward.*

Returns. *Repeat food orders/Second helping of dish.*

Rosie. *Refuse bin.*

Rounds. *Captain's inspection (Chief Officer if Master unavailable).*

Running sitting. *Continuous service of meal (Passenger liners).*

Scupper. *Drain.*

Scuttle. *Porthole.*

Seven-bell breakfast. *Seven-thirty am breakfast for officers and engineers on eight till twelve watch.*

Sheds. *Passengers' accommodation.*

Show. *Waiter's table section (Passenger liners).*

Side doors. *Doors in side of ship used when passengers are embarking or disembarking. Also used for taking aboard stores, baggage, etc., (Usually passenger liners).*

Side job. *Working routine between meals.*

Silver. *Table cutlery, etc.*

Slops. *Clothing, shoes and other items available for sale to crew.*

Smoke-ho. *Morning and afternoon breaks for deckhands and engine room crew.*

SOS. *Senior ordinary seaman.*

Sparky. *Radio Officer (Not electrician).*

Sub. *Allowance from pay.*

Sugi (Sometimes Soogee). *Hot soapy water.*

Strapping up. *Washing dishes, silver, pots and pans, etc.*

Single change. *Changing one sheet or pillow case only on a bed or bunk.*

Starboard. *Right side of ship facing forward.*

Swing the lamp. *Reminisce.*

Tabnabs. *Cakes and pastries.*

Topside. *Upper decks on a ship (First Class on passenger liners).*

Tiger. *Captain's personal steward.*

Tick on. *Report for duty (Mostly, but not always, aboard passenger liners).*

Well-Deck. *Open space on the main deck of a ship where cargo hatches are located, usually fore and aft of the central accommodation area.*

Whites. *White tropical uniform.*

Winger. *Waiter (Mostly passenger liners).*

Working alleyway. *Alleyway off which most of a vessel's principal working areas are located: Galley, lockers, storerooms, etc. Also, mostly aboard cargo vessels, off which catering staff accommodation is situated.*

Printed in Great Britain
by Amazon